EYES OF GARNET

Eyes of Garnet

Mary Duncan

Sense of Wonder Press
JAMES A. ROCK & COMPANY, PUBLISHERS
ROCKVILLE • MARYLAND

Eyes of Garnet by Mary Duncan

SENSE OF WONDER PRESS
is an imprint of JAMES A. ROCK & CO., PUBLISHERS

Address comments and inquiries to:

SENSE OF WONDER PRESS
James A. Rock & Company, Publishers
9710 Traville Gateway Drive, #305
Rockville, MD 20850

E-mail:
jrock@rockpublishing.com   lrock@rockpublishing.com
Internet URL: www.rockpublishing.com

Trade Paperback ISBN: 1-59663-515-0
Library of Congress Control Number: 2006926207

Limited Edition Hardcover ISBN: 1-59663-517-7
Library of Congress Control Number: 2006926209

Printed in the United States of America

First Edition: 2006

Cover Design by Mary Duncan

For Dan

Partner, muse and Scotsman

ॐ

acknowledgments

The author would like to thank

My husband, Dan Duncan, for his unwavering support, his willingness to listen and catch timeline errors, and for being honest enough to say, "That makes no sense, Mare"; my sister, Cathy Emmons, for being my second pair of eyes, and to make sure a perpetual reader would actually believe this story; Wayne Smith, teacher extraordinaire, and Barbara "Sass" Sassaman, continual visitor of Scotland, for the *Gàidhlig* lessons to ensure authenticity in my story, and assuring me that, "They would never have said 'Lying Bastard!' in the 18th century"; O. William Robertson, International Vice Chairman of Clan Donnachaidh, for supplying me with the actual poems of Alexander Robertson, 13th Chief of Clan Donnachaidh, and other tidbits of the Chief's life; Aileen Peterson, stone reader, for giving me the go-ahead in a reading to take the dream to write and turn it into a reality, and the loan of books on Seers of the 18th century; and finally, my Dad, Paul Thonis, for not laughing when I said, "Move over J.K. Rowling." He said, "If you're going to dream, it might as well be big."

part one

loch rannoch, scotland
1738

stirrings

Even playing with the new lambs behind the barn didn't quell the nauseous feeling that ravaged Catrìona Robertson's stomach this morning. The nightmare she experienced last night had far greater detail than usual. She dreamt of holding an egg-shaped crystal that, when hit by the sunlight, splashed miniature prisms everywhere. The stone itself held a force of power that brought about death, or gave life, seemingly at its whim. As the stone warmed in her hand, its power flowed into her — she could foretell the future.

Trying to shake off the mood, Catrìona sat on the fence and lifted her face to the sun, noting the curious milky-blue sky of a warmer season. The odd warmth of this early April day was like an omen of strange things to come. A voice in her head kept whispering "see." She had no idea what it meant.

Her eyes went to the woods; her favorite place. She had spent many hours under those huge oaks watching the ravens do their aerial acrobatics, feeling a deep connection to the place. These things she could not explain to her brothers when they found her out there. She knew they didn't share her awareness.

As her eyes scanned further, she saw a doe and fawn crossing the glen in the distance, mesmerizing her. Suddenly the doe spooked, and with a flash of light, Cat got a sense of dread so acute it made her dizzy. She slid down from the fence and sat on the ground, propping herself up on the railing hoping to regain her balance. The world spun wildly, so she lay back on the ground and closed her eyes. Her whole body vibrated. She broke out in a cold sweat, her fingers tingled, and her lips went dry. Incredible colors undulated behind her eyelids, and she breathed so hard her heart felt as though it would burst from her chest.

The world went black, and she perceived that she had become something else, something not human. She had a different posture, a different sense of smell and hearing. Fear overtook her, ruling her entire life, and she felt no reason behind her thoughts — only instinct.

As quickly as the phenomenon began, it was over, and normalcy returned to her body. Cat actually felt like she had become the doe for a brief instant, and it scared her. The sun was warm on her face as she lay on the cool ground. When she opened her eyes, Lachlan was standing over her.

"Cat, Cat, what's wrong wi' ye? Did ye fall?" Lachlan shouted in a panicky voice, looking her over to see if she was hurt.

She sat up on her own, noting the fear in his eyes. He knelt down to cradle her, ready to listen to her explanation.

"I had such a strange thing happen to me, Lachlan. I was sittin' on the fence one minute, recountin' my nightmare o' last night; about a crystal that I used to tell the future wi', all the while a voice in my heid kept tellin' me to 'see,' then in the next minute, I was lyin' on the ground all froze up, and I was that doe in the glen wi' her fawn, scairt to death," she said, watching the doe trot out of sight. "What do ye think is wrong wi' me?"

She could tell he had an idea of her malady from the look in his eyes, but he wasn't ready to share it with her yet.

He said, instead, "I canna be certain, Cat. Let's go into the house, maybe Mam can tell ye," helping her to her feet.

"Och, I'm all right," she waved him off, "Besides, I've probably spent too much time out here anyway."

Wiping straw from her dress, she left her brother by the barn.

❧

"Damn it, where is that lass?" Angus Robertson ranted to his wife, Isobel, for the sixth time. "She's supposed to be in here helpin' ye, no' out playin' wi' the wee lambs!" Continuing with some choice words in Gaelic.

The tall, one-armed, barrel-chested leader of the Robertson clan of Aulich had little patience, especially with his youngest child. He was the laird of *Slios Mìn aig Aulich*, which meant Smooth Slope at Aulich, six thousand acres that bordered the north-central shore of Loch Rannoch.

Because of Catrìona, he was late getting to the high shieling to tend the cattle. His large herd of prime beef was a temptation to any cattle thief for miles around. Rumors were spreading of another raid by the Campbells, and he loathed leaving any of the beasts unattended.

Pacing in front of the window, he spied Catrìona coming out from behind the barn. He was right, she had been playing with the lambs. He walked over to the door, his wide shoulders filling the frame, and let out all of his frustration on her.

"If I hae to be tellin' ye anymore about helpin' yer Mam, I'll hae to be takin' the strap to yer backside, understood?" he growled as she got within earshot.

"Sorry, Da," she said, rubbing her stomach.

Whenever he was angry with her — which seemed to be quite often these days — an anxious feeling rumbled in her belly. She knew why, but was helpless to do anything about it. In her usual peace-keeping way, she tried to lighten the situation by saying in her best cheery voice, "A wee lamb needed me."

"Hmmm! No more about it, now get in here and help yer Mam," he said, then grabbed her arm and whispered in her ear, "She's no' feelin' well again today, so be sure to mind and fetch me quick if ye need to."

Angus caught Cat's concerned expression, gave her a quick squeeze, then looked her over. She would be a tall one, he thought, her head already fitting just under his chin. Her oval face, framed by long, dark auburn hair, and her mother's big eyes, but in a rare shade of violet-gray, made even more striking because they were surrounded by nearly black lashes. She was also the only one of his children who had Isobel's dimples.

Now that the household was back in order, his mood became more amicable and it was time for him to leave. He walked over to Isobel, pressed a kiss on her cheek, then patted her bottom lovingly. "I'm off to the upper shieling to check on the kine, and I'll be takin' the laddies wi' me." Kissing her again, he walked towards the door, stopped, and gave one last set of instructions to his frail wife. "And I want ye to let Cat do the work for ye today. She's plenty capable enough."

He ambled his way out towards the barn with a wrapped bundle of bannocks and cheese under his arm. In his big hand, he carried four stone bottles of ale; lunch for him and the lads.

"Mam, tell me again how Da lost his arm in the war," Cat asked, as she watched him walk away.

"Why Cat? Hae ye no' heard it more times than I can recollect?" Isobel asked wearily, but gave in when she saw Cat watching her retreating father through the doorway. She walked over to stand next to her daughter and draped an arm over her shoulder.

"It was durin' the last Risin' of 1715. Some of the Jacobite clans rallied together to regain the throne of Scotland for King James VIII," she said. "It was on the first day of the battle in Prestonpans when he was hit in the arm with grapeshot, takin' it off just below the elbow. Thank *Brighid* the clan surgeon was there — he was a good one too — for many died from fever from less wounds. Being only 16 at the time, he had no business bein' there, but ye ken yer Da, there's no keepin' him from a fight, even today. Many good, brave men died in that battle," she concluded. For a moment, she wore a far-away look on her face, seeing the battle in her mind's eye. Then the look was gone, replaced with one of fatigue.

Isobel closed the door and leaned on it, exhausted. Today would not be a good day. She wasn't well, but tried to conceal it from her family, even though they all knew it. Some days — like today — it was impossible to hide. Angus got mad at Catrìona for not being in the house all the time to help her, but she refused to confine her daughter like a prisoner. Catrìona had a special purpose; Isobel only hoped she would see it come to fruition.

Isobel wished her mother had taught her the healing ways, but Catherine Macinroy was not around long enough to pass on what she knew. Being a Seeress was a dangerous business, and Catherine was very good at it. Unfortunately, being honest about what was seen was not always the best policy for a long life.

"Mam?" Cat asked quietly, twirling a thick strand of hair around her finger.

"Aye?"

"I had a verra strange thing happen to me while I was outside."

Isobel looked hard at Cat, feeling this was something more than playing with the lambs.

"Let's hear it, then."

Isobel listened to the details of her daughter's episode, knowing exactly what had happened, but trying to tell Catrìona why and what would be happening to her from now on was not going to be easy.

"Yer Grandmam was the same as ye are, lass. She had the *dà shealladh*; Second Sight. The Clan Chief called upon her many times to tell him the outcome of a battle, or anything else he needed to ken," she said.

But how could she explain Second Sight to her daughter when she herself didn't understand how it worked? She didn't know what triggered the start of the Sight, but had heard it was when a lass started her monthly courses. First blood signalled big changes in a lasses life, and thought perhaps Catrìona had started hers, or was very close to it.

With that idea, Isobel asked, "Hae ye started ye courses then, lass?"

Cat was sitting at the table staring at her hands. At this question, she jolted upright and looked at her mother with soft violet eyes full of expectancy, clueless to a reply.

"I heard tell that's when lasses get their Sight; hae ye started then?" she pressed.

Finding her voice, Cat said, "No, Mam, but I hae been feelin' verra strange today. Do ye think it will happen today then?"

Before Isobel could answer the thousand questions she knew Cat had, the door flew partially open, hitting Isobel on the back, making her nearly jump out of her skin. With her hand over her heart, making sure it was still beating, she turned to find Lachlan poking his head in.

"What is it, man! Ye nearly killed me!" she blasted, the color drained from her face.

"Mam, I must catch up to Da or he'll hae my head, but I need to ken if Cat was feelin' okay, and Da wanted me to make sure ye didna need anythin' before I left, that's why I'm here," he said all in one breath.

"Och, aye, she's fine lad," waving the episode off. "And tell yer Da that Mrs. Stark will be o'er shortly to help me wi' the chores." She was just about to close the door, when she added, "Oh, and dinna tell yer Da of what went on wi' Cat, mind me now." With that she closed the door on him and walked over to sit with Catrìona at the table, ready to be barraged by questions she knew Cat wanted to ask.

ã&

About an hour later, Mrs. Stark came in, and the daily routine resumed. Catrìona still had many unanswered questions, but one phrase her mother said kept looming in the forefront. She said that all of her senses would be more heightened now. Cat wasn't sure how that was possible after the doe incident. Is that what the voice in her head was trying to tell her? Would she faint every time she had a vision? Would she have time to prepare herself beforehand? Would the visions always be so traumatic and fearful, or would she have good ones as well? She had to learn these things … and quickly. Maybe her brothers would know who to ask.

Later that afternoon, while in the barn milking the cow, she heard hoof beats. Her father and brothers were home. Moments later, Lachlan appeared in the doorway with the horses and saw her on the stool. He walked over to her with concern on his face and asked in Gaelic, "*Ciamar a tha thu?*"

"*Tha gu math*, just fine," she said.

"Really? How can ye be fine? I've been thinkin' all day about yer experience this mornin'. Do ye ken it might be the Sight that ye hae?

She looked hard at him for a second. "How did ye ken I hae the Sight? Did Mam tell ye?"

He shook his head from side to side. "I heard stories o' Grandmam and figured that was how ye heard the voice in yer heid and became the doe."

He was silent for a moment before continuing, again considering if he should voice his opinion.

"Rabbie Duncanson's auntie has the Sight. Rabbie says that she has to stay away from everyone because all she has to do is look at ye to see what will happen to ye. And it's always bad! She can see when someone will die or get hurt, and how it will happen!"

Cat felt his anxiousness and was not prepared for the validation of seeing only bad things. And the thought of having to live away from her family was not something she was ready for either. The more she thought, the more worked up she got.

"Do ye mean to be tellin' me that I'll hae to move away and live by myself?" she whispered, the color draining from her cheeks. "Where am I to live? How am I to live? I'm no' even twelve yet! I canna be takin' to the heather and livin' in a wee cave for the rest o' my life just so I dinna hae to see people. I wilna do it!" Panic crept into her voice. She stopped milking the cow and pushed herself away from the beast. She was twirling her hair now; not a good sign. "I'll stop haeing the sight! I'll make myself stop!" She was shouting now.

"Cat, I dinna think ye can just stop it just because ye dinna want it." His voice was full of sympathy, wishing with all his heart he had never brought up the subject.

"Come on wi' me to the house. The sun's goin' down and Mam will be wantin' her milk." Taking Catrìona's arm, he guided her out of the barn, stooping to pick up the bucket on the way.

Cat stopped him, looked deep into his blue eyes and softly said, "I can look at *ye* and no' see anythin' bad to come to ye, Lachlan. Does it mean that maybe I wilna be like Rabbie's auntie?"

"We'll hae to wait and see."

all the preparations
in the world...

It was an uneventful two and a half months for Catrìona. Was that day with the doe just a one-time event? Maybe she really didn't have the Sight. She had started her courses later that day, as her mother predicted, but since then, nothing else out of the ordinary had occurred.

It was the week before the Gathering of the Clan and the Highland Games. The eighteen-mile wagon journey to Blair Atholl and Blair Castle, where the Games were held, took a day and a half. The Robertsons would be gone for almost a week.

The Games were very exciting to all of Cat's brothers. Seumas, her oldest brother by seven years, was especially uncontainable. For the past two years, her father had been teaching him the battle arts in preparation for these events. Seumas practiced with Iain every spare moment with the broadsword, claymore, and dirk to compete with the men this year. Iain, more graceful and athletic than Seumas, but not as strong, was competing in the sword dancing.

Lachlan, too young to participate in the games, was giving Catrìona dirk lessons. Many Highland women carried, and were quite capable in the use of the dagger. Nearly the same height, brother and sister made a good match. Cat was strong and took to the moves naturally. She kilted her skirts up between her legs to give her more freedom of movement for lunging and back-stepping. In one smooth movement, she grabbed the dirk handle from its sheath on her belt, making sure she had a good grip on it and it was in the correct position. With practiced speed, and feeling in control, she lunged in one quick motion towards Lachlan.

"Arrhh! Ye nearly got me that time!" Lachlan yelped, nearly tripping as he back-stepped out of her reach. "If I didna ken better, I'd think ye were tryin' to kill me!" He squinted at her and cocked his head. "Ye're no', are ye?"

Cat let out a belly laugh at the look on her brother's face. "I really did give ye a fright, didna I, big brother." With her dimples deep, she continued the heckling by coyly batting her eyes at him. "Ye ken I would ne'er harm ye, but ye do want me to do it right, dinna ye?"

Angus had been sitting on the fence watching his two youngest, and let out a roar of laughter at the look on Lachlan's face. "Cat, ye'll make a fine battle-woman, but yer Mam will hae me head for it! I dinna think she'll be wantin' another lad around the house," he said, the adoration showing in his eyes.

"I'll no' tell her if ye dinna, Da!" Still giggling, she made another swipe at her brother. He was much more wary of her skills now, and she came nowhere close to him.

"Come on, the lot o' ye. 'Tis near time for supper," he bellowed to his tribe, getting down from the fence. "There's plenty o' time for all o' this tomorrow."

"But Da, I was just gettin' started!" Cat cried.

"I think ye had enough for today, Cat," Lachlan said. "Or maybe it's me who has had enough," he continued under his breath, along with other mumblings in Gaelic.

Angus scooped Catrìona up and flung her over his shoulder amidst gales of laughter. They all walked back to the house with smiles on their faces.

❧

That night, Catrìona lay in her bed thinking of the day's events. She laid in the dark with a smile still on her face, remembering Lachlan's horrified look. Tomorrow they would begin the trip to Blair Atholl.

Sleep eluded her, she was just too excited to keep still. Quietly, she got up and went to the window. Her room — only slightly larger than her bed — was hers alone. It was a safe haven where she could think without interruption. The full moon lit up the night as she looked out the window. In its glow, she could see the cattle and sheep behind the barn. They looked like apparitions. There was no color or details to them, just dark shapes on the land. Crickets were chirping, and a nightingale could be heard in the distance. The night was peaceful.

After a while, she went back to her straw-filled bed, closed her eyes and laid very still, becoming one with the night. All thoughts retreated from her mind. She became the darkness. There was no body attached to her anymore, no face, no hands, no legs. She just was — like pure essence — the energy of life itself.

Slowly it started. The tingling of her hands where she had none just a moment before. The dryness of her lips, the cold sweat and heavy breathing. She saw nothing. Everything was still and black, but there was a sense of something. What was it? She tried to stay calm. Maybe she could control this. Breathe. Breathe. Breathe.

With a suddenness that startled her, she was Seumas! She was at the Games testing her skills against Alex Maclagan with the claymore. How wonderful it felt to be so strong and big. The two-handed sword was very heavy, yet she wielded it as if it were a dirk. The sound of the steel clanging together, and her agility to dodge the blows was as real as if it were actually happening. It was just her and Alex; no crowds or distractions around them. Her kilt was flying; her hair was blowing in the wind; her feet were light. Dodging and thrusting, secure, confident steps were hers to win the contest. Adrenaline rushed through her veins as the contest continued.

They battled together for a long time, each man the other's equal. Blades crashed together with such force, she felt the teeth-chattering reverberation go right through her entire body. Her hands ached from gripping the iron shaft with all her might in an extreme effort not to lose the sword when it was slammed upon.

Then, a series of blows made Alex's sword lift high over his head, coming down hard onto its mark. In the very next instant, excruciating pain. She looked down on her right leg. The shear force from the blow cut so deep into her leg, the blade severed the thick muscle and stuck into the bone, breaking it. Blood pooled around her as she lay on the ground, then everything faded to black.

Catrìona slowly came out of the vision. She laid there, her nightdress drenched in sweat, as the feelings came back to her body. The tingling was subsiding in her hands and she licked her lips to bring the moisture back to them. She sat up and leaned against the bedpost, exhausted.

How was she going to explain this to Seumas? Would he believe her? Was there any reason to tell him about it at all? What if it was just a dream from watching him practice today? Her mind was whirling. No one would believe her.

જે

Light from the rapidly appearing dawn filled the kitchen with a pinkish-orange hue. It was going to be a very warm day for traveling through the Highlands. Catrìona and Isobel, still clad in their night-clothes, were having tea at the table.

"What was goin' on in yer room last night?" Isobel asked over the rim of her cup.

Cat froze for an instant, then regained a little composure. "Och, it was just a bad dream."

"Are ye sure that's all it was?"

"Aye."

"No' another vision?" Isobel pressed.

Cat looked sideways at her mother, knowing full well she knew it was a vision, but continued denying it. Her mother had not mentioned the vision she had over two months ago to her father — neither had Lachlan — wanting to be absolutely sure before breaking such news to anyone. In the Highlands, Second Sight was a fairly common occurrence. More times than not it was the lasses, not the lads, being "blessed" with it, but everyone knew what it meant to have a Seer in the family. In earlier times, Seers were considered witches, and persecuted for their "crimes." Even now, one had to be very cautious as to who was told.

In all of Clan Donnachaidh, Cat knew of at least three others who had the Sight, but they were much older women. She was the youngest she knew of, but didn't know whether that was a good thing or a bad.

Angus strolled into the kitchen, belting his kilt around his trim waist. He was stopped mid-stroke at the sight of his two beauties sitting at the table in the glow of the morning. "*Madainn mhath mo nighean mhaiseach.* What are ye both doin' up so early? Are ye well?" Concern edging into his voice.

"Come sit wi' us, *a ghaoil*, we hae somethin' to tell ye," Isobel said.

Cat looked at her mother sharply. She wasn't going to tell him, was she?

Isobel waited for him to sit, then put her hand over his and said, "Angus, yer daughter has the Sight."

Cat watched his face run the gamut of emotions; bewilderment, frustration, anger, pity, awe, and finally resting on blankness. She watched her father's blue eyes change intensity with every emotion he felt, creating that pit in her stomach again. She was about to say something when he stood and rushed out the kitchen door, heading for the barn. Cat's hurt violet gaze rested on his back, and she said dryly, "That went well." Cat and her mother both pushed away from the table at the same time. Subject closed … for now. They went upstairs to get dressed and prepare for the journey. It was going to be a long trip.

                                    ❧

By the time all of the tenants who were going to the Gathering arrived, it was mid-morning. Many came on horseback with pack horses in tow, but there were also three wagons that would be loaded with supplies and people. It would be a slow, dusty, hot trip on the rutted trail. Roads were a new addition in the Highlands, thanks to General George Wade about twenty years earlier, but they wouldn't reach one until they were almost to the castle.

Catrìona got permission to ride with the Murrays so she could talk with her friend Janet. She didn't want to be too close to her father, who was still steaming over the morning's news. Cat knew he would talk to her when he was ready, and not a minute earlier. Pursuing an answer from him in his silent mood always caused more grief than good.

She climbed into the back of the Murray's wagon to sit with Janet. The two were like night and day sitting close to each other; their legs dangling over the edge of the wagon. Janet's light blonde hair and peachy complexion was a perfect compliment to Cat's darker tones. She had a pouty, small mouth, a scattering of freckles on her nose, and was nearly six inches shorter than Cat. Born only two weeks apart, Janet being the oldest, they shared no trace of the same personality. Janet was much more of a serious girl, never seeing the humor Catrìona found in almost every situation. She always said Cat was probably the happiest person she knew.

That's why Janet was so disturbed now to see Cat twirling her hair around her fingers. It was rare for her to be bothered to this extent. "What's wrong wi' ye, Cat?" she asked, using her best adult voice.

"It happened again last night, Janet," Cat whispered, mesmerized by the dust rolling up from the wheels on the dirt road.

"What did?" Janet moved closer, her light green eyes full of curiosity.

"Another vision, only this time it was about Seumas. I saw him get hurt verra badly at the Games." She chewed on her lower lip as she met Janet's eyes.

"What did he say when you told him?" She was watching Cat closely, wanting to know all the details. Not that she would gossip about it to anyone, but everything interesting always seemed to happen to someone other than herself.

"I dinna tell him yet." Cat was still trying to figure out if she should even tell him. Her usual bright, beaming face, always so full of joy for the sheer pleasure of life was now haunted.

Janet was at a loss as to how to console her, but after a few miles of silence, her eyes got large and a smiled played along her lips.

"Cat, do ye think ye can wait to tell Seumas about the vision 'til we get to the Gatherin'? There's bound to be at least one Seer there we could ask."

Catrìona dropped the twisted lock of hair, and beamed a bright, dimpled smile on her friend at the suggestion. "O' course! Why didna I think of that?" she asked, full of excitement at the prospect of getting some legitimate answers from a peer. The day was getting brighter by the minute as they bounced their way down the rutted dirt path.

ॐ

After the entire day of being thrashed in the wagons, the whole entourage stopped by a wooded burn to make camp for the night. The men unhitched and hobbled the horses, and the women got the cook fires started. To make better time, they had eaten oatcakes or bannocks and cheese for lunch, but now it was time for a hot meal. Some of the women were erecting lean-tos and draping canvas over them as shelter for the night. Others, mostly the men, would just sleep in the open. It was getting cloudy and cooler. Hopefully, it wouldn't be an all out deluge tomorrow, but Cat could smell rain in the air. Mud would make travel much slower, and her father even more distant.

Cat and Isobel made for the burn to get in a wash before the weather turned too cold. They were both filthy from the dust and sweat of the day. Many people didn't seem to mind that they smelled and looked like animals, with dirt streaks running down their faces and necks. While they may not be able to keep their clothes clean on the journey, they sure could do something about removing the grit from their skin.

Cat's brothers were finding their friends to get in some practice time for the competitions. The air was filled with the sounds of swords clanging together, grunts, laughter, and congratulations when a good strike was made. When the wind changed, the beats of the *bodhran* or skirl of the pipes could be heard from those who were dancing and competing on the *phìob-mhòr*.

When supper was finished, Isobel sat next to her daughter on the log by the fire to keep warm. She wanted to know what Cat felt about their conversation that morning. She knew Angus was still in a quandary about what to do with his youngest child, and was still very withdrawn. *He* may not talk while he was in that state, but Isobel always made the effort to tell him of any further developments — good or bad.

"Cat, would ye like to tell me o' yer dream yet?" Her light blue eyes reflected the flames, and her wispy, white brows arched in question.

Catrìona met her mother's gaze, but ignored the question, instead told her about the plan to find a Seer at the Gathering. "It would seem that I could be findin' the solution there, dinna ye think, Mam?" she asked in lighthearted tone. "It was Janet's idea really, but I agree wi' her."

"Aye, that is a good idea, lass, we should hae thought o' that earlier," Isobel said, tapping her finger on her chin. A strategy was forming. Catrìona should have a real teacher, not just someone to explain what was happening to her. It was the best — no, the only way — Cat would be able to learn how her gift worked. For the first time in almost three months, Isobel felt this was a step in the right direction.

"I ken just the one to ask, too … if she comes." Isobel excused herself with a pat on Cat's shoulder, and got up to find Angus to give him the news.

ॐ

Angus was by the burn sitting on a large rock when Isobel found him. He was so deep in his own contemplations that when she put her hand on his shoulder, he jumped. "Damn it, woman! Hae ye no sense comin' up behind a man in the dark, and ye as quiet as a mouse? Ye near made me draw me dirk!"

"Well, if that's all it took to get ye to speak to me, I would hae done that years ago, ye auld gudgeon!" she said with a giggle in her voice. "I hae some news about Catrìona ye may want to hear."

Angus reached around and gathered in his wife around her waist, drew her in front of him between his legs and laid his head on her breasts. "Sorry I'm such a fool sometimes Isobel," he said, his voice muffled in her bodice. She smelled of onions and bread and stew. Her fingers were in his long, wavy hair that he had untied from its plait. Rubbing his head and combing out the snarls, the tension started to release its hold on him.

"Aye, then, let's hear what ye hae to tell me, *a ghaoil,*" he said.

"Cat thinks we should seek out a teacher for her at the Gatherin'," she said, still rubbing his head. "I thought it was a good idea. I also thought that we should go a bit further … to see if Cat could stay wi' her until she has learned about the Sight."

He looked up at her at this, but kept her close. "Who were ye plannin' on askin', Anna Macpherson? She's the one Alexander consults when he needs answers, and he swears by her," he said, referring to his cousin, the thirteenth Clan Chief.

"Aye, just so. The Mistress is all alone and maybe wouldna mind the comp'ny of a young woman for awhile. Cat has no one else to go to. What do ye say?" The folds of her skirt hid her crossed fingers hoping he would agree with the plan.

Angus thought for a moment, then nodded his head in agreement. "How long do ye think she would hae to be away? I think I miss the lass already."

"Cat has so much of the Sight in her already that maybe it wilna be too long." She felt about as unhappy as her husband at the prospect of losing her daughter — for any length of time.

"I hae ne'er seen Cat use stones or wee plants to get her visions," she said. "She just seems to hae them on her own. I ken from my own Mam that there's much to learn about the Seer's ways."

"Seumas tells me that when they hunt together, she always tells him where to find the stags, and under which fallen trees the rabbits are hidin'. When he asks her how she kent those things, she just says, 'If ye dinna already ken, there's naught I can say to tell ye.' After a kill, she'll pray quietly over the dead beast. He doesna ken where she got the idea to do that, but told me that he and the lads ne'er mention it to her. They just let her be about it, thinkin' it's some kind of lasses way."

Angus stood up from the rock where he was resting to lead Isobel back towards the fire. "She's just such a wee lass yet. I'm fearful for her … but a teacher is what she'll be needin' to get through this. Best we go tell her, aye?"

Arm in arm, they walked back to the where Catrìona was sitting, taking a seat on either side of her on the log she occupied. Cat looked back and forth at both of them as they told her of their plan for her.

"But how long will I hae to gone from ye both? Who will help Mam in the house?" She sent her questioning gaze to her father. "Why canna I do the learnin' at home?" And a hundred other questions were in queue to be asked.

"Whoa, lass, whoa now." Angus held up his hand as if that would stop the bombardment of unanswerable questions. "We wilna ken anythin' until we speak wi' Mistress Macpherson and see if she'll take ye on as an apprentice of sorts."

"Cat, let's take one day at a time on this. It's goin' to be verra hard on all of us for a while," Isobel said, putting her arm around her daughter's shoulder. It would definitely be hardest on her. She counted on Cat to help with the chores, and just to have another female around to offset the male dominance in the household. Her strength would just have to hold its own until Cat was taught the healing arts. Isobel only hoped it wouldn't take too long.

"That's enough talk for tonight, lass. Off to bed wi' ye now. Yer Mam will be wi' ye in a while," Angus said, getting up from the log and pulling Cat to her feet. He gave her a hug and she squeezed him back, then standing on tip-toes, kissed his cheek.

"Good night, Da, and I'm sorry for all the bother I'm causin' ye," she said, looking him in the eyes. "I'll just hae to make ye proud of me for haeing the Sight."

He saw in her eyes the absolute resolve to do just that. "I'm already proud of ye, lass, now go on to bed," and kissed her forehead.

Catrìona bent to kiss her mother on the cheek, but when she did, she tasted salty tears.

"What's wrong, Mam?" she asked, kneeling in front of her mother and putting her arms around her neck.

"Och, Cat, ye are growin' up right fast and becomin' quite a woman. I'm verra proud of ye, too," she said, wiping the wetness from her face with her *arisaid*. "I'll be wi' ye shortly, now off ye go."

ॐ

It had been a very long day, yet she was exhausted and exhilarated all at the same time. Cat crawled inside the small, covered space, wrapped herself in the blanket, and before she could even say her thanks for the day, she was sound asleep. Sometime later, she heard her mother come in beside her, but immediately fell back into a deep sleep.

She dreamt of lying in a field of heather on her back, looking up at the clouds. She could see shapes in them, as if they were telling her a story. Many were of animals, like horses and seals, but the one that startled her out of her slumber was a swan.

Lachlan had told her something about a swan being very important to a Seer. Rabbie Duncanson's aunt had said it was a bird of the air, the water and the land, and where they met was a sacred place where the Seer could transform herself into the swan. It was a very powerful omen.

Cat stirred, waking her mother.

"Are ye haeing another vision, *nighean*?" Isobel asked softly.

"No, Mam … at least I dinna think so," she whispered back sleepily. "I was just dreamin' that I was a swan made from a cloud. It was verra beautiful."

Isobel rolled onto her side facing Catrìona, and cradled spoon-like along side her daughter's body. They fell back to sleep interlocked together until morning came.

ॐ

Angus woke up his wife and daughter just in time for them to grab a bite to eat and pack up their lean-to. He had been watching them sleep together like babes, knowing they were exhausted from the journey and lack of sleep the night before. Making sure that Isobel kept up her strength was paramount, so he let her sleep as long as he could. All of his tenants readily pitched in to help her whenever they could, and making breakfast for two more mouths was a minor addition to the daily routine.

"Did ye both sleep well?" He was squatting in front of the lean-to watching them fold the canvas and blankets they used for the night.

In harmonized unison, the two of them answered, "Aye, just fine," then looked at each other and burst into giggles. How alike they looked sometimes, Angus thought. How were they going to handle not being together all of the time? He had already decided to have a couple of his tenants' daughters move in to help keep the house. There was too much to do for Isobel and Mrs. Stark to do alone.

The rain scented air of last night led to only a sprinkle, and now the sun was trying to burn through the fog that shrouded the area. The scent of grass and heather was dense enough to be a tangible object. Not as hot as it had been yesterday, it looked like the makings of a fine day to complete their journey to the castle.

"Will ye be ridin' wi' the Murrays again today, Cat?" It didn't matter to Isobel if she did or not. Now that Angus was in a better mood, she would enjoy his company alone for a change.

"No. If it agrees wi' ye both, I would rather like to spend some time wi' ye in case I dinna get to for a while." Cat wasn't sure when, or if she would become a Seer's apprentice, but felt that she needed to be with her parents for the rest of the trip.

While Cat ate her breakfast, she told Janet about the plan her parents had forged. "I'll see ye at the camp tonight, Janet. I hae a lot of questions to ask Mam and Da yet, and I may no' get another chance if I hae to move away for a time." With that, they went to their separate wagons to begin the jostling, dusty day apart.

≥❧

The wagon train followed the River Tummel east, passing Loch Tummel. At Killiecrankie, they would head north to Blair Atholl. The passing countryside was in such a riotous summer frenzy of wildflowers and lush green fields, Cat hardly said a word for the entire day. Areas of thick woods interrupted the views of the seemingly impassable bens that loomed from the horizon. There were long, empty heather and broom-covered moors, with huge granite outcroppings covered in multi-colored lichens. Here and there, a cairn to mark a trail, or a pictish cross to mark a crossroad. They passed small villages with stone kirks and thatch-roofed cottages.

Shaggy Highland cows and black-faced sheep dotted the pastureland, with tenders and their dogs never far away.

It was visual overload for Catrìona. She rarely ever went far from home, finding what surrounded her astonishing when she did. Desire to walk through the fields of flag irises, orchids and honeysuckle, breathe in their heady aromas and gather them into a bouquet nearly consumed her. She listened to the myriad of songbirds that changed as quickly as the scenery.

She was smiling from ear to ear when she happened to see her parents watching her. A blush brightened her cheeks as if caught with her soul open. Strange. She had never felt like that before. Why did she feel like she needed this moment to be private? Her smile faded, replaced with a small crease between her brows.

Catrìona always had an expressive face, although not always readable. She could feel her mother remembering her own mother going through these very same things. The distancing from other people was crucial to a Seer.

The three of them were deep in their own thoughts when, in the distance, the white harled façade of the tower of Blair Castle came into view. The lush green Grampian Mountains were the backdrop for the small palace surrounded by woods. Long, green fields allowed the castle to be seen from a distance, but it was still about an hour away.

Camp would be made outside the castle walls. Tomorrow, the Clan Chief would welcome all the clansmen to the Great Hall with a feast to usher in the Games the following day. Since the middle of the eleventh century, when the first Highland Games were held on the Braes of Mar to choose the best soldiers and guards for the King, hundreds of clansmen would attend. A great hunt for boar would also take place, testing the skills of the Highlander's hunting prowess in the woods. It was a dangerous sport that sometimes proved fatal, not only for the boar, but for the men as well.

Highlander men were always gentlemen until they got to the Games. When they all got together, something came over them — mostly the plentiful flow of whisky and ale — turning them all into barbarians. Many would spend the entire week in a drunken stupor. Women were safest in large groups, if they chose to venture into the castle to watch the ceremonies after the great feast. This is when all the clansmen would swear their oath to the Chief, to protect him with their lives if necessary.

The fierce-looking Highlanders entered the Great Hall in their full war regalia. These were wild men, with their long hair, most with full beards. Each sept of the clan wore plaids of different colors in seemingly endless variations of tartan. Gold, silver, bronze, or tin brooches sparkling on their shoulders held their long plaids in place. Sporrans at their waists of every imaginable material from the skins of animals, such as badgers, to intricately tooled leather. Dirks were in their sheaths, broadswords hung from their belts, and the *sgian dhu*, or black knife, rested in the tops of their stockings. Some even brandished their pistols in their belted waists. To top off the ensemble, each wore a woolen bonnet with their clan crest and plant sprig on it.

All of this weaponry was proclaimed illegal by the English after the 1715 Rising, but the English were not there to police them. Their cocky confidence and indomitable bravado could terrify even their own kind, to say nothing of what it did to their enemies. Attempting to reckon with undisciplined Scots terrorized even the most seasoned troops.

⁊❧

Finding a secluded spot under a copse of birch near the Glengarry River, Angus stopped the wagon to make camp. The others in the group went off to make their own camps with a little privacy. The weather was holding, but Isobel still preferred to sleep under a lean-to. Angus set up a private one for the two of them, then set Cat up with one all to herself, making it close by, just in case.

Cat had already started the fire when Isobel got back from making sleeping arrangements. They were about to get supper started when Angus announced that he and the lads were off to the castle to register for the competitions. He promised his two lasses they would be back as soon as possible. Isobel knew that meant they wouldn't be back until early the next morning; another reason to have Angus set the lean-to's up close to each other. Once the whisky started flowing, only daylight would bring him back.

"Angus, would ye ask Alexander where to locate Anna Macpherson? We'll be needin' to meet up wi' her to see about lessons for Cat before we leave here."

"Aye," he said, sobering before even getting started on the drink. "Aye, I'll do that." He stood at his full height, accepting the enormous burden of responsibility, then bent to kiss her cheek. Isobel patted his bottom as he turned to leave for the castle, and he let out a deep chuckle.

Isobel and Cat cooked supper for themselves, then went off for a bath in the river. They took turns watching out for their privacy, even getting a chance to wash their clothes. They weren't alone though. Many of the other clanswomen had the same idea, and it turned out to be a small *ceilidh* of their own. It was a chance to get reacquainted with friends they had not seen since last year.

As Cat sat on the rocky shore drying herself off, a raven landed on a branch in the tree above her. It was so close that if she wanted to, she could have reached out and touched its blue-black feathers.

"Hallò wee raven. What is it ye're lookin' for?"

The raven cocked its head, staring at her with its black eyes that reflected Cat's image in them. Cat had the definite feeling that it was looking for *her*. A smile touched her mouth when she realized that it was sent to find her. She didn't know how she knew this, she just did. Ravens were messengers, but who sent it, and why? Was she supposed to give it a message back? No ... her reflection in its eyes was all that was needed by whomever sent it. She really needed to find Mistress Macpherson in the morning.

By the time darkness fell, Isobel and Catrìona were back by the fire drying their clothes. Cat didn't feel the need to apprise her exhausted mother about the raven, so they went off to their separate lean-tos. It had been another long day, and Isobel was asleep immediately. Catrìona, on the other hand, was still wide awake. Between the noise from the women still having their party, the shouts of the men at the castle, and pipes in the distance, there was little peace in which to sleep.

Cat looked up at the star-filled sky to watch the moon make its descent into the oblivion behind the mountains. Once again, she felt the oneness with the Earth and sky. Blocking out the noises all around her, she became the ground she laid on; she became invisible. A cool breeze stirred the thin muslin of her shift. She imagined herself as the grass in a field that waved in the wind. Small beasts hid in her shelter. Deer nibbled at her stalks. As she relaxed, the tingling started in her hands. She waited for the rest of the usual symptoms to happen, but this time they remained elusive. She was calm, dreamlike, and knew she would have another vision.

In her vision, Cat saw an old woman walking towards her. Cat didn't know who she was, there was too much distance between them to make out her face, but there was a certain familiarity to her. The woman had a beautiful red fox walking beside her. The fox kept looking at Cat, but how, wasn't she invisible? Suddenly, the woman held out her arms to Cat, beckoning Cat to go with her. Who was she? What did she want with her? How did she see her? Catrìona heard her name being called. It was the old woman speaking to her. How did she know her name?

"*Come to me, Catrìona, there is much to teach ye,*" the voice said. Cat then realized that it wasn't actually in her ears that she heard the summons, it was in her head. No one had spoken to her in other visions. This one was different.

With a start, she came out of her trance. She glanced over to her mother's lean-to to see if she woke her, but her mother remained sleeping. What was that all about? She didn't want to wake her mother to ask, but she didn't think she'd be able to sleep after that vision. She wondered who the woman could be. Why was she familiar? Cat knew they had never met. It would have to wait until morning, or maybe if her father got back soon, she could ask him.

⁊⬩

Day dawned a metallic gray with clouds racing in from the west. It looked as though the heavens would open up anytime to inundate the camp in a torrent of water. Rain happened with such frequency that life could not be stopped for the sake of staying dry. Scots went about their business, no matter what the weather. Just after breakfast was started, a heavy rain washed over the area.

Angus and the lads returned from the castle ravenous after being out the entire night. Isobel timed their arrival just right and breakfast was ready for them. The entire family was sitting under the trees finishing off their meal, when Angus broached the subject.

"So Catrìona, hae ye somethin' ye would like to be tellin' yer brothers?"

Cat was still thinking about her latest vision when she heard her father ask her to come forward with her gift. She looked up to see all of them waiting to hear what she had to say.

Seumas looked at Cat, his eyes full of curiosity and said, "What is it lass?"

Cat had regained a little composure by then and blurted out, "I hae the Sight, Seumas." She gave them all a moment to take that in. He looked at his parents for acknowledgement, unsure whether Cat was serious. They both gave a nod. He caught Lachlan's eye; a nod was given indicating it was true. Iain's eyes couldn't get any larger; he obviously didn't know. Seumas hid his emotions well, and if he was shocked by the revelation, it didn't show.

Seumas just sat there looking at her, shaking his head. Maybe it was because of their large age difference, but out of all of her brothers, she knew he found her the most peculiar. Cat got up, patted him on the shoulder, pressed a kiss on his forehead, and walked away. Iain asked if anyone else needed a drink, got a unanimous "Aye," and went to fetch the whisky.

෴

Catrìona wandered down to the river. She needed to hear the sound of the water to carry her burden away; needed to be cleansed. Kneeling in the wet grass on the bank, she cupped her hands to fill them with water. With her hands full, she stood, raised them over her head, and let the cold water drizzle down onto her face. She did this four times to each of the four *airts*, always moving sunwards, and ending in the west; all the while murmuring thanks in Gaelic.

She had no knowledge of being taught this. It was more of an instinct she followed from another time ... when she was here before ... as someone else.

Unaware of her parents standing beside a large oak tree behind her, they came to see if she was all right, not expecting to see such a pagan ritual being performed. Though it seemed like it was the most natural thing in the world for her to be doing, they gave each other a questioning look mirroring the same thought — *where did she learn that?*

"I told ye that she just kens about these things, Angus," Isobel whispered. "I'm thinkin' my Mam's blood runs thick in her veins."

"Aye, well, it sure isna from my family!" Angus whispered back. "I wasna sure I really believed she had the Sight until just this verra moment."

Cat had turned around to find her parents standing there watching her. Again, that strange feeling that her privacy was being invaded. Picking up her skirts, she dried her face, then walked over to see what questions she could get answered.

seeing it coming

nna Macpherson was preparing for a meeting. She had seen this day coming for a long time, and now it was finally here. Last night, she actually saw her young apprentice in a vision. She had no idea Catrìona would be so young, but because of her youth, would not have misunderstood notions of the Sight, and teaching her might actually be easier.

Anna's cottage was almost a mile away from the castle, tucked in the woods, well away from people. It sat on a knoll beside a burn with Blair Castle in the distance. She lived alone, never marrying or having relationships with anyone. Her energy needed to remain free from interference to attain clear visions. When she was needed, she would be summoned by a rider, and always go to them. Only by her invitation would anyone ever set foot in her house.

There was much to do in preparation for her new student. All the plants and stones to start her teachings with had to be collected, though she would let Catrìona choose her own power elements for her amulet. These may be stones, horns, feathers, shells, or even a bound lock of hair. Anything to which a strong attachment was formed due to the color, texture, or omen it represented.

Anna had sent the raven to locate her young student and report back with news of her arrival. Last night, the red fox guided her through the veil of duality to connect with Catrìona's inner self; the self that allows the Sight — and other abilities — to happen. She knew Catrìona saw her in the vision and would be looking for her by day's end. That commitment to find a teacher was an indication of her abilities and intent to learn.

Having taught only two others how to harness the power of the Sight, only students with great potential from the start would have the benefit of her tutelage. It had been over forty years since her last student.

Anna was said to be ninety seven years old, but even she didn't know that for sure. She had long, steel gray hair, which she always wore in a long plait; large black eyes, and not a tooth left in her head. To look at her, she was an old woman, but physically she was still able to run her own cottage and garden.

A long staff of gnarled oak, rubbed smooth from time and wear, was her power tool. Topping the oak staff was a purple amethyst crystal the size of an egg, enveloped inside the wood while it grew. Just below the crystal, encircling the staff, was the ancient Celtic interlace design carved into the wood. This provided protection against negative forces, confusing unwanted energies. With this tool, she had seen many battles won and lost; chiefs born and killed; time come and go. She had seen the other side of the veil.

Anna was the current holder of the *clach na brataich* or ensign stone. The crystal was unearthed when the Clan Donnachaidh standard pole was pulled from the ground at the battle of Bannockburn in 1314. The Clan Chief, *Donnachaidh Reamhair* or "Stout Duncan," saw it as a good omen because they were victorious. It had been carried by all the Robertson Chiefs since then, when leading the clan to battle.

The current Clan Chief, Alexander Robertson, would seek out Anna's advice before the clan went to any battle. The crystal was handed to him for good luck. If Anna saw the battle was to be lost, it was up to the Chief to make the final decision to fight or not. The omen would have to be very bad to keep a Scot from a fight.

In the Rising of 1715, the *clach na brataich* was handed to Alexander, and he was horrified to find a crack in it. This was a bad omen indeed, but the clan chose to fight anyway. Many men in the clan died during that rebellion, which led to the tight control the English held over the Scots.

ᘓ

The rain finally stopped just before noon. A thick fog was hanging over the area, yet the sun was seen now and then, like an apparition in the sky above. The campsite was a quagmire; impossible to start a cooking fire, so bannocks, hard tack and ale were lunch. Tonight, they would all eat heartily at the great feast in the castle, so filling the belly now was not important.

Angus remembered the request his wife asked last night, and went over to fill her in. She was sitting on a log with her *arisaid* wrapped tight around her shoulders.

"Are ye cold, *a ghaoil?*" he asked, cradling her into his big chest.

"Aye, a bit, but no' anymore wi' ye here to warm me," she said, cuddling into him to capture all of his heat.

Not wishing to get everyone riled up all over again about the subject, he whispered in her ear, "Alex told me that Anna Macpherson lives about a mile northeast o' here."

Isobel looked at Angus and simply asked, "When will ye go?"

"This afternoon. I'll take Cat wi' me to see her. Would ye like to come along?"

"No ... I mean aye ... what I mean is ye just canna go to her unannounced. Seers dinna allow anyone into their homes. Does she ken ye are comin'? Did ye send a messenger?" Isobel asked, getting anxious. She knew the proper protocol for getting an appointment.

"She kens we're here already. Cat told me of her latest vision, and the raven," he said, trying not to sound skeptical.

Isobel's white brows flew up at this revelation. "Raven? Vision? When?"

Cat told her father of her latest vision with the old woman after the camp finally settled down. When Cat described the woman to him, he knew exactly who she was.

"Cat told me a raven came to see her at the river when ye were washin' last night. She said it looked right at her, and she kent it was as a messenger. Do ye think it's really possible, Isobel?"

"I think anything's possible, Angus. What else did she say?"

"In her vision last night she described Anna to me; said that Anna called her by name and told her to come for her teachin'." Angus watched his wife grow pale during the story.

"Dear *Brighid*, Angus! This is happenin' verra fast." Isobel got to her feet and started pacing back and forth in front of him, fiddling with the ends of her shawl. "If Anna kens that Cat is here for her studies, will she want her to remain wi' her today?"

Angus stood and folded her into him, holding her close. "*A ghaoil*, I'm sure we can tell Anna that we will bring her back for her teachin' in a week or so. She wilna expect us to make this decision right away."

With a deep breath, Isobel agreed. After all, they had just formulated the plan for Cat on the way here. How could Anna expect Cat immediately?

Angus kissed the top of her head, breathing in the scent of camomile soap, and asked her again if she wanted to accompany them to see Anna. "Come wi' us, my love. Ye'll feel better to meet Anna and ask yer questions."

"Aye, maybe I will at that." It would definitely reassure her if she could speak with Anna herself, and also see Catrìona's reaction to her new teacher. She squeezed his waist, grateful for his understanding of her feelings and concerns.

"I'll get the horses saddled and we'll be ready in a wee bit. Go fetch Cat and let the lads ken where we'll be goin'. We should only be gone for a couple of hours and be back in time for the feast tonight." He tossed the last statement over his shoulder as he walked towards the horses.

ॐ

By the time the threesome started riding, the sun had finally burned its way through the fog. Every step the horses took squished in the soggy ground. When they arrived at the crossroad that led to Anna's cottage, Cat saw the raven on the pictish cross that marked the juncture.

"Stop at the crossroad, Da, Mistress Macpherson will meet us here. We are no' to go any further." Her eyes were fixed on the raven, as if in a trance.

"How do ye ken this, Cat?" Angus questioned. He was looking back and forth from his daughter to the raven.

Isobel, who was also watching Cat, had seen this look before in her mother. "Angus, the raven spoke for Mistress Macpherson, we need to do as it asks."

"I heard nothin'. How did it speak to her? Did ye hear it speak?" He was more than a little spooked by this.

"It was in her heid that she heard it, Angus. There's no other way to describe it. My Mam often described the voice to me. She said it was how she knew things."

Cat caught a movement out of the corner of her eye to see Anna walking towards them. She was all alone, carrying a large staff that glittered deep purple at the top. The raven took flight, landing in the tree that Anna was walking by.

All three dismounted and waited for Anna to reach them, not going any further, as instructed by the raven. When Anna got closer, Cat realized that she was the old woman in her vision last night. She looked around for the beautiful red fox that had accompanied the woman in the vision, but didn't see it.

"Where's yer wee fox, Mistress Macpherson?" Cat asked, still hoping it would show itself from the woods.

"Ahhh, so ye did see *mo shionnach* that led me to ye last night. Gooood," she crooned. "Ye will only see him in visions, but this ye'll learn soon."

"Will ye be able to teach our daughter then, Mistress?" Isobel asked, wanting to get the conversation back to a more familiar realm.

Cat watched Anna tear her obsidian gaze from her to look at Isobel. At first, she wasn't sure if the old woman had heard her mother; she just stared at her for a minute. It was like Anna was seeing right into her.

"So that's where she gets it from," Anna said to Isobel, as if she had just learned a secret. "Ye did ken that ye have the power as well, aye?"

Isobel's large eyes got even larger, while her wispy, white brows shot up to her hairline.

"No, 'twas my Mam who had the Sight, no' me." Isobel said, fidgeting with her *arisaid*.

"Aye ..." Anna said slowly, seemingly looking right through Isobel. "Aye, ye have it too, ye just dinna ken how to use it. Ye're no' well, are ye?"

Isobel had gone quite pale, and Angus quickly went to her side to steady her. Anna shifted her gaze up to Angus this time, who appeared unphased by her attention. Again, Anna just stared at him.

"Be sure to tell yer eldest son to take care wi' his sword tomorrow," she said ominously.

Cat froze. Then it wasn't a dream. Anna looked sharply at Catrìona, sensing that the vision had not been shared with her family yet.

"It's yer duty to tell those ye hae seen in a vision what will come o' them, Catrìona."

Then Anna turned her black stare back to Isobel, and said, "To answer yer question, Mistress Robertson, aye, I will teach Catrìona about her powers, and she'll stay wi' me for a period of three years. I ken that ye are no' ready for me to take her just now, so bring her back in one week." Then, without another word, turned and started back down the lane towards her cottage.

One question remained and Cat asked it loudly. "Will I be permitted to go home now and again, Mistress?"

Anna stopped in her tracks, and without turning around said, "Only once," then resumed her journey home.

Before any of them could comment, Anna was out of sight. The three of them rode back to camp in silence; each burdened by their own thoughts. The wind had picked up and the sun was disappearing behind the eerie fog again.

᷾

Anna knew the news she gave the Robertson's was a bit cryptic, but it had to be said. She did not adhere to the belief that if a vision was spoken, it would bring it about. She knew from long experience that when she saw something, it always came to be. Fear of invoking the power of what was seen caused many Seers to use a substitute word for the proper name. Anna believed that the power of the spoken word was commanded by intent. It was up to the person in the vision to make the changes necessary for it not to occur, not her.

After meeting Catrìona, Anna knew that she would be her brightest student yet. It was as if Cat was already attuned to all the powers of nature. Could she be a reincarnate? She would employ a divination to see who Catrìona was in a past life, when she became her pupil. This was one of many tools a Seer used, so Catrìona would experience how it worked first hand. For the first time in years, Anna was excited about the prospect of teaching again.

Anna smiled to herself as she walked up the path to her cottage, the scent of herbs and flowers wafted on the air as she passed by her gardens. One corner of each garden was left uncultivated as offerings to the land faeries. This acknowledged that Mother Nature was the ultimate cultivator. The protective Rowan tree beside the house was already starting its berry clusters that would turn a bright red in the autumn.

Her one room cottage was made of stone with a thatched roof. The only door faced east to greet the morning sun. As payment for her services long ago, she was given a window; it was in the west end of the cottage to let the warm light in. This setup allowed the flow of the cottage to follow the direction of the Sun and Moon cycles, keeping harmony with nature inside the home.

The smell of peat smoke from the hearth rose from the vent in the roof. The hearth fire was rarely extinguished. The only exceptions were on the sun festivals of Beltaine, Samhain, and Imbolc, when a new fire would be lit from a central bonfire and brought into the house. Three white circles were carved into the hearth as protection against evil entering her home. Beside the hearth, a narrow table held stones, bones, feathers and candles; a sacred area.

Unlike the normal custom, no animals lived in the cottage with her. The animals she communed with were all wild. The fox, deer, raven, owl, falcon, and many years ago, the wolf. Living as one with the natural world was easier than trying to conform it to human standards.

Anna was also a healer, so herbs were hung to dry on the walls, lower rafters, and stored in jars. Teas, infusions, and poultices awaited preparation for those who became ill or were wounded. Mostly, she tended only her own clan, but sometimes, it would be a two or three day trip to the far-off Highlanders who needed her assistance. This was the life of a Seer, and soon she would be sharing it with her new student.

&

"I think now would be a good time to tell us o' the vision ye had, Catrìona," Isobel demanded when they returned to camp.

The whole family was seated around the fire staring at Cat, waiting for her explanation. She picked up a lock of hair and began twisting it around her fingers. Out of their own volition, her eyes went directly to Seumas and remained on him.

"Since it's me that ye singled out, I take it ye had a vision about me then?" He got up and moved closer to her, looking deep into her eyes for the answer.

"Aye, Seumas, I hae. It will be at the claymore competition. Ye'll be fightin' wi' Alex Maclagan ..."

"Wait," Seumas interrupted, "How did ye ken I drew Alex for the competition? I hae no' even told Da yet!"

"What do ye think haein' the Sight means, Seumas?" Cat said. "I ken what will happen before ye do."

"Oh, right." He settled back and asked her to continue. "Sorry for interruptin' ye, go on."

"Ye were doin' right well and seemed to hae control, when all o' a sudden, Alex's sword cut into yer right leg." With a valiant attempt to keep her own feelings checked, she told him what she saw. She didn't need to look at him to feel the range of emotions he was going through.

"Did I die?" he whispered.

Cat held his gaze, choking on what she had to tell him.

"Did I?" A look of horror changed his face.

"No, but it crippled ye, Seumas."

The sharp intake of everyone's breath summed it up.

"Cat, why didna ye tell us this sooner?" Isobel asked through gritted teeth, trying to contain her frustration.

Cat couldn't meet their eyes. She just sat there shaking her head, staring at her feet.

Angus got up and grabbed her shoulder, shaking her back to reality. "Why, Cat?"

She took in her family's glares and her tears let loose.

"I didna believe it myself. How would ye hae believed it?" she cried, then ran into the woods.

ہ▲

It was nearly dusk before Cat had enough courage to go back to camp. Her absence gave everyone enough time to discuss what they would do. In the end, Seumas decided that since he knew about the incident, he could change the outcome without getting hurt. Cat wasn't sure if that was possible. Her mother said it was tempting the fates, and after repeated pleading, still couldn't get Seumas to back out of the claymore competition.

Angus said that since he knew nothing of how visions worked, he felt like Seumas did; with the knowledge, the outcome could be changed. He admitted that this would test the accuracy of Catrìona's vision, and to see if fate really could be changed. He wanted to see it all play out, whatever the outcome.

With everything out in the open, Cat felt a deep sense of relief. She wished she had told them earlier, but this was all so new to her. They believed her, mostly, and only time would reveal the outcome.

ہ▲

The thick fog showed signs of settling in for the night. A cool mist was falling on the eerie gray landscape, covering everything in a shimmering blanket. It would be a good night to be inside staying dry. With all the body heat, it would also be warm.

Angus and the lads wore the Robertson plaid of red, green and blue, with white linen shirts. The brooches holding the plaids at their shoulders were made of fine silver, hand-crafted by clan silversmiths bearing a pair of leaping wolves springing from a Highland interlace knot design. The design was an adaptation from the Robertson's of Straun shield, which had three silver wolves' heads on it.

Catrìona and Isobel proudly walked through the huge front gates of Blair Castle surrounded by their men. Already, drunken men brawled inside the gates, stopping long enough to see if they could elicit some new blood. Angus and Seumas just snarled at their disrespect and kept walking. Iain ignored them. Lachlan, of course, thinking he could take on the world, taunted them in Gaelic, saying he'd be back later. Angus, hearing this, cuffed him up side his head; the brawlers roared in laughter.

"Ye may be a braw laddie, but hae ye no sense at all?" Angus scolded quietly. "Maybe I should let ye come back later so I can watch the show myself." A chuckle entered his voice remembering his own fearlessness at Lachlan's age.

"Hmmm!" was the only word Lachlan used to show his indignation.

Once inside the Great Hall, Cat and Isobel sat on the benches near the front with the other women to watch the ceremony. Angus and the lads joined the loosely formed line gathering in the back to renew their clan oaths. Somehow, all three of them now carried cups of ale while talking with their cousins. Isobel, watching them, smiled and shook her head.

"What are ye smilin' at, Mam?" asked Catrìona, happy to see the earlier tension disappear.

"At how quickly the ale finds a man," Isobel said, dimples deepening in her cheeks.

Cat's belly rumbled at the thought of something to fill the void. She had not eaten since breakfast and now she was ravenous. Isobel, hearing the growling, said she would fetch them each a bite to eat from the long tables of food along the wall. Cat volunteered to go, but someone caught Isobel's attention, and she headed for the tables.

"Keep my seat for me, Cat. I'll be back directly. I see yer Da's sister, Emma, and I want to say hallò."

"Aye, Mam. I'll stay here, but hurry back, I'm starvin'!"

Cat looked around to see if Janet had arrived yet. She wanted to tell her about meeting Mistress Macpherson and her three year stint away. The hall was crowded and the smells of ale, unwashed bodies, and meat cooking was a potent mixture in her famished state. She was just about to head for the food tables when a hand on her shoulder stopped her.

"Och, Janet, I was just lookin' for ye." She stood up and gave her friend a hug, happy to see her.

"So tell me what's been happenin'," Janet said. "Did ye find a teacher? Will ye hae to leave? How long will ye be gone for? What did ..."

"Stop, stop," Cat said, holding up her hands and giggling at her friend's enthusiasm. "If ye let me get a word in, I'll tell ye all about it."

Halfway through the narrative of who, what, where, and when, Isobel came back with a huge plate of food; enough for the three of them.

"The cocks crow," Isobel said, letting her gaze travel to the men, "but the hens deliver the goods!"

She settled down in between Cat and Janet and set the plate on her lap. They all ate and talked about the beginning of Cat's new life; each expressing their own reasons for sadness at seeing Cat go.

"Do ye ken that ye'll be nearin' fifteen years old when ye get back, Cat?" Janet said with a sort of awe in her voice.

"So will ye, Janet." Sarcastically letting Janet know it wouldn't only be her that aged in the duration.

"Do ye think that Mistress Macpherson will let me come to visit ye?"

"I dinna think so, at least no' at her house, but maybe we could meet here at the castle once in a while." Cat looked at Isobel, waiting for a confirmation on this theory.

"I canna answer that. That's somethin' ye and Anna will hae to talk about."

The three of them finished their meal just as the distant pipers announced the beginning of the ceremonies. The Hall grew quieter as people heard the music play; those still talking were shushed. Everyone moved to take what seats were left. Even with three floors, people hovered at the railings on each floor maneuvering for the best observation position.

Six pipers came into the Hall in a slow march playing *Teachd Chlann Dhonnachaidh*, "The Coming of the Robertson's"; the sound of the pipes echoed beautifully off the stone walls. Clan Donnachaidh had many talented pipers, harpists and fiddlers, not to mention those with beautiful voices. After a few minutes, the pipers got to the front of the Hall and ended their tune.

From behind great double oak doors in the front of the Hall, with armed guards on either side, Alexander came in and took his seat, signaling to everyone that the formal ceremonies would commence. First on the Chief's agenda was to let everyone know that rents will be collected after the Games tomorrow. Second was to find out who in the clan were to be married. The Chief often chose who might be suited to each other when men and women came of age, or if a widow or widower needed to be cared for. If love was involved from the start, all the better, but mostly, marriage was a necessity.

After these formalities were completed, the third, and final item on the agenda before the oath taking was to dole out punishments to those who broke the law. The "law" was dictated by what the Chief deemed correct for the clan. The feudal system worked by keeping order and a sense of authority by the Chief. Crimes were anything from adultery to theft to murder; punishments ranged from fines to public flogging, and could be as harsh as hanging. "Public" meant in the Hall that night with all the clanspeople watching. Luckily, this night would only see a few fines handed out, but those who were accused still had to suffer the humiliation of being charged in front of the entire clan.

Finally, with the business end of the ceremonies complete, it was time for the oath taking. The men were assembled in a neat, orderly row now. There was a hierarchy in the line up. Angus, since he was a laird and a direct cousin to Alexander, was up near the front of the column, with two chieftans in the lead. This hierarchy was visible by the feathers they wore in their bonnets. Alexander, being the Chief, wore three feathers, his chieftans wore two, and the lairds wore one.

To toast their allegiance, claret replaced the ale in their cups. Each one of the clansmen were to go up to Alexander and proclaim his loyalty. It was Angus' turn, and being at least six inches taller than most of the men there, he was easy to spot in the crowd. He approached his cousin, who sat in his richly carved mahogany chair, got down on one knee, held his dirk up high by the point, and said in his deep, clear voice, "I swear by all that is sacred and by this holy iron I hold, to give ye my fealty, and my loyalty to Clan Donnachaidh. If ever my hand shall be raised against ye, I ask that this iron shall be used to end my life."

With his oath sworn, Angus rose, gave Alexander a warm clap on the shoulder, then bent and whispered something in his ear. Alexander nodded in response, then directed his eyes to the next clansman in line.

Isobel was watching this transpire, wondering what her husband was up to now. Instead of going back to sit with her, Angus walked towards Alexander's private quarters. She fought the urge to follow him, as she would have lost him in the throngs of men long before she could get to him. She would have to find him after the rest of the clansmen swore their allegiance.

❧

The night's festivities came to an end for many after midnight. Isobel had not seen Angus since the swearing-in ceremony. She had left word with Lachlan that she wanted to speak to his father as soon as possible, but he said he had not seen him either.

"Besides," he said, "I hae other things on my mind at the moment," staring at a pretty lass getting two plates of food from the feasting tables.

Isobel followed Lachlan's gaze and smiled at his choice. She thought she was George Reid's youngest daughter, Sara, but wasn't positive. She had white-blond hair, light blue eyes, and was barely five feet tall. As Isobel and Lachlan stared, Sara caught their eyes on her, and blushed a pretty shade of pink, making Lachlan break out in a sweat.

Isobel laughed, patted her son on the arm, and said, "A fine choice ye hae made lad," then walked away, leaving her son to work out his own affairs. She was just about to fetch Cat and Janet to head back to camp, when she spied Seumas and Iain getting refitted with new mugs of ale.

"Where's yer Da, lads. Hae ye seen him?"

"No Mam, no' since the oath takin'," Seumas said with a slight slur to his speech.

Isobel looked at her sons, put her hands on her hips, and said, "Do ye no' ken it's only a few hours 'til the Games? Hae ye no sense for the drink, both of ye? How are ye goin' to fight and dance when ye wilna even be able to stand by the looks of it?"

"Aye, Mam," they both said in unison.

"We'll make this one be the last, aye?" Iain said, looking desperately for a place to sit down.

"Do that," she said, then shook her head and resumed her quest.

When Isobel and Catrìona left with a mob of other women, the mist had stopped, and the moon was making brief appearances from behind the clouds. Cat and Janet were still working out plans for the future between themselves. Isobel was only half listening to the conversation, when movement in the courtyard caught her eye. It was Angus and Alexander sitting on a bench under the Rowan tree. Too far away to catch all of what they were saying, she could hear bits of Angus' deep voice float on the breeze to her.

"... but I'll need ... provisions ... safety ... witch hunt."

Isobel stopped in her tracks. Witch hunt? What were they talking about? *Who* were they talking about? Surely not Anna Macpherson. They haven't had a witch hunt for nearly a hundred years here, thank God. Scotland was notorious for being excessive in its pursuit of witches ... or those whom they deemed as witches. It was only in 1735 that the death penalty was finally abolished for witchcraft.

Cat had continued walking with Janet and turned to include her mother in the conversation, only to find that she wasn't there. She looked back to see her mother in front of the courtyard they had just passed.

"Mam, are ye all right?" she called.

No answer came from her mother, so Cat told Janet to go ahead, she'd see her in the morning. Cat walked back, hoping to glimpse what had her mother's attention thoroughly enough to not hear a summons. She laid her hand on her mother's shoulder, giving Isobel a guilty start.

"Dear *Brighid*, Cat, ye scairt me!"

"What are ye doin' Mam? Are ye listenin' in on Da's conversation?" Cat whispered.

"No, I mean aye, I mean ... och, ne'er ye mind, now. Let's get back to camp, aye?" Isobel said, flustered.

Cat giggled. "Yer secret is safe wi' me, Mam."
"Hmmm."

❧

Morning dawned cool and the sky was white with the promise of more showers to come. The Games would continue no matter what the weather. Rain, however, always made it harder to keep a grip on blades. This fact made Cat even more nervous for Seumas. He somehow managed to be standing this morning after all the drink he had last night. Iain and Lachlan didn't seem any worse for the wear either.

Isobel was huddled next to Angus eating their breakfast on the log in front of the fire. They seemed to be in deep conversation. Cat smiled at her mother eavesdropping on her father last night, but their conversation now didn't seem to be a light one. She wondered what they were talking about. Her mother wore a heavy look at what her father was telling her, making Cat get that funny feeling in the pit of her stomach again.

She was unable to hear the conversation, yet somehow knew it was about her and it wasn't good. What did cousin Alexander have to do with it? Mam was so intrigued when she saw him talking with Da last night. She had to find out what her parents were talking about.

Closing her eyes, she cleared her head of all other sounds. She felt herself moving towards the fire to stand beside her parents. She could feel the warmth from the flames. The voices were clearer now.

"But Angus, a Seer is different. Nearly all the clans have Seers to aid them in their decisions. Like it or no', Cat has the Sight. There's naught we can do to change it, is there? Better to teach her how to use it so it can keep her out of danger, aye?"

"I honestly dinna ken what else to do, *a ghaoil.* Do ye think we should be tellin' her about this, though?" He pounded the log next to him in frustration, making a dull thud. "She's still so innocent about so many things!"

"Aye, we must … for her own safety … and maybe ours as well."

They fell silent now, huddled together on the log in their own thoughts. Cat stepped back into herself, and opened her eyes to find she had not moved an inch from where she had been standing. How did she do that? Each new experience was stranger than the one before it. But what was the conversation her parents just had really about? What about this "danger" part? She had heard tales from Janet about how some Seers were condemned as witches a long time ago, but that was just it; a long time ago. Why was it coming up now, and how could it be affecting her?

This time, she physically walked over to her parents and stood by the fire. They hadn't heard her come up behind them until she was standing there. As if expecting her, her father motioned for her to sit down.

"What is it, Da? Why am I in danger?"

Both her parents' eyebrows shot up at this query.

"How do ye ken what we were talkin' about, Cat?" asked Isobel, more than a little curious.

"I canna explain it, but I was standin' right where I am now, listenin' to ye when ye were talkin' a minute ago. When I opened my eyes again, I was still standin' o'er by those trees behind ye."

Angus just gawked at his daughter with his mouth hanging open.

Isobel looked at Angus and said, "She must be taught the ways, Angus. I canna stand the thought o' the same thing happenin' to her as what happened to my Mam."

"Aye," he said, nodding. Never taking his eyes off his daughter, his face had gone a very unnatural shade of white. He was genuinely scared. Even more frightened than he had been when he was lying on the battlefield with half of his arm gone all those years ago.

❧

"I think it would be best for two of the lads to take Cat to Mistress Macpherson's next week," Angus announced, relaxing in camp before heading to the Games.

"I'll go," Lachlan said unhappily. "Three years. She'll be all grown up when she gets back wi' us. We wilna even ken her anymore."

"Lachlan, did ye forget?" Isobel asked. "Ye'll be goin' to the castle next year yerself for yer teachin'. Ye'll be right next to Cat, and be able to see her as often as Mistress Macpherson allows it."

"I did forget," he said, the light dawning. "That'll be all right then. I dinna think I could stand to be away from her for so long wi'out seein' her whenever I liked."

"I'll go too," Iain chimed in. "I would like to spend a little time at the castle with the new books that just arrived from cousin William in France."

So far, no one brought up the one time Cat would be allowed to return home.

"That'll do then. Lachlan, I trust ye'll be able to stay busy there for a few days, so ye both can travel back home together, aye?" Angus asked, his deep blue eyes holding more than a hint of mischief.

Cat watched Lachlan flush a bit at this and then look away. Seumas was watching him and wearing a grin from ear to ear. Cat smiled, remembering that Lachlan had met a pretty lass at the castle last night. Obviously, his father and brother noticed him following her around like a lost pup, and were now going to tease him about it.

Seumas had been quiet during the conversation; just listening. He was busy checking and rechecking his chain mail armor looking for any defects. Every precaution was being taken to prevent the injury from happening. Cat understood his need to compete. He had spent years practicing for this day. She truly hoped he could change his fate as he left with Iain and Lachlan for the Games.

૨ⴰ

The Games were well under way when Catrìona and her parents finally decided to walk over to the grounds. The air was still dry, but for how much longer, no one knew. After her brothers left, Angus relayed as much as he could to Cat about the rumors of witches being persecuted again by a few zealous clergymen.

Her family was not religious. Aware of the Protestant and Catholic religions, they were more free-thinking. Even her cousin Alexander, who had been educated at the university of St. Andrew's as a clergyman, never followed that path. Organized religion seemed an affront to their ways of thinking. If they were called heathens for it, it was of no consequence to the Robertsons.

Seumas' turn in the claymore competition wasn't for another hour, but Iain was up next in the sword dance. The competition was stiff this year, with sixteen other men vying for the title of the best in the clan. Exuding confidence, Iain took his place next to Jamie Reid. They competed in doubles on the flat, grassless ground that was their stage. A piper was filling the bellows, and another man was ready to beat out a rhythm on the *bodhran*.

Iain and Jamie were each in their stance when the *bodhran* started to beat. After first bowing to the *airts*, they started to dance skillfully over the crossed swords. Kilts flew, showing strong legs, but Iain unquestionably had the grace and skill over Jamie. Lighter than air, Iain masterfully leapt over the swords, never touching them. In memorized placement of where his feet had to be at all times, he closed his eyes. Jamie had already kicked the swords twice, clearly intimidated by Iain's performance. He gave up gracefully, even before the pipes had stopped.

There was a roar from the crowd at Iain's skill. Many of the men bet no one would even come close to beating that performance. Angus got in on that bet, with a sidelong look from Isobel.

"What? Ye dinna think he'll win?" he said with the glimmer in his eye that always made her smile.

"Oh, aye, I hae no doubt of it. I was just thinkin' it was takin' advantage a bit."

"Phaaa! Takin' advantage o'er this lot? Lass, ye hae a lot to learn about men," he said in a lofty tone of superiority.

"Phaaa! yerself, Angus Robertson! I hae all I need to ken about the lot o' ye, to ken that I'll hae a more intelligent conversation wi' a stone!" She giggled, stretched up on tiptoes, gave him a kiss on the cheek, then turned and headed for the nearest rock pile.

❧

Cat watched the claymore competition with more interest than anyone there. Janet tried to involve her in conversation, but Cat just stood there twirling her hair, eyeing each move the swordsmen made. Janet finally gave up. Isobel inched through the crowd towards Cat and Janet to secure a good spot to watch Seumas' match, which was coming up next. A minute behind her was Angus and Lachlan. Iain was still competing and would be unable to watch the outcome of this ill-omened battle.

Angus protectively stood behind Isobel, hand on her shoulder, and Lachlan, not realizing it, did the same to Cat. Tension ran high as Seumas appeared in full chain mail to face Alex Maclagan, also fully armored. They stood facing each other; legs apart, braced for the ready, twisted at the waist, swords raised above their heads, the light blazing off the crossed blades.

Seumas was a full head taller than Alex, his claymore reflected his height by being over five feet long. Alex's sword was about four feet long, but knowing what lay ahead, no less deadly. This was not a contest to the death, just to wound. The first man to draw blood was the victor.

The two men stood perfectly still, staring intently at each other, waiting for the signal to begin. All at once a flag was dropped, and the battle began with a loud *clang!* of steel. Seumas got the first blow in and knocked Alex off balance. Alex regained his equilibrium quickly, slashing his blade back and forth in a frenzy, not giving Seumas a chance to do anything except fend off each impact.

Angus was not the only one in the crowd yelling at the top of his lungs coaching his son, but surely one of the loudest. Isobel moved Catrìona and Janet out of reach of the flailing arms of the men around them. Cat was glued to the action, silently watching, willing Seumas to be safe in the battle of steel.

It was a good contest, each of the men had expertise and speed. Thrust after thrust, a counter blow resounded from each volley they threw at each other. The crowd had to move further and further from the fray to keep from getting maimed. The physical exertion of wielding the five pound sword was enormous, and sweat streamed down each of their faces, plastering their hair to their heads.

In a quick succession of moves, Seumas was able to catch Alex's blade with his own, almost pulling it out of Alex's grasp. Alex's blade went up into the air, seemingly out of control. The only way Alex kept hold of the heavy sword was by the downsloping quillons on either side of the hilt. The mighty sword swung around Alex's head, and he twirled around with the blade, making a large downward sweep. Cat, Isobel, Angus, and Lachlan all saw it at the same time, knowing what would happen in the very next instant, yet unable to do anything but watch.

When Alex's blade swept around, Seumas was struck on the right leg. The force of Alex's swing was sufficient to break through the chain mail and penetrate to the bone. Seumas was thrown to the ground from the force of the blow; Alex's sword stuck in his leg. Seumas writhed in agony and the clan physician was called over.

Catrìona turned to her father just in time to see him faint to the ground in a heap. For such a huge man, his fall was rather graceful. She knew how much he wanted *not* to believe in her vision, but was unprepared to see him this disturbed.

❧

Angus came to with his head cradled on Catrìona's lap, hearing soothing words in Gaelic crooned to him. Lachlan, who had gone quite white, knelt on the ground beside his father, at a total loss as to how to help. Isobel was with the clan physician, and was unaware of Angus' uncontrolled exit to the ground.

"I'm all right, lass." Angus gazed up into his daughter's concerned eyes. His eyelids were heavy, but he wore a blissful smile on his face.

"Are ye sure, Da? I dinna ken if ye hurt yerself when ye hit the ground," Cat said, brushing the hair from his forehead, touching his smoothly shaven cheeks.

A crowd had gathered around to see what had happened, and Cat was embarrassed for her father. Angus suddenly realized where he was and what had happened, as faces slowly came into focus around him. A look of shame appeared on his face. He quickly tried to get up, but the world spun wildly. He broke out in a cold sweat, slumping back into Cat's lap, unable to rectify the situation.

"Lachlan, get them all away!" Cat barked, using an authoritative tone that left no room for argument.

Seeing that her brother had not fully recovered yet, she said, a little softer this time, "Da is fine, but he needs some air, aye?"

Lachlan did a nice job of dispersing the crowd in short order, while Cat helped Angus get to his feet. The three of them supported each other to a small clump of birch trees, sat, and regained some composure.

The scene had played out exactly as Cat had envisioned it. The entire performance was going through their minds over and over again. Each of them trying to glimpse a different outcome, yet none were to be had, except for the destined one. Fate.

"I guess I wasna sure I believed in yer vision, Cat," Angus said, fully revived now, "but ye got it right to the last detail ... that's what scairt me so."

He was unable to meet his children's looks. He always thought he could handle anything. He was the laird of *Slios Mìn aig Aulich* and all its people and property. If he couldn't handle this, what else would he fail to control when the situation arose?

Cat was watching his struggle. His emotions lay bare in his eyes for all to see. She had to say something to help him, but what? What could she possibly say to the larger-than-life man who was Angus Robertson? She looked at Lachlan, who had been quiet during the entire time, hoping to get some reassurance from him. He just lifted a shoulder in a shrug with total bafflement in his eyes. She countered his look with a, *ye are a big help,* look of her own.

"Da?" she asked, trying to snap him out of his depression.

"Aye Cat?"

"Ye could always tell everyone that it was my cookin' that made yer belly ache so, that ye fell to the ground in agony."

He looked at her for a long moment, then started shaking. She thought she had said the wrong thing for sure, and now he was getting furious. All of a sudden, he burst into laughter with such abandon that tears ran down his cheeks. Lachlan looked at Cat. At first, a smile came to his face, then he too broke into laughter. She stared at both of them with a look of astonishment on her face, which of course made them go deeper into hysterics.

"What? What?" she pleaded with each of them.

"Och, Cat, ye always did ken the right thing to say," Angus sputtered, after a few more minutes of gut-splitting whoops.

the journey

By the end of the week it was time for Catrìona to be delivered to her new life. Iain and Lachlan were taking the wagon so Cat could bring the few personal items she owned with her. Three years was a long time.

"I dinna ken why I hae to bring my own bed," Cat said to her mother for the fifth time.

"Because Anna only has her own bed wi' no room for guests. 'Tis a wee cottage, aye? Do ye think she entertains, bein' who she is?" Isobel snapped, instantly regretting her terse answer.

Cat stopped packing to watch her mother. This separation was very painful for both of them, and tempers were getting the upper hand. Last night, Isobel told Cat that this was the only way she knew of to learn the ways of the Sight, telling her that she had to learn to be comfortable in her own solitude by detaching herself from everyone. But Cat saw something more in her mother's eyes. Remembering what Anna had said about the one time she would be allowed to come home, she instinctively knew it was when her mother died, and it appeared that her mother knew it, too. The only question was when.

Isobel stopped fidgeting in the wagon when she saw Cat watching her. Silently, she stepped out of the wagon, walked into Cat's arms and embraced her tightly. No words needed to be said; the mind connection was strong enough to say what neither could voice out loud.

Lachlan did not interrupt them when he brought out the last of Cat's parcels. He quietly put them in the back of the wagon and went back into the house to wait for their summons to leave. Angus and Iain waited at the kitchen table. Each understood the mother-daughter bond was different than what they shared with her, but it was still hard to see Cat go.

After a few minutes, Angus said, "We'd better get this overwi' now, lads. It'll no' get any easier the longer we wait," realizing that left to his women, this journey would never get underway.

Cat saw them come out of the house, aware it was an attempt to break up this long goodbye. She released her embrace first, but kept hold of her mother's hand.

"Mam, it's time for me to go. The weather should hold fine 'til I get to Blair Castle," Catrìona said, trying to lighten the moment.

"Aye, it should at that," Isobel said, trying her best to collect herself. "Be sure to mind Mistress Macpherson and yer studies. Dinna forget to write when ye can. I'll get a letter to ye once a week so ye can stay acquainted wi' all the happenin's around here. Janet said she would write ye, too."

Angus guided Catrìona towards the wagon. He gave her a long hug, and a quick kiss on the forehead.

ॐ

Seumas sat in the best room with his leg propped up on the settee. He was in a lot of pain, and while the physician told him that he would heal, he also said that he would probably walk with a limp for the rest of his life. Just like Cat predicted. He was angry that he couldn't change the outcome of what she saw. Like a witch chanting an incantation, she *made* the vision come true. He wondered if that could be true. The more he thought about it, the more he convinced himself that was why he was maimed.

When he heard the rest of his family saying their good-byes, he debated whether or not to make the attempt to say farewell. The fact that Cat was leaving for three years was his only inspiration to make the effort.

The settee was near enough to the window that all he had to do was turn around. Pushing open the sash, he rested his arms on the sill and waited for Cat to notice him. With a strange, brooding pettiness, he decided he wouldn't be the one to initiate the gesture. He even toyed with the idea of slipping back away from the window, so she would have to be the one making all the effort to look for him and say good-bye. Before he could implement his plan, Cat caught sight of him and waved.

≥∙

Cat saw Seumas in the window and waved her good-bye. At first she didn't think he was going to wave back. She suddenly got the distinct impression he was angry with her for something, though she couldn't fathom anything to warrant such behavior. After a long moment, he finally lifted his hand in a half-hearted attempt, then disappeared from the window.

Iain and Lachlan were anxious to be underway and told her to hurry along. The horses, feeling their tension, stomped in agreement. With everyone loaded, Iain clicked the reins for the journey to begin. Cat took a seat in back of the wagon waving her farewell. The tears started flowing again and Seumas' attitude was forgotten.

≥∙

The ride was very quiet. Neither brother spoke. Each was in their own world; one too bleak to share. By early evening, they made camp beside the river. Cat started the fire while her brothers went rabbit hunting. In no time, they each returned with a hare that was cleaned and put on a spit to cook. Cat fetched some water and set up a lean-to for herself. The weather was good, so her brothers would sleep in the open.

By the time the rabbits were cooked, the sun was a vermilion orb hanging on the horizon, casting a rosy glow over the countryside. The birch trees turned pink, and the grass blazed in the warm radiance. Crickets made themselves heard all around, and songbirds headed to their night roosts.

"I'm all right, ye ken," Cat said to no one in particular.

Iain and Lachlan stopped chewing, startled, just now remembering she was there.

"Aye Cat, we ken ye'll be all right," Iain said, talking around the meat in his mouth.

"We just wanted to give ye some time to yerself. We kent ye would speak to us when ye were able," Lachlan added.

"Dinna be daft, the both of ye. O' course I'm able. I hae just been thinkin' about how to be tellin' ye of my vision."

Iain and Lachlan focused intently on their sister at this announcement, the succulent rabbit totally forgotten.

"What vision?" They said in unison. No one mentioned anything to them about Cat having another vision. That meant … what did that mean?

Lachlan timidly broached the question first.

"Who was the vision about, Cat?"

Looking at both of them, she knew from her short experience with the Sight she just had to tell them exactly what she saw.

"It was about Mam," she said, then went right into it. "We all ken that she's verra ill and dyin' slow. Mistress Macpherson said that I'll be able to come home only once. Mam kent, just as I did, it would be when she died. In my vision last night, Mam fell off a horse and hit her heid on a rock. She died where she fell."

Her brothers were shocked at the calmness in which she explained the details of their mother's death. They just sat cross-legged on the grass, their mouths open in a look of horror.

Recovering a bit from the jolt of the news, Iain asked, "Cat, do ye ken when it will happen?"

"No, but when was the last time ye kent Mam to get on a horse?" Cat asked, twirling her hair. "Seems like it would hae to be somethin' dire to make that happen, aye?" she continued, expressing her thoughts out loud.

"Aye," Lachlan stated, trying to work out the scenario in his head. "So all we hae to do is keep her from gettin' on a horse then?"

"That's what Seumas said about the claymore competition," Iain said in a tone marked with hopelessness. "Ye ken we canna change fate."

"We dinna ken that, Iain," Cat said. "Seumas went through wi' his competition; he didna back out of it to change the outcome."

"So yer sayin' that if we prevent Mam from gettin' on a horse, she wilna die?" Iain asked, hope ringing in his voice.

"'Twould seem likely, would it no'?" Cat stated, looking for confirmation.

"'Twould seem like we should make sure she ne'er even gets near a horse," Lachlan said.

The fire was little more than embers, and the stars shone bright in the night sky by the time all of their options were exhausted. Drained, they went to bed; no doubt to dream of their entire conversations all over again, only to receive the same outcome. Everything they spoke of was only speculation. They had no real facts to base their conclusions on, but it seemed like a plausible method to change fate.

Cat mulled over these questions and more, until she finally fell into a restless sleep. In her dreams, she searched for an answer to fate. Was it really so set in stone? How could they keep the circumstance that forced their mother get on a horse from happening? Could they find someone to heal their mother so she didn't die from her sickness? She had already seen the clan surgeon many times, and he didn't know what was wrong with her.

Tossing and turning, sleep would only be a wishful event this night. Dreams of strange people and places made for restless dozing. When she awoke with a start, it was light; the sky was a pale grayish-pink. A spider had taken up residence on the ceiling of her lean-to. She watched it for a while, spinning its web. Had she really thought of an answer in that fitful nap? She had heard of people with the Sight being healers as well. Maybe she could learn the healing arts from Mistress Macpherson in time to save her mother. The more she thought about it, the more resolved she became to learn as fast as she could.

She lay there quietly asking for help. From where this help would come was of no consequence. Appealing for guidance to those of the Otherworld with more knowledge than herself, and those who came before her that had miraculous healing abilities. She asked that she be directed to the answer.

Being careful not to wake her brothers, she got up and quietly walked down to the river to make her offerings to the four *airts* with a blood sacrifice to the Earth. With her dirk, she made a small slice on her thumb, causing a hissing noise to emanate from her lips as the blade cut into her soft flesh. She faced North and let a few drops of her life force fall onto the ground; then to the East, and South, and ending in the West. All the while she chanted a prayer in the Gaelic.

> *To the North I ask for strength and power*
> *To the East I ask for wisdom.*
> *To the South I ask for inspiration*
> *To the West I ask for a clear mind.*
> *Grant me these abilities so that I may learn to heal others.*

⁊❧

After sitting on the bank of the river for a while, Cat headed back to camp, picking up wood for the fire on the way. A movement in the trees caught her eye. A raspy gargle let her know it was a raven.

The black bird hopped down the branches like stairs, ending up eye-level with Cat. She dropped the collected wood to concentrate on the message the raven was to deliver. Its shiny black eyes locked onto hers, and a voice filled her head. It sounded much like Anna Macpherson's voice.

All ye seek is here, 'Garnet'.

Garnet? Who's Garnet? No one ever called her anything but Cat or Catrìona. Was this message meant for someone else? She didn't think that was possible. It was Anna's voice for sure, but did this new name have some meaning she didn't know of yet?

Instantly, she heard a soft giggle in her head. Was Anna laughing at her? The raven was obviously acting as a conduit between the two minds, so her thoughts were not her own. Anna must have heard her questions, thinking they were funny. If that were the case:

Why did ye call me Garnet, *Mistress?* Cat asked telepathically, still locked in eye contact with the raven.

The name Garnet stands for fiery, independent, determined and courageous; all the things ye are, lass, came Anna's voice in her head.

Cat did not think any of those qualities belonged to her.

Ah, but they will … they will.

Startled by an intruder, the raven broke eye contact with Cat, and flew back up into the tree.

"There ye are. I woke up and found yer wee tent empty. Are ye all right, then?" Lachlan looked like he had as rough a night as she did. His shoulder-length hair was a tangled mess, like he had been running his hands through it all night.

"Aye, I'm fine. Are ye all right? Ye look a bit worse for wear," she said, her dimples hinting at the humor she found at his dishevelment.

"If I slept at all I would be surprised. Iain as well," he said, suppressing a deep yawn. Then he caught the appearance of her dimples. "I dinna ken what ye find so amusin'. 'Tis all because of ye that we didna get a wink."

"Aye, well, I may have an answer. Help me wi' the wood and I'll tell ye both," she said.

૨**ও**

After relaying her communication with the raven and Mistress Macpherson to her brothers, they ate breakfast and broke camp. Either they were all crazy, or they were just immune to the fact that Cat could speak to ravens, because it was beginning to feel normal. The sun shone warmly by the time the wagon was loaded for the completion of their trip. Blair Castle was about a half a day's ride away, and all were in better spirits than yesterday.

"Do ye think Garnet is a good name for me?" Cat asked whoever was listening, twirling her hair.

"Why *Garnet*?" Iain asked.

"It means fiery, independent, determined and courageous," she said, repeating Anna's words.

"I dinna ken of any occasion ye ever had to show those qualities, Cat," Iain said, trying to recollect a time when she even got angry.

"I dinna ken that I want to be the one who backs ye into a corner to find out, though," he added with a smile that reached his eyes. He did look as tired as Lachlan, with dark circles under his eyes.

Cat laughed at that improbable circumstance, and dropped the hair she had twisted around her finger. For the rest of the morning they all talked amiably between themselves. Iain proclaimed his excitement over the chance to delve into the newest books in the castle library. Lachlan spoke of the new love he would get better acquainted with while waiting for Iain to finish his reading. By mid-morning, they stopped for a quick bite to eat by the burn in Tomanbuidhe.

Iain and Lachlan requested to rest for a few minutes before continuing the teeth-rattling travel. They laid down under a birch tree for a short cat nap to make up for last night's lack of sleep, and were asleep immediately.

Cat watched her brothers in sleepy bliss, but she wasn't tired. Her restless energy needed to be worked off, and walking always did the trick. She followed a burn up into the woods, where it ended in a waterfall so inviting, that she took off all her clothes and sat on the rocks it was cascading onto. The cool water was very refreshing, doing wonders to relieve her tension. She watched a young stag come to drink from the pool she had her feet dangling in. He grazed on the small leaves of the birch and willow, unafraid, ambling out of sight.

All of a sudden, the hairs on Cat's neck stood up on end. She froze when she saw a man coming into the clearing. He had his bow at the ready, tracking the young stag that had just been so peaceful there. The intruder hadn't seen her yet, but she was unable to move without catching his eye. Her clothes were on the opposite bank he was on, so maybe he wouldn't notice them. The waterfall behind her was about five feet tall. Could she slide back on the rock and slip behind it without him noticing the movement? She had to try. She couldn't take the chance of being found naked and alone. Her brothers were not within shouting distance, and probably sleeping so soundly that they wouldn't hear her anyway.

The man bent down to inspect the tracks more closely, then turned to follow the path the deer had taken. Now was her chance. With the quickness of her youth, she slid her legs up on the rock and stood up straight, then took a step back, instantly hidden by the veil of rushing water. The sound of the water changed as she went through, instantly alerting him. Had he seen her? Could he see her now behind the falls? She could see him, though not clearly. She watched him scan the area up and down the waterfall for a very long time. She was shaking now, not only from the cold, but from fear.

Suddenly, the man whirled around at a noise in the woods behind him. A snapping of a branch. Was the stag returning to the water? He lifted his bow, firing an arrow towards the sound. It must have hit its mark, for he ran off, eliminating the danger.

Emerging from the behind the falls, she scurried off the rock to the bank where her clothes were. She tried to dress hastily, but being wet only made it slower, the cloth adhering to her dripping body like glue. Finally, using her muslin shift as a towel, she was able to finish putting the rest of her clothes on.

The urge to run back to camp, to the safety of her brothers was strong, but she knew the hunter was still close, so she had to proceed quietly. Her russet-colored homespun dress allowed her to blend into the woods, just as the deer had. Slowly, she made her way back towards camp, staying close to the trees and bushes for cover, letting out a sigh of relief when she saw the wagon. She walked over to her sleeping brothers and nudged them both awake.

"C'mon the both o' ye or we'll ne'er get to the castle by nightfall, aye?"

They groggily awoke with tendon-popping stretches and wide-mouthed yawns. Iain sat up first, noticing that Cat's hair was wet. So were her clothes in spots.

"Where hae ye been, lass?" Iain asked.

"Och, I went for a swim. There's a waterfall up the burn a ways. It was beautiful." She tried to sound casual, but wasn't very convincing.

"Ye went alone?" Lachlan asked, shaking off the sleep.

"Aye," she said, not meeting his eyes.

"What happened?" Lachlan asked, sensing that she was disturbed about something.

"'Twas naught anythin' to be concerned about," she stated, stubbornly lifting her head a little higher.

"What happened?" This time both her brothers asked the question in unison.

"I was ne'er in any danger."

Lachlan stood up, grabbed Cat by the shoulders, and gave her a shake.

"If ye dinna start talkin', I'll hae to shake it out o' ye, now what happened?"

She looked up at her brother, and turned a very becoming shade of red. That got Iain's attention, and got up to intimidate her into to revealing her misadventure.

"Och, all right, the both o' ye. I'll tell ye, just let go o' me!" she sputtered, wriggling out of Lachlan's grip.

"I was almost caught swimmin' naked by a hunter who was chasing a young stag that came for water at the pool that I was in," she said all in one breath. As she spoke, the redness faded from her cheeks, only to be replaced by tears.

Iain and Lachlan looked at each other and burst out laughing. Laughing so hard, they had tears of their own running down their cheeks. Cat just stood there. Her hands rolled up into fists at her sides. So many emotions were going through her at once, she didn't know which one to act on. For the first time in her life, she felt rage. Her fists pummeled her brothers' backs and arms; whatever they could land on. She wanted to do some damage at their careless disregard for her feelings.

A blow struck Lachlan hard in the side and he let out a *yelp!* to her delight.

"Hey, that hurt!" he said, holding the spot where she caught him.

Cat set the fury in her eyes on Iain next, but he quickly side-stepped her punch.

"Whoa now, Cat," Iain said, holding both of her arms in a vice-like grip. She was strong and almost wriggled out of his hold. Lachlan recovered enough to realize she was not playing around, and went to aid Iain.

"Calm yerself, *a ghaoil mo chridhe*," Lachlan crooned, holding her tight from behind, waiting for her to regain control of herself.

"We dinna ken it bothered ye so, or we wouldna hae made a joke of it, aye?" Iain said, holding Cat's face in his hands to look her in the eyes.

As quickly as the rage manifested itself, it was over. Cat relaxed in Lachlan's arms when she realized how silly the flare-up was. When she thought about it, she could see the humor in the situation, but the unreleased fear made her lash out when they started to laugh.

Both of them released her and stepped back, keeping a wary eye just in case the wrath wasn't over. Cat sat down, exhausted. She was breathing hard from the exertion, cradling her knees and rocking back and forth. It took her a few minutes to settle down completely. Her brothers sat down beside her, waiting for her to explain the sudden outburst.

"Why did it bother ye so Cat? We swim naked together all the time," Lachlan asked, not wanting to rekindle the fire still in her eyes.

"I was afraid," she whispered.

That hit both her brothers at the same time. She watched the light dawning in their eyes when they thought of what could have happened.

"Let's forget it, aye? It was stupid of me to go so far from ye all alone to begin wi'." Then, in an attempt to lighten the moment, with a smirk on her face, she asked, "Did I hurt ye, Lachlan?"

"Oh, aye. Ye pack quite a punch … for a lass." Then quickly got out of the way to avoid another show of her fighting skills.

They all got up and strode arm in arm back to the wagon to continue the last leg of their journey. Catrìona was sitting in the back of the wagon thinking how that rage felt. She had never experienced anything so powerful before, '... *fiery, independent, deter-*

mined and courageous; all the things ye are, lass,' Anna had said. *'I dinna ken that I want to be the one who backs ye into a corner to find out,'* Iain had said. Well, now she knew what it took to get her fired up enough to be called *Garnet*.

❧

Later that afternoon, they reached the castle without further incident. Bone tired, Cat got a bite to eat, then retired to her room for some much needed sleep. Not even looking around to assess her surroundings, she shed her dress and shoes, fell onto the soft featherbed with a blissful sigh, and was asleep instantly.

When she awoke early the next morning, she didn't even remember dreaming, so sound was her slumber. Feeling more like herself again, she stretched out languidly in the soft comfort of her bed. Sounds from the yard below announced a new day beginning, and she inhaled the savory smells coming from the kitchen.

Suddenly, she remembered why she was there, and scooted out of bed to get dressed. She ran down the stairs to the kitchen to find her brothers. They hadn't discussed when they would take her to Mistress Macpherson's house.

"Hold on there lass," said Mrs. Macgregor, the cook. "What's the hurry, ye just got here."

"Hae ye seen my brothers? Hae they been down yet?" Cat asked, looking out the window.

"No lass. They're still in bed for all I ken."

"Oh good," she said, releasing a heavy breath. "I thought I might hae missed them." Needing something to keep her busy until her brothers got up, she asked, "Might I be helpin' ye wi' breakfast then?"

"No. Most e'eryone has already ate and gone about their business. Might I fix ye somethin' to eat though?"

"Aye. Whatever ye got handy. I dinna want to be a bother." Cat sat at the kitchen table absently twirling her hair.

Mrs. Macgregor cooked up some eggs and sausage, and served them to Cat with a hot biscuit dripping with fresh butter. Cat ate the sumptuous meal without any enthusiasm. Her mind was on the end of the journey, and she wanted to get it over with as soon as possible. She had to learn the healing ways quickly for her mother's sake.

practical magick

Lachlan drove Catrìona to Anna Macpherson's house later that morning in a thick fog. A light mist gathered on Cat's face, helping to hide her tears. This was even harder than leaving her parents two days ago, and her mood was black. She pulled her *arisaid* tighter around her shoulders, although the chill she felt was not from the weather.

Cat noticed that Lachlan kept his eyes on the road ahead, unwilling to look at her. She knew just how he felt. Iain had said his good-byes at the castle, understanding her relationship with Lachlan. She was glad for his thoughtfulness.

It was the shortest mile of their lives. Lachlan stopped the horses at the crossroads leading to the house where Cat would spend the next three years. Cat looked for the raven, but it was nowhere in sight. They were alone, and alone was exactly how she felt. She was torn between staying where she was as a normal eleven year old, and moving into a new world. The only thing that made her choose the latter was the potential to help her mother get well again.

"Cat, I ken ye'll do well in yer studies because ye hae the gift. We all hae seen it. Ye'll be a rare fine healer too, and I ken ye want to do it for Mam. I'll be doin' my studies at the castle come spring, and I'll be able to see ye as often as Mistress Macpherson allows." Lachlan had been talking without looking at her, fidgeting with the reins. Time stopped in her eyes when he finally met them.

Cat took his hand in hers and stretched over to kiss him. Lachlan kissed her back, then fiercely hugged her to his chest, waiting to compose themselves enough to let go. Lachlan loosened his grip as

Cat pulled a handkerchief from her sleeve to blow her nose. She made a tooting sound that made Lachlan smile, despite himself.

"Ye always do smile when I blow my nose," she said, showing her dimples and drying her eyes.

"Aye, and I'll be missin' that noise. Well, we'd better be off before ye get all teary again," he said, clicking the reins and making the turn into Cat's future.

ƻ▰

The mist had stopped when Anna went out into her garden. She already knew Catrìona was at the crossroads saying her farewell. Anna was anxious to start working with her new student, thinking she may even learn things from her. In fact, she was sure of it. Catrìona inherited a rare talent, the type that only needed to be fine-tuned, not taught.

A few minutes later, the wagon rounded the corner then drew up close to the house to unload Cat's belongings into Anna's small cottage. Anna noticed the strong young man with Catrìona was heavyhearted. She sensed a closeness of family and of fierce protection. This was good. Catrìona would need to have protectors with her abilities.

"Hallò, *Garnet*," she called, waving her oak staff as she walked towards them in greeting.

"Hallò, Mistress Macpherson. This is my brother, Lachlan," Cat said when Anna got close enough. Cat touched her brother's shoulder, trying to muster some cheerfulness in her voice.

"Glad to meet ye, Mistress," Lachlan said, wondering how such an old woman would manage to keep his sister occupied.

Anna stared at Lachlan for a minute, searching him. A smile cracked her face following the deep creases of age.

"I'm glad ye'll be here in the spring, Lachlan. Catrìona will need her protector then."

Lachlan just stared wide-eyed at her as if to say, *how did you ken that.* Cat smiled at him, taking the parcel from his arms to start the unpacking process. Lachlan passed the same look to Cat, who just shook her head.

"*A ghaoil mo chridhe*, ye should ken who ye are talkin' to. All Mistress Macpherson needs to do is look at ye to ken all about ye. Maybe I'll be able to do that when ye get here in the spring, aye?"

"I'm no' sure I'd like that," he mumbled to himself, retrieving another package from the back of the wagon.

Cat and Anna laughed together, sharing the private joke. Anna announced that she would make some tea, while the two of them finished putting Cat's life into her home.

❧

After all of Cat's belongings were brought in and set up, they all shared some tea. Lachlan was very quiet, careful not to meet Anna's eyes, thinking that's how she saw into his future. He didn't want that. He just wanted to know that Cat was going to be all right out here on her own. He knew he was overly protective of his little sister, but he couldn't help it.

After tea, they all walked out together to say their good-byes. Lachlan gave Cat another big squeeze and a kiss on the tip of her nose, then hopped up into the wagon and grabbed the reins. Before he clicked them, he just sat there, deep in thought, then asked, "Mistress, when will our Mam die?"

Cat inhaled sharply at the blunt question, and gave her brother an incredulous look.

Anna didn't seem to be phased at all by the question. Her eyes locked with his, seeing into his very core.

"*When* is no' a thing I can be givin' ye, lad. There are too many paths that can be taken before we ken — Catrìona bein' one of those paths."

"Can we change the fate?" he asked, undaunted by the look boring into his soul.

"Aye, sometimes ... if all involved are willin' to help change it," she stated, then turned and walked back into the house.

Cat and Lachlan just stared at the door she had walked through, awaiting an encore. None came. When they finished their good-byes, Lachlan clicked the reins and was off. Cat stared after him until he was out of sight. The raven landed on the fence near the house and Cat asked it to return to her when Lachlan got safely to the castle. It flew off to do her bidding and returned a little while later.

❧

Anna had been watching through the window when her new student enlisted the raven's aid. How quickly Catrìona learned. *Learned?* She was not *taught* that, she just watched and applied it to the situation. The raven had never done the bidding anyone else had requested of it before. No other student she taught had been able to make a beast understand, yet here was this young lass with no training, able to speak through the mind as if she had done it all her life. Maybe she *had* been doing it all her life.

Anna never asked questions of a student's skills. She knew from experience that parents were very biased in their opinions of their children. She wanted to see for herself what a student knew, or didn't know, in order to teach that student better.

Anna would measure Catrìona's abilities through a series of tests planned for her. These were usually easy lessons to assess a student's proficiency in reading the minds of others and reading signs of the future. Different tests were applied to see if a student could be a healer. Anna already knew Catrìona could read beasts' minds, as well as see into the future of her family. Catrìona had also expressed a keen interest in being a healer for her mother's illness. Anna would have to rethink how to go about "training" Catrìona, already knowing it would be different than the others. Catrìona would be more like a skilled apprentice working directly along side her, getting involved in all that Anna did and saw.

❧

Almost a week had passed since Catrìona came to Anna's cottage to learn the art of Second Sight. In that week, Anna took her to two crofts and the castle, delighting Cat in a visit with Iain and Lachlan. The three of them spent the morning together while Anna waited to meet with Alexander.

"So, what are ye learnin' about, Cat?" Iain asked, smothering a warm oatcake with boysenberry jam.

"I'm no' sure yet. I think Anna just wants to see what I ken for now. But I hae been out to the Duncan's and the Macgregor's this week to treat some ailments, so I hae learned about some wee plants to make into tea to fix their sicknesses." Taking the newly jammed oatcake off Iain's plate, she promptly took a bite out of it, despite his look of annoyance.

"Didna I predict ye would be a rare fine healer Cat?" Lachlan said, buttering his own oatcake.

"Aye, ye did, *mo bhràthair*, that ye did," she said, licking the jam off her fingers.

Before she could finish her meal, a movement caught her eye. In the doorway, Anna motioned that it was time to see Alexander. Without a word, Cat left the table and followed Anna. Cat had rarely spoken with her much older, important cousin, and she certainly never had any occasion to visit with him in his private chambers. It was rather exciting.

Through the double doors, they passed two guards that nodded to Anna, then walked into a richly paneled room. The fireplace radiated a glorious warmth against the damp day. On one side of the fire, Alexander sat in a light blue silk brocade chair, and Anna automatically took the matching chair on the other side. A crystal glass of whisky rested on the table next to him, but he made no offer of a dram to Anna.

On the floor was a thick piled rug of deep pinks, royal blues, and sage greens in a vine and floral pattern. Life-size oil paintings of the previous Donnachaidh Clan Chiefs were hanging on the walls in ornate gold-gilt frames. Cat recognized none of them.

In the far corner stood a beautifully carved rosewood longbase clock. It made a deep, loud tic-tock noise. On its face was a painting of Mary, Queen of Scots being rescued in a boat; kilted Scotsmen and tartan-clad women in each corner. Catrìona saw that it was ten-fifteen.

Behind a large desk were shelves of leather-bound books. Some looked new, while others had an ancient appearance. She couldn't see the titles from where she stood, but thought Iain would love to get his hands on any one of them.

Scanning the room further, on the other side of the table near Alexander, lay the biggest dog she ever saw. He was the size of a small pony! Somehow knowing he was being sized up, with a groan, he got up and stretched — adding to his enormity. Cat stood her ground as he walked up to her and sat at her feet. Without having to bend over, she laid her hand on his scruffy light gray head and scratched behind his ears. He closed his brown eyes in bliss, enjoying the attention.

Alexander watched this bonding of dog and child in wonder.

"What is he?" Cat asked her cousin in awe.

"An Irish Wolfhound; I call him Curr."

Alexander bent over the sidearm of the chair and whispered to Anna, never taking his eyes from his young cousin. "He has never let anyone touch him before. I keep him as a hunter and as a protector," his eyebrows lifting high in amazement.

"She has a rare gift, that one," Anna whispered back.

"Tell me what he's thinkin', Catrìona," Anna asked, louder this time so Cat could hear.

Cat looked up, surprised to hear someone speak, so entranced with the dog, she forgot where she was. When she saw Anna and Alexander watching her, she turned a few shades of pink.

"Oh, uh, sorry Mistress. What did ye say?"

"Where were ye, lass?" Anna asked, a smile entering her voice.

"Och, well, me and the big lad here were off in the forest for a good run chasing a stag. He loves to run. He sees verra well, but doesna smell too good, even though he has a big nose," she said, running her fingers down its length.

Alexander stared at Cat open-mouthed. He turned to Anna and asked in his soft Scottish accent, "Does she do that all the time? I mean read beasts' minds?"

"Was she right?" Anna asked, ignoring his question.

"Aye, she was right. We had a stag chase just yesterday. He's in his glory when he can run, and he sees very well, indeed." Alexander scratched his head under his wig, watching his dog become fast friends with his young cousin.

"Maybe we should get on wi' it then, aye?" Anna broke the spell, and Cat sat on the little ottoman that matched the chairs next to Anna. The dog returned to Alexander, and lay down by his master's feet.

"Aye, we should at that, Mistress," he said, shaking his head at what he just witnessed to focus on what they were all there for.

"What might I be helpin' ye wi' today, Alexander?"

"Well Mistress, it seems we have a thief here at Blair Castle. The silver collected from the rents at the Gathering is missing," he said, back to business.

"And ye want me to be tellin' ye who took it?" asked Anna.

"Aye, and I need ye to be absolutely sure about it, as it's a hanging offence, ye see," he stated, unwilling to believe it was someone in his own household.

Cat watched her mentor with interest. Anna took a few deep breaths, then her eyes went lifeless. Tuning herself to Anna's mind, she saw the steps Anna was taking to find who the culprit was. In childhood ignorance, no trance-state was needed to do what Anna was doing. She just focused on the question and went there.

In the psychic realm, Cat followed Anna up the stairs to the room where the silver was kept. A guard was by the door of the small room; it was Gregor. The giant was asleep in a chair. The room was in a part of the castle she had never been before. She looked around to get her bearings. Through a small, thin window across from the sleeping man, she determined that the only place they could be was in the tower. The entire countryside was visible from this vantage point. At least Gregor had a beautiful view for such a lonely job.

A door opened behind her, and she turned to see Anna going into the little room. Gregor never stirred; some guard, she thought. Had he been awake, no one could have gotten passed the huge man. If the thief knew what kind of sentry was on duty, it was no wonder the silver was stolen. Following Anna inside the dark, windowless room, they stood near the open door waiting for something to happen.

As Cat looked around, she saw a small, portable chest on top of a simple wooden desk. Suddenly, a shadow filled the doorway, blocking out the light for an instant. She strained to see who entered, but didn't recognize him, so thankfully, he was probably not from Alexander's staff. He had fair blonde hair, green eyes, was of medium height with a stocky build. His plaid was dark blue and green, and on his shoulder was a brooch she would never forget. It was about a four inch silver disk with a dark blue stone in the center, surrounded with an interlace knot pattern.

Catrìona watched him empty the rents into a leather satchel hiding under his plaid, then he quietly slipped out of the room passed Gregor, who never moved from his slumber. Maybe he was dead. No. As she looked closer, she could see Gregor's chest moving up and down. No wonder the disappearance of the silver was a mystery. From the looks of it, there were no witnesses.

Anna headed for the exit, then instantly, they were back in Alexander's chambers. Cat shook her head in an effort to clear it, attempting to figure out what was real again. She looked over at Anna and watched her come out of her trance. Anna turned to Cat, beaming with child-like enthusiasm, smiling a toothless smile that reminded Cat of a toad.

"Ye saw it too, aye?" Anna asked excitedly.

"Aye, but I dinna ken who it was. I'll ne'er forget that brooch, though," she said, matching Anna's tone.

"Well, are either of ye going to tell me or do ye mean to keep it to yerselves?" asked Alexander.

"Oh, aye. I apologize, Alexander. The man ye're lookin' for wore a four inch silver brooch wi' a blue sapphire in the center, had fair colored hair and green eyes," Anna recounted in a more professional voice, while Cat bobbed her head in agreement.

"Blue sapphire … fair hair … green eyes …" Alexander muttered to himself, tugging on his earlobe trying to recollect who wore that brooch. "Wait, wait a minute. How did this man get by Gregor? Was he not on guard?"

Cat and Anna looked at each other with wide eyes. Such a pointed question could not be dismissed, it had to be answered truthfully. The last thing they intended was for Gregor to be blamed for shirking his duty, but truth be told, if he were doing his duty, the robbery would never have taken place. Cat could not look at Alexander, knowing her eyes would give her away, so she looked at her feet instead.

"Aye, he was on guard, but he was sleepin' in his chair," Anna answered regretfully.

Alexander rose from his chair and walked over to the double doors, put a hand on the knob and paused, contemplating what to do next. He rubbed the back of his neck in troubled thought for a couple of minutes. Cat could feel his turmoil, hoping her cousin would not be too harsh with Gregor.

Coming to a conclusion, Alexander opened the door and spoke to the guard outside — too softly for her to hear what was said. He came back into the room, walked over to his desk, and sat down heavily in the leather chair. Pulling open the top drawer, he lifted out a small pouch, setting it on the desk with a clink. Without a word, Anna got up, took the pouch and left the room.

Cat stayed seated, expecting Anna to come back. Alexander looked up, surprised to see her still sitting there.

"Ye may go now, cousin. We're finished."

"Oh … I'm sorry, I dinna ken," she said, the pink rising to her cheeks in embarrassment.

She rose from the ottoman and started for the door, but before she left the room, she turned to her cousin and asked, "What will become of Gregor, then?"

"'Tis no concern of yers, Catrìona. Go on now, I have work to do." He waved her off in a tone of dismissal.

ᘒ

Neither Anna nor Cat spoke of the outcome of the vision they shared. *It was not for them to be concerned with.* Anna reiterated Alexander's words on the walk back to their cottage. What *was* talked about was how well Cat had done on her first exercise.

"Ye did real fine, lass. I was quite startled to see ye wi' me in my vision. How did ye ken what to do?" Anna asked.

"I concentrated on the question of who stole the rents, then in my heid, I was wi' ye on the stairs. Did I do it right, Mistress?"

"Och, aye, ye did lass, though I dinna ken that there's a right or a wrong to it. We all hae our own ways wi' the Sight, though most will ne'er be able to do what we did," Anna said, looking at Catrìona, her black eyes filled with wonder.

"I ... uh ... hae a experiment for ye that I need yer help wi'. Are ye up for it?" Anna asked.

"Aye. What sort of experiment?" Cat met Anna's black stare with her own smoky-violet one, searching for the reason for the odd tone Anna used. Cat was getting to know her mentor's personality very well, but this hinted at something deeper than they had gone before.

"I want to ken who ye were ... before," she asked.

"Och, aye, me too!" Cat said. "What do we do?"

"Weel, I put ye into a trance, then ask ye about dates and places, and ye tell me anythin' ye can about who ye were, and where ye were at the time, aye?"

"All right."

They arrived back at the cottage, unsure who was more excited. Anna instructed Catrìona to lie on her bed and get comfortable. It was late afternoon and the sun flooded through the west window, casting long shadows on the floor. From the cupboard, Anna took out a candle, some catnip, mugwort, rowan berries, and valerian she had ground into powder for just this purpose. From the sideboard, she removed a midnight blue square of silk the size of a handkerchief, and laid it on the table. She set the candle in the center and lit it, then sprinkled some of the powdered herbs over the flame so it gave off a wonderful aroma.

"Mmmm. What's that smell, Mistress?" Cat asked.

"Hush, lass. Just relax yer whole body, and clear yer mind of e'erythin' but the sound of my voice, aye?" Anna sat at the table with a sheet of parchment, inkwell and a quill ready to write down all Catrìona could tell her.

She waited until Cat was in such a relaxed state that she was no longer herself. Now, her past lives could be read like chapters in a book.

"Now, I'm goin' to say some dates and I want ye to see if any of them belong to ye from before," she said quietly. "1600 … 1621 … 1650 … 1683 …"

"1683 was when I was born," came the odd statement in a voice so soft Anna barely heard it. She moved her chair closer to Cat to hear her better.

"Where do ye live?"

"Drumachuine, at the base of Schiehallion, the faerie hill," Cat said.

"What's yer name?"

"Catherine. Catherine Reid."

Anna wrote the name on the parchment.

"Are ye marrit, Catherine?"

"Aye. To Robert Macinroy. We have a bairn. A daughter named Isobel," Cat whispered in a voice not quite her own.

If Catrìona wasn't in a trance, she would have known just who she was, and why she had the Sight. Catherine Macinroy returned to help heal her daughter through the granddaughter she never knew. Anna took Catrìona's hand and held it while she brought her young student out of the trance.

"Are ye all right, lass?" she asked at the first sight of Cat's alertness.

"Aye. Did I say anythin' of use to ye, Mistress?" Cat asked, wiping her eyes and stretching out on the bed before rising to sit on the edge.

"Look for yerself, Catrìona. I wrote it all down for ye," she said, handing Cat the parchment with her eerie past on it.

Cat took the parchment and read it, then read it again, twirling her hair this time. An odd frown indicated that she did not believe what she was reading. Cat looked up from the small script searching Anna's obsidian eyes.

"Aye, Catrìona. Ye were yer Grandmam before." Anna let that sink in for a minute before continuing.

"Do ye ken why ye're here now, and why ye have the Sight so strong?" Anna asked.

A thousand questions filled Cat's head, yet she already knew the answers to them. She just sat, twirling her hair with a far away look on her face.

Cat got up from her bed to stand next to the window, just in time to watch the sun fade behind the clouds on the western horizon. A warm breeze spilled in and the sound of crickets filled the air. Catrìona was left to work out what she needed to in her own mind, as Anna moved quietly around the small cottage.

By the time Catrìona left the window, only a sliver of color was left on the horizon. She dropped the hair that was twisted around her fingers in resolution. When she turned from the window, she saw that the candles were lit and supper was waiting for her on the table. From the looks of things, Anna had already eaten and was sitting at the table knitting in the dim light. Cat hadn't heard a thing while she was thinking. She hadn't smelled supper being prepared either. How long had she been standing at the window? Time must have stopped, and apparently, she stopped with it.

Anna looked up from her knitting to meet Cat's eyes, but did not initiate a conversation.

"I think maybe I kent who I was all along," Cat said, as if permission had finally been given to her to voice her belief. She sat down to eat her supper without another word.

ða

Summer passed and the golden grasses waved in the cold mid-autumn wind. It was the morning of October thirty-first; Catrìona's birthday. Anna didn't seem surprised that her apprentice was born on this day. It was Samhain, the transition period between summer and winter; the night when the veil between the realm of the living and dead is the thinnest. To make the life force of Catherine Macinroy transition into Catrìona Robertson took great planning. It was the perfect time for a spirit with unfinished work in the physical realm to reincarnate and complete their task.

Anna and Catrìona were expected at the castle to give divinations for the upcoming months, and to join in on the feast and traditional bonfire celebrating the past year. The entire clan was invited, since it was usually the last time they would all get together until the next spring. Winter was long, dark and cold in the Highlands. Not many ventured far from home.

Over the past few months, Cat had learned many of the herbs that were used in healing and how to prepare them. All during the summer and early autumn, leaves, roots and flowers were collected to pound into powders, make into to ointments, or dry for poultices, teas and infusions. Cat enjoyed this time very much, yet there was so much more to learn about the uses of each plant.

She had not had any visions of her family since she came to stay with Anna. Cat thought of her mother every day hoping to find a cure for her illness, though she had a very strong feeling the answer would not be in time to save her mother.

"Mistress, do ye ken if my family will be at the *ceilidh* tonight?" Her back was toward Anna as she pounded nettles into a fine powder.

"Why are ye askin' me, lass? Ye hae all the answers ye seek at yer own fingertips. Get the answer for yerself, aye?" Anna said, making a chuckling noise that sounded like a chicken.

"Och, aye, I forgot!" Cat giggled. "I was too involved in these darn nettles to remember."

"They are a rare stubborn herb to pummel," Anna said, "and I'm verra glad ye're here to do it for me, lass. After I thrash on them for a few hours, me hands will ache for days."

"I dinna mind the task to help ye, Mistress, but would ye pardon me then, I hae an answer to get." Cat put down her mortar and pestle, wrapped her shawl tightly around her shoulders, and walked outside to ask for the raven's assistance.

The wind blew a cool mist in her face as soon as she opened the door. Cat concentrated on the raven, and shortly he appeared on the gate, waiting for instructions. He flew off with her request, and Cat went in search of some eggs for lunch. The chickens would lay them anywhere, but usually they were found under the thickest bushes. She scouted under all the normal shrubbery in vain. Finally, twigs stuck in her hair for her effort, she walked over to the root cellar on the other side of the garden. There she noticed something she had never seen before.

The fog made the landscape look very different. Certain landmarks disappeared completely and others stood out more. She saw a strange mound about fifty feet from the edge of the woods in back of the cellar. Scanning the area in search for other similar anomalies, it became even more conspicuous, since there were no other such heaps on the flat piece of moor. With all thoughts of eggs gone from her mind, she approached it. As she did, the hair on her arms started to rise. There was something very odd about this place. In all the time she had been here at Anna's, why had she not noticed it? Maybe it was the weather playing tricks on her making it look so spooky. She stood in front of the piece of rounded earth. An urge to pay tribute to it was so strong, she knew it had to be a burial place for someone. Scanning the area around it again, she found no marker or cairn indicating who was buried here.

She bent over, laying her hand in the wet grass that topped it. All at once she got a vision of a warrior. He was dressed very differently than anyone in her own time. How long ago did this man die? Where was he from? Did he die in battle or was this a burial site of a king? Cat had many questions for this man and wanted some answers.

The warrior turned to look at Cat. He told her that he was Crinan Macduncan and he was killed in 1045 by his nephew Macbeth, after attempting a rebellion against the English. Crinan had been chief financier of King Malcolm II, and as such, was a very powerful man in the kingdom. His family lived near here then and that was why he was buried here. He went on to tell Cat that he had married King Malcolm's daughter Bethoc, and that he was the father of King Duncan I. After recounting his story, he turned again, and disappeared.

Catrìona stood up. This was a kings burial place, then. This was a great, great, great, grandsire to her clan. After all, *Clann Donnachaidh* means Children of Duncan. Did Anna know about this place and who was buried in her back yard? She thought she had to have known, but why no marker? Vowing to find out more, she ran back to the cottage, totally forgetting about lunch.

❧

"Aye, of course I ken of the burial place." Anna wiped her green, rosemary-powdered fingers on her apron, eyeing her pupil dubiously. She had just finished pouring the fine powder in a stone jar for safekeeping.

"Did ye ken who's buried there, then?" Cat asked, taking off her wet shawl to hang it near the fire to dry.

"Crinan Macduncan. Catrìona, has no one e'er told ye about the past here?" Anna asked.

Cat stopped in mid-motion and thought for a moment. She knew of her ancestors, of course; all Scots knew of their genealogy, but most could not recount that far back.

"Och, aye, Mistress, I ken what went on here, but I just ne'er thought I would meet one of my ancestors," she said in an awe-struck voice, resuming her activity.

"*Meetin'* isna exactly what I would hae called what ye did, Catrìona," Anna laughed. "Let's hae lunch, aye? I'm hungry."

Without a word, Cat walked back to the fire, took her wet shawl from the peg, wrapped it around her shoulders again, and walked out the door to fetch the eggs she forgot. She heard Anna's laughter all the way to the garden. A smile played on her own lips at her one track mind.

≥◆

By early afternoon, the fog had burned off revealing a crisp, cool day. In preparation for the walk to the castle, Cat filled a satchel with the items they needed for the divination tonight. At the cross-roads, the raven waited on the post for Cat. She nearly forgot sending it to confirm that her family would be at the castle. The raven told her they were not there.

Cat wondered what happened to keep them from their traditional year-end *ceilidh.* Not that she and her family would go every year, but for most of her life, felt as if the entire clan was celebrating her birthday on Samhain. She hoped everything, and everyone, was all right.

Story telling, a favorite pastime of all Scots, started on this night, continuing every night, all the way to Beltaine on May first. It was how the past stayed alive. This wasn't to say that history wasn't embellished on, of course.

By the time Anna and Cat arrived at the castle, it was already a full house. The tables in the Great Hall were filled with meats, breads and other savories, and the ale was flowing freely, as usual. Cat remembered that the Seer would always give a divination in the private chambers of the Chief. She had never been privy to what the outcome of those divinations were, but since all seemed to be peaceful in the clan, the visions must have been favorable. How these divinations were done was a mystery, but tonight she would be in the chambers with Anna and her cousin to see first hand.

Anna told Cat she would be waiting in Alexander's chambers getting prepared, and asked if she would bring her a plate of food and meet her there. Cat accompanied Anna to the chambers, went back into the Great Hall for some food for the two of them, and to see if Janet was here tonight.

As she filled the two plates, the hair on the back of her neck rose. Slowly, she looked around to see why, then spotted the reason. It was the hunter from the woods. He was talking with Duncan Robertson and hadn't seen her yet. Why did alarm bells go off each time she saw this man? Was he really someone to be afraid of? Was he going to do her harm in some way? She didn't even know who he was, but she was definitely going to find out before this night was over.

After loading the two plates, she jostled her way back to the chambers through the throng of people talking and laughing. Any attempt to seek out Janet in the melee was futile. She would scout her out after she ate and before the ceremonies started.

Noticing Catrìona coming back to the chambers, the guard opened the doors for her with an unexpectedly friendly smile. She gave him her own dimples back, then walked into the room to see Anna at a round table covered with cards.

"What hae ye got there, Mistress?" Cat stood across the table from Anna, watching in fascination.

"These are Tarot cards, lass. 'Tis one of the ways I tell the future of the clan," Anna said, laying her Celtic Cross spread on the table. "Who was it ye met in the Hall?"

Cat gave her mentor a squinted look, attempting to see if Anna had sent the man herself.

"Do ye ken who he is, then?"

"Aye, a bad sort, that one," Anna said, keeping her eyes on the cards.

"What has he done, Mistress? 'Tis the second time I've met the man, and each time the hair raises on me," she said, twirling her hair.

Cat noticed Anna's hesitation, instantly going on the defensive.

Anna laid the cards down, and looked up into eyes that demanded an answer. Catrìona sensed she was not in danger with the man, but she saw Janet in those black eyes.

"He likes to touch wee lasses. But only ones wi' verra light colored hair," indicating her insight of Cat's safety.

Cat inhaled sharply and ran out through the chamber doors, startling the guard outside, and ignoring Anna's call. She had to find Janet now.

Though she was tall, Janet was very short, and would not be easily seen from the floor of the Hall. Cat ran up to the second floor landing to get a better view. She scanned the entire room, but didn't even see Janet's parents anywhere. Maybe they weren't here. She made another visual sweep, then went back downstairs.

"What is it lass?" asked the guard who had smiled at her before, looking genuinely concerned.

"Do ye ken if the Murray's are here tonight?" she asked.

"I've no' seen them. Do ye wish for me to look out for them for ye?" he asked, making a scan of the room himself.

Before she could answer, the chamber door whipped opened, and Anna said, "No, they'll no' be here tonight," giving Cat a look that said, *come in here at once, this is no way for a Seer to act.*

"Thank ye anyway." Cat said, looking shyly at the guard, and pulling the door closed after herself.

Anna verbally pounced on her as soon as the door was firmly shut.

"What were ye thinkin', lass? Did ye no' hear me callin' for ye before ye ran out?" Severely agitated, Anna paced the room, waiting for Catrìona to answer.

Cat didn't understand why Anna was so angry. All she wanted to do was protect her best friend from a fiend. She sat heavily into one of the brocade chairs near the fireplace. The two plates of food sat on the little table; forgotten. Twirling her hair, she watched Anna wear a path in the thick rug.

"No Mistress, I didna hear ye call to me," she said, looking down at her feet. "Did ye already ken that Janet wasna here?"

"Aye, of course I did! So would ye hae if ye didna let yer emotions get in the way of yer thinkin' straight," she scolded, trying her best not to shout as she pounded her hand on the table, sending the Tarot cards flying off in every direction.

The color started to rise in Cat's face at this abusive barrage. Dropping the twisted hair, she listened to Anna rant on. Finally, unwilling to take anymore of this berating, she stood up, put her hands on her hips, and in a very controlled voice that belied her young age, said, "Sit down!"

Anna stopped in her tracks, in mid-sentence of the next outburst to look at Cat. It seemed that's what she was waiting for.

Anna aimed one of her toothless grins at Cat, which took Cat totally off guard, then sat in the chair as she was told, while Cat watched, utterly perplexed. She sat down next to her mentor, eying her with suspicion, twirling her hair again.

"What are ye doin' to me, Mistress?" she asked. The color had receded from her face, but she still was furious.

"Weel, it wasna somethin' I was expectin' to hae to show ye so soon, but ye forced me hand," Anna said, fingering the amethyst crystal on her staff, trying to keep the smile from her face.

"I want to ken what ye mean," Cat said, still holding her ground.

"I wanted to be sure that ye could stay true to yerself if someone tried to undermine what ye saw. If ye feel strong about a vision or a feelin', yet allow yerself to be swayed by someone's opinion, ye'll ne'er believe in yerself again. Ye'll hae doubt and doubt is the biggest adversary ye'll encounter as a Seer, *Garnet*. Remember that, and ye'll be fine."

The light dawned in Catrìona's eyes and dimples formed in her cheeks.

"Ye did real fine, lass, and now that ye ken about the doubt, ye'll stay true in a reading, aye?"

"Aye, I will. Now tell me about the divination," she said, picking up her plate of food to eat her supper.

ૢ

A while later, Alexander came into his chambers, and the readings began. As the cards were placed in the proper positions for the past, present, future, obstacles and final outcome, Anna told Alexander what each card meant in the position it was in, and in conjunction with the cards already there. Cat wondered how so many meanings could possibly be remembered for each card. It seemed an impossible task. Why didn't Anna just look into the future instead of having cards tell it for her?

After listening to questions and explanations for some time, Catrìona wanted to see into the future of the clan on her own. Anna and Alexander were so engrossed in the cards, they didn't notice when she quietly got up to sit in a darkened corner on the other side of the room. She caught the eye of the Wolfhound and he made a motion to get up. Holding up her hand, she silently asked him to wait until she finished her task. He lay his big, shaggy head back down on his mammoth paws, and let out a small groan, conceding to her request.

Cat sat back in the chair and concentrated on the clan; her family and friends, the crops, the beasts, life in general. At first, everything was status quo. Life in the Highlands was never easy, but Highlanders always made do with what they had, thriving in whatever nature, or man, could send their way. There were the same old problems to trouble about — the weather, keeping the herds in tact, the occasional bickering between themselves or neighbors — nothing out of the ordinary.

An image of her mother living through spring was a relief. Running down a mental checklist, she noted that the rest of her family and friends would be well in the coming months. But she wanted more.

Then, out of the blue, the hunter appeared, making her skin break out in goose flesh. She saw him plain as day. He was holding a little girl's hand; her hair almost white, and her eyes a sad blue. Who was this little lass? Not that Catrìona knew all the children in the clan, but she thought she was acquainted with most.

Her brows furrowed together as she concentrated on the little girl more, asking for her name. The lass looked at Cat, saying her name was Caroline Menzies. Caroline said the man was her father, and she lived in Fortingall with her mother. Cat broached the question, asking if he hurt her. Caroline told Cat that she rarely saw her father, but that he would never hurt her.

Was the hunter deprived of his own daughter? Is that why he sought out young girls who reminded him of his own flesh and blood?

Becoming very tired, Cat opened her eyes, familiarizing herself with her surroundings again. The room had gone quiet. Anna and Alexander were nowhere to be found. She looked over to see if Curr was still sleeping behind the chair. He had been watching her, and now saw that she had completed her task. He stretched out with a big yawn, walked slowly over to Cat's chair, then proceeded to rest his big head on her lap.

Cat smiled at the way he made himself at home with her. Taking his ears, she rubbed the soft tips until pure bliss registered on his face. A noise outside the door made him lift his head from Cat's loving attentions to see who was entering. Anna walked though the door, and Curr went back to his place behind the chair.

"How did ye do, lass?" asked Anna. She had a small pouch in her hand again. Payment for the divination from Alexander.

"It looks like another good winter, Mistress." Cat stood up and stretched out to get some circulation back in her legs.

"Anything else?" asked Anna in an all-knowing manner.

The look Cat returned led Anna to believe that there was, but Cat wasn't ready to divulge what she saw just yet. There was information she wanted to get on her own. Anna read this fleeting thought and let the matter drop. Catrìona would tell her when she was ready.

≥●

Winter came early, the first snow falling not two weeks after the Samhain festivities. The days were very short this time of year, and except for hunting, most people did not venture far from their crofts. It was a time to be with family, tell stories, and sleep.

This was no quiet time for Cat, however. This was a time to hone her skills and develop new ones. Working on telepathy, Anna set up tests enabling Cat to explore that unseen realm. Cat's natural ability, enhanced by her grandmother's life force flowing in her veins, required no aids of herbs, crystals or trances to hear other's thoughts. Cat became so good at this, on some days, words were rarely spoken.

One morning, as the snow fell lazily from the milk-white sky like goose down after a pillow fight, Anna asked Catrìona if she wanted more of a challenge. Cat was definitely ready for something new.

"What can we try now, Mistress?" she asked, as they sat together eating porridge at the kitchen table.

"I want ye to go into someone else's thoughts."

"Oh? Whose?" Her spoon was put down, forgotten in her bowl.

"Gregor's. Do ye remember him?" Anna asked, watching

Catrìona's expression when she brought up his name. Cat had told her that she didn't want to know his fate for letting the thief steal the rents.

"Aye, o' course I remember him."

"I want ye to tell me what happened to him."

Catrìona walked over to the window twirling her hair. She absently watched three deer cross the snow-covered moor through the wavy glass. When she turned to face Anna, letting the twisted lock fall to her chest, her eyes had gone to dark amethyst sparkling with tears.

"He was sentenced to be flogged, and was relieved of his duty as a guard. He's now workin' in the stables," she cried.

Anna went to her and cradled her like a small child.

"It was no' yer fault what happened to Gregor, lass. Askin' for Gregor's fate was a hard request, but with yer abilities, learnin' to mask yer emotions is imperative, or it will tear ye apart. Ye ken that, dinna ye?"

"Aye," she sniffed, pulling out a handkerchief from her sleeve and blowing a little toot. Anna let out a deep chuckle at the strange noise emanating from Catrìona's nose.

"Weel, that lifts the spirits, aye?" Anna said, unable to suppress the giggle she felt as she replayed the toot in her mind.

Despite herself, Cat smiled too; her dimples getting deeper hearing Anna laugh.

"My brother, Lachlan, always laughs when I blow my nose, too." The laughter made her feel a little better. Stuffing her handkerchief back up her sleeve, she finished her porridge.

❧

The snow that fell in mid-November had all melted, the ground was now bare. A winter thaw on that Hogmanay eve led to the celebration at the castle of the age old tradition of First Footing. The Great Hall once again accommodated a small feast for those few who braved the winter night.

Folklore dictated that if a dark-haired man should be the first to cross the threshold after the stroke of midnight, it was good luck to that household. If a fair-haired person, a woman or a child be the first to cross, it was bad luck. If a red-haired person was first, it was most unlucky. Catrìona and her mother were only allowed to go into a house well after their men. No sense leaving anything to chance.

This year, Catrìona would not be attending the First Footing at the castle since her family wouldn't be there. She and Anna were going to have a small feast of their own to celebrate Hogmanay. Two rabbits and a ham were brought by yesterday, as payment for some healing services they had performed on one of George Reid's children.

Gavin, Mr. Reid's eldest son, came by last week asking for Anna's help with his sick brother. He told her that young Archie had a terrible cough and fever. Cat packed up some chamomile, camphor, peppermint oil, fenugreek, garlic, thyme, mullein and marshmallow, as Anna instructed. She said that these herbs, made into tea, would break the fever and relieve the mucus from the lungs. The camphor and peppermint oil would be rubbed onto the boy's chest to help clear the lungs and sinuses.

Cat and Anna went with Gavin in his wagon and was taken to his family's croft, some three hours away. Cat instantly got the impression that he was scrutinizing her every move — taking in her every detail. For the most part, she ignored him. She was getting used to piercing looks and close examination by nearly everyone she came into contact with. It was a natural curiosity, she thought. Being such a young Seer would attract attention.

Feeling his eyes on her, she looked up and flashed her dimples, unaware of the effect she had on him. Immediately, she sensed him become very uncomfortable as he quickly turned to face forward, grasping the reins in a death grip. When he attempted to ask if they were ready to leave, he had no voice. Cat watched his mouth attempt to form words, but he remained silent.

"Are ye all right, then?" Cat asked for the third time, oblivious to the reason for his strange behavior.

"Uh, oh, uhm … och, aye," he sputtered, doing his best to regain some composure. His face blazed as Anna giggled like a schoolgirl in the back of the wagon.

"We're ready to go then … Gavin, is it?" She tossed the question over her shoulder, carefully stepping over crates and hay to the back of the wagon to sit next to Anna. Just as she got settled, the reins clicked fiercely. The wagon was off with a lurch that made both of them nearly come unseated. This made Anna whoop with laughter even more.

❧

For the next three hours, Anna and Cat rode in semi-silence, punctuated only by Anna's occasional giggle that Cat still didn't comprehend, nor did Anna shed any light on. Cat was very curious about Mr. Reid's youngest daughter, Sara, the lass Lachlan was so smitten with. Wondering if there was any resemblance to Gavin, she studied his back as he drove the wagon. He had blonde hair and small shoulders on a wiry frame. When she looked into his eyes earlier, they were soft blue highlighting a friendly face with a small mouth. All in all, he looked rather girlish, she thought, which led her to believe that Sara was probably rather pretty.

When they arrived at the Reids' small stone croft, it was dusk. Mr. Reid came out to meet them and helped Anna out of the wagon as Cat gathered the satchel, bringing up the rear. Inside, the crowded two room cott was warm from the peat fire and body heat. In front of the fire, a small boy wrapped in a blanket lay on a pallet. His mother, Màiri, was sitting in a chair next to him, knitting. She never looked up as the blast of winter air entered the room with her guests.

Anna walked over to young Archie, bending to feel his head and listen to his breathing. Cat brought a chair over for her, along with the satchel of remedies.

"Hae ye some hot water for tea, Mrs. Reid?" Cat asked.

"I'll put it on for ye," Mr. Reid volunteered, not even giving his wife a glance. She still hadn't moved from her chair, or acknowledged them in any way.

"Has he been able to eat or drink anythin' lately?" Anna asked to no one in particular, putting her gnarled hands on the boy's chest.

"No. No' since early this mornin', that's why I sent for ye," Mr. Reid answered. Crouching down next to his son, he tenderly wiped the blonde locks from the lad's damp forehead.

"Do ye ken what's wrong wi' him, then, Mistress?" he asked, searching Anna's face for any clues to his son's ailment.

"A touch of the ague, sounds to me. What do ye think, Catrìona?"

Cat was pouring the hot water over the herbs to steep for a tea. Putting the cover on the pot, she turned to face Anna, catching the "play along" look in her eyes.

"Aye Mistress, and the rest o' the family may get it soon, so I'm makin' a big pot for the whole family," she said, sure there was something decidedly strange going on. Mrs. Reid. What was wrong with her? Why didn't she acknowledge anyone's presence? It was unnerving. Cat felt a kind of malevolence emanating from her. Did Mrs. Reid have something to do with her son's ailment?

"Mistress, a word wi' ye, please?" Cat asked softly.

Cat heard her mentor's reply to the unasked question in her head. *Aye, she's a spell caster, and she's put a spell on him.*

Can she hear us when we talk like this? Cat asked telepathically.

No. She's no' powerful enough. See if ye can get into her thoughts and find out why she did this to wee Archie, aye? But be careful! Dinna let her be aware that ye are there.

Cat turned to the kitchen table, pretending to check on the tea. Still learning the art of masking her emotions, she stood with her back facing the room, not trusting herself to be unaffected by the results.

Concentrating on Màiri Reid, Cat became a shadow and went inside. The shadow found many odd things about Mrs. Reid. Come to find out, Màiri Reid was quite aware of their presence in her house. She was trying to put up a barrier around herself so Anna, at least, would not find out who, or what she was. It wasn't working very well, Cat thought. Anna said she wasn't powerful enough, although she was powerful enough to make her own child very ill. Why? That's what she needed to know.

Cat went deeper into Màiri's thoughts; stealthily as the shadow she was. It seemed that her young son was a test to become a spell caster. Make him ill then make him well again. Unfortunately, the part about making him well again wasn't working, that's why Anna was called. Màiri was actually terrified of what may happen if Anna could not reverse the spell. The coven leader told her it was an easy spell, but if she failed, would not be allowed to learn more about the arts.

Cat was snapped out of her mind meld with Mrs. Reid when Anna asked if she could help with the tea.

What did ye find out? Anna asked telepathically.

She put a spell on him and doesna ken how to break it to make him well again. She's verra scairt.

That she should be; damned fool woman. I think I ken who she's goin' to for this magick, too, and he doesna even hae the power, just charm. Good work, lass. I'll take it from here whilst ye pour a cup o' that tea for each o' the family.

As Cat poured, Anna walked over to Mrs. Reid and yanked the knitting from her hand. Màiri, about to put up an argument, stopped when she saw the look in Anna's eyes, daring her to say a word. Màiri knew she'd been found out, and pleaded with her eyes to not say anything to her family. Anna made it known that if this ever happened again, that the whole clan would know of her *dabblings*.

With the rest of the family kept busy with Catrìona's tea dispensing, Anna and Màiri went about quietly undoing the spell. A little later, Archie started coming around. Anna kept pouring Cat's tea into the boy, giving it the appearance of a miracle cure to the rest of the family. It wouldn't hurt him any to make sure no real infection began in his lungs.

It was well into the night by the time young Archie was feeling like himself again, and the Reid's made room in the cramped croft for their guests. Màiri Reid couldn't do enough for Anna for making her son well again, *and* keeping the secret of why he was sick to begin with. They all shared a savory lamb stew with biscuits for supper. Afterwards, Gavin gave up his bed for Anna and Cat to sleep in, saying he would take the floor near his wee brother to keep watch over him.

When all had retired for the evening, Cat finally had the chance to ask Anna what was so amusing on the journey this afternoon. Anna had been facing the wall in the small bed with Cat cradled in along side her. Cat felt the bed shake as Anna started to giggle again.

"What is so funny?" she demanded in a whisper, propping herself up on her elbow.

"Ye dinna even notice the poor wee lad, did ye?" Anna asked, thoroughly amused.

"Who?"

"Gavin, lass, Gavin!"

"Well, o' course I noticed him. He drove us here," she said, still not understanding.

"He's quite smitten wi' ye," Anna said, chuckling.

"What?"

"He thinks ye're his age; almost 18, and he's smitten wi' ye."

"Shite!"

That expletive did Anna in, and she let out a whoop sure to wake the entire family.

"Shhhh, shhhh, quiet! Ye'll wake the dead, ne'er mind the Reid's!"

Cat said, crawling on top of Anna to put her hand over her mentor's mouth. The bed was shaking so hard, Cat feared it would fall in from both of their weights. Now, seeing the humor in the whole situation, Cat started to giggle herself. Anna and Cat buried their faces deep into their pillows until they were composed, which seemed to take quite some time. They both fell asleep with smiles on their faces, cradled together in a spoon-like position. If the Reid's did hear them, no one came to see what was so funny.

whispers of rebellion

It was early afternoon in the beginning of the new year. Isobel sat close to the smoldering peat fire doing her mending. Lately, no matter how close she sat to the blaze, she was unable to get warm enough. On the damp, cold days when it rained or snowed, her entire body ached. She barely moved from her chair to do her chores; the life drained from her day by day.

She missed Catrìona more than she thought possible. After six months of separation she thought she would be used to it. Sure, the house was full of women to help her cook, clean, and do the wash, but none were her daughter. Each night, she cried herself to sleep, hoping Catrìona was learning her craft well enough to return home soon. Angus did his best to cheer her up, but truth be told, only her daughter could do that right now.

Isobel looked up when the best room door opened. Lizzie Stark's daughter Maggie, brought in a hot cup of tea and a warm scone with jam. Maggie was two years older than Catrìona, and was a great help in the house, tending to Isobel like a mother to a child, but Isobel knew it was more from a sense of duty than anything else. Maggie bore no resentment, but carried no warmth either, not like Catrìona would have responded with.

Isobel laid her mending in her lap, and smiled up at her, taking the presented cup of tea. Maggie put the dish with the scone on the little table next to Isobel's chair.

"Shall I be gettin' the candles lit for ye, Mrs. Robertson?" Without waiting for an answer, Maggie was already heading for the desk drawer to get a new pair of tapers.

"Aye, please, it's gettin' dark in here." Isobel blew on the steamy liquid in her cup trying not to give away the anxious feeling in the pit of her stomach. "Are Angus and the lads back yet?"

"No. Or at least they hae no' made it into the house yet," she said, blowing out the twig she used brighten the room.

"Will ye fetch me when ye see them, then?" Isobel asked.

"Aye, I will," Maggie answered, then left the room to Isobel.

Angus had taken the lads to the Hermitage, Alexander's country home in Carie, on the southern shores of Loch Rannoch, to talk about the imminent war between England and Spain. He needed to know where Alexander's sympathies lay; for the Jacobites and King James, or the Hanoverians, the House of Orange, and King George. Alexander didn't recognize any established form of government, going about things his own way. In the '15, where Angus lost his arm, Alexander raised his men to fight with the Jacobites, but over the years ideals changed.

Even though Scotland had not seen a war in over thirty years, Scottish soldiers were trained and sent abroad to fight in France, as allies with the English. With the English spread thin fighting Spain, and ever prepared for the French, the Scots could beat the English on their own ground. Word was, Prince Charles was petitioning Spain and France to finance a Jacobite invasion against England, to put his father, King James, back in power. This sparked new rumblings of a rebellion against the English. It was the chance Scotland waited for, to be its own sovereign country again, free from English rule.

Isobel wondered what the outcome of these rumblings would be this time. She knew if it actually came to blows, she would lose Seumas — even though still limping badly from his broken leg — and Iain to the military. If Lachlan were older, he would follow his brothers as well.

It was full dark when Isobel was notified of Angus' return. The lads would sit down immediately to eat, and this would give her and Angus a chance to talk alone about the meeting. She heard his footsteps coming down the hall, then the door opened with a whoosh of cold air. Angus lumbered over to her, tiredly planting a kiss on the top of her head.

"Tell me all about it, then. What went on?" she asked, straining her neck to take in his full height.

With a deep sigh, Angus sat heavily in the chair next to the fireplace to warm his feet.

"It seems that an Association has been formed that includes the Duke of Perth; John Drummond; Simon Fraser, Lord Lovat, the Chief of Clan Fraser; young Donald Cameron of Lochiel, Chief of Clan Cameron; and William Macgregor of Balhaldie."

"What does it all mean, Angus?" The mending was dropped in her lap, all but forgotten.

"Simply, it means that if King James and Prince Charles can persuade Spain and Cardinal Fleury, chief minister to King Louis XV of France to finance a war with England, a Scottish rebellion will begin."

à.

For the next few months, talk was tense. Every man in every tavern had an opinion on the matter, deciding who should command the rebellion. Angus worked as Alexander's ears and eyes, gaining as much information as he could, leaving its reliability to Alexander. Seumas, Iain and Lachlan also got involved where they could. It all just seemed to be talk and bravado; no solid facts about anything.

By early spring, the rumblings died, and life in the Highlands returned to normal. With the lambing and calving season upon them, the men of Clan Donnachaidh became too busy with the beasts and the planting of barley, to think of the far-flung idea of war.

It was nearing time for Lachlan to do his studies at Blair Castle. Isobel was not looking forward to loosing another one of her children for a year, but at least it was a safe place for him to be. He and Catrìona would be able to visit each other often; something he had not stopped talking about since she left.

Cat had written many letters during the long winter, and they became a journal of her time with Anna Macpherson. They were about what she was learning, who she was treating for what ailments, the making of remedies from herbs, and about the divinations at the castle. Letters would arrive in a stack from whoever came from Blair Atholl. Isobel sent hers and Janet's back with anyone going in that direction. Normally, only every couple of months Isobel received her letters, then it was a reading frenzy for the entire family to see what had been going on with their youngest.

Sometimes, Cat would address a letter to Isobel alone. These were the most difficult ones to read ... and write, Isobel assumed. So far, there had been two like that. The first was when Cat found out why she had the Sight so strong. Isobel had pulled that letter out of the stack so it wouldn't be read by the rest of the family. When her men were out in the field, she read it. Then read it again. She wasn't sure if it were true, but it made her feel good to know that her mother was watching out for her through her own daughter. Knowing information of that magnitude would be too difficult for Angus and the lads to comprehend, she was glad Cat took it upon herself to keep them sheltered.

Today, Isobel got the second privately addressed letter from Catrìona. She waited for the men to leave, then went up to her room to read it. It was sealed with wax and imprinted with what looked like a leaf. Cat had no jewellery of her own to imprint it with, and Isobel smiled at her daughter's ingenuity. Breaking the wax seal, she unfolded the parchment carefully, and took a seat at the edge of her bed. Never knowing what to expect in these letters, she didn't want to land on the floor if she fainted.

2 January, 1739

Dearest Mam,

I'm writing to you this way as a matter of some urgency. I have had a Vision about Janet and I would like you to see what can be done about it. It seems that a Man named Fergal Menzies has been in the area, and he likes to make indecent advances on young, blonde-haired lasses. He has a young Daughter of his own that he is not able to be with for some reason, so he seeks "her" company from others. I'm not sure he means it to be wicked, but I'm quite sure it's interpreted that way by his Victims.

Anna does not see that Janet is in any danger, but I cannot help thinking about him. I myself have seen him twice - neither time has he taken any notice of me, and both times it was in or near Blair Castle. I know that Janet is unlikely to come here, but I'm unsure of Mr. Menzie's whereabouts and intentions.

Would it be possible to warn her and her parents to watch out for the man? He is of average height with light hair and blue eyes. I do not wish to alarm anyone, but he frightens me.

*I'll leave this in your capable hands to find a way to keep harm
from coming to Janet.*
   Your Loving Daughter,
   Catrìona

At that moment, Isobel found it very difficult to believe her
daughter was only twelve years old. Catrìona's shoulders were much
too narrow to bear that kind of responsibility. Isobel carefully folded
the parchment and tucked it under the mattress. She wouldn't let
the lads read it, but she would show it to Angus, since it would be
him that brought the news to the Murray's.

She wondered if Angus knew of this man, Menzies. From the
sound of it, he was very troubled. She hoped he never set foot on
Robertson land for fear of what Angus would do to him. Isobel hoped
she would have an answer for Cat about Janet before Lachlan made
his trip to the castle tomorrow.

Isobel carefully trod down the stairs to see if she could help in
the kitchen. If not, she would go back to her chair in the sun to
mend the never ending pile of clothes. Winter had taken a toll on
her, but as the warmth of the early spring days came, she felt a new
energy in herself. By no means well, she at least could do small chores
again, making herself feel useful.

When she opened the kitchen door, Lizzie Stark was kneading
dough and Maggie was half finished plucking three chickens for
tonight's supper. A half completed crust for a dried apple pie waited
for some attention on the table. Isobel was planning a going away
supper for Lachlan, preparing all of his favorites.

"Might I be a help wi' the pie crust, Lizzie?" Isobel asked, already rolling up her sleeves and strapping on an apron.

"Oh, aye, Isobel … if ye feel ye're up to it, that is." Lizzie caught
Maggie's hazel green look of concern, but then took in Isobel's apparent vigor, however fleeting. "Ye look like yerself this day, are ye
feelin' well then?"

"I do feel like myself today, like a new beginnin'," she said,
smiling a dimpled grin at Lizzie. With each roll of the wooden
rolling pin, she felt vitality flow through her veins. Maybe she
really was on the mend and the chronic fatigue would finally
subside.

の

The sun stayed in the sky longer each day, the fields had all been
plowed, and the seeding of barley was almost complete. The good
weather allowed for an early start on planting. Lachlan, a great help,
would be sorely missed, especially when it came to the end of the
calving and lambing. All the men were needed at this time, but it
was also very important for him to start his studies.

Atop the great dappled gray Percheron, Uallach, Angus looked
over at his youngest son from his elevated perch. He smiled at the
resemblance Lachlan had to himself. A swell of pride engulfed his
heart for all of his children. They were a fine lot. A man could not
ask for better. Then he thought of Isobel. She would miss so much if
she passed on before her time. She needed Catrìona home again,
but it was not to be.

At least the talk of rebellion had ceased … for now. He knew it
would never really go away until it happened, but he was glad for
the quieting, because he knew Isobel couldn't bear seeing her sons
become soldiers. He didn't like the idea much either.

Squeezing the sides of the great horse and clucking his tongue,
he rode down the hill to help his sons gather in the kine for the
evening. So far, the calving and lambing was going very well. The
warm winter attributed to only a few of the priceless beasts' deaths,
unlike the year before when almost one quarter were lost to the
freezing cold and late storms.

As Angus rode into the glen, a rider crested the hill that he had
just come down. Iain, noticing the rider first, pointed him out. They
all waited in silence for the stranger to ride down and introduce
himself. In the heart of Robertson land, an unfamiliar face put all of
them on alert. What was a stranger doing so far out of his way?

As the stranger neared, Angus took in everything about the man.
His fair hair, his green plaid, the bow he had slung over his shoulder,
and as he got closer, his blue eyes. Angus saw his sons do the same
thing. He looked beyond the outlander to see if anyone else was
with him on the hill, but the man appeared to be alone.

"What can we be doin' for ye, sir?" Angus asked, towering over
the smaller man and his pony.

"Will ye be Angus Robertson then?" the stranger asked.

"Aye, and who may ye be?"

"My name is Fergal Menzies. I heard that ye may be needin' a man to run yer sheep," he said in a cordial voice that kept cracking.

"And where did ye hear that from, Mr. Menzies?" Angus asked, looking the man up and down boldly, as if he were some kind of prey.

"I was at Blair Castle last Samhain and spoke wi' Duncan Robertson who said ye may be needin' help come spring. Is it true then? Are ye in need of an extra man for a while?" Fergal asked, squirming a bit in his saddle as Angus blatantly scrutinized him.

"No. I thought I may be needin' help the autumn last, but wi' the mild winter, I hae it under control," Angus said, his face showing no emotion.

Seumas and Iain exchanged quick glances, wondering why their father just turned away a perfect candidate for tending the sheep while Lachlan was gone. Both said nothing; neither would dare question their father in front of this stranger to usurp his authority. They knew their father well enough to go by what he said for reasons their youth and inexperience could not comprehend.

"Aye then. Sorry to hae bothered ye. Do ye ken of anyone else who may be needin' help?" Fergal asked, almost glad the big man said no. It was unnerving the way he was being examined.

"No. No one that I'm aware of in these parts. Ye may try the Campbell's to the southwest, but that's all I can tell ye," Angus said, then turned his mount in dismissal to continue with his work. Taking the hint, Fergal turned his pony southwest in search of more friendly company.

All four of them watched the outlander until he was over the rise out and of site before speaking. The strange tension in the air was released when he disappeared.

"What was that all about, Da? O' course we need a man," Seumas challenged, rubbing his thigh.

"There's somethin' verra odd about that man. Did none of ye feel it?" Angus asked quietly. He rubbed the stubble on his chin, watching where Fergal disappeared over the hill, thinking he may reappear at any moment.

"He did hae a nervous air about him. What else, Da?" Iain asked, his eyes locked on the same place his father's were.

"Like he had no spirit left in him," Lachlan whispered, he too watching the empty hillside.

Lachlan was right, something was lost in the man. Something broke him. Angus was glad he went by his gut feelings on the man.

Fergal Menzies was not someone he wanted anywhere near his family.

"Let's get back to it then, lads. The kine wilna move on their own, aye?" Angus commanded, putting the situation behind him, breaking the spell cast by the stranger.

❧

The day ended with a sunset that took one's breath away. The sky was on fire with deep rose, lilac and peach. The snow that topped the Grampians blazed with its reflection as the riders pressed for home. The breeze freshened from the west, bringing with it the smell of supper, as they neared the house.

"Take the horses into the barn, *mo ghille*," Angus said, handing his reins over to Lachlan. "We'll meet ye in the house for supper, aye?"

"Aye, Da. I'll be there in no time. The smell of that chicken will be drivin' me to distraction all the while," Lachlan said, breathing deeply as he gathered the reins from the horses and walked them into the barn.

As soon as Lachlan was out of sight, Angus and Iain bolted for the house, with Seumas limping up the rear, and burst into the kitchen. Isobel had told them when to be home for Lachlan's going away supper, and they wanted to get cleaned up a bit before they sat down to eat. The smell of that chicken was making their mouths water.

"Ah, good, right on time, Angus," Isobel commented, pulling the fresh hot bread out of the oven.

Angus was quite surprised to see her in the kitchen. He looked over at Lizzie for assurance, and she gave him a nod and a smile. He planted a kiss on Isobel's cheek, then stood there, just staring at her.

"What is it, Angus? Ye act like ye ne'er seen me in the kitchen before," Isobel said, her dimples deepening.

"Ye ne'er cease to amaze me, *a ghaoil*." Smiling and shaking his head, he turned to the wash bowl to get cleaned up.

Lachlan walked in a few minutes later. "What's goin' on?" he asked, wiping his freshly washed hands on the linen towel. Something was awry. They were all seated and none of the food had been touched yet.

"'Tis yer goin' away supper, Lachlan," Maggie said, sheepishly, the color rising in her cheeks.

"Och, aye! I nearly forgot that I'm leavin' in the mornin'," he said, pulling out his chair to take a seat.

"So ye did all this cookin' just for me then, Maggie?" Lachlan teased.

"No, my Mam and yer Mam helped," she said, in full bloom now.

"Well Mam, ye are lookin' rare fine tonight," Seumas stated, looking at his mother trying to remember the last time she looked this healthy.

"Thank ye, Seumas, I'm feelin' verra well today," she said, starting the rotation of food to Angus. "We got a few letters from yer sister today. Andrew Murray brought them by this mornin'. They're in the livin' room, if anyone wants to read them."

Iain jumped from his chair, nearly knocking it over. Anything new to read was a rare delight, and he seized the opportunity, running to the best room to get them. Angus chuckled to think, to Iain, reading was even more important than eating, taking half a chicken and passing the platter along to Seumas.

It was a feast. They all sat at the table and ate until there wasn't a scrap left of anything. Lachlan sat back in his chair when the last piece of pie was eaten, belched, and smiled at Maggie.

"Weel Maggie, lass," he said, exaggerating the Scottish lilt in his voice. "Ye outdid yerself, makin' that meal just for me." He pat his stomach and watched the color rise in her face again.

Angus noticed that this comment provoked a kick from Isobel to Lachlan's shin under the table, along with a look charged with daggers. Obviously, Lachlan understood it, because he excused himself to go pack for the trip tomorrow.

After the meal was over and the dishes were washed and put away, Angus requested that Isobel join him in the best room. He sat in his chair and pulled her onto his lap.

"Are ye really feelin' better then, or are ye just tryin' to put on a show for Lachlan?" he questioned into her hair. "And what was the kick to Lachlan's shins for?"

"He kens how Maggie feels about him. I dinna care for the way he was teasin' her." She snuggled into him, melding herself to his body. "And I do feel like myself again, Angus. I dinna ken how long it will last, but for now let us take advantage of it, aye?" she purred into the side of his neck, sending him into gooseflesh.

He looked down at her, catching the meaning in her light blue gaze. She wrapped her arms around his thick neck, and he lifted her light body to his chest to take her upstairs.

❧

The next morning, as Isobel was making the bed, she found the letter from Catrìona she forgot to show to Angus. Bringing it down to breakfast with her, she asked if he would stay for a few minutes after the lads left to do their chores.

"When did ye get this?" he asked, taking the presented parchment from Isobel.

"A week ago last. I tucked it under the mattress, then forgot about it until it fell out this morning while I was makin' the bed," she said, clearing the table.

Angus unfolded it and read it. Isobel turned to see his reaction to the delicate script and noticed he was finding it hard to catch his breath.

"What is it, Angus?"

"Ye say ye received this letter a week ago?"

"Aye," she said nervously, standing next to her husband. "What's the matter? Ye're givin' me a fright."

"A week ago last, a man — this man — came to me and the lads in the glen where we pasture the kine, lookin' for work," he said, paled by the thought. "I kent from the moment I saw him that there was somethin' wrong wi' him. So did Lachlan. He said it was if he had lost his spirit. Now I ken why."

"What did ye tell the man?" Isobel asked, sitting down at the table before her legs buckled under her.

"I told him that I didna need any help, to try the Campbell's."

She watched the emotions he let show on his face run the gamut from relief to rage as he replayed the scene in his head.

"Do ye ken what might hae happened if I took on Menzies?" he asked. "Lord, I go weak just thinkin' about it. He needs to be found. I'll no' hae a man like that in my back yard. I'll go tell Andrew about him, then see who I can spare from the farmin' to help me search for him." He was up and pacing now, determining which of his men were the best trackers, and how to cover as much territory as possible.

"I'm verra sorry for forgettin' it, Angus. Wi' Lachlan leaving, I guess my mind was on other things," she said in a deflated tone.

"Och, dinna fash yerself about it," he scoffed, putting his big hand on her shoulder when he saw how white she had gone. "Will ye mind some company?"

"Mòrag and Janet, ye mean?" Reading his mind, she covered his hand with her own. After twenty years of marriage, she knew him better than he knew himself, and she saw him smile.

"Aye. I'll be taking Andrew wi' me. Seumas and Iain will stay here. Gregor will be by later this mornin' to fetch Lachlan. Too late to stop that now. I'll hae scouts patrollin' around to make sure Menzies is caught, if he comes back this way."

It was no use in asking how long he would be gone. Who knows where the man ended up. Isobel knew it could be a few days to a few weeks.

"What will ye do when ye find him, Angus?" she asked quietly, not knowing whether she really wanted the answer or not.

"I've been thinkin' on that, and the only thing I can come up wi' is to bring him to Alexander to be dealt wi'. That is unless he does somethin' in the mean time that he's caught at. Then I reckon it will be my responsibility to see that he's punished fair."

That was enough to let her know that the man would indeed be punished, but that she didn't need to be privy to all the details.

ঽৡ

Mòrag and Janet Murray were right at home with Isobel. It wasn't just Catrìona and Janet that were close, Isobel and Mòrag had known each other most of their lives. Mòrag was like the sister Isobel never had. Though Isobel felt better each day, she still didn't understand what happened to turn her health around, but was taking full advantage of her good fortune. Having her dearest friend stay with her also lifted her spirits. Angus knew what he was doing when he had asked them to stay with her. She wasn't sure how much these new events would have set her health back, with only worry on her mind.

A week had gone by with no word from Angus or Andrew. They all knew it could be a while before any notification was delivered. Seumas and Iain, armed to the teeth, stayed close to home; always within shouting distance of the house. This, of course, meant the cattle and sheep were close as well. It wouldn't be long before the beasts would have to be moved to stay in green grass further from the house.

"Dinna worry, Mam," Seumas announced at the supper table one evening. "It's no' like the kine need tendin' the entire day, and we hae enough men to keep the sheep tended. Iain and I will take turns bein' here, and watchin' the kine from the low shieling from now on."

"Aye, and if Da is in Campbell territory, they surely wilna be here," Iain said. The deep smirk on his face indicating his father will be keeping the Campbell's too busy to be contemplating the theft of Robertson cattle.

Isobel looked at Iain, and despite herself, laughed out loud; a sound that had not been heard in the house for some time. A picture formed in her head of Angus rousing the Campbell clan with his small army of Robertson Highlanders, on a search and destroy mission.

"All I ken is I will be right glad when the fiend is found and punished," Janet said in a serious voice. "What in the world would make someone do such wicked things?"

They all sobered at this question, the lads shifted in their seats uncomfortably.

"No one kens what's in a troubled mind, lass. That's why yer Da is out lookin' for him … to stop him," Mòrag said, reaching over to stroke her daughter's long blonde hair.

After a moment of uneasy silence, Seumas pushed away from the table, with Iain right behind him.

"Uh, we had better go take a last look around before dark," Seumas said. Iain bobbed his head in agreement, then they were out the door.

Isobel pushed her own chair from the table to begin the clean up process, leaving Mòrag to talk to Janet in private. She didn't know how much had been divulged to Janet, until just this night. With the distraction of the two of them in her house, she forgot the sobering fact that a man was being hunted for serious crimes against young girls. Making light of it certainly did not distract Janet, and Isobel could see that the lass was truly frightened.

Isobel finished cleaning up the kitchen, leaving the dishes on the table for Mòrag to do when she finished having her say. Suddenly feeling very tired, she went into the best room, stoked the fire for the night and went up to bed.

આ

It was a restless night for Isobel. She missed Angus and desperately needed to know if he was all right. She dreamt of dark woods, long, lonely moors and an ever-present shadow following her. This shadow never made itself known, but an evil emanated from it. She awoke to the beginnings of dawn in a sweat that soaked her shift through to the skin. Getting out from under the covers, she stripped off the wet muslin, then sat next to the open window to let the cool breeze chase the excess warmth from her body. The early hour was devoid of all sounds as she peeked out the window for any sign of movement. Even the rooster wasn't up yet.

Suddenly, the bedroom door opened, and even in the dark, she could tell it was Angus filling the doorframe. Her movement at the window caught his eye.

"Are ye all right, Isobel?" he whispered, careful not wake the rest of the house. He walked over to her, stopping short by her nakedness.

"Were ye expectin' me then?" he asked, with a smile in his deep velvet voice.

"No, but I'm verra glad ye're home," she said, then stood to wrap herself around him in a loving embrace. "I had a nightmare and woke in a sweat. I was tryin' to cool off. I ne'er even heard yer horse."

"The men and horses are wi' Andrew behind the barn." He was rubbing his hand up and down her back, reaching down to cup her bottom. "We found Menzies and are off to deposit him into Alexander's capable hands," he said into her chamomile-scented hair. "I just wanted to tell ye of our progress."

She was getting a chill standing by the open window, despite the heat emanating from Angus, and wriggled out of his embrace.

"Did ye ask him if he did those terrible things?" she asked, walking over to the bed to wrap herself in a blanket.

"Aye, but he hasna spoken since we found him. Wilna say a word no matter what I threaten him wi'," he said. "But there's a strangeness about him that I canna place. I'll be glad to let Alexander deal wi' him."

"Mòrag and Janet will stay here until ye and Andrew return, aye?" she asked.

"If that's what ye want, my love," he said, pulling her against his big chest once again. "I best be off so I can get back within the week."

She hugged him tightly, stood on tiptoes, and pressed a kiss softly on his lips. "Hurry back."

"Aye," he said hoarsely, then kissed her soundly on the mouth. He released her slowly, then walked to the door and was gone. She listened for his footsteps down the stairs, but he was silent. She always wondered how a man his size did that. Going back to the window, she watched his shadowy form walk towards the barn. A moment later, the string of riders without shape or definition ambled across the hillside and out of sight.

She got dressed and went down stairs to start breakfast. After the tenseness of last night, this morning's news should lighten the household a little. When she got into the kitchen, she saw Iain by the doorway looking outside.

"It was yer Da," she whispered to his back.

Startled, he turned with the agility of a cat ready for the fight before realizing it was her, and relaxed his guard.

"Did ye speak wi' him then? Did he find Menzies?" he asked, trying not to speak too loud.

"Aye, they found him. Yer Da said the man hasna spoken since his capture. He's bringin' him to the castle to let Alexander deal wi' him." She rolled up her sleeves to start the porridge and sausage.

"What do ye suppose will happen to him?" Iain asked, relighting the fire for his mother.

"It's no' of our concern, Iain," she said. "Now go wake yer brother, ye hae lots o' work to do today. The kine can go back to their regular shieling."

❧

Angus and his men rode in silence in the slate-gray dawn. Tired from sitting a horse for a week, the thought of a few more days astride made them a bit edgy. They all wanted to return to their families, and their own beds. Sleeping in the heather for long periods of time was not as romantic as it sounded.

Fergal Menzies' hands were tied in front of him, and his feet were tied under the belly of his horse. Of all the people to be complaining, one would have thought it would be him. Angus glanced at him every so often, wondering what was going on in the man's mind. In a way, he admired him for his perseverance. Angus could tell Menzies was a soldier, feeling like the man was acting on orders not to divulge the troops' whereabouts under penalty of death. If he wouldn't talk, that's exactly what would happen to him when Alexander got a hold of him.

Angus sidled up to Menzies, riding step for step with him for about three miles, never saying a word. When they stopped for water and food, Angus allowed Fergal to stretch. Curiosity was getting the better of Angus. He wondered what he could say to get Menzies to talk.

Angus sat next to Menzies, while the rest of his men chose to be in small groups away from the laird to talk quietly between themselves as they ate. Angus passed the hardtack to Fergal, chewed on a piece of his own, then started talking about his children; how much he missed his daughter, who was away; his sons, how well they were growing up. Angus talked as if speaking to himself, never looking in Menzies' direction. Out of the corner of his eye, he could see Menzies watching him, though. Every so often, it looked like Fergal wanted to say something, but then looked away, silent.

This went on for the better part of half an hour. Angus couldn't remember ever speaking for that long all at once, especially to himself. He had all but given up, when in the small silence between recalling another anecdote, a voice so soft it was barely audible, interjected.

"My daughter's name is Caroline. My wife took her away from me, and wilna let me see her but a few times a year. I miss her as ye must miss ye arm, Mr. Robertson," Fergal said, running his hands through his fair hair. His voice held a quiet anguish.

The men must not have heard him because the talking continued in each of the groups.

"Come wi' me, Mr. Menzies," Angus said, getting up off the ground. Fergal's hands were still tied, but he could walk fine. The few men who looked up probably assumed Angus was taking Fergal for some privacy to do his business. Fergal got up, following Angus to a small clearing in the woods, taking a seat on a large chunk of granite.

"I'll get right to the point, Mr. Menzies. Did ye do those wicked deeds to the wee lassies?"

Angus wasn't sure if Menzies was going to speak again or not. Just then, Fergal lifted his head and looked Angus square in the eyes, searching for something. Trust? A soft shoulder? Understanding?

Angus kept his face blank. If Fergal was going to say anything, Angus was giving no quarter. Angus knew the need to remain dispassionate for an unbiased opinion. He also wanted to talk to the lasses Menzies was said to have molested, so he would have all the facts to present to Alexander.

Fergal stared at the ground shaking his head in silence for a long while.

"I just wanted to hold them; to love them. I pretended that they were my Caroline. I touched their hair and face and ..." He looked over at Angus, searching, but the big man still wore his indifferent expression. All of a sudden, Angus noticed a realization dawn on Fergal's face.

"Wait a minute. Did the wee lasses think I was goin' to hurt them?" he choked. Hearing the words sickened him. His face turned the color of sun-bleached linen, and he started shaking all over. "Dear God in heaven."

In despair, Fergal offered Angus all the details of his life without his daughter, and how it happened. By the end of the account, Angus was convinced he was indeed a sound man, but one dealt a rotten hand.

Getting up from the rock, Angus took out his dirk and cut the ropes that bound Fergal's hands. He patted Fergal on the shoulder — his only show of sympathy — then quietly turned and walked back to camp to leave the man in peace. The bond between a child and a parent was strong, and he was unable to contemplate his own reaction if forced into the same position.

❧

Angus came back into camp alone, stood in the clearing, and attempted to figure out an explanation. One by one, his men took notice, rising to hear what he had to say.

"I'm lettin' Menzies go," he said to his tired men.

An uproar came from them at their laird's hasty conclusion.

"Are ye daft, Angus? We hae spent a long time trackin' down that fiend, and now ye just want to set him free? What did he say to ye to make ye believe he didna do those unspeakable things to those lasses?" Andrew sputtered.

Angus held up his hand to quiet the men. He knew that they would react this way, but could see no way around it. He knew he would have to tell them why he changed his mind.

"All of ye hae bairns, aye?" Angus asked, pacing back and forth, rubbing his chin in an effort to choose his words carefully. Knowing he would only get one chance to explain, he had to get it right the first time.

"O' course … Aye … That's why we came wi' ye …" they each answered, eyeing their laird with concern.

"What if ye could ne'er see them again? How would ye feel?" he asked, watching their expressions ponder the unthinkable.

"I would ne'er let that happen," Andrew stated, folding his arms over his chest, as if he had control over every detail in his life.

Angus lifted a brow, letting Andrew know how preposterous that sounded, but Andrew held his ground.

"What if ye went to war and came back to find out that yer wife was told ye were dead, was remarrit to another man, and the only bairn ye had was but a wean when ye left, and doesna remember ye? Now yer wife has a new life, and doesna feel any obligation to ye to let ye see a wean ye ne'er kent. How would ye feel if we go to war wi' England and this happens to ye?" His voice was soft and even, not letting any emotion enter into it.

The men looked at each other with their mouths open. A few uncomfortably shuffled their feet. Some had heard of such circumstances; of how things were never the same after a war, even hearing that some men never went back to their families. Being a soldier was not an easy life.

"But that doesna account for his behavior towards the wee lassies," George Reid said, still unconvinced. He, after all, had a young, blonde daughter of his own, and was afraid for her safety.

Some of the men rallied again with George's statement. Angus quieted his men again with a lifted hand.

"What if it was ne'er done to harm? What if every fair-haired, blue-eyed lass reminded ye of the child ye will ne'er see again?" he said, driving home the severity of the loss.

Silence again, and this time, pity registered on many of their faces.

"Are ye sayin' he didna realize what he was doin'?" Andrew asked, still very skeptical.

"Aye, that's what I'm sayin'. If ye had seen the look on his face …" Angus said shaking his head. "'Twas as if I drove my dirk through his heart to hae others think he meant any harm to the lasses."

"What will ye do wi' him now?" asked George, still not wanting the man near his family, no matter if he meant to harm or not.

"Take him back to the Campbell's. They were willin' to take him on, and he'll be far enough away from our families so that we dinna hae to worry for them," Angus answered, reading George's mind, and probably a few others.

The men were appeased by their laird's decision. Angus heard them talk amongst themselves saying that it was the right thing to do. Others said Fergal was to be pitied.

Angus began breaking up camp; one by one, his men followed suit. All of them were anxious to be on their way home. Fergal quietly emerged from the woods and walked over to Angus. Angus glimpsed the tear-stained streaks through the dust on Fergal's face, and patted him on the shoulder again.

"Go back to yer families, aye?" he told his men. "I'll take Fergal back on my own."

Reunion

Though Lachlan wished he could stay on to see what came about with Menzie's, he couldn't. Gregor had arrived in the wagon to drop off supplies from the castle and was instructed to bring Lachlan back with him. Lachlan wasn't sure why the Chief's guard was reduced to doing such a lowly task, but felt it was not his place to comment.

Lachlan carried with him a stack of letters to deliver to Catrìona. He was unsure what he was more excited about — to be at the castle for the next year, or to be close enough to see his little sister. He suspected it was the latter. He sure missed her. His brothers didn't feel Cat's absence the way he did — especially Seumas — nor did he consider it odd having such powerful feelings for his sister. She was a part of him somehow. Never judging, he never had to prove anything to her as he did with his brothers and father. He could be himself. A sense of calm and peace surrounded him in her presence.

The trip was a quiet one; Gregor was a man of few words. This gave Lachlan plenty of time to contemplate his future. He would be near his sweetheart, Sara; he would be close to Catrìona, and he would be learning the art of war and his ancestral history from the Chief of the Clan.

There was a certain mystique about Blair Castle. He thought in amazement of the ancient tower that was built over five hundred years ago by a squatter named John Comyns. "Red Comyns", so called for his red hair, took up residence there when the Clan Chief was fighting in the crusades in the 12th century. As testimony to how much he cared for the small palace, the tower he built still stands today.

Lachlan loved exploring the castle whenever he was there for any length of time. Now he had an entire year to discover its secrets, and share them with his sister.

Catrìona was very much like him in regards to archeology. A few years ago, they found ancient artifacts buried near the River Garry that runs in front of the castle. On an outing with their family, they unearthed an ancient targe and a decaying sword from the long ago wars fought against the Norse, from whom he and many Highlanders were descended. A wild spring storm caused the water to overflow its banks and tear away at the tree roots that lined it. They were walking along the banks when the end of the sword was discovered protruding from the muddy shore. He remembered the look on Cat's face at the sight of the disintegrating metal.

"What do ye suppose it is, Lachlan?" she had whispered. Her eyes were as big as purple Alliums. She had nudged its tip with her toe, as if it were an entity that would reach up and grab her. They excitedly began the excavation of it from the tree roots which held it there for over a thousand years.

After a few hours of painstaking digging, not only did the sword appear, but the targe as well. If they had gone just a little further, they would have found the bones of the man who died with them. Later that year, Cat had found some old coins with funny looking profiles on them. When she showed the coins to Alexander, he said they were from the first century Romans, when Emperor Claudius' men tried to conquer the wild Highlands ... and failed. Who knows what other finds they will get a chance to discover during his stay?

❧

The next day, as the wagon rounded the long moor overlooking the fields, the castle's tower came into view. Lachlan needed to get word to Cat somehow that he had arrived. He didn't really want to interrupt the brooding Gregor, but his question could be answered with a nod or a shake of the head.

"Does Mistress Macpherson come by the castle regularly?"

At Anna's name, Lachlan felt the big, quiet man stiffen in his seat. Gregor turned to face Lachlan with a cold look that spoke volumes. He never said a word, but Lachlan knew the meaning of one of those looks when he saw one. Ok, so now he had more questions.

Why did Gregor have such disdain for Anna Macpherson? Was she the reason he was doing this mundane task? What had he done to merit his demotion? He vowed to make solving this mystery be one of his first tasks when he got to Blair Castle. Surely someone there would have the answers.

The wagon bumped and jostled its way to the front of the castle gates, where it came to an abrupt halt. Lachlan, all too eager to remove himself from Gregor's disquieting presence, jumped from the seat to the hard ground with a quiet thump. Without waiting for assistance, Lachlan gathered all of his belongings from the back of the wagon, and tossed them to the ground.

"I'll bring these in myself, Gregor." The tone he used indicated he wanted no help from the brooding giant.

Without a word in response, Gregor clicked the reins, leaving Lachlan to fend for himself as he wished. Lachlan picked up his satchel and weaponry and started for the huge front door, when out of the corner of his eye, he caught a movement at the gate. At the top of the iron crossbar sat a raven.

❧

Catrìona was in the garden tending to her herbs on that warm spring afternoon. Lachlan was expected at the castle any day now, and she was desperate to learn of the news back home. Having dispatched the raven three days ago to keep watch for him and report back to her, so far there was no news.

It was nearing Beltaine, the first of May, and she made preparations for appeasing the faeries for the aid of plentiful crops. A little milk and bread was left out on the doorstep in return for protection of the Earthly realm they shared with humans.

As with most of the Fire Festivals, a feast was being held at the castle for the beginning of the new season. This would be the first time since Samhain for many of the clan to get out and renew old friendships. Cat and Anna were expected at the castle to give another divination for the upcoming months. Hopefully, Lachlan would have arrived by then.

Most Highland children were born in the spring, and Anna was called out to mid-wife on several occasions. Cat always went to attend her and was getting quite an education. Having a child in the winter months was very dangerous, not only for the mother, but for the child as well. With the smoky peat fires burning all day, every day, the extreme cold, and no windows in most of the crofts, winter babies had a very high mortality rate.

Catrìona was finishing her work in the garden when she heard the raven signal his return. He landed in the apple tree near the house and waited for her. She walked over to him meeting his polished ebony eyes; Lachlan was at the castle.

She walked into the house humming to herself.

"Lachlan made it then," Anna stated, watching her apprentice flutter about the house.

"Aye, he did." Making herself busy, she put her basket away, and sorted out the herbs she brought in earlier, not meeting Anna's eyes. Knowing full well secrets were impossible with Anna, Catrìona posed a question to her, "Mistress?"

Cat saw Anna already shuffling the Tarot cards to answer the question drifting from her mind. Anna laid out an advice spread as Cat sat next to her, awaiting the outcome of her silent request. Anna asked the cards if Catrìona could stay with her brother at the castle for a few days. Cat smiled when she heard Anna say her exact question.

"Aye, ye can stay for two days wi' yer brother," Anna replied after seeing the favorable outcome. "Ye'll be gettin' some good news from the lad as well, the cards tell me."

"Oh?" Catrìona walked over to the window and started twirling her auburn locks. She stared out through its wavy view for a few minutes while Anna watched.

"'Tis my Mam," she said to the window. "She's been feelin' better o' late, though I fear it will be short-lived." Cat let the twisted lock fall to her chest, and met Anna's eyes, looking for confirmation. Anna refused to comment on the statement and looked away.

❧

The morning dawned with a gale force wind blowing in from the west, bringing with it the scent of the sea, and a few gulls that were blown off course. Spring storms were never taken lightly in the Highlands. At the moment it wasn't cold enough to snow, but many times, a late season blizzard would take many of the new lambs. The young calves seemed better equipped to brave the storms without much pause.

Cat tried to occupy herself enough to not count the hours until she and Anna went to the castle. She could hardly restrain herself from running the mile to the castle, giving her brother a huge hug, and running back before Anna realized she was even gone. Knowing that wasn't possible, instead she stared off in the direction of Blair Castle, and sent an image to Lachlan's mind. It was early still, and she felt he was still sleeping; a sleeping mind was easier to penetrate than an alert one. He would wake to remember a dream of the two of them reuniting today, not realizing it was a message from his sister.

Cat left the cottage with her basket to collect some eggs for breakfast.

"It sure is a gale out there, Mistress. Do ye think Alexander will send a coach to fetch us this afternoon?"

"Oh, aye. I hae already *sent word*, so to speak," indicating the telepathic message she sent out to Alexander, winking an obsidian eye at Catrìona.

She laughed at the uncanny resemblance to an owl Anna had when she winked. Cat sat in the rocking chair by the fire and picked up her knitting, hoping to finish the stockings she was giving Lachlan as a present tonight. They had a dark blue background with a yellow and cream argyle pattern. Even though all of her brothers could knit their own stockings, she thought it would be a nice gift just the same.

Realizing Anna might need help with her preparations for the divination tonight, she asked, "Is there anythin' ye want me to be helpin' ye wi', Mistress, or can I finish my present to Lachlan?" Her knitting needles stopped in mid-air, waiting for the answer.

"No, finish yer wee present for the lad. I hae a poultice to prepare for someone tonight," she stated absently, taking down some of the stone jars of herbs she had on the shelves; the lids clinking together as she set them on the table.

Cat smiled at Anna's certainty of the proper herbs and preparations for almost any situation. She hoped that someday she too would have that assurance, and hoped beyond hope it would be in time to heal her mother. Cat thought about the good news Lachlan would deliver to her tonight about their mother's apparent remission of illness. As her knitting needles clicked out the knit and purl, she wondered why this was happening. Was it really a remission or just a momentary lull before she took a turn for the worse? In her divination last Samhain, it showed her mother living through this spring. Tonight she would look again to see if there were any changes.

On a lighter note, Cat was thrilled to be able to stay at the castle with Lachlan for a couple of days. She hadn't seen him in almost a year, and wanted to hear of everything that went on at *Slios Mìn aig Aulich* in her absence. She knew she would miss her home, but not to the extent that she had. Even with her studies — which she loved and was consumed with — she missed her family beyond belief.

She completed the end row of the stocking and tied it off. With her teeth, she bit off the end of the nubby yarn, and held up her handiwork. The flash of color caught Anna's eye and she looked up from her herbal creation.

"He will cherish them, lass," she said, smiling as she stirred in the rest of the ingredients. She wrapped the sticky, vile smelling goo into a muslin square then enclosed it in a leather pouch. "Ready to go then, *Garnet?*"

"Aye. I hear the coach comin'. Let me fetch the satchel and we'll be on our way," she said, quickly placing everything into the woven bag they needed for trip.

ॐ

Alexander's personal coach was the mode of transportation used this afternoon. Cat was delighted to think that she and Anna were thought of so highly. The wind was still howling, and the driver was encased in a heavy cloak that whipped around him, making him look as if he could fly. As he got down to open the door for them, Cat caught a glimpse of the mystery man under the dark hood. It was Gregor. He never raised his eyes to meet hers, but she could feel a very unnatural emotion emanating from him. Not that she really knew the man all that well, but in the past he had always been courteous to her. Surely she hadn't changed enough for him to not recognize her.

"*Hallò a Ghregoir.* 'Tis I, Catrìona Robertson. *Ciamar a tha sibh?*" she asked in a cheerful voice.

He met her eyes with a look that made her feel very uneasy.

"Fine, Miss," he answered, as if it hurt him to say the words.

Cat climbed up into the coach and waited for Anna, who forgot her staff, and went back to the cottage for it. Cat's eyes stayed fixed on Gregor, trying to figure out why he was acting so strangely. It took Anna a few minutes to retrieve her staff, so Cat went into Gregor's thoughts to find the answer. As she probed, she saw the reason. In his opinion, Anna was the cause of his dismissal as a guard, and why he was doing all these menial tasks. He never took into consideration that if he hadn't been sleeping on duty, he would still have his job.

"She was only the messenger, Gregor," she said, hoping he wouldn't lunge at her throat for saying it.

It was loud enough for Gregor to hear because he turned to look at her. She breathed in sharply at the extent of the hatred in his eyes, and turned to look out the window. This was not going to be a comfortable ride, even if it was only a mile. Where was Anna? What was taking her so long? She had just returned her gaze to the cottage when the atmosphere changed.

Anna emerged with her staff over her head; her own cloak writhing around her in a frenzy from the gale. She was saying something inaudible into the formidable wind. Every so often, as the wind blew towards her, Cat heard a word or two in Gaelic. Anna was chanting! Whatever the spell was that she was casting, it seemed to have a profound effect on Gregor. Cat could feel the animosity ebb in the big man, as he went to meet Anna. Extending his elbow for her to hold onto, he guided her to the door of the coach.

When Catrìona saw Gregor's face again, he no longer wore a murderous look on it. Now, a kind of peace radiated from him. Cat definitely wanted to know what her mentor had said to change the giant's attitude so rapidly.

Anna stepped up into the coach and took her seat, while Gregor closed the door behind her. Cat could tell she was still in a trance, muttering unknown words in Gaelic. Was this some kind of ancient spell? One so old that the words were no longer used? She caught the meaning of some of it, but not all. She felt Gregor climb up into the driver's seat, his great weight shifting the coach to one side until he settled in the center. He clicked the reins and the coach slowly rolled down the bumpy track towards the castle.

Just as they reached the front door, Anna's mumblings stopped, and she came out of her trance. Gregor halted the coach and Cat felt him step down to open the door for her and Anna. She hoped the spell was still in effect. It must have been, for Gregor was the perfect gentleman, extending his huge hand to help them both down. Cat grabbed Anna's arm, quickly escorting her to the entrance just in time to meet Alexander opening the front door for them. He had a quirky smile on his face then broke into laughter.

"Did ye think I lost me touch, me laird?" Anna asked, her voice dripping with acidity. She broke out of Catrìona's grasp, disappearing out of sight before Cat could do anything about it. Her cousin was still chuckling until he caught Cat's fuming stare.

"What were ye tryin' to do to us, Alexander? Ye kent damned well that Gregor despises Anna, yet ye sent him to drive us here!" she snapped, her face the color of the stone she was named after.

"Do not use that tone on me, lass or I'll take ye o'er my knee; cousin or no," he stated, taken aback by her vehemence. "Did Anna not tell ye of the prank I was playing on her?"

She sobered a bit by this statement, allowing the color to slowly recede from her cheeks. Maybe she was angry at the wrong person. Maybe it was Anna she should be angry at for not telling her about this little prearranged scene.

"I'm sorry, Alexander. No, she didna tell me." She picked up a heavy lock of her hair and started twirling it. After a minute, she dropped the curl and smiled. "I should hae kent somethin' was goin' on when she called me *Garnet*." Patting Alexander's arm, she disappeared into the dark recesses of the castle, leaving him to scratch his head in wonder.

❧

Cat headed for Alexander's chambers to find Anna, but stopped when she heard footsteps on the stairs above her. She looked up to see Lachlan descending, and waited for him to notice her. He was about halfway down the ancient oak steps when he caught sight of her standing at the bottom. He stopped in his tracks, saying nothing, then ran down the last of the treads two and three at a time.

He grabbed her up into his arms, laughing like a madman, and squeezed her tight until she yelped for breath. When he finally released her, she wrapped her unpinned arms around his thickening neck, and kissed him furiously on his cheeks; giggling all the while.

"God I missed ye, *a ghaoil mo chridhe*," he said into her lavender scented hair. "I canna believe how ye hae changed in a year ... less than! Tell me everythin' that ye hae been doin' in yer studies. Tell me ye can stay here for a while. I had a dream this mornin' that we were together for a couple of days. Say it's true, say it's true!"

He was uncontainable, and she laughed as the words spilled from his mouth all at once.

"Aye, aye, I can stay for two days wi' ye," she said, sobering a bit. Two days wouldn't be nearly long enough to suit her. "I hae missed ye terrible, Lachlan."

Releasing her stranglehold on his neck, she stepped back, remembering her appointment with Anna, but she wasn't ready to leave her brother just yet.

"Can ye walk wi' me to Himself's chambers? I hae to get back to Mistress Macpherson soon, but I need to ask ye of Janet and Mr. Menzies. What happened?" Holding hands, they walked down the long hallway to the Great Hall.

"Naught as o' yet. Mam didna give Da yer letter until the night before I left to come here. She hid it and forgot about it for a week. Before I left, Da had raised a small army to go into Campbell territory to find the fiend. They left the mornin' I left to come here. I'm certain he'll find him and we'll hear about it soon."

"Och, enough of that now. What do ye want to do for the next two days?" she asked, shaking off the negative energy from their conversation.

"How does explorin' sound to ye?" he asked. "Do ye remember when we found the old targe and sword?"

"Oh, aye! I do indeed! Do ye ken where to find more relics like that? Maybe even more coins wi' funny faces on them!" The nine months apart vanished with each word they spoke. She was definitely ready for some adventure.

"No, I dinna ken of anyplace to find treasures like that, but how do ye feel about goin' up on the Faerie Dùn and do some diggin'?"

She stopped dead in her tracks and turned to face Lachlan; her look was of sheer joy. He laughed and hugged her again.

"I'll take that as aye," he said, continuing to the Hall.

When they entered the enormous stone room, it was filling up fast. Lachlan found a seat towards the back — nearest the food tables — and Cat made her exit into Alexander's chambers to find Anna. The friendly guard she had met before blocked the door, but realizing it was Catrìona, smiled and opened it for her. She started to go through the proffered door, when she paused.

"What's yer name, sir?" she asked, not realizing the implication that question had on the man.

The smile froze on his face. Cat noticed the bizarre behavior, wondering how asking him his name could mean anything but just that. He stammered for a minute, the thought process showing on his face, then he cleared his throat and stood at his full height, which was just an inch taller than Cat.

"I'm Robert James Alexander Collier, Miss," he announced with the dignity of a king.

"Glad to meet ye, Robert," she stated, then entered the chambers and Robert closed the door behind her.

When Catrìona entered the room, she found Anna smirking at her.

"Now what," Cat demanded.

Anna burst out laughing at this. "Do ye no' ken what ye did to that poor lad by askin' him for his name? Ye still dinna realize the effect ye hae on men, do ye? I ken that ye're only twelve, but ye easily carry yerself as a woman in her late teens; just as Gavin Reid thought. Yer height alone makes ye appear older than ye are."

"I was just tryin' to be friendly, since I see him e'ery time I come here," Cat said, unperturbed at the suggestion of misconduct.

"I think I'll ask Alexander for a lookin' glass for the divination payment, just so ye can see for yerself what the world sees of ye. Ye're a bonnie lass to be sure."

Anna laid out a new spread with her Tarot cards. Cat took the seat across from her, still trying to figure out what Anna saw in the cards.

"What advice are ye lookin' for, Mistress?" Cat asked, recognizing the particular spread Anna used when she had a simple question to ask.

"I had a vision of ye and yer brother bein' in dark place. I'm tryin' to get where and when this will happen. What were ye plannin' to do wi' yer brother for the next two days?" Anna asked, never looking up from her spread.

"We were goin' to go up to the Faerie Dùn to explore," she answered. "Someplace dark, ye say? I ken of no place like that up there. It's a shieling for the sheep — all grass and broom."

Cat was making a mental picture of the entire dùn.

"It's cold and damp ... oh, beneath the Earth," Anna determined, turning over another card. "A passageway!"

Anna had Cat's interest piqued now. "Really? Where is it? How do we find it? Does anyone else ken about it?"

"Good questions, lass. Let's see if the cards can give us some answers." A few more cards were laid out and the picture became clearer. "Ah … it was used by the ancient ones."

Cat racked her brain trying to figure out where something like that could hide.

Anna laid down the final card, then said, "It would please me if ye take the wee dog wi' ye when ye go."

ॐ

Alexander was very anxious for the divination. After all, he needed to know if Anna saw any more activity on the Jacobite front. He noticed dragoons more frequently around his homes in Carie, so he spent more time at the castle as a precaution.

Being quiet for so long, most of the Clan Chiefs thought a rebellion had once again failed. In fact, Spain refused to put up the funding for an invasion on English soil while the English army was in France. The English could just as easily turn the tables on Spain in retaliation.

Anna relayed the information of King James not getting financial support to raise an army, then the reading turned closer to home. Alexander and Anna were head to head at the table, so once again, Cat got a chance to do her own divination.

Relaxing in the chair away from her Chief and mentor, she was soon seeing into the future. Looking in on her family first, all looked well, except Seumas. There was a festering anger and resentment growing in him. She asked what it was pertaining to, and the answer she got stunned her.

It seemed he was holding her slightly responsible for his accident at the Games. Probing further to see where this would lead, it was unknown because his feelings had not reached the surface yet. Not even he knew about them. She concluded that as time went on he would release them and they probably would not affect their relationship.

Just about to close out of her session, she got a very disturbing sight. She saw dead plants. This was not an unusual occurrence in the Highlands, where the sparse soil and frequent spring and summer hail storms could decimate entire crops for the season. Those were hard times for the families it fell upon. Famine and starvation were no strangers to the Highlanders and island peoples.

She let her mind go back to find the last time her family had their crops fail. She could not remember a time when they did not have adequate grain for their clan throughout the winter. Dismissing this premonition as the failure of her own garden, she vowed to take better care of it, no matter how busy she got.

Her mind wandered to the passageway she and Lachlan could stumble onto tomorrow during their explorations. It fascinated her, especially never hearing of it until this very night. Did Alexander even know about it? She would ask him when they were finished, and also ask if she could take "Celt" with them in the morning, searching behind Alexander's chair to locate the big dog. He was there; his enormous head resting on his huge paws. His ear was twitching. Sensing her stare, he opened his nearly hidden brown eyes and looked at her. She telepathically asked him to stay where he was until she finished. Emanating a soft groan as if to say, *aye, I know the routine,* he closed his eyes.

Getting back to her divination, there was still no indication of the event tomorrow. Could it be that it wouldn't happen tomorrow? Still no answer. Could it be she wouldn't see things that may happen to her? She thought back. So far, she had never seen anything in her visions about herself. That made her a little uneasy. What if she really needed to be warned of something; would she see it coming? She promised to take this up with Anna later.

She was drifting again. Too many things were on her mind to stay focused, and she was about to give up. Then she remembered that this would be the time Anna would test her to see if she were doing her job thoroughly. Anna always seemed to know when to do this. Cat just started to refocus when she heard Anna's laugh in her head.

So, ye caught me. I'm verra proud of ye for rememberin' that I would test ye when ye least expected it, or wanted it, Anna's giggling voice said to Cat.

Aye. I'm catchin' on right quick to yer wicked ways, Cat replied back telepathically, laughing a little herself.

Now back to work, and go deeper wi' yer questions, Anna instructed.

Cat stole a look at Anna, unwilling to believe she could do such tedious work with the cards, and chastise her at the same time. Another laugh came into her head from Anna.

All right, all right, I'm workin'! Cat resigned, then settled back into herself and proceeded to dig deeper.

By the end of her session, Cat was unable to get any further than when she stopped the first time. Anna and Alexander were finishing up, and Cat just wanted to get back out to the Hall with Lachlan, but she knew she had to wait.

Alexander got up, and disappeared out through the big double doors. When he reappeared a few minutes later, he carried an ornate, gilded oval frame to his chest. Thinking it was a painting, Cat got up to look at it. When she saw her own reflection staring back at her, she remembered Anna's request for payment.

"Go ahead, Catrìona, look. Ye have the makings of a fine woman," Alexander said with a touch of pride in his voice.

Cat saw in the reflective glass the color rising in her cheeks at Alexander's uncommonly affectionate comment. It made her uncomfortable to see herself this way; like she was being scrutinized, having her strong points being pointed out. "If her appearance was her strong point, what was her weak one?" she asked herself. She looked over the gold frame to meet Anna's eyes. Yes, Anna had heard her questioning thought.

Another time, was all Cat got in reply, then Anna headed into the Hall for her supper. That was Cat's cue.

"Alexander, a word wi' ye if I may?" Cat asked, stepping out of the mirror's critical view.

"Sit down, cousin. What is it?" he asked, making himself comfortable in his brocade chair by the warmth of the fire.

Cat sat in the matching chair and rubbed her hands together over the peat flame. Celt got up, as if beckoned, and walked over to rest his big head on her lap. She absently rubbed his ears, then looked up to speak, but Alexander spoke first.

"Ye're still the only person he will allow to touch him, especially when I'm near," he said, puzzled.

"Och, we hae an understandin', ye see. He kens I mean ye no harm and he kens I mean him no harm. What would be the sense in gettin' all ruffled over naught, aye?" she stated logically in her cheeriest voice.

Alexander's thick eyebrows shot up on his forehead, and he let out a big guffaw at her candidness.

"Aye, well, would it not be nice to know that about everyone," he attested. "Now, what is it ye want to speak with me about?"

"Lachlan and I want to go explorin' tomorrow up on the Faerie Dùn, and Anna asked that we take Celt, uh Curr, wi' us. Would ye allow it?"

"Did she say why she wants ye to take the beast?" he asked, sitting straighter in he chair, intrigued.

"She sees us in a passageway," she stated, still rubbing Celt's ears.

"A passageway? Up on the hill?" he asked, rubbing his chin trying to recollect the entire area. "No such thing, cousin. Are ye sure that's where she saw it?"

"Why, is there a passageway somewhere else?" Cat asked, undeterred.

"Not on this estate, I can assure ye," he informed her confidently. "But, if Anna saw it, then aye, I'll allow ye to take … what did ye call him?"

"Celt. He says he prefers that name to Curr." Hearing his name — both of them — he looked at his master as if waiting for a verdict on the choice. Cat laughed and patted him on the head, while her cousin shook his head, smiling.

"Aye, ye may take *Celt*," exaggerating the big dog's name, "with ye in yer travels tomorrow. I'll expect a full report on yer findings as well, although I would be quite surprised to hear of ye finding a passageway."

"Thank ye, cousin. Is this where I can fetch Celt in the mornin'?" Cat asked, standing up from her toasty seat by the fire.

"Aye, he'll be here. Good night then, cousin," he said in a distracted tone, already looking through his storehouse of books for any clues to a secret passageway. As an afterthought with Cat almost out the door he mumbled into a large journal, its contents filled with ancient parchment, "Be careful tomorrow."

secrets of the faerie dun

The sky hung low the next morning, obscuring the normally breathtaking view of the mountains. The clouds literally touched the ground, allowing only close views of the newly budding woods surrounding the castle.

Catrìona woke before dawn. She couldn't remember having any dreams to decipher, so she lay in her soft feather bed listening to the silence. It was cold in her room, and even as excited as she was to get Lachlan up and start their adventurous day, this warm cocoon was too much like heaven. She rolled over to watch the mist hit the windows and roll down to plop on the roof just below it.

Just as she started to doze off again, she heard her door open. Lachlan quietly stepped in, bringing with him the smells of the kitchen, and her stomach instantly started growling.

"I'm up," she said groggily, rolling to face him.

"C'mon Cat! We're wastin' daylight," he whispered. Walking over to her bed, he pulled the covers out from around her and she let out a squeal in protest.

"Shh, ye'll wake the household!" he reprimanded, laughing at her struggles to keep the bedclothes around her.

"I told ye I was up, now get out while I dress," she told him with a giggle in her voice. "I'll meet ye in the kitchen, aye?"

"All right, but hurry." He bolted out of the room, leaving the door open behind him.

Cat muttered a few curses in Gaelic, got up to shut the door, then hurried to get dressed before she froze. Wearing her wool dress and carrying her cloak, she walked down the cold stairway into the

Great Hall. She stopped to fetch Celt on her way to the kitchen to make sure he had some food before he went on the long excursion. No guards were posted at the huge double doors this early, so Cat just walked right into her cousin's chambers. Sensing her arrival, Celt waited in front of the door wagging his tail in anticipation of a romp outside.

"That's a good lad! Are ye ready then?" she asked the enormous beast, patting his head.

Obviously ready, he loped passed her through the doorway, and she followed him out, closing the door behind her. He waited for her just outside, and she led the way to the kitchen.

At the sight of Cat and her companion entering the warm room, Lachlan smiled.

"Ye always did find the beasts, didna ye?" he asked, admiring the size and manners of the dog.

"This is Celt and he's coming along wi' us today to help us find our way through the passage," she stated, absently, splitting a hot oatcake and spreading jam on it for herself. As it was cooling, she went into the pantry to find something for Celt to eat, returning with a plateful of meat left over from last night's party, and set it on the floor in front of him. Mrs. Macgregor just shook her head, smiling as she watched in silence, her arms white up to the elbows with flour, kneading dough for bread.

"What passage?" Lachlan asked, stopping in mid-chew of his spoonful of porridge.

"Oh, I ne'er did find ye last night to tell ye of the vision Anna had of us in a passageway," she said, sitting down to eat her cooled breakfast.

"A passageway? There are no passageways here. Did ye speak wi' Alexander about it?"

"Aye. He said the same thing."

Lachlan pondered a thought while he continued his breakfast.

"Didna ye see it too? The vision I mean," he asked, under the misconception that all Seers could see the same thing.

"No. That's the odd thing about it. I couldna see it at all, no matter how hard I tried, which has me verra worrit about what else I canna see," she confessed. "That's why Celt here is comin' wi' us."

Celt wagged his tail at the sound of his name being spoken, but never looked up from his plate of food.

"Well, good thing ye're feedin' him now," he said chuckling. "I wouldna want to be lost in a dark passageway wi' him hungry, aye?"

Finishing their breakfast at the same time, Cat and Lachlan bid farewell to Mrs. Macgregor, who had packaged up some hard tack and cheese for their lunch. Celt sprinted for the front door, knowing they were ready to leave. Lachlan and Cat weren't far behind, but just before they reached the door, Alexander halted them from the top of the stairs. They waited for him to descend the creaky oak treads before asking what he wanted.

"Ye hae no' changed yer mind about us takin' Celt, hae ye cousin?" Cat asked.

"No, no, it will do him good to be out. I only wanted to tell ye that I was up most of the night looking for any reference to a passageway on the estate, but found none. However, I'll be most anxious to hear of yer adventures when ye get back," he said. "Go on now, the three of ye, and make me proud like ye have in the past."

"We will," Cat and Lachlan said in unison, and were off towards the clouds following Celt.

ð

It was a raw morning, the mist dampening everything it landed on. By the time they were at the base of the Faerie Dùn, Celt looked like a giant drowned rat, and wool or no, Cat and Lachlan were damp to the skin, but warm from their exertion.

They spoke amiably between themselves, each getting caught up with the events of the past year. Cat told Lachlan all about what she had learned since she last saw him, but his favorite story was of her finding the grave of Crinan Macduncan.

"Ye actually saw him?" he asked, not quite fathoming how.

"Aye, but it was no' like ye think. I didna see him wi' my eyes, I saw him in my heid," she said, watching for comprehension.

Lachlan thought about it for a minute, then said, "Ye mean like in a dream ... only ye were awake?"

"Aye! That's exactly it!" she said, knowing he would understand.

Walking up and down the hillsides through the wet grass, so engrossed in getting caught up, they didn't realize they had reached the flat top of the Faerie Dùn. Celt sniffed the ground to get acquainted with the new aromas.

On the north side of the dùn sat a single huge granite boulder.

Curiosity drove them to investigate how something so out of place came to be up here. They walked around it, brushing away last years grass from the base. Celt got in on the action, thinking there must be something of interest here if the two of them were giving this rock so much attention.

"I guess that's why it's called the Faerie Dùn. 'Tis the only explanation for it gettin' up here," Lachlan conceded, pushing the granite monolith to see if he could move it. Of course it didn't budge.

Celt started digging under it. Sod flew out from between his legs as his huge paws churned the wet earth. Cat stood back and watched the two of them expel great amounts of energy on this futile attempt ... for what? Maybe it was just what males of any species did, because she saw no other explanation for it.

"What do ye hope to find under somethin' so big that it canna be moved?" she asked, patiently.

"Maybe the faeries put it here to cover somethin' up," he said, breathing heavily.

"Hmmm," was her only comment.

After a while, Lachlan had dug a trench all the way around the boulder. He was on his own now; even Celt saw the futility in it, but continued to watch. Bored with their folly, Cat walked around the flat hill, stopping now and then to peer over the edge. When she reached the opposite end of the dùn, she spotted a place where erosion had left a bare patch of dirt exposed to the elements. She crouched down to get a closer look at what appeared to be a partially exposed iron ring.

"Lachlan, can ye tear yerself away from the wee stone for a moment to come see this?" she called over her shoulder.

Ceasing his excavating for a minute to locate where she was calling him from, he spotted her on the east side of the dùn; all that was visible was the top of her hood. Celt was already racing over to her. Lachlan wiped his muddy hands in the wet grass, and walked over to where his sister's interest was focused.

"Look," she pointed a cold-reddened finger down towards the ring. "What do ye suppose that is?"

Lachlan strained to see it, but needed to get a closer look for true identification.

"I dinna ken what it is," he said, looking around for a way down the steep embankment, "but I'm goin' to find out. Are ye comin' wi' me?"

"Ye couldna keep me from it!" She pulled her cloak a little tighter to keep it from getting in the way when she climbed down the embankment.

Giving Celt the lead, they followed him down a long worn deer trail. It was a roundabout way of getting there, but it was safe. The wet ground was slippery, and it was steep on this side of the dùn. They slowly edged their way over to the escarpment, grabbing at roots that stuck out. The trail ended a short distance from where they had seen the ring.

Celt was already digging when Lachlan and Cat got there. His long toenails were hitting something hard and scratching on it. Lachlan brushed aside the mud that clung hard to the planking the ring was attached to. Upon completion of the excavation, he looked at Cat with such excitement on his face, she couldn't help but laugh.

"I think it's a door!" he said.

"Can ye open it?" she asked, nearly as excited as her brother. She had maneuvered closer to him to help wipe away all the dirt until the entire door was exposed.

Lachlan lifted the pitted iron ring and gave it a pull. Nothing happened. He pulled harder this time, trying to keep his balance on the precarious cliff. It wouldn't budge. Cat tried pulling with him this time, and it made a little creak, but still didn't open.

"Maybe it's bolted on the other side," Cat said. "Do ye hae ye *sgian dhu* wi' ye? My dirk blade is too thick."

"Good idea." Lachlan pulled the small knife from his stocking, and slid it in between the frame and door to determine if there was a bolt holding it in place. The thin blade went in and slid the entire length without obstruction. Ancient water-engorged wood was all that held the warped door shut. In an attempt to loosen it, he slid the blade in again. It caught a few times, but eventually made it all around.

Getting a firm grip on the ring, they both slowly pulled on it until the door opened with a loud groan, awakened from its ancient slumber. Air from a time longer than could be recollected filled their nostrils, smelling of earth and mildew. The entrance was barely large enough for a person to squeeze through. Celt stuck his head into the darkened void filled with cobwebs and roots, but had no inclination to go further.

"Can ye ask yer wee dog to move so I can get in, Cat?" Lachlan asked, not wanting to get into a wrestling match on the side of the slippery embankment.

After considering the request, Celt shook the webs from his head, then moved to the other side of the door. He obediently took a seat, watching intently to see what Lachlan was going to do next.

"Thank ye," he said to Celt.

Catrìona laughed and said, "He understands ye fine wi'out having me speak for ye." She took a seat, just as Celt did, to watch Lachlan's plan unfold.

"Ye're no' goin' in there wi'out a torch are ye? This must go right through the dùn," she said, standing up to judge the distance across the top of the flat hill.

"I just want to make sure it goes in far enough to need a torch. If it does, we can come back wi' some lanterns. Hold the door open so the light comes in, aye? I'm goin' in."

He cleared away the sticky webs from around the entrance and went in headfirst. It took a little squirming, but after a moment, the soles of his shoes were all that were left of him.

Celt looked at Cat with his head cocked to one side, wondering if this was such a good idea.

"He wilna be long," she assured him.

Getting up, Celt peered into the hole Lachlan disappeared into, still unwilling to follow him in.

After a few minutes, there was no sound or indication that this was just a shallow cubby hole. Lachlan must have indeed gone quite a ways in. Curious now, Cat moved Celt's big head out of the way, searching for any sign of her brother. All she saw was pitch blackness.

"Lachlan?" she called, getting a little worried now. "Can ye hear me, Lachlan?"

She listened for an answer, but there was only silence. Celt let out little whimpers, indicating he too, was uncomfortable with the situation.

"Lachlan can ye hear me?" she shouted into the hole. Her ears strained to hear any noise emanating from the passageway. Nothing. She glanced over at Celt. She could tell he hoped she wouldn't ask *him* to go in after the fool. Even with his superior hearing, no sound could be heard. "We'll give him a few more minutes."

After a few more anxious moments, Celt cocked his head and started wagging his tail at the entrance. Cat strained to hear what Celt had detected by sticking her head into the hole.

"Lachlan, are ye there?" she shouted, her voice muffled by the earthen entrance. From an unimaginable distance, she heard him reply. With relief, she sat back down to wait for his exit from the dark tomb. Moments later, Celt had his head back in the hole, furiously wagging his tail at the emergence of Lachlan's dirt-covered hands.

Cat stood and pulled him out of the small entrance. He was covered from head to toe with dirt and cobwebs. She brushed him off as best as she could, all the while listening to him extol the grandeur of the find.

"It goes for a short way as a narrow tunnel the same size as the entrance," he said, "then it opens to where ye can almost stand up straight. I walked for a hundred paces before I came to another wooden door that was definitely bolted from the inside."

"The inside of where?" Cat asked, still brushing off his back.

"I dinna ken. It was too dark in there, but it's a straight line passageway, so the light from the wee door here allowed me to see a little. Are ye up for a look after we get some lanterns?"

The sky had lifted since Lachlan's immersion into the depths, and the mist had stopped. They easily had time to return to the castle and retrieve a couple of lanterns to get a better look at the door inside.

"Aye, let's go, but we canna tell cousin Alexander just yet about our find. I want to ken where it goes first."

Lachlan agreed, and they retraced their steps down the dùn, sliding halfway down on the wet, slippery grass. Neither one said much on the trek back to the castle, each consumed by their own fantasies of where the tunnel would lead.

At the front gate, they stopped. Wanting to remain unseen, they scuttled around the west side of the white harled walls to the stables where the lanterns were kept. Seeing all was clear, they scurried to the side of the stable wall. This would be the hard part. They both knew Gregor was working in there and neither relished a confrontation with him.

Standing quietly, with their backs up against the wall, they listened for tell-tale noises from inside to see if they could wait out the big man. It sounded like he was pitching hay from the loft.

"This could take too long," Lachlan said impatiently. "We need a distraction so one of us can get in and get the lanterns unnoticed. Gregor is no' verra fond o' me right now. Would ye go in and talk wi' him?"

Cat looked at her big brother and suppressed a giggle at his cowardice. Here was this tall, strong, brave man-child afraid to go in and talk to a man pitching hay.

"This is no' the proudest day in yer life now, is it *mo bhràthair mòr*," she said. Squaring her shoulders and pulling herself up to her full height, she would be the brave one. Truth be known, she was not looking forward to meeting Gregor again either, but she wasn't going to let that stop her from the find of a lifetime.

Surveying the area, she looked for something to call Gregor's attention to so he could be brought outside. Noticing a wagon in back of the stables, she motioned for Lachlan to follow her. They stealthily crouched over to it.

In a whisper she asked, "How hard is it to loosen a wheel to the point where it's ready to fall off, making it too dangerous to use?"

Lachlan looked at his sister through squinted eyes, his head cocked to one side.

"Where did ye learn to be so clever? Surely Mistress Macpherson is no' teachin' about the evil ways, is she?" He ran his hand through his long hair, eying her suspiciously. It was a good idea, however; one he should have thought of. He crawled around the wheels, looking for a weakness that could be exploited.

"Look," Cat stated, pointing to a rusted iron pin holding the front wheel on. "Can ye break this so it looks as if the wheel will roll right off if no' replaced?"

Lachlan inspected the rust-pitted pin and tested it for its strength. Sure enough, with a couple of small tugs, it broke into two sections. He held them up with a devious smirk on his face and a conspiratorial twinkle in his eyes. Throwing the pieces into the bushes, he took a handful of dirt, rubbing it over the area he worked to make it look like dust from the road. Now, the diversion.

"Ready?" he whispered to Cat.

"Aye. Gregor will be thinkin' I had a vision about the wagon, and he'll come out to check it. Then you sneak in, get the lanterns, and meet me by the front gate. Stay out of sight, though," she warned in a hushed voice.

Getting back to the stable wall, Catrìona walked to the front doors and disappeared inside. Lachlan could hear her muffled voice talking to Gregor. He heard the big man's footfalls as he stepped down the ladder to meet her. Gregor sounded like he was in a better mood than yesterday, and now Lachlan felt like a fool for sending Cat in to do his work.

"Och, aye. I noticed there was nothin' holdin' the wheel on. That canna be a good thing," she stated, walking out of the stable with Gregor in tow.

"Ye had a vision then?" he asked, intrigued, eyeing the young Seer with new respect.

"I saw it all happen," she said truthfully.

Once at the wagon, Gregor got down on his knees, brushing away the dirt that covered the missing pin to see what he needed to repair it with. This would keep the giant busy for a while. Out of the corner of Cat's eye, she saw Lachlan stealthily run into the stable to do his part. She began some idle chatter with Gregor to cover any noise Lachlan might make from inside. A few minutes later, he caught her eye again by holding up the two lanterns. She excused herself from Gregor, and met up with Lachlan at the front gate.

"Great! Let's get back up there then. I want to be back before dark, aye?" Cat said, staying low to keep from being seen by anyone in the castle.

"Aye. If only we kent where it came out," Lachlan said, referring to the passageway. "Maybe we can get yer wee dog to go in and search around?"

Catrìona looked at Celt, already knowing that he would have no part in that adventure.

"He wilna go into such a small space. His legs dinna work verra well when he crawls," speaking for the big dog.

"Well, he can stand guard then. We dinna want to be trapped in there when no one kens where we are," he said, looking back to make sure no one was following them up through the fields.

"We'll take no chances, agreed?" she said. His apprehension of a face to face confrontation surprised Cat, even if it was with Gregor, but she knew he would be fearless when it came to exploring.

Lachlan eyed her, judging to see how far he could to go with her definition of 'chances,' but knew he had better play it safe. "Agreed," he promised.

By the time they reached the top of the Faerie Dùn, the storm clouds were retreating, and shafts of warm sunlight swept across the grassy knoll. Cat shed her cloak, and kilted her skirts between her legs, making it easier to crawl through the passageway. She kept her dirk sheathed in her belt; she might need it in there, although she felt nothing about this being a dangerous venture.

Lighting the lanterns, Lachlan went in first. Cat stole a look at Celt to make sure he understood his role in this exploit. He wagged his tail in affirmation, and she plunged into the abyss head first.

She wriggled her way through the short tunnel, and just as Lachlan described, it opened up to where she was almost able to stand up straight. Lachlan waited for her there, the light from the lantern showing nothing but dirt, roots and rocky ledge.

"Here's where I started counting one hundred paces to the door. Even wi' these lanterns ye canna see it from here," he said bewildered, his voice sounded muffled even though he stood only a few feet from her. "It's like the Earth swallows up the light."

"Aye, there's an odd feelin' in here. I canna describe it, except that it's like a sacred place where we shouldna be," she said, shivering despite the warmth of the earthen catacomb.

"C'mon, let's see if we can get the door open," he said, already on his way.

They plodded through the tunnel, and finally, the light from Lachlan's lantern hit the wooden door. It looked as solid as the day it was put up. Thick oak planks held together by long, wrought iron hinges kept many generations from learning the secrets that lay beyond it.

"What do ye plan on doin' about gettin' through?" Cat asked, trying her best to shake the feeling of entombment from creeping up her spine.

"I dinna ken, yet. I wanted some light to see about the bolt before I made any decisions. Here, hold this for me," he said, passing the lantern to her so he could have both hands free to work with.

She watched as he pulled a long, thin strip of metal from his belt she had not noticed before. He knelt on the dirt floor, slid the strip in between the swollen jamb and door, then slowly shimmied it upwards. About a third of the way up, the strip hit something metal on the other side.

Now Cat understood what he was trying to do. If the bolt holding the door closed was only a latch, Lachlan could lift it up out of its cradle and open it.

Cat concentrated on the lock on the other side. Slowly, the door came into view. Even though it was dark on the opposite side, she could see the lock. It wasn't a latch like Lachlan hoped, it was a bolt — two of them in fact — one where he had his metal strip, and another about a foot higher. No matter how much he tried to work it free, he would not succeed.

She wondered if she could make it slide. If she could see it, why couldn't she move it as well? Concentrating harder, she mentally put her fingers on the iron bolt, feeling its coldness. She raised it out of its locked position to start the movement. Feeling the tension of years of disuse, she applied more pressure to make it move smoothly. Gradually, the more she envisioned it to move, the more it did move. Perspiration formed along her brow from the effort.

❧

Lachlan, still trying to make the metal strip lift the latch, looked over to see why Cat was so quiet. What he saw amazed him. There she stood, a lantern in one hand held high to shed light where he was working — her face shimmering moist in the warm light — in her eyes, the most distant look he had ever witnessed. He wasn't sure where she was, but was positive it wasn't with him.

Not wanting to do anything that would disturb her, he quietly removed the metal strip out from the between the door and jamb to watch what she would do. He could tell she was working at something. Her free hand was in a grasping position, moving sideways very slowly.

All of a sudden he heard a scraping sound like metal sliding on metal. He looked at the door, then at Catrìona, then back at the door. He heard a release from the other side, and expected it to open at any moment. When it didn't, he looked at his sister again. Her hand was in the same position, only now it was higher up. There must be two bolts to unlock.

This bolt must have been stuck, because she was wiggling her hand, as if trying to loosen it. He heard the click when she got it to slide, then the release of it altogether. When he saw her eyes brighten and familiar expressions return to her face, he knew she was back in the room with him. Her hand dropped, and she looked around to get her bearings.

ଈ

Lachlan stood and took the lantern from her. She smiled at him, not knowing if he knew what she just did.

"I saw it, Lachlan," she said, awestruck at what she was able to accomplish with her mind.

"I ken ye did. I heard ye workin' on the other side of the door. I heard the second bolt get stuck, and saw yer wee hand workin' to free it. I heard both bolts release. How did ye do it?" he asked, as much in awe as she was, and proud to be there to witness the event.

"I just concentrated on what was holdin' the door shut, then figured if I could see it, why couldna I move it? And it moved!" Glancing at the oak door, she tried to recall what was on the other side.

"What's on the other side?" he asked, reading her expression.

In the warm glow of the lanterns, she turned a blushed pink and started to giggle. "I dinna ken. I ne'er looked."

It was Lachlan's turn to laugh this time. "I guess ye really were concentratin' then, lass! Ye didna turn around at all?"

"No," she said, thinking how ridiculous it sounded that she wouldn't have thought to take a look. "Why dinna we open it and find out for ourselves, aye?"

Just realizing the door really could be opened, Lachlan stopped laughing, looked at the door, then back at Cat. She burst out laughing at the look on his face.

He walked over to the heavy planks and gave the iron ring a pull. Sure enough, the door grudgingly creaked open. Cat held up her lantern, passed the other one to Lachlan, and they stepped inside the black room.

As the light from the two lanterns illuminated the space, they were able to see wooden benches along the walls. The room itself was long and narrow; about four times wider than the tunnel. Lachlan figured it could hold about fifty men. They searched around to see if anything would indicate what date this place was last used, and by whom. Lachlan found a couple of thin leather strips under the benches. He picked them up to inspect them closer, but gleaned nothing of their use.

Cat walked to the end of the narrow room finding it made a sharp turn down a short hallway. As she ventured further, she elatedly realized it ended at a stairway.

"Ye better bring yer lantern o'er here. It looks like we hae some stairs to follow," she said, looking to see what Lachlan was doing.

At this announcement, the leather thongs were stuffed into his plaidie, and he hurried over to see what she had found. He stopped beside her, holding up their lanterns to shed some light into the narrow, dark shaft.

"After ye," Catrìona said, waving her hand in front of her.

Lachlan started down the small steps, wiping thick cobwebs out of the way for Catrìona. She watched him disappear down the stairs following a curved wall. When she finally ventured forth, all that remained of him was the faint light from his lantern. She put her hand on the curving stone wall and quickly trotted down the steps to catch up with him.

The stones felt cool to the touch; familiar somehow. Instantly, she got a vision in her mind of a tower. Her steps slowed as she tried to get a clearer image; her hand skimming the surface of the rough stones. She had a sense of being enveloped by the Earth herself, a different feeling from the entrance into this chamber. Here, she was a welcomed guest, not an invasive intruder. Why? What was the difference? She was still underground, but somehow this man-made place held a different energy. Or was it *man*-made? Was this the reason it was the called the Faerie Dùn?

Drawn out of her thoughts by Lachlan's urgent voice calling to her to hurry up, she picked up the pace and dashed down the rest of granite treads. When she reached the bottom, Lachlan pointed to the floor. It was wooden. They looked at each other in amazement, then surveyed their surroundings.

The ceiling was high; about ten feet. There were sconces on the stone walls where ancient fires once lit the room. As they walked further into the room, they noticed that the far wall was made of wooden planks.

"What is this place?" Cat asked in amazement, taking in what she could see by her lantern's glow.

"I dinna ken," he replied.

Up against the wood-planked wall stood three tables adorned with wooden bowls. A few carved bone spoons sat in a pile; unused for how long? The cobwebs covering them suggested quite a while.

Catrìona stood in front of one of the tables and picked up a bowl. She instantly got an image of many people filling the room. They were small people in a very strange dress she had not seen before. There were some families, but mostly men. Some of them had blue paint on their faces, carrying spears and targes.

Were they faeries? She didn't think so. Intrigued, she put the bowl down and turned to Lachlan.

"Do ye ken of any blue-faced people in yer studies?" she asked.

Lachlan walked over to the tables where Cat was standing to get a better understanding of her question. He saw the bowls and spoons, but nothing else that would indicate people with blue faces.

"Are ye asking if faeries hae blue faces?" he asked, perplexed.

"When I picked up the bowl, I saw small people wi' their faces painted blue. They were no' faeries. I was wonderin' if ye recall anythin' about who may hae lived here."

"How small?" he persisted, convinced that they were indeed faeries.

She recounted the vision, trying to gauge their height to hers.

"Most o' the men were just to here," she said, her hand skimming the bottom of her chin, implying they were just about five feet tall. "They were no' faeries," she stated firmly. "They were real people wi' families, and armed wi' spears."

"Well, they dinna sound like Romans; too short," he said, running his hand through his black hair, pondering the question. "Wait, I remember Iain telling stories of strange people who lived here in Scotland before the Romans came. I think they were called "Picts." The castle library will hae tales of them. We'll look when we return."

"Picts. Aye, that's them! I also remember Iain tellin' about how they would paint their faces blue when they went to fight their enemies," she recounted. "But how did they get in here? That passageway isna the only way in, surely?"

Lifting their lanterns higher, they walked all around the room, but found no indication of a door. Cat touched some of the stones hoping for an image of the entrance. As she walked behind the tables to touch the wood walls, she noticed an extra wide space between some of the planking. Pushing slightly on one side of it, a door opened inward leading to another stone stairway. Upon closer inspection, she felt fresh air blowing in from its entrance.

"I found it," Cat said, standing at the mysterious entranceway.

They entered the darkened void with lanterns held high; Cat staying close behind him this time. They went down only about twenty steps before finding themselves in another dirt tunnel very similar to the entrance they came in. It still wasn't tall enough for them to stand up straight in, but the Picts, being of shorter stature, must have been able to. This tunnel wasn't a straight shot to a doorway like the other entrance. As they walked, the tunnel turned a sharp left corner. At the end of it, they could see a faint light in the distance.

"This must be the true entrance!" Lachlan said.

"Hurry! I want to see where we are!" Cat said, pushing her brother to quicken his pace.

The tunnel ended at what looked like another ancient wooden door. This one wasn't in nearly as good condition as the interior one; hence the light coming through. Lachlan bent to take a peek out through a section of the rotted wood to get his bearings.

When he got a look, all he saw was water. The entrance was behind a waterfall about eight feet high and fifteen feet across. No wonder it remained hidden from everyone on the estate. He lifted the rusted, iron latch and pulled the door open, crumbling some of the wood at the top and bottom in the process. Standing in a heavy mist in the ancient doorway, the noise nearly deafening as the River Garry raged over the granite ledge above.

Cat waited at the entrance while Lachlan picked his way down the rocks to a path still visible behind the water. She watched him go behind a huge boulder, then disappear. Through the falls she could see his distorted figure walking along the river bank. He stopped and turned to see if the entrance was visible from where he stood, then ran his hand through his hair; a sure sign he was baffled.

Smiling at his conundrum, she started down the rocks to see what the mystery was. She found the path, then saw the boulder he disappeared behind. Behind the boulder was an opening through some gorse and two ancient, sprawling oaks. She walked out into the opening and found Lachlan. He smiled at her when she emerged from the hidden path.

"Can ye believe it? Hidden right in plain sight for all this time, and no one kent it was here!" His voice nearly drowned out by the sound of the water.

Cat walked over to where he stood, and turned to see what baffled him so. No matter how hard she looked, she saw no sign of a path or an entrance. No one would have ever suspected there would be anything there but a waterfall.

"It's truly invisible," she said, audible only to her ears. She looked around to see where she was, but couldn't get her bearings. "Where are we?"

Lachlan said he remembered riding by this place quite a few times, admiring it for its beauty, yet never realizing he was passing by a perfectly concealed hideout.

"We're behind the Faerie Dùn. If ye follow the river, ye'll come right back around and see the castle," he stated.

The light was starting to fade from the sky; the sun making its final appearance just as they emerged from behind the falls.

"We'd better be gettin' back, it'll be dark soon. We still hae to get Celt, and my cloak is up on the dùn, too," she said, starting for the entrance.

"Where are ye goin'?" he asked. "It's shorter to go back up the dùn this way."

Cat stopped to look where he was pointing, and concluded that he was right, but she really wanted to go back through the passageway. As she looked at the deteriorating light from the graying sky, she knew it would have to wait for another time.

❧

The three of them wandered back to the castle in the fading June light. Catrìona's stomach was growling, having totally forgotten about eating her lunch. She unwrapped the hardtack and started to bite on it, when she caught Celt's stare.

"I'm sure ye are hungry too, big lad. Here's some cheese," she said, tossing the creamy substance over to Celt, who caught it and swallowed it in one gulp. "Do ye want a bite, Lachlan?"

"Aye, I'll take one," he said absently. "I was wonderin' if we should tell Alexander of our find. What do ye think?"

She looked at him for a moment, wondering if he was thinking the same thing she was.

"Aye, I think we should tell him, but *only* him, no one else," she said. "I hae an odd feelin' about it, like we may need its secrecy soon.

"My thoughts exactly," he said, smiling at Cat's perception to not share this discovery with everyone.

"Speakin' o' secrecy, why are ye so afraid o' wee Gregor all of a sudden?" she asked with a smile in her voice, watching his reaction to her question.

He stopped in his tracks as if struck. He turned to her, ready to deny it, then shook his head.

"He came to fetch me in the wagon the other day. I wondered why *he* would be the one doing such a task, but I said naught about it. Then, when I asked if Mistress Macpherson came to the castle regularly, he acted as if I had just cursed him. He gave me a look that sent chills down my spine. Ye ken I'm no' afraid of anythin', but he's a braw man that I wouldna want to fight wi'out a friend to help me out o' the heather when he finished wi' me."

Cat smiled at the image in her mind, but knew exactly what Lachlan had experienced. She recounted her own trip to the castle to him, and the reason why Gregor felt so strongly towards Anna.

"Ye say the man who stole the rents wore a large silver brooch wi' a blue sapphire?" he asked, totally dismissing Gregor. "And his plaid was dark blue and green?"

"Aye to both. It was a Campbell plaid for sure, but I didna recognize the man," she stated, wondering if Lachlan knew who it was.

"Da must ken of the man, did Alexander ask him?"

"I dinna ken. It happened after the Games the summer last, when the rents were collected. I ne'er heard if the man was caught or no'," Cat said, trying to recollect any other information that might be helpful.

"I'll get word to Da and ask him if he kens of the scoundrel," he said, boldly taking on the responsibility of apprehending the thief on his own.

Cat wanted to laugh at his brazenness, but didn't want to hurt his feelings. Who knows, maybe he would find the man and get the rents retrieved for Alexander.

꿎

They arrived at the castle entrance just before dark. It was a full day for all three of them, and they were exhausted and hungry. Celt bolted through the door, heading straight for the kitchen, with Cat and Lachlan lagging a bit further behind.

When they got there, Alexander was feeding Celt a plate of scraps.

"So ye didna get lost after all," he said, stating the obvious. "I saw that ye came back for some lanterns earlier. Did ye find anything of interest then?"

Cat and Lachlan exchanged guilty looks, but thought better about denying it to their cousin. Alexander read their looks and chuckled.

"Do ye really think anything gets by me in my own back yard, children?" Shaking his head, he took a large swallow of the whisky and honey concoction he usually favored in the morning.

Cat felt Lachlan bristle at being called a child, but he remained quiet.

"Can we talk in yer chambers about it, cousin? We would rather no' let other ears hear what we found," Cat said, acting as the spokesperson.

"By all means," he said, "but how about a bite to eat first." Without waiting for their replies, he brought out a plate of venison and some bread from supper, then sat and waited for them to finish.

After they ate their fill, he refreshed his drink, and headed for his chambers with all of them in tow. Celt went behind his master's chair, lay down with a groan, and promptly fell asleep.

"Right then, what is it that ye have found that needs to be kept such a secret?" Alexander asked, curiously, taking a deep swallow of his drink.

Cat glanced at Lachlan, wondering if this was such a good time to tell him in his inebriated state, but decided it may be the best time.

"We found a secret passageway where the Picts used to hide behind the waterfall on the other side of the Faerie Dùn," Lachlan said, watching Alexander's reaction to his statement.

He went on to tell Alexander where they found the door, how it went right through the dùn, and out the other side. Cat told him she knew it was the Picts by their painted blue faces. This seemed to sober him a bit; enough so he stood up to search his books for the one that carried that information. After a minute, he pulled an ancient, leather-bound book off the highest shelf and leafed through it.

"Here," he pointed, "Here is where it recounts when the Romans came to raid the ancient people who inhabited Scotland, then known as Caledonia. These "Picts", as they were called, would disappear into the landscape, leaving the Romans to think the wildmen were ghosts. After a while, the Romans stopped coming, leaving the Picts and this inhospitable land, alone."

He closed the book, but kept it on his lap, laying a protective hand on it. After a minute, he returned the book to the shelf and remained there, trying to decide whether to say something or not. Cat and Lachlan just watched him, waiting for him to make up his mind.

"I'll have to ask you both to keep this passageway a secret. Ancient tales told about tunnels up there, but never finding any, everyone just thought they were legends. This place may prove to be very useful later," he said cryptically. "We'll go up together and check it out in the morning, so ye had better be off to bed. We'll leave at first light so we wilna be seen."

Cat and Lachlan got up to leave, glad to be heading for bed, but before they got to the doors, Alexander stopped them.

"Thank ye both for not letting on about what ye found. Good night to ye both." It was a dismissal, as he was already back to his books to see what else he could find on the subject.

Catrìona felt like she had just gotten to sleep when Lachlan woke her, saying Alexander was waiting for them downstairs. She quickly got dressed, and quietly went down to join them.

Her cloak, wrapped tightly around her, kept the early morning chill from her tired body. The sky started to show signs of the dawn with an almost imperceptible hint of yellow on the eastern horizon. The fresh morning air smelled of sweet grass and new leaves as they trudged through the fields and woods.

Alexander, at seventy-one years of age, was not a very healthy man, but was enjoying this hill-walk very much. Cat wished she had his stamina this morning, as she followed behind him and Lachlan. He couldn't have had any more sleep than she did, but there was no evidence that he was fatigued.

Just as the sun brightened the sky, its illumination caused the falls to shimmer in rainbows. They stopped for a moment to admire the beauty of it, while Alexander scratched his head in amazement.

"Literally hundreds of times my men and I rode passed here. When the dragoons were after me during the '15 Rising, I sure wish I kent of this place."

They eased through the gorse and ancient twin oaks to the entrance of the passageway. Each carried their own lantern, which they lit before opening the rotted wooden door. One by one, they stooped in the short, earthen tunnel, winding their way up the stairs to the large room with the wooden floor.

Alexander's face was awestruck. The experience was too new for Lachlan and Cat not be feel the same. They took their time making a more thorough search of the room for any artifacts they may have missed yesterday. Still, the only items to be recovered were the bowls and spoons on the tables. They continued on to the second set of stairs that curved around up to the narrow room, where Lachlan found the leather thongs. He showed them to Alexander, but Alexander could not deduce their function either.

Lachlan suggested that they go back out the entranceway and walk up the Faerie Dùn from there to see the exit. Alexander agreed; he had no desire to crawl through the tunnel either.

They backtracked through the passageways, leaving one of the lanterns just inside the entrance for future use, then exited. Before emerging from the falls, they heard horses and men, and immediately stopped to identify the intruders. At first, no one was recognizable, but then Cat noticed the blue and green kilt, and the fair colored hair of one man.

Cat placed her hand on Alexander's arm and whispered who he was. Alexander questioned her certainty with his eyes. She nodded and whispered the same to Lachlan. Prudently, the three remained hidden until all the men were out of sight.

A few minutes later, the threesome emerged from behind the falls and quickly headed back to the castle. None of them wanted to risk a chance at being seen near the hidden passageway.

misinterpretations

In the thick air of the sultry mid-July day, the aromas of the estate took on a heady fragrance. Anna had been summoned to attend to Davie Collier's infected finger, one of Alexander's tenants who lived a few miles up in the Grampians. Anna appointed Cat the duty, declaring that it was time her apprentice started assuming some responsibility of her own.

Cat prepared a poultice, collected clean linen bandages, made an herbal tea concoction to keep the infection from spreading, and was on her way. The fragrance emanating from her satchel was pungent and earthy. As she rode her horse through the open fields of the estate, the sweet fragrance of the grasses and wildflowers made their way to her nose. She breathed them in deeply, closing her eyes and smiling at the sheer joy of living.

By mid-afternoon, she arrived at the Collier's croft. Like most tenants' homes, it was windowless and small. The only door, left open in hopes of capturing any wisp of a breeze, also let the smoke out from the ever-burning peat fire. Cat heard muffled voices inside after dismounting from her horse and hobbling him.

"Hallò in the house," Cat called from outside the doorway.

In an instant, a small, round-faced, towheaded boy poked his head out from behind the door. He looked up at Catrìona radiating a perfectly angelic smile. Cat couldn't help but return the grin.

"I'm Catrìona Robertson. Does someone here hae a sore finger?" she asked the little cherub, squatting down to meet his eyes.

Never saying a word, he opened the door a little wider, still smiling. Cat took that as an invitation, and walked in behind the boy. As she let her eyes adjust to the dark space, she felt a small hand grasp hers and pull her to the other side of the room. In the corner, dimly lit by the peat fire, was Davie Collier asleep in his bed. She didn't have to see his finger to know it was indeed infected. In this humid air, she could smell the festering wound, and the stink of sweat from his fever.

Davie was maybe twenty years old. His younger wife Margaret, not much older than Catrìona herself, was preparing supper over the fire. It was too stifling and too dark for Catrìona to work in the croft; she needed fresh air and light to administer any kind of aid to the wretched finger. She looked around for the young boy, then found him standing right behind her.

"Would ye ask yer Mam if she could boil some water for my poultice and tea, laddie?" she asked quietly, not wanting to wake Davie yet. "Oh, and what's yer name?"

The little towhead looked up at her with his enormous light blue eyes and stated simply, "Robert." He went over to his mother and whispered Cat's request, while Cat got her remedies ready. Margaret caught Cat's eye and nodded in affirmation from the fire.

In no time, the water was boiled for the tea and poultice, and was ready to be administered. Cat went over to where Davie lay, putting her hand gently on his shoulder to wake him. After a moment, he opened his eyes, trying to focus in on the unknown face in front of him.

"Ye're no' Mistress Macpherson," he stated groggily.

"No, sir. I'm Catrìona Robertson. Mistress sent me in her place. Would ye be able to get up and come outside wi' me? I need to get a better look at yer finger."

Without argument, he slowly got up from his bed and shakily crossed the room, sweating profusely. Wee Robert watched his father's struggle, and with great forethought for one so young, up-ended a log for his father to sit on when he finally reached his destination. Cat gave him a dimpled smile, then patted him on his head.

"Robert, would ye fetch my satchel? I left it by yer Da's bed," she asked, making him feel essential in his father's road to recovery. He ran into the house, and within seconds, was back with the satchel, which he promptly dropped at Cat's feet.

Margaret appeared by her husband's side with the prescribed cup of the herbal tea, holding it up to her husband's cracked lips for him to sip. He put his hands around his young wife's hands to steady the cup, and took at few small sips.

Cat watched the young couple, knowing they cared for each other deeply just from that simple action. Smiling to herself, she rummaged through her satchel for her knife. Now the hard part. She would have to open up the wound on Davie's finger to clean out whatever was causing the infection. In the light, she saw that it was filthy, swollen, and brilliant crimson with fever.

"Mrs. Collier, would ye put some hot water in a wash basin, and bring out a clean linen?"

Margaret nodded, handed the cup of tea to wee Robert, and went inside to get what was requested. Robert deftly took over his mother's position, as if he had done it many times before. A few minutes later, she arrived with a steaming basin and a linen towel over her shoulder.

Even after washing the dirt from Davie's finger, she found it impossible to assess the problem due to the swelling. This called for a different way of "seeing". She closed her eyes and concentrated on the swollen finger. A moment later, she saw the gorse thorn that lodged itself in very deep, causing the infection to spread through his body. She knew the procedure, but hoped when she explained it to Davie, he would be strong enough to take the news.

She opened her eyes to find Davie, Margaret and wee Robert watching her in fascination. She smiled at them, unperturbed, and feigned looking for something in her satchel, stalling for a little time.

"What is it?" Davie asked outright, wilting in his makeshift seat. The look on her face indicated bad news was about to be delivered.

Cat looked up from her search, catching the meaning clearly in his dark blue eyes.

"I'll hae to open yer finger to get the gorse thorn out. I wilna lie to ye, it's goin' to hurt a bit. Are ye up to it?" she asked, emotionlessly, her dusty-violet eyes never leaving his when she spoke.

She saw his jaw muscles working, knowing full well he would never let his wife and son see he hadn't bollocks enough to remove a wee thorn. He was a Highlander, after all. She smiled, thinking that's exactly how her father or brothers would have reacted in the same situation.

"Aye, I'm up to it," he said, sitting up a little straighter on the log.

With what appeared to be years of practice, Cat took the knife and quickly sliced open the festering wound, pinching his finger between her own so she could see inside it. Davie made a hissing noise, but never jerked away his finger. She dabbed a clean linen on the wound to soak up the puss and blood that oozed from the opening. When she pulled the linen away, the thorn caught on it and easily slid out.

"There, that wasna so bad," she said triumphantly, showing the thorn to Robert, who was quite interested in seeing what made his Da so sick.

Spying her patient's ashen color, she decided he probably didn't care what it was, as long as it was out. She cleaned the wound as best she could, then applied her poultice of purple cone flower, hyssop, marigold, marshmallow, and thyme. She carefully wrapped the linen bandage around the finger with instructions to leave it on for three days. After that, the infection would be out enough to permit the finger to just stay wrapped in a bandage until it was healed completely.

"And it's verra important to keep it clean. Keep feedin' him this tea three times a day 'til the bandage comes off, aye?" she instructed Margaret, putting her tools away after washing them in the hot water.

Cat watched Margaret help Davie back into the house, with Robert right behind them. Ready to put her foot in the stirrup, wee Robert bounded out of the house with a small package for her. Without a word, he handed it to her with the same angelic smile he wore since she arrived.

"What's this, then?" she asked, taking the wrapped linen from him. It was warm and had the aroma of fresh bread rising through the material. "Tell yer Mam, *tapadh leibh*."

ॐ

On the ride home, ominous gray storm clouds rolled in from the northwest like stallions in the sky. The air was still very thick and calm, only now there was a sense of urgency to make it to shelter. Feeling this wasn't going to be a regular storm, Cat squeezed the sides of her horse, picking up the pace to a canter. She was still a couple miles from home.

From behind her, a flash of lightning, then very shortly afterwards, deep, rolling thunder echoed off the mountains. She kicked her horse into a full gallop. At least it wasn't raining ... yet. Another flash of lightning, then another. The smell of rain permeated the air now. The storm was coming upon her much faster than she could outrace it.

Frantically, she thought of where to hide from the storm's fury. Nowhere here that she knew of. Still no rain. Good. She raced through the wooded area just before the fields surrounding the castle. The wind started whipping into a frenzy, as she watched leaves and small branches fly past her. Her inner compass told her she was equidistant to the castle and Anna's — which one should she head for?

A brilliant flash of lightning hit the birch tree directly in front of her, filling the air with the odor of sulfur. The exploding tree sent her horse into a panic, thus making the decision for her. He reared up, catching her off guard enough that his neck smashed into her face, cutting her lip open; the taste of blood filled her mouth. He was headed for Anna's and there was no stopping him. She let him have his head, knowing he wanted to reach safety as much as she did. Her dress flew out behind her as she held on for dear life. Somewhere on this hellbent ride, she spit out a mouthful of blood; the massive dose of adrenaline flowing through her eliminated the pain.

Suddenly, Cat felt things hitting her back and face. They were bouncing everywhere and started to turn the ground white. Hail! It was pea-sized now, but for how long? She had heard stories of hail killing entire flocks of new lambs. About a mile to go. Lightning seemed to be all around her and the thunder was constant. The hail stones were getting larger now, not just stinging anymore, but bruising.

Her cheek was brushing the side of her horse's neck. Fear raged in his eye; the brown iris was totally surrounded by white. She tried to eliminate her own fear so he could calm down, but that didn't seem likely to happen, as another lightning strike hit the ground in front of her. In an effort to swerve from the strike, her horse stumbled, and Cat was thrown to the ground with such force, the wind was knocked from her. The hail stones were piling up on the ground around her; each ragged piece of ice about the size of an acorn.

In her struggle for breath, she thought surreally how beautiful they were. The pain of being pelted by them started to surface now, as the air charged into her lungs. Sitting up, she used the back of her dress as a shelter. She searched for her horse, but he was long gone. She didn't blame him, she wouldn't have waited either.

Anna's cott was in sight now; just a little ways to go. She got to her feet, assessing the damage. Nothing seemed broken, so she made a dash for the house.

Noticing the horse come into the yard, Anna went outside to open the barn door for him. Cat could see Anna looking around for her, holding her *arisaid* over her head to keep from being pelted. Cat started waving her arms and screaming at the top of her lungs, as she ran towards the house. Anna saw her, realized she was all right, then headed back inside out of harms way.

A minute later, Catrìona ran through the doorway.

"Are ye okay?" Anna asked, frantically, ready with a blanket to wrap her in. "When I saw that auld clot heid come back wi'out ye in this terrible storm ... weel, ye scairt the life out o' me, lass!"

Cat was enfolded in the blanket by Anna, who started viciously rubbing her down.

"Ouch! I'll be beaten enough for one day, Mistress!" Pulling away from Anna, she stood shivering in front of the fireplace. She started picking ice balls from her hair, then stripped out of her soaked clothes, letting them fall into a puddle at her feet. Catching sight of Catrìona's naked back as she removed her shift, Anna saw the bruises already appearing.

"My, my, lass! No wonder ye didna want me to rub ye down. Ye'll be full black and blue by mornin'! I'll fetch some oil of arnica and rub on ye ... gently." Anna emphasized the word when she saw the beginnings of an objection forming. "It'll take the pain away."

Before Cat could protest, Anna had already located the remedy. Cat began drying her hair with the ends of the blanket, feeling the bumps on her skull from the battering she had taken. She would definitely be in pain tomorrow.

After the heat from the fire permeated her naked body, she walked over to the western window. The storm was over. She could see the clearing line on the horizon. Cat looked out at her garden and inhaled sharply, causing Anna to look up from her efforts.

"What's wrong, Catrìona?" Anna asked, walking over to the window to see what made her so upset.

"My divination on Beltaine. I saw dead plants, but I thought it was just *my* garden. This hail storm will hae destroyed all the barley and oat crops it went o'er." Tears rolled from Cat's eyes, and she felt Anna wrap a blanket around her like a cocoon.

"*Mo nighean mhaiseach,*" Anna said to Cat's warm back, "ye canna think to take this onto yer own shoulders. Ye hae a rare gift for the Sight, but ye're just learnin' how to use it proper. Many times what a Seer sees is a riddle. Mostly, we just get a wee slice o' the incident and hae to figure out who it's for, when it might happen, and how it might happen. Ye hae the ability to see much clearer than anyone else I e'er kent, but ye still may no' get it right e'ery time."

Cat silently trembled as Anna rocked her gently from side to side for a few moments. Finally, Catrìona lifted her hands to wipe away her tears, then patted Anna's arm in a gesture of thanks.

She slid out of Anna's embrace to get some dry clothes on, all the time wondering how far the damage to the crops had gone. She had to see for herself, no matter how irrational it was, no matter how impossible it would have been to prevent, even if she had voiced the premonition.

"How far will ye go, lass?" Anna asked.

Catrìona looked up, not realizing her plans were already public knowledge.

"As far as the damage goes. The hail didna start until I was just north o' the castle, so I'll head east," Cat said. "There's still some daylight left. Wi' any luck, I'll be back before nightfall."

She wrapped a bit of cheese and a crust of bread in a linen, then stopped.

"How's "clot heid" doin'? Was he hurt from the hail?" Cat asked about the horse with concern in her voice, remembering she would be riding him to survey the damage.

Anna let out a little chuckle, which seemed to break to thick air in the house. Cat smiled a little herself, releasing some of the weight of the afternoon's insanity.

"I ne'er put a name to a beast, but this afternoon that horse was a "clot heid"!" Anna said, still smiling.

"Och, I would hae done the same as him if I were in his place," Cat giggled. "It really must o' looked amusin', if it were no' so painful."

The electric charge in the air had totally diminished now. Catrìona unfold the linen, took a bite out of the cheese, then walked over to the table to sit and finish the meal. She finally saw the futility in actually seeing how much was laid to ruin.

"Would ye rub some oil of arnica on my back now, Mistress? Then I want to go to bed."

Spoken like the child she was.

Still smiling, Anna got up from the table, got the oil, then directed Catrìona to her bed to rub it on her bruised body.

tReachery of a Campbell

Lachlan received a letter from his father positively identifying the man he saw on the Faerie Dùn with Catrìona and Alexander almost two months before. He was indeed a Campbell, and from what his father described in the letter, he was hunting the Macgregors … any Macgregor.

Under royal orders from as far back as the late fifteenth century, King James IV passed an act on thievery to dissuade the Macgregor cattle raids. Under the tyranny that was beset upon them, the Macgregors were forced to raid the countryside for food for their very existence. In 1502, further charters were enacted to allow the pursuit of the Macgregor clan with fire and sword. In other words, Macgregors were fair game to kill. Under the King's orders, they were to be exterminated from the countryside. The Campbells had taken their lands from them in the late 1300's. Now, the few Macgregors who did not fear the penalty of death for using their own names, lived as tenants on their own lands in servitude and squalor; subject to any abuse the Campbells wanted to inflict upon them.

Over the years, Clan Donnachaidh would take in these broken Macgregors, allowing them to work the land in peace. The only problem with this policy was that Campbell land bordered Robertson land. Once the Campbells found out about the whereabouts of a Macgregor, they felt it was their duty to purge them from their new found peace.

Angus reminded Lachlan in his letter about the most notorious Macgregor of them all, the one they called Rob Roy or Red Robert, for his red hair.

> ... of course he was so Successful because he was Honest about it. Rob kept Records and gave Receipt for all of his acquired Stock and Grain. His Blackmailing was started due to the Savage abuse the Duke of Montrose's men inflicted upon his Wife in his own home while trying to capture him for forfeiture on a debt owed. She called for Vengeance for the shameful act, and after the Duke attempted to take possession of Rob's lands, Rob vowed he would make the Duke rue the day he quarreled with him.
>
> For Thirty Years, Rob Roy stole only from the Duke's estate — and in broad daylight. Having given Previous Notice to all of the Cattle District he was aiming for on a certain day, all the Black Cattle belonging to the Duke would be gathered up, and Rob, being an expert drover, would drive them in safety, under the Protection of the Duke of Argyll. Since the cattle were driven from the Duke's tenants in this manner, the tenants paid no rents, so the Duke of Montrose Suffered Greatly.

Lachlan remembered hearing these stories when he was younger. Rob Roy had died only a few years ago, but his name would live on forever in the tales that were told around a peat fire with a blizzard howling outside. He read on further.

> ... the man you are looking for sounds like William Campbell. He will Travel with two or three men at all times. I have had the Pleasure of being in an altercation with him myself, about fifteen years back. He was not a very braw Fellow, but he was very quick. I did, however, get the upper hand on him, and he went home worse for the wear! I will expect his men do his fighting for him now.
>
> Be careful of him, Lachlan. He is very smart, and has been doing this for many years. Please Promise me that you will not attempt to face him on your own. Let Alexander handle this. It is not your fight.

Lachlan finished the letter, folded it back up, then tucked in the top drawer of his dresser. He wished he could show it to Cat to get her opinion of it before showing it to Alexander. Maybe now would be a good time to try the experiment he had conceived.

He sat on the edge of his bed and closed his eyes. In his mind, he called up Catrìona's face. She came up instantly, and he smiled. Concentrating all of his thoughts on getting a message to her, he indicated the urgency of seeing her immediately. He didn't want to alarm her, but was at a loss as to how to accomplish that. Remembering the original reason for contacting her in the first place, he called up a vision of Gregor, then the wooden box with the rents in it, and released the thought to his sister.

He opened his eyes, hoping that was all he needed to do. Now, all he could do was wait. He would give her a day.

૨૦

Catrìona was still quite sore from the battering she took in the hail storm a few days earlier. Great patches of dark blue and purple splotches were evident from her shoulders to her hips, and even a few on her arms and legs.

Anna walked in from what was left of the garden as Cat studied herself in the looking glass Alexander gave Anna at Beltaine.

"Ye're verra lucky nothin' was broken, Catrìona," Anna stated, looking her over with a critical eye.

"Aye. Would ye rub a little more oil of arnica here … and here?" she asked, pointing to her right shoulder blade, and just above her left kidney.

"Take a seat while I fetch the bottle," Anna instructed, heading for the kitchen cabinet where it was stored.

Cat sat on the little stool beside the fire and closed her eyes. The warmth permeated her flesh, relaxing her to the point of daydreaming. She got a vision of Lachlan smiling, and she instinctively smiled back. Then she got a vision of Gregor and the room where the wooden box that held the rents were kept. Why would she think of that? Concentrating harder, she wondered why Lachlan would be in the same vision as Gregor and the stolen rents?

She tried to figure it out in her head, but could find no logical reason for those seemingly unrelated people and items to be linked together. Her eyes opened to find Anna watching her.

"Go deeper," Anna said.

"Do ye mean it might be a message?" Cat asked. The small line between her brow was showing, and she started twirling her hair around her fingers.

"Ye hae the answer inside. Go deeper," she said, closing her own eyes.

Cat closed her eyes again, forgetting the reason for the oil of arnica for the moment. Would Lachlan attempt to send her a message? Putting that possibility into the equation, why would he show her an image of Gregor and the rent box?

Suddenly her eyes flew open! He found out who stole the rent money from under Gregor's sleeping nose!

Anna smiled and poured a little oil into the palm of her ancient hand.

"He's a rare smart lad, yer brother," she said, rubbing the soothing oil onto Cat's shoulder blade.

"May I go to him to see what he's found out, Mistress?"

"Just as soon as I finish rubbin' this on ye, we'll both go. Alexander is goin' to want to ken more about this," Anna said, moving to the kidney area now.

❧

It was a autumn-like day, crisp, yet warm, with a crystal clear cerulean blue sky. Puffy white clouds peeked their heads over the mountains in a game of hide and seek. The westerly breeze was fresh-scented with grasses and heather.

As Catrìona and Anna walked to the castle, it struck Cat that while the hail storm was devastating to some areas, the native plants faired well. In the amiable silence, she wondered absently if the *sìdhichean* were angry at her for something, therefore causing that catastrophe. When she returned home, she would give an offering for more protection.

As they arrived at the front gate, Lachlan met them at the door.

"It worked then! Ye *are* here because ye received my message, right?" he asked, meeting Cat to give her a hug, then holding out his arms for Anna and Cat to take.

Cat giggled and Anna smiled from ear to ear, as they entered the castle arm-in-arm like the three musketeers.

"Mistress says ye were quite clever to send me that message. It took me a few minutes to figure out, because I didna realize ye would e'er think to do that. I'm verra proud of ye, *a ghaoil mo chridhe.* And just to make sure I did get the message right, ye ken who stole the rents from Alexander, aye?"

"Aye, ye got it right. Remember I told ye I would write to Da to see if he kent of the man we saw?" She nodded and he continued. "Well, Da kent the man all right. Oh, there's also somethin' in the letter about Mr. Menzies. Da caught up wi' him in Campbell territory. He was on his way here to deliver the man to Alexander, but changed his mind. Da didna give all the details, but said it was somethin' to do wi' him bein' a soldier and comin' back from the war to find his life turned all wrong. He wasna meanin' to be doin' harm to the lassies, he just missed his daughter."

"Is Janet safe, then?" she asked.

"Aye, all the fair-haired lassies are safe. The man was sick when he found out the lassies thought he was doin' them harm. He really dinna ken it was wrong."

"Thank ye for tellin' me, though I'm still no' sure why he makes me so uneasy. Maybe it's the fact that he was a soldier, and he is livin' wi' more than he can bear." She stared off to some far away place for a moment.

"Let me fetch the letter and ye can read it for yerself." He released his arms from Anna and his sister, then ran up the steps to his room. A moment later, he was back.

"Here," handing the letter to Cat. "Let's go into the Hall and read it, then we can discuss what to do next."

They took a bench in the back, with Catrìona sitting in between Anna and Lachlan so they all could read it together.

"Let's hear what ye hae in mind to do about this," Cat said to her brother, after completing the letter.

"If it were up to me, I'd tell Gregor and let him settle the matter. After all, this man is the reason Gregor is workin' in the stables now, instead of bein' a guard."

"Gregor and who else? Ye canna just send one man for this task. When Da says to be careful of a man, he would ken better, aye?" Cat stated.

"What would ye do, then?" he asked his sister, haughtily.

"I'd let Alexander handle the entire thing. It was his money that was stolen, under his care, and in his own house. I do, however, think Gregor should hae a hand in bringin' the man to justice, like ye said," she agreed.

"What do ye think, Mistress?" Cat asked.

"I think I'll wait for Alexander's decision."

As if on cue, Alexander came out of his chambers to find the unique gathering in the back of his Hall.

He smiled, put his hands on his hips, and said, "Well, what have we here? Did I miss a summons to have a meeting with the three of ye, or are ye all here of yer own volition?"

The three of them looked at each other, silently designating a spokesperson. Since Lachlan was the one who initiated the deed, he was chosen by the simple, yet direct gesture of Anna and Cat crossing their arms over their chests, and looking straight ahead.

Alexander watched this play of authority and laughed out loud. "Well, my lad, it looks as though ye're the man who'll tell me what's going on."

Lachlan sent a dirty look over to the ladies, then stood to tell his cousin of his findings. As soon as the words "rents" came out of Lachlan's mouth, Alexander's eyes widened, and he held up his hand for Lachlan to say no more.

"Please, all of ye, come into my chambers. I would prefer not to have this overheard by anyone," he said, retreating inside with the three of them in tow.

Once they were all safely behind closed doors, Alexander implored Lachlan to continue with his findings. Lachlan handed his cousin the letter from his father, implicating one William Campbell.

"Have you shown this to anyone else?" Alexander asked, fearing the answer.

"No, sir," Lachlan answered. "We in this room are the only ones who hae read it."

"Good," Alexander said, letting out a heavy sigh of relief. He took a large swallow of the whisky he perpetually had on his table, then got up and started pacing. From his position behind the chair, Celt's eyes followed his master back and forth. Cat twirled her hair, while Lachlan, unable to just sit and wait for his cousin to make a decision, got up and did some pacing of his own. Anna was the only calm one in the bunch.

As if they had been doing it for years, Anna and Cat looked at each other to make a silent communication.

He's leavin' here, that's why his decision is so difficult, Cat relayed to Anna telepathically.

Aye, he's goin' to France on business and doesna ken who to assign this task to, Anna returned.

My Da would seem the likely choice, since he kens the man already, and he has men wi' him he can trust, Cat concluded.

'Tis a wise choice, I agree, but there's somethin' else goin' on here. Alexander isna wantin' to leave, he's bein' made to. The Sassenachs are runnin' him out o' the country like they hae in the past.

Before Anna and Cat finished their *conversation,* Alexander voiced his decision.

"Lachlan, I know ye're in your studies here, but I would be grateful to ye to ride home, tell yer father to find this William Campbell, and get my rents back … any way he can," his last few words carried an ominous meaning.

"Would it be advantageous to my Da if Gregor came along wi' us?" he asked.

"It would be an excellent idea for Gregor to go along with yer *father.* Ye, my brave man, are not going on a man hunt … *and* before ye make any objections, ye know full well that yer father will not allow it either. Ye are only to bring Gregor to your father with the letter of instructions I'll send along with ye, and return here immediately. Understood?" Alexander held Lachlan's eyes in a stare that dared him to argue.

Whereas Lachlan may disobey his father's *requests,* he would never dare disobey an order from his Chief.

"Aye, I understand, sir. When shall I leave?"

"I'll tell Gregor immediately, and ye'll both leave at first light," he instructed.

ॐ

By the time dawn came the next morning, Lachlan and Gregor were on their way. Gregor was his same quiet self, but ever since Anna cast the spell on him, he at least wasn't as brooding. He had expressed his gratitude to Lachlan for suggesting that he aid in the capture of the thief. The fact that the thief was a Campbell was just an added bonus for Gregor.

Gregor was a proud man, as was his father, and his father's father before him. Proud to be Macgregor's, never considering to change their names to hide in another clan; especially the clan Campbell. When his father told him of the treachery the Campbell's employed to get Macgregor lands, in defiance of the Campbell's, he was proud to bear the name Gregor Macgregor.

As they rode passed the fields, Lachlan saw the barley and oat crops rotting in the ground from the hail storm Catrìona had been caught in. It would indeed be a lean winter for many. Nearing *Slios Mìn*, Lachlan was amazed to see how much a place could change in just a few short months.

Walking to the barn, Iain caught sight of riders coming in from the east. He could tell right away one of them was Lachlan, but didn't recognize the man his brother was with. As the distance closed, Iain realized it was Gregor from the castle. What in the world was that unlikely duo doing riding here?

He waited for them to get to the barn so he could tend to their horses. Since it was late afternoon, they would obviously be spending the night.

"Hallò, Lachlan ... Gregor. To what do we owe this pleasure?" Iain asked. He took the reins from them and led the horses into the barn.

"Good to see ye again, Iain," Lachlan said, following his older brother into the barn. "We'll all be needin' to speak to Da. Is he about?" Not giving away his purpose for the journey home just yet.

"Aye, he's in the house. We're just about ready to hae supper, would ye both join us?"

"I'll just stay out here wi' the horses and hae some hard tack," Gregor said, clearly uncomfortable with the prospect of taking supper with the laird and his family.

"Ye'll do no such thing, *mo charaid.*"

Gregor whirled around to see Angus standing in the doorway. A twinkle appeared in Gregor's eyes that Lachlan had never seen, or ever thought would exist.

"*My friend,* hey? We barely speak in fifteen years and ye think I'm still yer *caraidh?*" The acidity from Gregor's tone was unmistakable.

Lachlan and Iain were uncertain about the underlying current running through the barn. Watching their father saunter in, they moved back out of the way of the brawl that seemed eminent. Lachlan caught sight of yet another odd appearance on Gregor's face. Could that have been a smile?

Before he could make the determination, the two men were giving each other bear hugs, pounding each other's backs, and growling their greetings enthusiastically in Gaelic. Lachlan tossed a shrugging look at Iain, leaving the strange camaraderie to the two big men.

≥∙

Following supper, the men retired to the best room. Lachlan gave his father the letter from Alexander with his instructions on it. After reading it, Angus asked Gregor if he knew what it said. Gregor acknowledged its contents, and indicated he was willing to help in every way possible. Lachlan and Gregor then brought everyone up to date on the circumstances that led to this point.

"Lachlan, ye say Campbell ne'er saw ye wi' Alexander by the Faerie Dùn?" asked Angus.

"Aye. We stayed behind the falls until they were gone."

"I'll gather a few more men in the mornin', givin' them as little information as possible, wi' the exception of Andrew. Then we'll see if we can find Mr. Campbell … and the rents."

Several hours later, they all emerged from the best room with a plan well thought out and ready to enforce. Ready for bed, they each headed for their rooms, while Gregor took the rug on the floor in front of the fireplace.

≥∙

"How long will ye be gone for, Angus?" Isobel asked softly in the candlelight. Her head was resting in the crook of Angus' shoulder, while she combed her fingers through the black hair on his chest.

"I wish I could say," he said absently, playing with Isobel's hair. "I'll be takin' Andrew wi' me, and I'll hae Mòrag and Janet come here while we're gone, aye?"

"Thank ye, Angus," she said with a sigh of relief. "Ye'll no' be takin' the lads, will ye?"

"Only Seumas. Lachlan has been ordered to go back to the castle by Alexander, bless him. He must already be aware of Lachlan's determined tendencies," he said chuckling. "Iain will stay here wi' ye."

"Good. I dinna want to be here wi'out a man about," she said. "I dinna hae a good feelin' about this excursion to the Campbell's. Usually, ye just go there to *trade* cattle," smiling as Angus clucked his tongue at her belittling tone, "but this time it's a man ye are after."

"Och, dinna fash, Isobel. I'll hae the best men wi' me to see me home safe, ye ken that. Besides, he'll be taken unaware so he'll be less of a threat; maybe even wi'out his own men around him," Angus boasted, running his hand down her spine, smiling as he felt her quiver at his touch.

He blew out the candle, and found Isobel's mouth in the dark; all thoughts of tomorrow were gone.

ಶ

Angus lay on his side facing the window, watching for the moment when dark turns to light. This imperceptible change went unnoticed as he slipped out of bed, careful not to wake Isobel. He had truly been blessed with an extension of her life. He secretly wondered if Anna Macpherson had anything to with it, or maybe even his own daughter. Just as long as it kept his beloved with him longer, it didn't matter where the reprieve came from.

Silently, he dressed and went downstairs to meet Seumas and Gregor. Mrs. Stark had packed some food for them last night; it was waiting on the table. Seumas took out a few bannocks for himself and his father, storing them in his sporran to eat on the trail. Gregor was content with his hard tack for breakfast.

Angus headed for the barn to gather his broadsword and pistols; his dirk never left his side and he patted the handle of it. He hoped he would not have to use all this weaponry, but knew who he was up against. Telling Isobel he would catch William Campbell unaware was an illusion for her only. He knew full well that Willie was never unaware. Knew it all too well.

Andrew and six men rode up to see if their laird was ready to ride. Seumas had just finished saddling the horses and was leading them out towards the front of the barn.

"Ready then?" asked Andrew in a whisper. He too had left before Mòrag awoke. They had said their farewells last night, just as the rest of the men did.

Angus nodded, then he, Gregor, and Seumas mounted their horses. The platoon set out, walking their horses until they were out of sight of the house before bringing them to an easy canter. Andrew brought Angus up to date on what he had learned from the network of clansmen.

"Seems Dougal Macinroy saw Willie three days ago ridin' wi' his two men towards the Talla Bheith forest. Stopped and talked wi' him even," Andrew paused for effect. Getting the eye from Angus persuaded him to continue without further hesitation. He cleared his throat and continued, "Willie asked Dougal if he had seen any Macgregor's. Dougal said he didna, then asked Willie if there was someone specific he was lookin' for. Willie said it didna matter, they were all to be hung."

"He said that? That they were *all* to be hung?" Angus asked, shaking his head, unable to believe his ears. "I ken the royal decree has no' been changed to pardon the Macgregor's, but it was so long ago. I thought they would hae forgotten about it by now, especially since Rob Roy died some years back."

"Dougal also said that Willie was headed for the forest because it was reported that many o' the Macgregor's hid there," Andrew said.

"Christ, if we hae to go in there to find Willie, we'll hae to be on our guard day and night. It's no' an easy place to ride either, but a damn good place to hide. We'll be needin' a plan," Angus concluded, rubbing the short bristles on his chin, silently hoping he would be back home before he had a full beard.

❧

By mid-morning, the warmth of the day was beginning to be felt. The sun blazed overhead in a hazy blue sky. Some of the men removed their shirts and wrapped their plaids around their waists, laying bare as much area to catch the cooling breeze. Ten men rode silently through the warmth of the open heather, then up into the dense, cool tree line.

Angus quietly instructed his men to fan out, keep their eyes open, and arms at the ready. Flanked by Seumas and Gregor, the group rode quietly through the thickening woods of oak and fir. It was impossible to see more than a hundred feet in front of themselves. Willie was right, it was good place to hide.

By noon, Angus gave the sign to break, dismounting next to a small burn to water his horse. Seumas and Gregor dismounted a little ways further downstream. Squatting on the bank, Angus cupped his hand for some water of his own. In the water's reflection, he noticed a movement behind him. Not wanting to let on that he saw anything, he rose from the bank, keeping his back towards the unknown observer, while he walked his horse over towards Seumas.

Seumas, sitting on the bank rubbing feeling back into his leg, looked up when he heard hoof beats approaching. He caught the look his father gave him and searched for who, or what was watching them. Seumas shook his head slightly, indicating he saw nothing.

Gregor, kneeling at the water, watched this play of observations, until he heard a stick break behind Angus. Seumas and Angus must have heard it also, and ceased all movement. Gregor caught Angus' questioning look, silently asking if he could see what it was or not. Gregor gave a negligible nod, then looked upwards with his eyes, indicating it was in the trees.

Angus slowly placed his hand on his pistol, never taking his eyes off of Gregor. Gregor again gave a nod. Seumas, now able to see that it was indeed a man in the tree behind his father, also slowly reached for his pistol. Assuming there would be more than one, he surveyed the area with his eyes. There, a little further up, a few trees further behind, was another man.

Gregor slowly rose from the water when he heard Andrew and the others approach. Feeling the tension in the air, Andrew gave the alarm sign to the rest of the men. They were all on alert now. Andrew followed the direction Seumas and Gregor were looking, and saw the two men in the trees. He passed on this information with more silent signals, and slowly the men spread out, surrounding the two in the trees.

Angus felt a trap. This was too easy for Willie's brand of strategy. With a blood-curdling scream, Angus gave the war cry of the clan, *garg'n uair dhuisgear!*, fierce when roused. All at once, as if practiced for years, his men had pistols and swords drawn.

A shot was fired from the trees and hit a rock next to Angus' feet. Standing his ground, Seumas fired at the form in the tree and hit his mark. The man fell to the ground with a sickening thud. Angus and Gregor raced there in a heartbeat, trying to glean the identity of the man.

"Aye, he's one o' Willie's henchman. He would be the other one," Gregor said indicating with a nod of his head the man still in the tree. "Unfortunately, now e'eryone in these woods will ken we are here."

"Good shot *a Sheamuis*," Angus said, patting his son on the back. Walking over to the tree the second man was still clinging to, Angus aimed his pistol and simply said "Get down, or die."

The man chose wisely and shortly was in the custody of Angus' not-so-gentle men.

"Who was he?" Angus asked his prisoner in a deep growl, pointing to the dead man.

No answer was given. The man just glared at Seumas with a look of death in his eyes.

"Maybe I should ask him, Da. He looks as though he wants to tell me somethin'," Seumas said, smirking at the prisoner.

As Seumas approached the man close enough to see the color of his eyes, the prisoner spat vehemently in Seumas' face. Seumas remained unphased while Gregor grabbed the prisoner's arms from behind, securing the smaller man easily.

With the back of his hand, Seumas smashed the man in the mouth, then took the man's plaid to wipe away the spittle from his face. The cut on the prisoner's lip was bleeding, and he ran his tongue over it, never taking his eyes off of Seumas.

"Who was he, and who are ye? And if ye spit at me again, it'll be a hard kick to yer bollocks," he promised.

Still no answer, but no spittle either. Another backhand; again no answer. After a few more rounds of questions, Angus said it was enough. The prisoner was stripped naked, tied to the tree he was hiding in, and left there. Angus took his men and rode away to make camp well out of sight of him. With the superstitious nature of Highlanders, no man would choose to stay alone in the haunted woods at night. Angus figured it would give the man some time to think.

Just as the sun was setting, Angus and Seumas rode back to the prisoner to see if he was ready to talk. When they got to the tree, they found him slumped over. Thinking he was sleeping, Seumas grabbed his hair and pulled it back. When his head was lifted, a strange sucking noise came from his throat where it had been slit.

Seumas let out a yell, taken fully off guard, dropping the almost severed head. Angus had his pistol at the ready, waiting for any surprises. Obviously, Willie's *trusted* men could not be trusted with keeping his whereabouts a secret. It also obviously meant that they were not alone.

Having heard the yell from camp, Andrew and Gregor appeared within a few moments, breathing heavy from the sprint.

"Looks like our bait is workin'," Andrew stated, staring at the dead man. "At least we ken he's here."

"Aye, but that doesna make me feel any safer," Angus said, squinting in the fading light in an attempt to locate his enemy.

"How could he do that to his own man?" Seumas asked, still a bit shaky from the heinous encounter.

"This'll be his warnin' to us. To let us ken that he's no' afraid of us, nor unwillin' to kill us," Angus said. "This will be his strategy; split us up, then take us one by one. Let's get back to camp. We hae some plannin' to do."

⇃⬥

The night passed uneventfully. This in no way gave Angus, or his men, a sense of security. Everyone was alert and ready for anything. Angus had instructed his men to stay in threes, no matter where they went. Gregor, Andrew, and himself made up the leaders of the sets, with Seumas as the fourth under Angus' watchful eyes.

With dawn came a riotous flurry of bird calls. At first, the men all thought it would be impossible to hear anyone coming over their commotion, but soon realized that the opposite was true.

A routine had begun in the calm of the morning. The camp had semi-relaxed as they made their breakfast. Each team member stayed close to each other while getting water and doing their business; ever watchful, knowing full well this would be when a cunning man would strike.

Angus was about to take a bite from the rabbit Seumas had snared earlier, when the hair on the nape of his neck started to rise. At the very same moment, the woods went quiet. Not a chirp was heard anywhere. Instantly, the entire camp was on alert with pistols, swords and dirks in hand; each man scanning the area for the intruder.

The horses, hobbled near the burn, whinnied restlessly. Gregor and his team silently skulked through the trees to make sure they were not being stolen or released.

Angus signaled to Andrew to stay at camp, he was going to flank Gregor's team to make sure it wasn't a trap. Angus had a strange feeling there was more than just one man out there. On second thought, leaving Andrew with only two men wasn't wise. He resignaled Andrew to flank the right, and he would take the left.

As the two teams converged to meet Gregor, Angus heard hoof-beats galloping away from where the horses where hobbled. With his heart in his throat at the thought of something terrible happening to Gregor, or any of his men, he sprinted through the trees to the burn.

When he got there, Gregor had five horses by the reins, still hobbled, while the other two men in his team had the other five. Obviously, it wasn't one of Angus' horses he heard making a hasty getaway.

"Did ye get a good look at him?" asked Angus impatiently.

"Only his horse's arse," Gregor grumbled.

"Let's get after him!" urged Seumas, ready for a skirmish.

"That's just what he wants us to do. I think he has more men wi' him than the two we found," Angus concluded, looking at the three sets of tracks in the soft mud. "He'll ken I wilna send all my men after him; I'd leave at least half here. But he could do this all day long; strike and run, strike and run. We need to make him think we hae fallen into his trap by splitting up."

"'Tis a dangerous game ye are playin', Angus," Andrew stated. "If we split up, there's a better chance of him winnin' this game."

Angus was rubbing his chin, the stubble of his beard making a rasping noise.

"C'mon Da, tell us what ye are plannin'. I can smell yer thoughts from here," Seumas said with a smile, reclining by the cool burn looking up at the trees.

Angus followed his son's gaze, then suddenly realized it was the perfect plan.

"We'll wait for dark." He walked back to camp, his men following, knowing not to question him. He would tell them what they needed to know when they needed to know it.

ॐ

Dusk came late in mid-July, as the men had their supper around the cook fire. While it was still light enough to see properly, Angus instructed half of his men to each find a tree they could easily climb in semi-dark. After eating, they were to discreetly and quietly climb it, finding a place to safely wait out the short darkness of the Highland night.

If Willie and his men were watching, they would think Angus' men were splitting up when they didn't return to the fire, but hopefully, would not see them climb the trees.

The men remaining in camp were all on high alert. Angus, Gregor, Andrew, and two others were on the ground. Angus directed his marksmen to the trees, leaving his veterans on the ground for the hand-to-hand combat.

The short night passed without incident. At dawn, with the woodland creatures comfortable with men in the trees, the sound of bird calls once more made it impossible to hear any footfalls or snapping twigs that would give away the enemy.

Angus' men lingered around the fire, appearing unconcerned with who may be watching. Angus knew Willie would think it was a bluff, but he hoped it would too much of a temptation to resist ambushing only five men.

*

Andrew and Gregor went to the burn for some fresh water, and to check on the horses. They lingered there for quite awhile, checking each of the horses with exaggerated care, pretending indifference to any threat. This left the group split up even further. If Willie was out there, this would be the time to attack.

After what seemed the entire morning, they had no choice but to start back to camp. It had just started to mist. Obviously, no one was out there waiting for them with malice on their mind. Willie had called their bluff. He was long gone.

Andrew bent to pick up the sheep stomachs used to carry water in, and before he could stand up, a cold metal object was pressed hard against his temple. He froze, knowing to make any sudden moves would surely end his life. Where was Gregor? Had they got him too?

"Slowly," was all the threatening voice said.

Andrew did as he was told and rose slowly, still holding on to the sheep stomachs.

"Where are the rest of yer men?" asked the soft-spoken unknown assailant.

Andrew tried to look out of the corner of his eye at who was holding the pistol to his head. He couldn't see anyone else around, and hoped his attacker was alone.

"Who wants to ken?" Andrew said in his normal deep timbre, hoping Gregor would hear him, if he wasn't already in the same predicament.

Not taking kindly to this insolence, the assailant cold-cocked Andrew on the back of his head just hard enough to make him see stars. Andrew saw his chance. Pretending to stumble from the blow, instead of falling, he whipped the fully laden sheep stomachs up quick enough to catch the attacker off guard, knocking him to the ground.

The pistol went off, nicking Andrew on the side of his neck before he could disarm the man. With lightning speed, Andrew drew his own pistol, and turned the tables on the stranger. Sitting on the man's chest, Andrew pressed the gun hard into the assailant's cheek. The assassin was surprisingly young; only about sixteen or so.

"Now then, who are ye?" Andrew asked, holding his neck where a trickle of blood ran down. "And dinna be thinkin' of tryin' anything foolish. My men are on their way after that racket ye made."

Gregor appeared on the scene the same time Andrew took a seat on the stranger's chest.

"Who hae we here, Andrew?" Gregor asked with his hands on his hips, chuckling.

"I dinna ken just yet, we hae no' been properly introduced," Andrew said through an evil smile. Harshly pushing the pistol barrel deeper into the young man's cheek, he wiped his bloody hand on the lad's plaid.

Andrew wasn't a small man, but when the would-be attacker saw the size of Gregor, he went visibly white. Gregor had brought a club-like piece of oak with him and started striking it in the palm of his huge hand to further intimidate the lad.

"We'll be askin' ye once more; who are ye?" Gregor demanded, watching the lad's eyes follow the oak club.

"I'll be wantin' to ken the same thing," Angus growled, finally making it from camp.

The lad's eyes were wide with fright now. Taking in the gathering of men surrounding him, he surrendered.

"I work for William Campbell," he said, wincing from the pain of the gun barrel in his cheek.

"What a surprise," Gregor said.

"What's yer name?" Angus asked, kicking him hard in the thigh to show he was not going to take much more of this.

"Martin. Martin Campbell," he said.

"Get him up," Angus said gruffly.

With Gregor grabbing one arm and Andrew the other, they hoisted him unceremoniously to his feet. Angus looked him up and down, noting his tall, lean physique.

"Where's Willie?" Angus demanded.

"If I tell ye, I'll be killed," Martin mumbled, looking around for any sign of his leader, unsure which man he was more afraid of at the moment.

"And if ye wilna tell me, ye'll still be killed. Seems ye're in a no win situation, lad," Angus said matter-of-factly, so close he could smell the lad's fear.

Martin looked at Angus with his mouth open as if to say something, but then turned away silent.

"Ye wilna be hurt if ye tell me," Angus said trying to sooth him with the same calm voice he used on horses.

Martin looked at the ground and remained quiet; fear replacing any rational thinking.

"Bring him to camp. We'll deal wi' him there," Angus ordered, indicating the moment for leniency was over.

ॐ

Martin was tied to a tree while Angus, Andrew, and Gregor argued about what to do with him. The conversation got heated enough for the other two men in camp to look at each other with raised eyebrows, indicating they were glad the methods to make the lad talk weren't going to be applied to them.

"A hot poker always does the trick, Angus," said Gregor.

"No, no, man. Dinna ye ken anythin'?" Andrew said, whittling on a stick with his dirk. "One of these sharp sticks in the eye will always get 'em to tell ye whate'er ye want to ken."

"I think ye're both daft," said Angus. "Ye cut off a finger one at a time until he talks."

This continued for the better part of the day. Periodically, Angus stole a glance at the lad to gauge his reactions to the torture they planned to put him through. He didn't look well. His face was the color of old oatmeal, and he was perspiring so much that his plaid was soaked through. It also looked as though he had pissed himself.

Angus, silently giving the boy credit for his bravery, wondered how much more it would take before Martin cracked. Angus whispered instructions to Andrew to fetch the rest of the men out of the trees to get some supper. It did indeed appear as though Willie was long gone.

Andrew got up just in time to miss the arrow that whizzed by his head. Had he still been sitting, he would have been dead. The rest of the men dove to the ground, dirks flashing and pistols at the ready, searching frantically for the assailant.

Angus looked around for Seumas, who somehow managed to get up into a large fir, and wondered if he was able locate the attacker. Seumas had his pistol ready, but Angus could tell he had not been able to pinpoint the man.

Gregor was crawling over to Angus when another arrow whizzed passed, this time finding a mark. Following the gurgling noise, both men sought to find the wounded man.

"Willie really doesna trust his men, does he?" Gregor stated dryly, seeing the arrow protruding out of young Martin's throat.

"Damn it to hell!" Angus roared, pounding his big fist on the ground. "We were verra close to gettin' him to talk."

"It must hae been that Willie kent that too, aye?" Gregor said, shrugging indifferently. As far as he was concerned, the only good Campbell, was a dead Campbell.

A shot was fired from the trees above, then hoofbeats were heard retreating at a rapid pace. Angus and his ground force were on their feet in a heartbeat, running towards the fleeing culprit hoping to get another shot off before he escaped. They were too late, glimpsing only rooster-tails of sod disappearing into the trees.

Seumas had scurried down from the tree and caught up to his father.

"I got him!" he said. "I saw his shoulder jerk from the bullet!"

"Aye, he's right, Angus," Andrew said kneeling next to a small red stain that had darkened the ground. When he touched it, his fingers came away with the distinct red of fresh blood.

"*A Sheamuis,* get the rest of the men down from the trees. Hurry, we hae no time to waste. We'll get him now," Angus said, anxiously looking towards home. Funny time to think of Catrìona, but he had the distinct feeling she was with him at that moment. He smiled a little to himself, but in the next instant, paled. He tried to shake the odd feeling off, but couldn't.

Home … he had to get home.

Turning back to camp, he called out unnecessarily, "Gregor, Andrew, get the horses ready, quickly."

They were already heading that way.

shifting time

Catrìona awoke with a start. It was still dark outside, but the vision was so fresh in her mind that she was still in the daylight of the event. What in the world were her father's men doing in the trees?

She sat up in bed, letting her feet touch the cool wooden floor. Reviving the vision to ascertain any details she may have overlooked, she remembered seeing Seumas with a pistol taking aim at someone in the trees. Was he shooting one of her father's men?

Walking over to the open window, she let the cool air awaken her further. Her hair was being twisted at an alarming rate; each recalled tidbit only begging for more answers. Dawn had arrived; the western sky turned a pale lavender before she decided she was getting nowhere. Quietly, she got dressed and went outside. Maybe busying herself would clarify her reasoning.

The horse stall needed to be cleaned, eggs needed to be gathered, the cow had to be milked, wash had to be boiled, yarn needed to be spun. It was just what she needed to clear her mind. Hard, mindless, work.

The day went quickly, not stopping until all the chores were done. Anna, who she hadn't seen all day, knew to give her space when she had visions.

In an effort to interpret the vision on her own, she gave up after spending the entire day pondering it. This one just didn't make any sense. She needed some help.

Sitting next to Crinan Macduncan's last resting spot, she hoped for help from the other side. It didn't come. Watching the sky darken, she realized she hadn't eaten anything all day, and her stomach now made itself heard.

Before she rose, she affectionately patted the mound where her ancestor was buried, then headed for home. The aroma of cooking stew wafted passed her on the breeze, and her stomach directed her feet to quicken the pace. When she got to the garden, she stopped to pick some of the small wildflowers that had taken over after the hailstorm destroyed all other standing vegetation. They would brighten the table, since it was obviously nearing suppertime.

"Well, she is still alive," Anna said. "What hae ye been up to all day, lass? I thought we were goin' to the castle today."

Cat shot Anna a look as blank as a fog-shrouded sky. Anna could tell she had no recollection of the conversation they had the night before.

"We were? Why dinna ye come and find me?" Cat said, putting a strangle hold on the flowers in her hand.

"I kent ye had a vision last night that ye needed to figure out, and I ken how ye want to do it on yer own. Besides, yer brother isna back yet," she smiled, rolling out the dough for biscuits.

"That's it!" Catrìona declared, smashing the flowers onto the table. No need to find a jar to put them in now.

Anna lifted a steel gray eyebrow at the remnants of petals and leaves scattered all over the table. "Care to enlighten me wi' yer conclusion, then?"

"I couldna figure out why my Da and Seumas were in trees. I forgot that Lachlan had gone to tell Da that it was William Campbell who stole the rents. They must be hidin' in the trees," she said proud to have figured that part out. But the very next statement was said with a perplexed frown on her face. "Seumas shot someone."

Cat walked over to what Anna was now calling the vision glass — the west window — twisting her hair around her fingers. Now that the strange part was resolved, she sought to know if her father and brother were safe, or in further danger. She, and her stomach, had forgotten all about the stew.

❧

When Cat returned to reality, she focused on the raindrops sliding down the window in front of her. She turned to see Anna dishing up the stew, and placing biscuits on two plates.

"Are ye ready to eat, lass, or do ye need more time?" Anna asked, holding the two plates in front of her.

"Aye, I'm ready," Cat said absently, taking a plate from Anna and sitting down at the table. "I dinna like what I saw, Mistress, but I fear there is naught I can do about it."

"Ye ken there isna always a way to prevent what ye see from happenin', Catrìona."

"But there has to be a way." Her impatience was showing as she pushed around the stew on her plate.

They ate in silence for some time. Watching Cat's dismay and frustration made Anna think of another Seer in a similar predicament.

"Hmmm," Anna mused.

This seemed to bring Cat to full attention. "What is it?"

"There may be a way … if ye want to try it. Mind, I hae ne'er been able to do it myself, but ye hae the power more than I," Anna said, wheels turning in her head as to how to proceed. She looked at Catrìona and simply said "After supper."

ﻬ

Anna prepared the herbs, laid out the midnight blue silk scarf she used for such incantations, and sprinkled rowan berries and sage around the table. A candle was lit and placed in the center of the scarf. Cat sat close to Anna so they could hold hands. Anna wanted to "be there" when Cat went in. She had heard stories of others attempting this ritual, and never coming out.

Outside, the wind started to whip up; the heavy rain hit the window with loud pops. Every so often, Cat got distracted by the eerie noise the wind made when it blew through the roof. It took her a little time to get into the relaxed mode needed to go where she was going.

Ancient prayers for protection were mumbled in Gaelic by both of them, assuring them of a safe "trip" back.

> *Goddess Diana, ruler of the Otherworld,*
> *Give my eyes vision to see all my quest,*
> *With sight that shall never fail before me,*
> *That shall never quench or dim.*

With her eyes closed, Anna instructed Cat to walk *deiseil,* around the house until she reached the door. To judge the outcome of the journey, Cat needed an omen. This would be done by looking through a circle made with her fingers. When she opened her eyes, the first thing seen was the omen.

Anna opened the door and the wind whipped in. With her fingers up to her eyes, Cat opened them and saw a dove in the rowan tree just outside the house; a sure sign of a safe, productive journey.

The candle's flame flickered from the draft in the cottage, and a fox bark was heard nearby. Cat smiled, knowing the *sionnach* would guide her to her father and brother.

Back at the table, they sat down and took each other's hands. Anna's black eyes looked intently into Cat's in the dim of the lone flame, then, giving Cat a toothless grin, said "Let's begin."

Catrìona closed her eyes to recollect the vision. This time she saw Anna beside her looking into the dense woods. She squeezed Anna's hands to acknowledge her presence, and got a squeeze back.

This was different than the earlier vision. This time, they stood beside the campfire with Angus and Gregor. There was a dead boy beside a tree. Her father's men where coming in from the woods one by one.

Sensing Cat's confusion, Anna explained. "We are with yer Da *now*, no' in the past."

Catrìona nodded, showing she understood, yet unsure if she should speak. Again, sensing the question, Anna explained that it was like they were in another room listening through a wall. This made Cat giggle, now that she knew she couldn't be heard.

"So we canna interfere wi' what's happenin' here?" Cat asked, walking closer to her father.

"No, we're just observers. No one can see, or hear us."

"Then how will we see what danger they're in?" Cat asked, putting her hand on her father's arm. "How can we get ahead of this time to warn them?"

"Let's go back and try it again wi' that intent, aye?" Anna said, taking Catrìona's hand.

When Cat opened her eyes, she was back at the kitchen table with Anna. She gave Anna a dimpled smile and excitedly said, "It worked."

"Aye, but will it work to go into the future, then go back to warn them, if need be?" Anna got up to fetch some more herbs, her staff, and the *clach na brataich*.

"The ensign stone, Mistress? What would ye use that for?" Cat asked.

"We need all the help we can get for this. The *clach na brataich* is just a crystal, after all, and the crystal and my amethyst will keep us protected. Here," Anna said, placing the milky, translucent stone into the palm of Cat's hand. "Hold onto this stone 'til we get back."

Cat closed her hand around the stone, feeling a strange power emanating from it. Instead of it feeling cold, it was warm and made her entire hand tingle. She sat there staring at it for a moment, silently directing it to protect her on her journey.

"Are ye ready then, lass?" Anna whispered, not wanting to interrupt, but feeling they needed to continue.

Cat looked up, gave a nod, took Anna's hands, and closed her eyes. Anna's staff lay across her lap to enable freedom of both hands, yet still have contact with her protective stone.

"Let's ask to start in the mornin'. That should be enough time to see what danger they may be in, and allow time to get back to warn them," Anna directed.

Cat took in a deep breath and was transported into the future. It was light. A heavy mist was falling. Cat looked around to get her bearings. She turned to see Anna standing next to Gregor and Seumas by the camp fire. Anna motioned for her to come over.

As Cat got closer, she could hear them speaking. They seemed upset about something, but arriving in the middle of the conversation wasn't shedding any light on what had happened during the night.

"Can ye make out what they are talkin' about, Mistress?" Cat asked.

"Seems that yer Da thinks they should go back to *Slios Mìn*. He's told the men he has a feelin' Willie Campbell may be headin' that way. Says he's seen this tactic used by Willie before."

"Mam!" Cat looked at Anna with horror on her face.

"What?"

"We hae to go back now. It's no' my Da who's in danger, it's my Mam! We hae to see if we can prevent what I saw in my vision last year," Cat said, thoroughly riled.

A moment later, they were back at the kitchen table. Shaken to the core, Cat got up, wrapped her *arisaid* around her shoulders and walked to the door.

"Where are ye goin', Garnet?" Anna asked, just before Cat opened the door.

"I'm goin' to the castle to see if Alexander can send some of his men to *Slios Mìn* to protect Mam. If they leave now, they can be there by mornin'," she said, challenging Anna to stop her.

"Alexander is no' there, remember?" Anna stated calmly.

No, she didn't remember. This fact made her loose a little momentum, but she was still defiant.

"Then I'll go myself."

"How will ye be able to help her?" Anna asked, noticing the slight waver.

"I'll kill Willie Campbell myself," Cat uttered through her teeth, her fists in tight balls, and tears forming in her eyes.

"What if I told ye that together, we can go back to yer Da to tell him what may happen. He's already got a feelin' that somethin' is no' right. Let's go tell him to take all his men with him and go to *Slios Mìn* to protect yer Mam."

Anna watched Cat's struggle to quell her feelings in order to think logically and rationally. Her face was as flush as the stone she was named after. Anna had to tread carefully this time. One wrong word, or attempt to push her into changing her mind, would make her walk out the door. Anna held onto her staff, directing the clarifying properties of the amethyst towards Cat in an effort to calm her down. Her will was very strong for someone so young.

"What if it doesna work? What if we're too late?" Cat asked, wiping her nose on her sleeve, desperately wanting to believe something could be done metaphysically instead of physically.

"Och, lass, ye ken better than to ask those questions," Anna said, sensing her apprentices rationality coming back. "C'mon, let's go back," she coaxed.

Catrìona stood there, unsure of which path to take. Instinctively, her hand went to her hair to begin the deep thought process of hair twirling in a determined effort to calm herself down. Anna let out the breath she had been holding for that entire time.

"Right, then. Let's go back to last night and get yer Da to leave camp immediately. How would ye get him to see it's yer Mam who's in danger?" Anna asked, wanting this to be done by Catrìona. She was only there as a guide.

Cat thought for a minute. "When I was there the first time, I touched Da's arm. I had a strange feelin' he felt it. Do ye think he did?"

"Aye, it's possible. Many a tale hae been told about just such things. Not that long ago, auld John Gordon was trapped in a cave wi' his leg broke. His wife, Emma, had died the year before, and his children wouldna ken he was missin' for a few days yet. The weather was gettin' real cold and he feared for his life. No one kent where he was."

"Night came, and wi' no way to make a fire for warmth, no food or water, he lay down as comfortable as he could get, and resolved himself to die. No' long after he closed his eyes, he heard someone callin' his name outside the cave. He sat up to make sure he wasna dreamin'."

"All of a sudden, his Emma walked into the cave."

Cat inhaled sharply, her eyes wide with anticipation. "He really saw his dead wife?"

Anna continued the story, knowing all of Cat's questions would be answered.

"He rubbed his eyes to make sure he was really seein' what he thought he was seein'. He asked her what she was doin' in this world again, and she said she wasna really here. He thought for sure that meant he was in the Otherworld wi' her."

"She asked auld John if he wanted help. He said of course he did, but how was he going to get it when the only person who kent where he was, was dead. Emma told him that she would return in the mornin' wi' their sons, but he would hae to fend for himself this night. He told her that he would manage, but to hae them hurry."

"The night went on, and auld John managed to get a little sleep, even though he was verra cold. As the dawn came the next mornin', he heard voices outside the cave again. Figurin' it was Emma, he called out to her. The voices got quiet, so he called out again. This time, instead of Emma walkin' into the cave, his three sons walked in, with a litter to carry him home in."

"What did they say to him? How did they ken where he was?" Cat asked, literally on the edge of her seat.

"He asked them those verra questions. They told him that their dear Mam came to each of them in a dream, tellin' of how their Da was hurt in a cave, and would hae to be carried home. They all met at the eldest son's croft; each telling of the dream they had. It was exactly the same for each, so they kent it was a real sign from their Mam."

"They left before it was light. It took them a bit to figure out which cave he could be in, but on the second try they heard their Da callin' for their Mam and kent their dreams were true. They had found him and brought him home safely," Anna concluded, knowing she had convinced Catrìona to go back to warn her father.

"What are we waitin' on, Mistress? We hae to go back, now!" Cat said impatiently, already in position at the table, waiting for her mentor.

ਣੈ

The rain had stopped, but the wind was still blowing, as Catrìona and Anna held each others hands to make the trip back. Anna looked tired in the dim light of the candle flame.

"Are ye well enough to make the trip, Mistress?" Cat asked, her dark violet eyes showing concern.

"Aye, but let's be quick about. It does seem to be wearin' me out a bit," Anna said.

"Let's go back to when my Da had the feelin' he should return home. Ready?" Cat asked.

Anna squeezed Cat's hands and closed her eyes. They were off. Just as before, they "landed" next to the camp fire. Cat took a seat next to her father on the log as he was explaining in morbid detail how to make a man talk. She looked up at Anna with such an expression of disgust on her face, it made Anna laugh.

"Ye do ken he's only tryin' to scare the lad." Anna said knowingly.

"Aye, and if I were him, I would be talkin' up a storm by now," Cat replied, still cringing at the thought of the torture.

Anna was standing next to Andrew, when he made a motion to stand. As he stood, an arrow whizzed in from the woods beside him, narrowly missing him. A second arrow found its mark in the lad tied to the tree. At that point all hell broke loose, and Cat crawled over to Anna, who was crouched down out of the way.

Huddled together, they watched her father search frantically for the assassin, then look up into the trees for something. Cat and Anna followed his gaze, finding who he was searching for. Seumas. He was taking aim and firing at something only he could see. Not long after the smoke from his pistol cleared, hoof beats were heard departing at a rapid pace.

Cat raced with her father to see who it was, when Seumas appeared beside them, claiming he winged the man. Anna showed up just then, and stood next to Andrew to verify that the man was indeed wounded, finding the blood on the ground.

Cat touched her father's arm again, smiling when she felt him acknowledge it from the other dimension.

"He feels me, Mistress," Cat whispered.

"All right then. Can ye tell what he's thinkin'?" Anna asked, walking over to stand on the other side of Angus.

Cat closed her eyes and smiled. She gave her father a hug around his neck and held on for a moment. Anna watched Angus' face during this interdimensional interaction to see how much was getting through. When she saw Angus smile, she knew Catrìona had made the connection. She also knew the instant Cat passed on the message of her mother being in danger, because he went white.

⁊❧

It was quite dark when Anna and Catrìona returned from their journey. They were both exhausted from the efforts of the mind. Cat blew out the remaining stub of the candle on the midnight blue scarf, stoked the fire, then helped Anna into bed. As tired as Cat was, she knew Anna must feel it even more. They would both need their strength in the morning.

Cat got out of her dress, and splashed some water on her face and neck, too tired to do anything more. She crawled into her small bed, curled into a ball, and was asleep in an instant.

Her body may have been exhausted, but her mind was still wide awake. She dreamt heavily, tossing and turning, trying to get home in time to save her mother. She ran as fast as she could, but never got anywhere.

Wings, she needed wings. That was the only way to get there before Willie Campbell. It was the only way to get there to save her mother.

Becoming a raven, she flew to *Slios Mìn*. When she arrived, still-

ness prevailed. She landed on the sill of her parent's window, hoping
to get a glimpse of her mother asleep. The curtains were drawn, but
she could hear her mother breathing; only the breathing was labored, as if in a struggle. She heard small whimpers, but no crying
for help. She listened harder. Someone had their hand over her
mother's mouth so she *couldn't* call for help!

Cat beat her wings at the window in a vain attempt to distract
whoever was causing her mother harm. She heard a sickening thud,
then all was quiet in the room.

A moment later, the front door opened and her mother came
running out. She was heading right for the barn. Where was Iain?
Why wasn't he able to help her? She flailed her wings in a frantic
effort to deter her mother from getting to the barn, knowing what
would happen if she got to a horse. She had to be stopped!

Suddenly, Cat was being violently shaken. Who was doing this?
Why wasn't she able to get to help her mother?

"Catrìona, Catrìona! Wake up, lass! Ye're having a nightmare,"
Anna shouted, grabbing Cat by the shoulders and shaking her.

Cat stopped flailing and woke from her dream. Soaked, her
muslin shift clung to her body like a second skin. She sat up, breathing heavily, and put her feet on the cool floor. Anna wiped the wet
locks from her face, hushing her like a young bairn. Cat looked up
with such tortured eyes, Anna nearly started crying.

Anna got a damp linen to cool Cat with. She had to do something; she couldn't bear to see those eyes again.

"Here lass, this will cool ye down a bit," Anna said, lifting Cat's
heavy, wet hair off her neck, placing the cool linen on her skin.

Cat let out a heavy sigh and hung her head so the linen would
stay on the back of her neck, not having the strength to hold it there
herself. Her hair fell in her face, but she made no motion to come
out from behind it. She wanted to hide there for a while as the tears
streamed down her cheeks, blending into her already wet shift as
they hit her legs.

Anna sat down beside her to rub her back, but remained silent.
Cat would tell her about it when she was ready. Feeling Cat's intense
emotions, for the first time in more years than she could remember,
she let her own tears start a puddle in her lap.

ₑ🐌·

Cat felt it was only a dream, not a vision. Dreams could be manipulated, that's why she could become a raven. But it still left her drained, scared, and anxious. Refusing to close her eyes again for the rest of the night, she sat in the rocking chair by the smoldering fire until dawn came. Anna managed to go back to sleep, thankfully. She didn't need to be burdened by someone else's fears.

Wrapping a shawl around her shoulders, Cat quietly stepped outside into the cool morning air. She closed the door silently behind her, and went barefooted out to the garden. The cool air and wet grass brought her skin to gooseflesh and she deeply breathed in the new day.

In the field, she watched a fox pounce on a mouse for his breakfast, flinging the little gray creature into the air in a twisted game of catch. In a tree at the opening of the woods sat an owl. She too was watching the fox, but for a different reason. That was her prey he was eating.

Catrìona sat on a slab of granite at the furthest end of the garden, twirling her hair. She watched as the sun made long shadows of the trees behind her, and turned the Grampians a deep burgundy. She sat there until Anna came to find her, a few hours later.

"How can I be helpin' ye, lass?" Anna asked, still in her nightdress, the dark shadows under her eyes giving away her exhausted state.

Cat looked up from her granite post with a smile, shaking her head, "I'll be askin' ye the same question, Mistress. Ye look tired, and I'm to blame for it."

Anna walked over and took a seat next to Cat, put her arms around her, and kissed her forehead. They sat there in silence for a time, just enjoying the warming day and each other's company.

Death Rides a Pale Horse

It had been a long, uneventful day for Iain. His father had only been on the manhunt for two days, no reason to look out for him at this early stage. The end of the day was nearing, and he was looking forward to getting back to the house to read the latest letters from Lachlan and Catrìona. Lachlan himself brought them, along with the news that Willie Campbell was the culprit who stole the rents from Alexander.

The sky was turning a clear yellow as the sun, which had finally made its appearance only hours ago, disappeared behind the mountains. Its reflection was mirrored perfectly in the still waters of Loch Rannoch. Water soothed him and cleared his mind. He stood at the edge of the loch skipping stones, breaking the duplicate image into a billion wavy fragments of color.

He was perfectly content to stay there for a while longer, but Maggie Stark, always knowing where to find him this time of the day, came out to tell him supper was waiting for him. Truth be told, he liked it when she went out of her way to find him. She was a sweet looking lass with big hazel eyes, long light brown hair that she always wore loose, and was filling out nicely, too; for fourteen.

Iain knew that Maggie only considered him another older brother. She was still quite taken with Lachlan, even though he only had eyes for the Reid girl.

Telling her that he would be home directly, he watched her walk away, not allowing himself to pursue his own feelings. He wasn't about to compete for a lass with his brother, even though Lachlan would probably give his blessings to be rid of her big-eyed stares, and stop being followed wherever he went. Of course, now that Lachlan was gone, his hope was that she might forget about him and set her sights to the next eligible man.

He walked to the house, following his nose towards the scent of fresh bread and rabbit stew. Once inside, his mother was there with a linen; her subtle suggestion to wash before sitting at the table. He took the proffered cloth, slung it over his shoulder, and filled the wash basin with water under the supervising eye of Lizzie Stark.

The house was a-buzz with women's voices all helping out in the house, and keeping his mother company while his father was gone. To his ears, it sounded much like a chicken coop when they all got talking and giggling.

He could only take it for a couple of hours, then he had to get out. Maybe the real reason he didn't pursue Maggie was because he was more like his cousin Alexander than he realized. Alexander never married, though he claimed to love women — even wrote poems about them — to one woman in particular named Phoebe.

Iain's favorite poem was called "Liberty Preserved: or, Love Destroyed", whichever suited the mood of the day.

> *At length the Bondage I have broke*
> *Which gave me so much Pain;*
> *I've slipt my Heart of out the Yoke,*
> *Never to drudge again;*
> *And, conscious of my long Disgrace,*
> *Have thrown my Chain at Cupid's Face.*
> *If ever he attempt again*
> *My freedom to enslave,*
> *I'll court the Godhead of Champain*
> *Which makes the Coward brave,*
> *And, when the Deity has heal'd my Soul,*
> *I'll drown the little Bastard in my Bowl.*

ॐ

After supper, Iain procured Lachlan's and Catrìona's letters, and retired to his room for the evening. He shrugged out of his shirt and lay on his bed in just his plaid and stockings. A humid breeze, remnants of the mist that fell earlier in the day, lifted the curtains and played over his naked chest.

Downstairs, the cackling was becoming unbearable, but he wanted to finish reading the letters. Afterwards, he would go out to the barn to make himself busy until the ladies went to bed. He smiled as he read about Cat's run-in with the hailstorm. As usual, she found the humorous side in a very dangerous situation. He missed her very much at that moment.

If she were here now, she would be making him laugh along *with* the chicken coop downstairs, not desire to run from it. He folded the letters up, put his shirt back on, and tried to judge where the women were so he could sneak out without being seen. Sometimes this worked, other times it didn't. When it didn't, he would be cornered into doing almost anything they needed help with. Last time, it was rolling yarn into balls! Hardly fitting work for the man of the house. Phhaa, for any man for that matter! he thought to himself.

They were still in the kitchen — no way for him to leave without being caught. He would have to take the window. It was about a fifteen-foot drop, and only used as a last resort. A man could hurt himself making a jump like that. Luckily, he thought of that this morning, and brought a good length of rope up at lunchtime.

The moon was rising nearly full, keeping the room adequately lit when he blew out the candle. Tying off one end of the rope to the legs of his oak armoire next to the window, he gave it a tug to be sure it was tight, then silently maneuvered his way down the stone wall to the ground. He would hoist it up when he got back inside.

Inside the barn, he grabbed the currycombs and started the task of brushing down the three horses. When he finished with them — well after midnight — they all had shiny coats. He peeked over at the house to see if the candles were still lit. They weren't. He listened for any tell-tale giggles. There were none. Finally. He could go to bed.

He blew out the lanterns, and went to close the barn doors. After closing one and starting on the other, a prickly feeling rose up his spine. He turned to assess this odd reaction, only to be struck with something very hard on the back of his head. He crumpled to the ground.

る

Isobel said good night to her housemates and walked upstairs. She observed Iain leaving earlier, skulking his way to the barn, thinking he was undetected. She understood Iain's reluctance at being in a house full of women, and smiled at his attempts to be polite.

Quietly opening the door to his room, she saw the rope glimmering in the moonlight at the window. Just to let him know she was aware of his escape, she pulled the rope up from its waiting position, coiled it up, then placed it in the middle of his bed.

"I dinna ken where ye are, laddie, but ye'll hae to be usin' the front door to get back in," she said to herself, smiling.

She closed the door behind her, then walked down the hall towards her own room. She paused for a moment outside of Catrìona's room, touching the wooden door as if it were her daughter. She could hear Maggie climbing into bed and fervently wished it was Catrìona instead.

"Good night, Catrìona," she murmured.

When she got to her room, a soft breeze played with the curtains, making the candle's flame dance. The crickets were out in full force, and from somewhere far away, a fox barked. She slipped out of her dress, untied her corset, then dropped her shift to the floor. It was too warm for anything to be touching her skin tonight.

She blew out the candle and slid onto the cool sheets, letting the breeze make love to her body. She remembered many nights with Angus this way, just holding hands, letting the magic of the night prepare them for coupling. The light from the moon was brilliant, illuminating her rising nipples, making them look like shiny, dark buttons.

Isobel lay there unmoving for quite some time, then rolled out of bed and put her shift back on, unfulfilled. When she got back into bed, she noticed all had gone quiet outside. The cricket serenade had been interrupted, but by who or what. Maybe Iain was coming back into the house.

She listened carefully for the front door to unlatch. Everything remained silent, only her beating heart filled her ears. Climbing out of bed again, she went to the window to see if it was Iain coming back to the house. He had been in the barn, but the doors were closed now. She listened harder. Still silence. Something wasn't right about this. There was a presence in her house that didn't belong there.

Going to the door, she quietly turned the knob, straining to hear any sound. Her heart was beating faster now. She opened the door a sliver and peered out, then tip-toed **down the** hallway to stand at the top of the stairs. It was perfectly **quiet.** Was she just imagining someone was there?

Grasping the railing, she slowly descended **the wooden** treads; stopping on each one to listen. When she **reached the** bottom, she walked through the kitchen — as bright as if **the candles** were still lit — and opened the front door. Silence.

Isobel shook her head, smiled and released the breath she was holding. "Foolish woman," she chided, closing the door. Just one more place to look, just to prove to herself she was letting her imagination run wild. She walked down the hall to the best room, where Janet and Mòrag had set up their beds. She stood at the door and saw the two of them curled up together. "There, are ye satisfied?" she scolded to herself.

By the time she went back upstairs to her room, the crickets had resumed their serenade. The curtains still lifted in the breeze, and all was quiet in the house. Since Iain had not come in, she concluded that he must be spending the night in the barn. She was just about to slide back into bed, when a hand came around from behind her and covered her mouth.

She tried desperately to escape, but a rock-solid arm had wrapped itself around her petite waist in a stranglehold, pulling her up against a hot, firm body, not much taller than herself.

"Keep still," the man's hot, rancid breath hissed.

She had no intention of keeping still. All she had to do was make enough noise to wake Maggie, Janet, Lizzie, or Mòrag, and he would have no chance. She wriggled like a fish, scratching at his sweaty arms, but this had no effect on him whatsoever. She kicked him in the shins with her bare feet, but she was so light, he just picked her up, walked over to her bed, and lay on top of her; his hand never leaving her mouth.

Squashed face first into the mattress by his weight, she felt him shift, reaching for something. Her attempts to wriggle out from under him were in vain, he was too heavy. Suddenly, she felt what he was reaching for; the rope from Iain's room. He attempted to tie up her kicking legs, but couldn't complete the task and keep her quiet at the same time.

"Keep still, I said or I'll hae to take drastic measures," he growled in her ear.

He was winded from the struggle to keep her subdued. Good, she was making him work. Her own heart felt as if it were going to explode from her chest, but there was some satisfaction in knowing she wasn't making it easy for him. She kicked at him again, but to no avail; he had her pinned down good.

She felt him reaching for something else, this time a little further out of his reach. Isobel knew this was her only chance. With all of her strength, she lifted him off balance, and he fell to the floor with a thud. She rolled off the bed with unnatural speed, and grabbed for the silver candle stick on the table beside the bed.

In the moonlight, the struggle was like a surreal dance. She saw him roll to his feet, then saw his face reflecting in the moonlight. Looking him square in the eye, she swung the candlestick with all her might, striking him on the cheek. Not waiting to see if she had done any damage, she screamed at the top of lungs and ran out of the room, almost getting caught again as her assailant lunged at her from behind.

By now, everyone in the house must be awake. Where was everyone? Why weren't they calling for her? Why weren't they coming to her aid?

She ran down the stairs, not willing to look back, hearing his footsteps not far behind her. She burst out the front door into the night, running for the barn. Her only thought was to get away; get to Iain for help. The unknown man must have done something terrible to the rest of the household. Couldn't think of that now. Had to run.

Isobel made it to the barn and managed to get inside before her assailant, slamming down the iron bar to lock him out. Standing perfectly still, she let her eyes adjust to the pitch black. The only thing on her mind now was to get to the stalls. She put out her hands to feel her way back then kicked something on the floor. It felt like a body. God, not Iain.

She felt around the body, searching for the head. It was Iain. Her hand came away with a sticky feeling, certain it was blood. He was still breathing, but unconscious. It was too dark to tell how badly he was wounded. Where was her attacker? All was silent outside the barn. He made no attempt to get in.

Allowing herself a moment to cradle her son, she forged a plan to escape. There were no two ways about it, she would have to go out the front door. He would be waiting for her. The last time she got on a horse had been more years than she could remember, but she saw no other way of getting out of this situation. She would have to ride out.

Isobel laid Iain's head down gently in the straw, and felt her way through the barn to the first stall. Running her hand up over its hind quarters, she realized the horse she found was Uallach. No time to see what other choices there were. She fumbled around for the bridle and put it on him, but couldn't lift his saddle, so she would have to ride him bareback. Hopefully, he would have no objection to this, even though his name meant "spirited fellow".

She envisioned how she was going to get past her assailant. Would the bold approach work? It was only a couple more hours 'til dawn. Should she wait to see better? No. If she could see better, than so could he. It would have to be done now.

Isobel opened the stall gate, climbed the fence and straddled the huge animal's back. She gave him a gentle squeeze. Nothing happened. For a moment, she thought she may be unable to do this. This time she squeezed a bit harder and the great beast did her bidding.

They walked out of the stall to where Iain was lying. The light gray horse looked like a ghost as he walked through the barn, catching the slim shafts of moonlight coming through the cracks between the boards. Isobel gave the area where Iain was a wide berth, since she couldn't see exactly where he was. She stopped just in front of the doors contemplating how to be quick about this.

Angling Uallach beside one of the doors, she reached out to lift the iron bar. She grabbed a handful of his mane, just in case he reared when he saw someone on the other side of the door, as she suspected he would.

"Ready, lad?" she whispered to the big horse. Then with all the strength she had, she whipped open the door, and kicked Uallach hard in the ribs.

Obviously, not as easily spooked as she was, the great beast lifted off the ground with such force, he almost lost his rider. Once clear of the doors, Isobel saw her attacker scrambling to get to his feet. He certainly wasn't expecting to see a giant horse storm out of the barn with his intended victim on its back, hell-bent for escape.

He shouted and waved his arms in an effort to rear the horse, but the great beast instead rode directly for him. At the last moment, he dove out of the way, landing hard on his wounded shoulder.

Isobel gave Uallach his head, knowing he could see better than she could. She rode hard northeast, for the hills, in a desperate attempt to get as much distance as possible from the madman. She needed to get help, or find a good hiding place until it was light.

ࢠ

Willie Campbell, in his wildest dreams, never thought he could lose a hostage. Most of the time they ended up dead before ransom could be posted, because he tired of them. They were too much trouble to bother with.

Many men he captured never put up such a fight as Isobel Robertson had. She was so small, so frail-looking, he figured he would be able to subdue her as easily as he had the rest of the house, even with a bullet in his shoulder. She proved to be a worthy opponent, indeed, especially when she struck him with that candlestick. He rubbed his cheek, feeling blood from the slice it made. He smiled.

Walking into the barn, he saw the boy still lying on the floor. He gave her even more credit for having the strength to leave her wounded child. Then he had an incredulous thought. "She knew," he said. "She knew I was after *her*. No one else."

He laughed out loud this time. He had heard of the lass' abilities as a Seer, but had no idea it ran in her mother as well. Laughing again, he went behind the barn to his horse, grabbed the pommel and lifted himself up, wincing, now that the adrenaline had worn off. He didn't know where she was headed, but that big horse would leave a trail a blind man could follow.

ࢠ

As the edge of day appeared on the horizon, Isobel slowed the big horse down. They had been at full speed from the beginning. She found herself in a wooded grove at the top of a ridge, but had no idea where she was.

She looked back from the direction she came, and saw the telltale signs of the big horse's hooves. Her heart sank as she realized she left a trail for her assailant to follow that led directly to her. In an effort to locate him, she strained her eyes for any movement below her, but there was none.

Realizing she couldn't stay on horseback, she slid off Uallach's back, then smacked him with such ferocity on his big rump, that it left her hand stinging. He may have been tired from the long run, but with this action, he knew the way home in a hurry. The gray ghost loped back in the general direction from where he came. Inspecting the indents the hoof prints made, she saw no difference in them when she dismounted.

Each moment that passed, it got lighter and easier to see. Her eyes scanned the ridge line for any kind of shelter. East, about a half a mile away, a thick grove of fir trees came into focus when the light hit their tops. By the time she got to the grove, she was exhausted. The entire night without sleep and the receding adrenaline was taking its toll on her frail body. She ached all over from the struggle with her attacker, and from riding the great horse.

After reaching a huge fir tree, she collapsed at its base, unable to take another step. The ground was cold, and it seeped through her shift making each ache more intense. She had to get off the ground.

Scanning the area, she noticed some smaller firs with branches within easy reach. In a great effort to get up, she broke off a few bows, and laid them on the ground. This would keep her off the cold earth. Breaking off one more to cover herself with, she laid down on her newly made bed, falling asleep within minutes, lulled by the fresh scent of balsam.

৯

Just as he suspected, the big horse left an easy trail to follow. Judging from the distance between the hoof prints, Isobel Robertson was not wasting any time getting to her destination. He had been trailing her at a canter, the tracks indicating she was on a dead run for the entire time. He wondered where she was going. There weren't any crofts out this way that he knew off, so therefore, no help.

The sun was just breaking over the mountains, casting long, orange-hued shadows on the dew-covered grass. Willie looked up the hill to a ridge line. The trail led straight up to it.

When he reached the wooded grove, he noticed his quarry had stopped, turned, and retreated back down the hill. She doubled back! He was beginning to like this game. Isobel Robertson turned out to be very clever giving him such a good chase. He studied the area for any other tell-tale signs of what transpired up here. From the appearance of the hoof prints, she didn't dismount. She mulled around, probably stopped here to see if he was following her. From this vantage point, she could see for quite a distance.

The sun was higher now, and as he surveyed further, he could see in the dew-covered grass the trails animals left earlier. He turned his horse to begin the descent when he noticed a different kind of trail, one made by a human. His eyes followed the path to a thick fir grove. He smiled. "No' as clever as ye thought now are ye, Mrs. Robertson?"

He dismounted and tied his horse to a tree. He would be quieter on foot. Staying inside the trees as much as possible, Willie silently crept to the fir grove. He had a strange feeling she hadn't gone far.

The sun was rapidly drying up the dew on the grass and forever erasing the trail. He picked up his pace. When he came to a small clearing about a hundred feet from the beginning of the grove, he got down on his belly and crawled the rest of the way, so he wouldn't be seen. This was very painful on his shoulder wound, and he involuntarily let out a soft groan.

ॐ

Isobel slept heavily from exhaustion and fatigue, the sun warming her cover of fir bows. She dreamt of being chased. Running through the thick woods, small twigs whipped her face as she tried to outrun her stalker. Flailing her arms, she tried to keep the branches from her face.

She felt her arms hit something on top of her. Opening her eyes, Isobel realized she had batted away the fir bow she covered herself with, and was now fully exposed. She lay very still, straining to hear anything unusual around her, but all she heard was her own pounding heartbeats. She was just about to get up, when she heard a moan. She froze and listened for it again, but couldn't make out where it came from.

The hair on her arms started to rise. There was definitely someone out there. She had to get out of the sun, and move further into the woods without being seen. She got on her belly and crawled behind the big tree she was under, crouching behind it in search of her stalker.

At first, she saw nothing. The breeze had picked up making the grass dance around as if being stroked by millions of unseen fingers.

Hugging the tree, she stood up for a better vantage point, then spotted him. His green and blue plaid blended into the Earth, making him almost invisible. He was looking around; looking for her. So far, he hadn't seen her. He was only about two hundred feet away. She had to run.

She crouched back down, hiked up her shift and tied it between her legs, giving her easier mobility. Wishing fervently to be in any other color but white, she abandoned the notion that she would blend into the forest. Scanning the woods, she searched for a hiding place, but still there were only trees.

Barefoot, she quietly trotted deeper into the darkness of the woods, trying to keep as close as she could to the trees for cover. Fear of stepping on a twig that would give her position away made it impossible to run.

She came upon a thicket of birch trees bordering a small clearing. Their white bark would allow her to blend in a bit more. Picking out a cluster of five trees, she lay down at their base, quickly covering herself with grass.

In the firs behind her, a twig snapped. She froze, hoping she had enough camouflage on her to keep from being spotted immediately. Slowly, she turned her head to watch his advance. Time measured itself in grievous increments until she finally caught a movement beside an enormous fir just fifty feet away.

He was wrapped in his plaid, the only thing visible was his face. He made sweeping looks with his eyes, taking in every detail of what he saw. She was afraid to blink.

The breeze had now become a wind, making lots of small noises all around, covering any sound she made — like the black and blue pounding of her heart. It also covered any sound he made.

Obviously satisfied that she wasn't there, he ducked back into the thickness and disappeared. Isobel relaxed a bit, willing her heart to slow down. She thought briefly of Iain, but couldn't afford to linger there. She needed all of her wits to get out of this alive.

How long should she wait? Time became an enigma. Had it stopped? Was it speeding up? She couldn't tell. The sun made its way across a leaf, indicating it had indeed continued on; not waiting for her.

ᶻ🪶

Willie had to be mistaken. She must not have retreated to these woods after all. There was no sign of her anywhere, and he knew no one was that quiet. Even he had stepped on that twig before he saw the clearing. He patiently waited to see if the noise would spook out his prey. In his experience, prey will freeze for just a moment, then blindly run from their own fear. He expected Isobel Robertson to fall neatly into that category, that's why he felt he had to be mistaken.

This meant she was probably already back at her house, prepared for him now. He would never get another chance like last night. He needed to rethink his entire plan. Angus and his men could not be far from *Slios Mìn* if they followed what he imagined to be a pretty good blood trail.

"Damn!" he swore out loud, convinced he was alone. He walked back through the forest, to the clearing overlooking where his horse was tied to a tree. He sat beside an enormous fir tree, picking at the needles of a bow that had fallen from it. *Think, man, think.*

After calming himself down a bit, he started to take notice of some overlooked details. He smiled. Then he began to laugh.

❧

Isobel had not seen or heard a thing for some time. She couldn't stay there. All she could think of was getting home. Still wary and watchful, she slowly uncovered herself, brushing off the grass that stuck to her shift. She walked quietly back through the forest, coming out a little west of where she went in, stopping at a clearing to survey her surroundings. Imagine her surprise when she spotted a horse tied to a tree.

Caution bells were going off in her head, but the overwhelming urge to flee overran her senses. One last look to make sure her stalker wasn't in sight. All she saw were trees.

She sprinted out into the open, not daring to look back. It was do or die; literally. Racing downhill faster than she could control, just before she reached the horse, she fell, making a *oofff!* sound that knocked the wind out of her. Concentrating on getting her breath back, she didn't hear the footfalls beside her until it was too late.

Totally at the mercy of the strong arms hoisting her onto the horse, she struggled to breathe. As she landed in the saddle, it jump-started her lungs into receiving air again. She coughed and sputtered, the fight in her forgotten, until her captor attempted to step up into the stirrup.

With an adrenaline rush that seared through her veins, she kicked her assailant in the shoulder, sending him to the ground in a thud and a deep groan. Trying to free the reins from the tree, she screamed at the top of her lungs in frustration. The reins wouldn't come loose without getting off the horse that was now doing a panicky dance around the man crawling towards him on the ground.

"There's nowhere to run, Mrs. Robertson," Willie said in an all-too-calm voice, standing now, holding his shoulder.

"Who are ye? What do ye want wi' me?" Isobel screamed, still pulling on the reins and kicking at the horse's sides.

"William Campbell, at yer service, Miss, and I want yer husband," he stated matter-of-factly, walking over to put a stop to her fight. He grabbed the halter roughly, and untied the reins from the tree. Isobel had not stopped kicking the horse, and he tried to rear up. Taking the reins, Willie whipped Isobel's legs a few times, leaving red, angry welts on her bare skin. She let out another scream, and tears streamed down her face.

"Enough!" he demanded, "or I'll whip ye 'til ye're raw."

Isobel stopped. She sat atop the horse and wept, all strength to fight was gone.

Willie waited a few minutes for his shoulder to stop throbbing, and to make sure Isobel was truly subdued. He was sweating profusely and really needed to sit down, but that fact he had to hide from her. One sign of weakness from him and frail or not, she would try something again.

"I'm goin' to get up on this horse wi' ye now. Dinna be tryin' anythin' else, mind?" he told her through gritted teeth.

Isobel just sat there, unmoving, tears drying on her face. Willie reached up and grabbed the pommel with his left hand. Isobel did nothing. He put his foot in the stirrup, and hoisted himself up behind her. Isobel sat there, as if in a trance. He slowly reached his arms around her, grasping the reins and squeezing the horse to start it moving. Isobel sat motionless up against Willie's hard chest.

They started down the hill; Willie convinced that Isobel was under control. They went about twenty yards, then Isobel heard voices. She searched around with her eyes, trying not to give away her readiness of escape.

To the east on the ridge line, a string of men came into view. They were about a half a mile off. Isobel didn't think William Campbell had seen or heard them; he wasn't taking any evasive action. Judging from the blood on the shoulder of his sark, he was wounded pretty badly. She had placed a hard kick there, and now figured he was too preoccupied with his pain to notice what was going on around him.

This was it. Her only chance to get away. With what little amount of strength she had left, she grabbed the reins, pulled hard, and screamed for all she was worth. The horse reared up, and caught off guard, Willie lost his balance, taking Isobel to the ground with him.

RETRIBUTION

Angus and his men rode until darkness prevented them from continuing safely. He was wary and alert of the invisible, as were all the men. He desperately needed to get home, but couldn't risk riding into an ambush; Willie's style.

Cat gave him a message that Isobel was in danger. She showed him Isobel riding Uallach, and knowing her aversion to the great beast, she would indeed have to be in dire straits for that to happen.

"Da, how do ye ken Willie's headed for *Slios Mìn?*" Seumas asked, laying under the stars, unable to sleep.

"Yer sister showed me," Angus said, his head resting in the crook of his arm, he too unable to sleep.

"When?" Seumas asked, frowning in the dark at his father.

"When ye shot Willie. I had a feelin' she was there wi' me. Then I saw in my heid yer Mam ridin' auld Uallach …

"What? Oh, Christ! It's happenin' just like Cat said!" Seumas rolled to his feet, severely agitated.

This got Angus' attention. Seumas rarely fretted about anything. What did his son know that he didn't?

"Make sense, man," Angus growled, sitting up to watch his son pace. "What's happenin' just like Cat said?"

"When Iain and Lachlan took Cat to Mistress Macpherson's, Cat told them of a vision she had where Mam was thrown off a horse. When she fell, she hit her heid on a rock and was killed. We dinna put much into it, as none o' us could remember the last time Mam got on a horse," Seumas said, then added, "She's makin' it happen."

187

"What do ye mean, she's makin' it happen?" Angus asked, frowning

"Naught would hae come out o' my competition wi' Alex, if Cat had no' said it out loud. She made it happen," he said again, already making preparations to leave. "We hae go now, Da! We hae get to Mam!"

Angus was stunned, his mouth open in disbelief. He quickly got to his feet and followed Seumas towards the horses.

"What's goin' on Angus?" Gregor asked curtly, having been interrupted from a sound sleep.

"Get the men up, we're leavin'. Now!"

℈

Twilight quickly became dawn as Angus and his men continued their journey southwest back to *Slios Mìn*. With almost two hours of hard riding to go, the band was on high alert, ever watchful of an ambush. They carefully picked their way through the thick forest just as the sun made its appearance, casting long shafts of yellow light through the firs.

At the edge of the woods, they found themselves on the ridge line overlooking the Robertson valley. One more hour.

Seumas was just about to kick his horse into action, when he noticed deep hoof prints coming straight up through the valley to the top of the ridge, just to the west of them, about fifty feet away.

"Da, I'm goin' to check out those tracks. Looks like a heavy horse made them," he said, trying not to read anything into them yet.

"I noticed them as well. Let's go hae a look," Angus agreed, his heart beating a little faster than it should.

As they reined their horses in that direction, they heard screaming and yelling coming from just below the tree line on the western ridge. They spied a man and a woman in a scuffle next to a horse; the new morning light illuminating the white of the woman's dress. Suddenly, the energy of the men was charged. As if they were one, the entire group spurred their horses towards the melee; Angus and Seumas leading. The pair was still unidentified, but certainly something was wrong if the woman was screaming like that.

It was hard to say who recognized her first, but realization registered as terror on their faces. As the two of them got closer, they heard Isobel scream, then saw her grab the reins in an attempt to dislodge her captor. To their horror, they watched the horse rear up, dislodging both riders to the ground.

Angus couldn't make his horse go any faster. It was like a bad childhood dream when he would run, but not get anywhere; his dreamscape stalkers easily catching him. Everything moved in slow motion. Try as he may, he would never reach Isobel in time.

❧

The sunrise was spectacular, but no one saw it. The air was fresh from the sea, yet no one smelled it. Angus and Seumas were devastated by what they witnessed, as were all the men. Somehow Willie managed to live, while Isobel did not. Willie broke the same arm he was shot in when she landed on him. He lay unconscious on the ground; a couple of the men stood guard over him.

Angus sat on the ground cradling Isobel on his lap, silently willing life to flow from his body back into hers, knowing the attempt would be futile. Seumas knelt beside her, holding her hand, his eyes overflowing onto her muslin shift. Both men were reliving the moment over and over, as if fate could be changed.

Moments later, Angus lay his wife's head on a blanket that was given to him; he didn't know by whom. His hand came away red from the fatal wound on the back of her head; he wiped it in the grass. He looked over at Seumas, as if just noticing him for the first time.

"I'm so sorry, *mo bhalach,*" Angus whispered, his own blue eyes bright with tears.

Seumas said nothing, unable to speak as tears streamed down his cheeks. It was a look Angus would never forget, one of sheer and utter desolation, and rage, as if Seumas blamed himself for not being able to reach his mother on time. He was not alone in that sentiment. Angus would feel that way for the rest of his life. A minute sooner, that's all he needed to save her. One minute.

Glancing over at Willie — still unconscious on the ground, his arm twisted at a unnatural angle — Angus' eyes immediately hardened, and the small muscles bunched in his jaw. He needed to think. What he wanted to do to Willie right now was tear off his arm and beat the life out of him with it. Nothing was too savage at the moment, but there were other matters to address first.

He got up and wandered, keeping his back towards the grizzly scene, finding solace on a chunk of granite. After a while, his mind cleared and rationality slowly reemerged. He thought of Iain, then all the women who were with Isobel when she fled; Andrew's wife and daughter, and Lizzie and Maggie. *Please let them all be unharmed!*

He called for Gregor, his voice hoarse with emotion. The big man was instantly at his side.

"What can I do to help ye, man?" Gregor placed his big hands on Angus' shoulders, ready to do whatever was asked.

"I need ye to go to *Slios Mìn* to make sure Iain and the women are safe and unharmed. Take a couple o' the men wi' ye; uh, Donald and Malcolm. If I'm correct, these tracks were made by Uallach, my Percheron. He kens his way home from the looks of the tracks goin' both ways. Hitch him to the wagon and bring it back here. Leave Donald and Malcolm there. I'll keep Andrew here wi' me." Angus' eyes locked with his friend's, making sure he was clear.

Gregor nodded in understanding, then he looked over Angus' shoulder at the unconscious Campbell. His big hands tightened into fists.

"I'd be obliged if ye wait for my return." His meaning unmistakable, referring to Willie's punishment.

ða

By the time Gregor and the two men made it back to *Slios Mìn*, it was mid-morning. He saw Uallach grazing not far from the barn. The beast did indeed know his way home.

The three men rode up to the barn; both doors were closed. Dismounting, they drew their dirks and pistols, and Gregor whispered to Malcolm to open one of the doors. Gregor and Donald waited in front of the other, ready to overtake anyone still inside.

As the door opened, it filled the dark area with light, catching on the brown of Iain's plaid. Gregor wasted no time reaching Iain's side, hoping the lad was still alive. Laying his big hand on Iain's head, he watched Iain's eyes flutter open and wince from the sunlight that caused explosions in his head. Malcolm and Donald quietly began searching the rest of the stalls to be sure no one was hiding in them. They came back shaking their heads, indicating the barn was clear.

Gregor smiled, as Iain focused in on the semi-familiar face.

"Good to see ye're still wi' us, lad. Yer Da will be verra happy to see ye." He sheathed his weapons and reached his big arm under Iain's shoulder to get him into a sitting position.

Iain moaned a little, reaching back to feel if his head was still in tact. It was, but he felt the dried blood that caked to his hair. "What did I get hit wi', a rock?"

Gregor looked around for the weapon in question, but found nothing close. "Dinna ken, lad. He must o' had it on him."

"Stay here while ye get yer wits about ye, I hae others to see about. Ye may no' be the only one in need o' help."

The three men trotted to the house, noticing the front door was wide open. They drew their weapons again, unsure of what they would find inside. Quietly, they walked into the kitchen. At this time of day, the house should be a bustle of activity. It was silent. Gregor instructed Malcolm to stay and guard the front door, while he and Donald walked down the hall to the best room. Gregor instantly noticed two women on the floor, bound in back by the wrists, and gagged.

When the women saw him, the young one tried to scream, letting out a muffled whimper through the gag.

"It's all right, lass," he said, holding up his hands. "I'm Gregor Macgregor, a friend of Angus'. He sent me to make sure ye werna harmed." Holding up his dirk, he quietly asked, "Is there anyone here I may need to use this on?"

The older woman recognized him from the castle and shook her head, but tears still rained down her cheeks. Gregor knelt down next to them and removed their gags, each trying to lick their lips with dry tongues, while Donald cut the ropes that bound them.

"Thank ye ... Gregor. I'm Mòrag ... Murray and this ... this is my daughter ... Janet," she said between hiccupping sobs.

Now he knew why Angus sent him, and kept Andrew there. His heart gave a little jump at the strength it took Angus to think clearly, putting someone else's feelings before his own after what he just went through.

"Is Isobel all right? Dear God, please tell me she is," Mòrag pleaded.

Gregor and Donald exchanged glances, looked over at young Janet, then back to Mòrag. Their looks told her all she needed to know, and she started sobbing anew. Janet had not caught their expressions and just held onto her mother, thinking she couldn't bear to know the answer. Gregor got up and left the room, leaving Donald to tend to the women. He had to check the rest of the house.

He silently walked up the stairs and stood at the top, straining to hear any sound. From a room down the hall, he heard whimpering. He opened the door to find two other women bound and gagged in the same fashion as the Murray's downstairs. Their wide-eyed looks of renewed fear led him to recite the same soothing words he had just moments ago.

Gregor removed their gags and cut their ropes, and before he could be barraged with questions he did not want to answer, he asked them to come downstairs when they were ready. He wanted a full recounting of how this happened.

Gregor instructed Donald and Malcolm to fetch Uallach and get him hitched to the wagon. He went back out to the barn to bring Iain inside the house.

"Come in when ye are done, lads."

❧

Gregor helped Iain into the kitchen. Iain held the back of his head, attempting to keep it on his shoulders. When Maggie saw dried blood on Iain's face and neck, she was instantly at his side surveying the damage. After her assessment, she went to fetch some bandages and whisky.

Gregor assumed by the speed which Maggie was attending to Iain, the young man was in good hands. All the women were together in the kitchen consoling each other.

"Ladies, Iain, can ye make time to come sit so we can hae a talk about last night? I'll be needin' to get back to Angus directly." Gregor waited for them all to settle down.

Not being his area of expertise, Gregor had no idea what to say to a room full of women. He wanted to just come out and say what he knew, get their information and leave, but with the two young lasses, he decided vague would be better if questions arose.

"Iain, let's start wi' ye. Tell me what happened last night."

Iain recounted his story to the sympathetic noises of the women. Maggie never left his side, tending to his wound as if she had been doctoring for years.

"So ye didna see who it was that hit ye?" Gregor asked.

"No. I was out cold 'til ye found me in the barn."

"Right then. What about you Mrs. Murray?"

"We had all said our good nights; Janet and I took our beds in the best room where ye found us. We were all havin' a good time, a *ceilidh,* if ye will, and time got away wi' us. I dinna ken about Janet, but I was asleep almost instantly. I was jostled awake by a hand coverin' my mouth, then heard the same thing happenin' to poor Janet," Mòrag said, cradling Janet in her arms.

"Wait. So ye're tellin' me there were two of them?" Gregor asked, instantly on guard. Iain seemed to catch the wariness and removed himself from the doctor to stand near the door; on the alert.

"Aye, otherwise he woulda ne'er gotten away wi' it," Mòrag stated with resentment in her voice, indicating that she, nor any of the other women in the household were incapable of defending themselves, especially in a group.

Gregor cleared his throat, silently agreeing; catching Iain's smile. It was true enough. A group of women, Highlanders or not, were a force to be reckoned with when one of their own was in danger.

"What happened then?" Gregor prompted.

"One o' the men stayed in the room wi' us, and the other went upstairs. Och, he went up quiet enough, but the third step from the top has a squeak if ye walk on it just right, and I heard the squeak."

"Anything else ye can tell me?"

"That was all 'til I heard all the commotion comin' down the stairs," Mòrag said. "The last thing I heard were hoof beats headin' off behind the house."

"Right. What about ye, lass?" Gregor giving his attention to Janet.

"It all happened so quickly. The only thing I remember is bein' scairt out o' my wits," Janet said candidly. "But it was just as Mam said."

"Mrs. Stark? Can ye add what happened upstairs for me?"

"I ne'er heard a thing 'cause I was struck on the head wi' somethin' hard; thought I was dreamin'. I heard Maggie whimperin', but could do naught to help her. It was like I was froze up," Lizzie recollected, feeling the bump on the side of her head. "Then he stuffed that dreadful rag in my mouth, tied me up, and left the room. I heard naught else 'til, just like Mòrag said, I heard the commotion goin' passed my door and down the stairs."

"Maggie?"

"It was just as Mam said, only I heard three sets of hoof beats all at different times."

Gregor thought quietly for a moment, trying to piece together what everyone had told him.

"Well, there are a couple things that dinna make sense," Gregor pondered, rubbing the rough whiskers on his chin. "Firstly, who was the second man and where did he go? We ken it was Willie Campbell who chased Isobel 'cause we caught him, but he was alone. Second, why was there such a space of time between riders?"

"I hae to get this information back to Angus. He's waitin' on me," he said, getting up quickly to leave before the questions started. There was only one person left he needed to speak with, that was Iain. He had to be told. Gregor thought it odd that the lad never asked about his mother's fate. Maybe he didn't want to know, or, like his father and brother, already *did* know.

"Iain, will ye walk wi' me?" Gregor asked before he left the room.

ॐ

"She's dead, isna she," Iain said emotionlessly. It wasn't a question, it was a statement.

Gregor just nodded, hoping not to be prodded into a full explanation of how.

"Willie killed her. She ne'er would hae gotten on a horse unless pressed into it, especially Uallach. She was afraid o' him," Iain said coldly, pacing back and forth in frustration beside the barn. "My sister told us that was how she would die. No' from her sickness, but from a horse. Cat wasna totally right though, was she?" he continued, sending a piercing look towards Gregor, daring him to deny any of it. "It was really Willie who killed her, not Uallach."

Gregor saw the same look in Iain's eyes as Angus and Seumas had in theirs. Willie was going to pay for his treacherous act, and it would not be quick, nor painless.

"The only one who kens about yer Mam is Mòrag. I'll leave it to the two of ye to tell the others, but now I hae to return to yer Da."

Gregor completed the few steps to the barn, where Donald and Malcolm had just finished hitching the wagon. "Ye two are to stay here," he directed to them, then lifted himself up into the wagon. "Keep a watchful eye, all of ye. We dinna ken who the other man was wi' Willie, or if there was more than one. I dinna believe they'll return here, but keep alert." He clicked the reins and started the trip back up to the ridge line.

ॐ

It was mid-afternoon by the time Gregor arrived in camp, giving Angus ample time to think about Willie. Angus had to employ all of his willpower not kill Willie and say to hell with the information about the stolen rents. But leaving the deed to Gregor would make sure it was a long, cruel death.

Before Angus could do anything, though, he had to get Isobel home. He had already decided the task would fall to Seumas, sparing his son the knowledge of what men were truly capable of. Life was hard enough without having to bear this gruesome deed on his conscience.

Interrupting his thoughts, Gregor appeared at his side to explain what happened at *Slios Min*. He reassured Angus that all the women, and Iain, were all right, and the fact that there were at least two men doing the deed.

"How many are we lookin' for then?" Angus asked, looking very tired.

"It sounds like there were three riders. We ken one was Willie and one was Isobel. We dinna ken who the third was."

"No one saw who the second man was then?" Angus asked.

"No, it was too dark, and they were bound and gagged before they ken what was happenin' to them."

"Where was Iain? He sleeps too light to be snuck up upon like that wi'out hearin' somethin'."

"He was in the barn and was hit verra hard on the head from behind. Lucky to be alive." Gregor regretted those words as soon as they were uttered when he saw the look that came over Angus' face. "Och, I'm sorry for sayin' that Angus ..."

"No ... no, man. Ye only said what ye saw, and I thank ye for bein' there for them all." Angus cleared his throat and told Gregor he wanted Seumas to take Isobel home.

Gregor nodded and said "I'll get her into the wagon. Shall I send Seumas to ye?"

"No, get the men together. I'll be there shortly. I'd like to tell them of what went on first ... wi' yer help o' course, then I'll speak to Seumas."

A few minutes later, Angus and Gregor recounted the events that led to this end amidst angry outcries, fists pounding on the logs they sat on, and a general fueling of a fire already burning nearly out of control.

Andrew was visible shaken, not from the account, but from the anger he felt towards Willie. He wanted nothing more than to slit Willie's throat that very instant, but that would be too quick, too forgiving. He stole a look at the culprit tied to a tree behind him, the sunlight hitting the sheen of sweat on Willie's face. He would enjoy each painful scream Willie would make for putting his family in danger.

When the story had been sufficiently reported and questions answered, Angus took Seumas aside.

"I need ye to take yer Mam home in the wagon," Angus said, holding up his hand to stop any argument that request may generate. "Take Johnnie and Robbie wi' ye. Ye'll hae to fetch Lachlan and Catrìona and bring them home."

Seumas stood perfectly still listening to him, but not really hearing him. Angus could tell the image of his mother falling from the horse consumed him. When Seumas finally spoke, it was in a voice he didn't recognize. "Ye wilna need to tell Catrìona. She already kens," then walked away without emotion or debate.

Angus watched his broken son head for the wagon, convinced sending him home was the right thing to do. Following a little behind Seumas, Angus arrived at the wagon just as Gregor lifted Isobel's lifeless body into the back. She had been wrapped in a blanket, so he was unable to see her beautiful face one last time. Tears ran unabated down his face, though he was unconscious of them. He reached into the wagon and laid his big hand on her head, his heart crushing under the emotional weight. "I will see ye again, *a ghaoil*," he whispered, then turned and walked towards the woods. No one followed.

❧

It was nightfall when Angus emerged from the woods. Even in the warm glow of the camp fire, he was not himself. He wore the look of retribution. Gregor and Andrew noticed it right off, never witnessing this emotion in Angus' eyes before. Angus had spent many hours contemplating how to make Willie pay for what he did. The mind festers on things like that. Now it looked as if he had come to a decision.

He sat down on the log beside Andrew, not saying a word. Rabbits were sizzling on the spit over the fire, ready to eat. Just realizing he was hungry, he got up, and with his dirk, sliced off a chunk of meat.

"Eat up men, we hae work yet to do." It was as if none of the day's events had occurred; it was business as usual. Slowly, each of the men got their food and sat eating in strange silence.

After supper was complete, Angus got up from his log and walked over to Willie. He squatted down in front of the wounded man and just stared at him. Gregor smiled and nudged Andrew in the ribs to get his attention. Andrew, his back towards Willie, had just started a quiet conversation with Norman and Tommie, and had not seen Angus get up. Andrew turned to Gregor to see what he wanted, and followed Gregor's gaze.

All conversation ceased. Ears strained to hear what Angus was saying to Willie, but he remained silent. He just squatted there and stared. Willie seemed unphased by this at first, but as time went by and Angus still hadn't spoken a word, only stared, then he began to get agitated.

"Say what ye want, man!" Willie growled through gritted teeth, his shot and broken arm throbbing.

Silence.

"Ye canna make me talk," Willie continued.

Silence.

"What are ye goin' to do, stare at me all night?" Willie scoffed.

Silence.

"I ne'er meant to harm yer wi — " he started to say, but was cut off by Angus' big hand clenching tightly around his sinewy throat.

Andrew made a move to get up, but Gregor put a hand on his arm to stop him. "Let him be for a minute. He kens he canna kill him wi'out questionin' him first. This is just part of the game."

Andrew sat back down, watching Willie's eyes bulge, and his face turn bright red in the glow of the fire. Norman and Tommie had never seen this side of their laird. Glancing at each other, they thought of the torturous deeds Angus, Andrew and Gregor had planned for young Martin, and wondered if they would actually have been carried out.

All at once, Angus let go, stood up, and walked back to the log to sit next to Gregor. Willie was coughing and sputtering, trying to catch his breath. Gregor smiled and patted Angus on the shoulder. "Well done, man."

"Where's his dirk?" Angus asked, never taking his eyes off of Willie.

Andrew held it out to Angus, who refused it, saying instead, "Put the blade in the coals. We'll need it red hot."

Andrew did as he was told, shoving the blade up to the hilt into the glowing coals, then returned to the log.

❧

Gregor recognized the game Angus was playing; and playing it very well, he might add. Willie, proficient in the art of torture, would know it as well. Many men would scare their intended victims by telling them what they would do to extract the information from them. Others would show their victims the tools they would be using; again, another scare tactic. But to the truly skilled, the art of silence was the most frightening. The victim was left to create his own worst fears. No other man could do that better than oneself.

There was also the time factor. The more time Angus took to let Willie stew in his own juices, the worse things Willie could conjure up. Take the dirk. Angus would heat it until it was cherry red, but that didn't mean Angus would use it on him right away; or at all, for that matter. Just another scare tactic. But Willie wouldn't know that. No, he'd try to second guess Angus; try to anticipate what he'd use the dirk for. The fear factor.

Suddenly, Angus got up, walked over to Willie and calmly kicked him hard in his broken arm. Willie let out a bloodcurdling scream, and as if nothing had happened, Angus returned to the log and sat down.

Gregor looked at Angus with a new appreciation in his eyes. He may have wanted to kill Willie himself for what the little man put him through, but watching this was just as enjoyable. He waited with delighted anticipation to see what would happen next.

❧

A short time had elapsed and the camp settled a bit. Just then, Angus got up again, charging the atmosphere of the camp. Willie sat up a little straighter against the tree. His arm was numb and the sweat poured from his body, giving off an odor of sickness and fear.

This was the last thing he expected from Angus Robertson. Gregor, yes, but Angus always had a soft streak when it came to this sort of thing. Angus always said that with patience, he could get a man to talk about anything. One never had to resort to barbarous violence.

Now, Willie saw Angus rise and start towards him again, tensing for whatever came next. He watched the big man grab his plaid like a mitt, and remove the dirk from the embers. Angus held it up, inspecting it. It was a brilliant glow of iron.

Angus walked passed Willie to somewhere behind the tree where he was tied. Now the fear factor was brought to a new high. Not only were no questions asked of him, but Angus had a glowing blade and was out of his range of vision. What could he do back there to hurt him? Only his hands were back there. What … ?

Before Willie finished the thought, he found out what Angus was doing back there. Pain seared through him, the likes of which he had never known. His eyes were wild and disbelieving. He opened his mouth to scream, yet nothing came out. Angus emerged from behind the tree to show Willie his handiwork. On the end of Willie's own dirk blade was his own finger. It was the last thing he saw before blackness enfolded him.

৵

The night sounds were obliterated by cheers when Angus held the blade high with the still-twitching finger on the end of it, and let out his own roar of release. All the men rose to their feet clamoring for a look. Gregor pounded Angus on the back, laughing at the spectacle. Walking over to the fire, Angus threw both dirk and finger into the flames, then went back to sit on the log.

"What will ye do next, Angus?" asked Andrew.

Angus turned to look at his friend, just realizing he wasn't alone. For a moment, Andrew was unsure Angus heard him, and was just about to repeat the question, when Angus said "Wait 'til mornin'. I'm verra tired." Angus sat down at the base of the nearest tree, rolled up in his plaid and went to sleep.

"It's been a long, hard day for him," Gregor said to Andrew's back. "I'm sure he wilna remember this in the mornin'. This isna Angus' way, but I like it fine."

"What do ye think he'll do to Willie in the mornin'?" Andrew asked, ever taking his eyes off of Angus, who was already sleeping.

"He has Willie so scairt now, he can probably ask him where the rents are and actually get the truth out o' him," Gregor chuckled.

Andrew smiled, found a tree near Angus, rolled up in his own plaidie, and did his best to get some sleep. Norman and Tommie were settling in to get some sleep of their own. Gregor was the only one too enlivened to rest, so he volunteered to keep a watchful eye.

ઢ

Morning began in a light mist. The sky was obscured by fog, yet an eerie yellow glow shone through. Angus opened his eyes when he felt drops of water dripping from his thick hair and run down his neck. At first, he was unsure of where he was. He didn't want to move; to bring back what was already filtering in from his subconscious. He squeezed his eyes shut, pressing water droplets from his lashes, trying to keep it from coming back.

Isobel.

His heart gave a huge lurch in his chest.

Isobel.

She was gone. What was he going to do without her? What were his sons going to do without her? Cat ... oh, God! Would Cat blame herself for this? He knew how hard she tried to find a cure for her mother. Then she saw this all happen. How could she take all this? Christ! She was only twelve years old! How could she take all this?

Angus sat up, still wrapped in his plaid, and stared off in the direction of *Slios Mìn.* From behind him, he heard his men talking quietly and starting breakfast. They all stayed away from him, sensing his need to be alone. Even Andrew, who spent the night not three feet away, got up without a word to him.

He needed a clear head before interrogating Willie as to the whereabouts of the rents. It wouldn't be easy. Willie may be impossible to crack, he thought.

When he walked over to check on Willie, he noticed the closer he got, the wider Willie's eyes got. The sheer terror that came over Willie's face seemed very odd. Why was he acting this way? Had Gregor told him something to scare him so? Well, good. Maybe getting the information he needed wouldn't be so difficult after all.

In a replay of last night, he squatted down in front of Willie, smelling the stench of his fear. Willie's face was pale and he was shivering with fever.

"What do ye want from me?" Willie asked in a pathetic tone.

"I want to ken where Alexander's rent money is." Angus said coldly.

A look of total disbelief came over Willie's face at this. "Ye what?"

"Ye heard me. I'll no' repeat myself to ye. Where is it?"

"That's what ye hae been huntin' me for; the rents I stole from a sleepin' giant almost one year last?" he said in taunting voice loud enough for Gregor to hear.

"Seems a new day makes this wee man a bit cocky, Angus," Gregor said behind him. "Maybe we should put another dirk in the coals and work on him some more, aye?"

Angus turned to face Gregor with a questioning look, confirming Gregor's suspicions that there would be no recollection of last night's events. Angus had been functioning in shock, but before Gregor could explain, Willie voiced his opposition.

"No, please. I dinna think I can take that again. Please. I'll tell ye," he pleaded.

Angus took Gregor aside out of hearing and demanded to know what went on last night.

"Weel, Angus, ye played him the only way a man like him deserves."

After giving a full description of what *did* happen last night, Angus wasn't sure he could continue those acts.

"Ye wilna hae to," Gregor whispered. "Look at him, he's cowerin' like a wee lamb. All ye hae to do is keep a hard eye and ask him where the rents are. He'll tell ye. He wants no more o' what ye gave him last night."

Angus composed himself for a moment before turning around. He wiped all emotion from his face, knowing the one thing that would bring back the hardness into his eyes was Isobel.

"Put the blade in the fire, Gregor," he said, sending a steely glance over Willie's way, then went and sat on the same log as the night before.

Gregor smiled and did as the laird requested. He did it with a little more relish than Angus would have, but the point was made. He spied a fresh bead of sweat on Willie's brow, indicating the act was still working. Willie would never know that Angus couldn't continue with what he started last night.

Angus was able to continue the silent treatment easily enough, and just stared at Willie. Andrew took the position on the log next to Angus for moral support. Shortly thereafter, Angus got up, and just like last night, grabbed the glowing dirk from the fire and walked around the back of Willie. Glimpsing his handiwork from the night before, he was thankful Willie couldn't see his face. He stood there hoping Willie would just tell him what he needed to know, but Willie remained silent. Angus bent down, roughly grabbed another finger, crushed it up against the tree, then pressed the searing blade up against it. Willie let out a scream.

"Where are the rents?" Angus demanded.

"Taymouth Castle ... please ..." Willie pleaded, breathing heavily.

Angus pressed harder on the finger; the hot blade made a hissing noise, the smell of burning flesh nearly overcoming him.

"Where?"

"What's left ... will be in ... the Chief's chambers," Willie growled between breaths.

"How many on guard?" Angus questioned.

"Ye'll ne'er ... get away wi' it," he said through gritted teeth.

Angus had no choice now. In slow motion, his blade went through the flesh and into the bone, making a sickening crunch. The finger fell to the ground, curling up like a worm. There was no sound from Willie. He must have passed out. Angus looked around to the front of the tree at Gregor, who still wore the smile on his face, to get confirmation of Willie's fate. Gregor just nodded, then Angus went back behind the tree and threw up.

Andrew heard the retching and brought a ladle of water. Angus looked up, almost as white as Willie, and said "I canna do that again."

"He'll be out for a spell, we hae enough information from him now anyway, dinna we?" Andrew asked.

"No," Angus said after a large gulp of water. "We still need the name of his other men."

They went back to sit on the log by the fire. The fog created a fine mist, and the heat from the fire felt good on Angus' legs. Gregor took a seat on the other side of Angus, rubbing his hands together over the flame; silent, yet still smiling. Angus stole a glance, and couldn't help but let out a little chuckle breath at the joy his friend exuded from all of this.

"Just one more time, Angus, that's all. Just find out who's been helpin' him and then I'll finish him," Gregor said, totally serious now.

"I hope he stays out for a long time. I'll need that time to work myself up to it again, *mo charaid.*"

"Who do ye think the man could be?" Andrew asked both men. "I dinna ken of anyone who uses a bow and arrow, do either of ye?"

Angus stared into the fire, not hearing.

Gregor just shrugged. To him it didn't matter. He knew where the rents were and vowed to return them to Alexander to get his old job back. One thing still puzzled him though, and that was how he slept so soundly that day in the tower. Sure, he had a few ales — it was the Games, after all — but he certainly wasn't drunk. He could never have slept heavy enough not to hear someone climbing the stairs. He'd ask Willie when he woke up.

❧

It was quite a while before Willie started stirring. Angus took his cue, getting back into torture mode. He hoped fervently this would be the last of it.

"Do ye want to answer me now, or do I need to repeat the performance, Willie?" Angus asked, holding the cold dirk in front of Willie's unfocusing eyes.

"Please … no more … what was … the question?"

"How many guards?"

"Eight."

"Now that wasna so hard, was it? Who else was helpin' ye in my house?"

"Fergal Menzies, that's all."

Angus almost dropped the blade. It was a good thing Willie wasn't all together at the moment, or he would have seen the look of surprise on his face. Angus stood and turned his back to Willie. Fergal? Oh, Christ, that's right! He should have remembered that Fergal used a bow and arrow, but why would he help Willie do this? He was quite convinced the man was harmless.

Angus walked over to the fire and squatted in front of it, rubbing his hands together, buying some time to think. Andrew caught the name and the look on Angus' face. He wasn't quite as convinced as Angus that Fergal was so harmless, and motioned for Angus and Gregor to talk in private.

They headed into the woods, well out of hearing range, and took their seats on a fallen tree. The first thing Gregor wanted to know was who Fergal Menzies was. Andrew explained about the molestations last year, and that it was Menzies who was doing it. He went on to explain that Angus had found out the reason, and gave the man a reprieve, so to speak. Angus had sent him to the Campbell's for work.

"I dinna understand why Fergal would do such a thing to our women," Angus said, picking off the bark from the large fir he was sitting on.

"He wouldna," came a voice out of the woods behind them, making all three of them jump.

They whipped around off the log; all three with their dirks and pistols ready. Fergal slowly emerged from his hiding place with his hands in the air.

"Ye had better explain, and quickly," Angus demanded, pointing his pistol squarely at Fergal's head.

"If Willie had his way, all yer women, and yer son would be dead now. He takes no prisoners. I convinced him that it wasna worth bein' hunted down by ye for the rest of his born days if he killed yer family. I also killed each of his men, as ye may recall," he said, slowly pointing to his bow that was slung over his shoulder.

"Almost got ye too," he continued, looking at Andrew, "by mistake. It wasna intentional. I did hit my mark, though."

"Aye, ye did at that," Andrew said coldly.

"So ye're tellin' us that ye were tryin' to undermine Willie's efforts to kill us?" Angus asked.

"Aye. Willie was boastin' about how he drugged a guard at Blair Castle last year at the Games, and stole the rents from under his nos ..."

"What?" Gregor cut him off before he could finish his explanation. "So that's why I was sleepin' so sound!"

"It was ye? Ye were the guard?" Fergal asked, in the cracking voice Angus remembered. He obviously used it when he was nervous.

Gregor stood a little taller, ready to kill the little man if he dared laugh at him.

Angus impatiently broke into the private conversation and asked, "Are ye familiar wi' Taymouth Castle, then?"

Fergal pulled his eyes from Gregor to look at Angus, and nodded.

"Was Willie tellin' the truth?"

"Aye, he was. I ne'er in my wildest dreams would hae thought Willie Campbell would break under any kind o' torture. He's a verra tough man. Cruel even, but ye kent how to get to him," Fergal smiled, appreciating the cunning it took to do what he did to Willie.

"I did what I had to do." He didn't know if Fergal knew of Isobel's fate or not, but didn't feel he had to mention it.

"What do we do wi' Willie now?" asked Andrew.

"If I may make a suggestion, Mr. Robertson?" Fergal asked.

Angus looked at him for a moment, debating on whether or not he needed a suggestion. He pretty much knew what had to be done with the man at this point.

"Go ahead."

"Kill him," Fergal stated simply.

That's pretty much what Angus had in mind to do anyway. If he let the man go, he would be the scourge of the Earth for him and his family. He also wanted retribution for Isobel's death.

"Gregor, ye hae the honors. Oh, and I dinna mean to be tellin' ye how to do yer business … but take yer time," Angus said tiredly, "I'm goin' home. Mr. Menzies, I can use ye at *Slios Mìn aig Aulich* if ye're lookin' for a job. I'll also need ye to help Gregor get the rents back from Taymouth Castle, if ye hae a mind for it. But first I hae to bury my wife."

the rest is silence

nna and Catrìona were startled awake at sunrise; both sat up straight in their beds breathing heavily. Catrìona looked over at Anna and asked if she saw it too.

"Aye, wi' frightenin' clarity, Garnet."

"Then it's true?" Cat asked in a defeated whisper, her eyes instantly misting over.

Anna got up and walked over to sit at the edge of Cat's bed ready to console her.

"Awe, lass," Anna cooed, taking Catrìona in her arms and rocking her gently. "I so hoped we could hae stopped it from happenin' to spare ye this grief."

Cat shook the bed with her sobs, and hung on to Anna as if she were the last person on Earth. Anna wept also, not for Isobel, but for Catrìona, knowing how much intent she gave to save her mother. How much of this would she blame on herself? How much would she blame on her father? Right now, the only thing clear was that Cat would be leaving for a while.

After a few minutes, Cat's sobbing turn to sniffles, then stopped altogether. This was the part Anna never cared for. She had called her *Garnet* for a reason when she awoke, never knowing what to expect from the young spitfire. For now, Cat was content to just be held and rocked. Anna didn't dare break the spell.

"Do ye think she suffered, Mistress?" Cat whispered.

"No, lass, I think she went verra quick."

"I wondered when I first saw it happen — so long ago it seems — whether it be better to die slow from her sickness, or to die quick from the fall. I wanted so much to help her get well again, now I fear my learnin' was all for naught," Cat said, pulling away from Anna's embrace to wipe her eyes and nose.

Anna took Catrìona by the shoulders and said "Lass, ye hae a gift. Ye dinna ken if it was only to help yer Mam or no', but one thing is for certain, what ye hae learned here was no' for naught."

Cat looked at her for a long moment, mentally assessing what she had learned in nearly a year and a half. She knew most of the plants that grew in the area, and what they were used for medicinally. Watched new life be brought into the world, then come full circle to watch it be taken away. Learned how to communicate telepathically and see into the future. She learned how to communicate with the dead ...

She had no more than completed that thought, when she realized she could still talk with her mother, just on a different level now. She looked at Anna with epiphany in her wide amethyst eyes.

"Why not?" was all Anna had to say, reading Cat's thoughts.

Cat stayed on the bed, her mind racing in every direction, her fingers twisting her dark locks. After a few minutes, she sent Anna a tortured look and said "I dinna ken what to say to her," and the tears started fresh.

Anna stroked Catrìona's long auburn hair, the sun catching it now, turning it to liquid fire. The deep claret, cinnabar, black, and burgundy running down in thick waves past Cat's waist had a mesmerizing effect.

"Did yer Mam like to brush yer hair?" Anna asked, spreading the dark flames out over Cat's shoulders.

At the memory of her mother brushing her hair every morning, Cat stopped crying.

"Aye, she did," Cat said in a wispy voice. Closing her eyes, she recalled how it felt and the conversations they would have while *making ye look lovely,* as her mother used to call it.

In what appeared to be a dream, Cat saw her mother standing beside her bed, still flesh and blood. Cat opened her eyes to be sure she wasn't dreaming. She wasn't. She reached out her hand and her mother grasped it. It wasn't the same as her mother's real touch, but she had made a connection.

"Did it hurt, Mam?" Cat asked out loud.

"No, lass, I felt nothin'," Isobel said to her daughter, then walked around the back of Catrìona to take over the duty of brushing her hair.

"Why didna Da get to ye on time?"

"Och, he tried, but was just a wee bit too late to stop what was meant to be. Seumas is takin' it verra hard. They'll be blamin' themselves, and I need ye to let them ken there was naught anyone could hae done to change the outcome … no' even ye. Ye'll need to be strong for them, Cat." Isobel said, pausing in mid-stroke for emphasis.

"I dinna ken how ye can say that, Mam. I saw it all happen. I told Lachlan and Iain about it, I made Da see it. There should hae been one o' us who could hae stopped it," Cat said, getting slightly agitated.

"I kent it was comin' too, Cat."

"Ye did? How?" Cat asked and turned to face her mother, unmindful of her mother *making her lovely.*

"I had been feelin' so much better of late, but kent I would die from my sickness before the year was over. The night yer Da left to find Willie Campbell, I kent somethin' wasna right. I didna want him to leave, but o' course Alexander bade it, so he had to go. A feelin' come o'er me that I couldna explain, still canna," she said. "I just kent I wouldna live to see yer Da again."

The tears started forming in Cat's eyes again, and ran down her cheeks.

"Dinna cry, *mo nighean mhaiseach,* this will no' be the hardest thing in yer life. I need ye to be strong for our men. I'll love ye always; I'll be wi' ye always. Ye only hae to whisper in yer heart and I'll be here for ye, but for now, ye need to get home," Isobel said, touching her daughter's tear-stained cheek. "I'm in a good place, Cat." Then slowly she faded before Cat's eyes.

Catrìona sat on the edge of her bed, staring at where her mother just sat, unable to assure herself that she had been really there. A moment later, Anna brought her a cup of tea. Cat looked up at Anna pleading with her eyes for the truth, Anna just nodded. Cat gave her a shaky smile.

❧

Catrìona was sure Lachlan didn't know about their mother yet. Cat packed up her clothes in her satchel, said a teary good-bye to

Anna, and walked the longest mile in her life to the castle. She told Anna she expected to be back before the snow came; hopefully this was enough time for her family.

As Cat neared the castle, glowing white in the mid-day sun, she pondered what she would do with her life now. She still had the Sight, but what would she use it for now? Did she want to be like Anna and work for the Chief, taking Anna's place when she died? She hoped fervently that wouldn't happen for many years to come. She wanted to continue learning about healing people; it made her feel good when she was able to help someone's pain go away.

Before she knew it, she was at the front entrance of the castle. She walked in and went straight to the kitchen. If anyone knew where Lachlan was, it was Mrs. Macgregor. Lachlan was never away from food for too long; he was a growing lad and perpetually hungry.

As luck would have it, Lachlan was just finishing his lunch in the company of Mrs. Macgregor, who was elbow deep in bread dough. She looked up when Cat walked in the room, and a big smile came over her face. Lachlan hadn't seen her come in, his back was to the door. He noticed Mrs. Macgregor smiling at something, and assumed someone walked into the room. Still chewing the last bite of his cheese, he nearly choked when he saw her standing there.

Cat smiled and pounded his back to get him to stop coughing. Red-faced and still coughing a little, he asked what she was doing there. Cat's smile froze on her face, unsure of how she would tell him.

"What's wrong, lass?" Mrs. Macgregor asked when she saw Cat's expression change.

Cat needed to sit down, so she took the chair next to Lachlan facing Mrs. Macgregor.

"It's Mam," she said, looking down at her hands. She knew if she saw either of their faces, especially Lachlan's now, she wouldn't be able to tell them what happened without breaking down in tears.

Lachlan took her hands and gently coaxed the explanation out of her. Mrs. Macgregor wiped her flour-covered hands on her apron, and sat on the other side of Cat, listening intently as the story unfolded, which took some time to fully satisfy Lachlan's interrogation. At first he didn't believe it really happened, figuring Cat must have just had a bad dream, but when she told him that Anna saw the same thing at the same time, he had no choice but to believe her.

"We hae to go home, Cat. Alexander is at his house in Carie, hiding from the dragoons. They hae been harrying him fierce lately …"

"The bastards!" Mrs. Macgregor swore under her breath, forgetting who was in the room.

Cat and Lachlan raised their eyebrows, but said nothing, silently agreeing with her assessment of the *Sassenachs.*

"I'll go get some clothes together, and we'll leave immediately," Lachlan said, already getting up to leave the room. "Oh, Cat, would ye go out to the barn and ask Alasdair to saddle a couple o' horses for us? I'll be down shortly."

Catrìona was up and out of the kitchen at a trot, not hearing the rest of Mrs. Macgregor's profanities towards the English, or the Campbell's.

By the time Lachlan met her in the barn, Cat had just finished helping Alasdair get the two horses ready. She felt better now that there was something to occupy her. She hooked the straps of her satchel over the pommel and mounted the sorrel-colored horse, while Lachlan mounted the bay. They would ride straight on until they got home. Neither wanted to stop for the night.

As they got to the front gate, Mrs. Macgregor was waiting for them with a sack of food. "Ye dinna think I would let ye both go off on empty stomachs, did ye?" she asked, with a glint of humor in her dark eyes, looking mostly at Lachlan.

For most of the trip, Lachlan was quiet. Cat didn't feel much like talking either, but it would have made the ride a little shorter. At sunset, they stopped at the river to water the horses and give them a rest.

"Do ye think she's all right where she is now?" Lachlan asked in a little voice, not making eye contact with his sister.

"She told me she was in a good place, and when I saw her, she looked beautiful," Cat answered, trying her best to console him. "She said there was no pain."

Lachlan looked at Cat for a moment. "Ye look just like her, ye ken."

Intuitively, Cat walked over and hugged him. *Ye'll need to be strong for our men, Cat.* She only hoped *she* would be strong enough.

❦

The night fell around them in a heavy cloak of warm August air. In the dark, travel was very treacherous. The moors were dangerous places if you got caught out in them; day or night. The muddy bogs would suck the shoes right off your feet and prevent your horse from moving at all.

Lachlan was in the lead when Cat heard him stop. He obviously had heard something, and she strained her own ears to hear it as well. But she didn't need to hear who was coming down the path; she saw them in her mind. She reined her horse up to stand beside Lachlan's and whispered, "It's Seumas."

In the faint light of the crescent moon, she saw Lachlan turn towards her, and whispered back, "Are ye sure? There hae been lots o' dragoons about of late."

"I'm sure."

A few minutes later, two riders came up to within fifty feet before they stopped to ask who was there.

"Seumas?" Lachlan called.

"Lachlan? Is that ye out there?" Seumas called back, wondering if his ears were playing tricks on him.

"Aye. Me and Cat. Hae ye come to tell us about Mam?"

There was no response from Seumas, he and the other rider reined their horses towards them. As they got closer, Lachlan recognized Johnnie with his older brother. All four of them dismounted.

"I kent ye wouldna need me to bring ye home. I told Da that, too," Seumas said coldly.

"I saw it this morning at sunrise. Is that when it happened?" Cat asked, feeling his anger.

"Aye. We watched and could do naught to help her. We were too far away." He let out a jagged breath, as if trying to contain his feelings.

"Is there somethin' else yer no' sayin', Seumas?" Cat asked, tingling from the tension in the air.

It took a moment, but finally Seumas said "No. Naught else. Let's go home."

❧

Somewhere in the predawn hours of the next day, Catrìona, Seumas, Lachlan, and Johnnie arrived in front of the barn doors at *Slios Mìn*. Spent, but not wanting to wake the household, they unsaddled their horses, and bedded down in the loft. They would take the new day as it came, knowing that was all they could do.

The sound of a mouse chewing something beside Cat's ear was what woke her as the sun rose. She rolled over to check out the culprit who interrupted her slumber, and found herself literally eye to eye with a wee brown field mouse. It obviously didn't mind her presence, but she would have preferred to be somewhere else, like inside the house in a comfortable bed.

"Ye couldna wait one more hour before ye had yer breakfast in my ear?" she whispered to the mouse. It stopped chewing for a moment, as if contemplating her wish, but then merrily resumed its nibbling of the hay chaff it was so fond of. "No, I guess no', then. I dinna blame ye, I'm hungry too."

She sat up and pulled the straw from her hair, quietly climbed down the ladder and opened the barn door, instantly embraced by the warm morning sun. She stood there with her eyes closed for a minute, a smile of contentment on her face. She was home.

Opening her eyes when she heard footsteps approaching, the smile remained on her face when she saw Iain. His smile was a bit pained, but a smile just the same. Cat ran to her brother and hugged him fiercely; Iain stroked her long hair, pulling out the pieces of straw she hadn't reached.

"I thought I heard ye come in last night," Iain said.

"More like this mornin'. I feel like I hae no' slept a wink." Pointing to his bandaged head, she asked, "What happened?"

"I'll fill ye in later."

Voices behind her indicated Seumas and Lachlan were up. Lachlan and Iain huddled around Catrìona like bees to honey, picking off straw from the back of her dress. She had forgotten what it was like to be around them; how they always made sure she was doted on. She remembered how she used to love it, but now found it rather smothering.

Right on cue, as if sensing her best friend's needs, Janet came running out of the house at full speed to the rescue, screaming at the top of her lungs.

"Cat! Cat!"

Cat and Janet hugged each other in a fit of giggles. Her brothers just stood there listening to the beautiful, melodious sound of Cat's laughter. It had always been contagious, yet now had a different tone to it; or maybe it was just that they hadn't heard it in so long; or maybe they just really needed to hear it now. Whatever it was, they all had smiles on their faces when Cat and Janet let go of each other.

"Welcome home, Cat! Och, I hae missed ye so!" Janet said, squeezing Cat around the waist. "Dear Lord, I think ye hae grown three inches since I saw ye last," her head coming just to Cat's chest. "Are ye hungry? Let's all go hae some breakfast!" Giving Cat no time to answer, Janet led them all into the house like the pied piper.

૨

Word got around the highlands faster than one could imagine. Messengers were dispatched to bring Alexander from Carie, gather all the tenants from Angus' lands, and the lairds from the neighboring Robertson clans to honor Isobel Helen Macinroy Robertson.

Wakes were not entirely gloomy events. They were a celebration of the person's life, as well as the prevention of the spirit of the person from wandering or interfering negatively with the affairs of the living. Long laments were spoken by those who wanted to eulogize their friend or loved one, along with clapping of hands, wailing of women, and of course, whisky.

Angus, Andrew, Tommie and Norman arrived back at *Slios Mìn* at mid-morning. Gregor and Fergal stayed behind to see what else they could get out of Willie before he was put to death. Gregor promised he would be back before the Isobel's *caithris,* giving him more than a day to work on Willie.

Angus reined his horse just outside the barn where he met Iain. They met each others eyes, but neither had words to speak. The wounds were too fresh; one wrong utterance would crumble their shaky façades. Andrew understood their silence, but did not think that it applied to him, so he asked how Iain was feeling; if his head hurt much. Iain's reply, as he took the reins and headed into the barn, was simply that he was all right. Norman and Tommie stayed with Iain to help unsaddle and brush down all the horses.

Cat had just left the confines of the crowded, noisy house when she saw her father come out of the barn. When their eyes met, she felt the enormity of his pain. She ran into his embrace and held him for a long time. Pulling away just far enough to look at him, not ready to let him go just yet, she noticed that he seemed much older, and very tired.

"Are ye all right, Da?"

For a moment, she thought she saw his eyes darken, but he smiled weakly and said "I am now, lass, I am now," then pulled her against him again in a tight embrace before letting her go. "I'd better get to the house to see about things."

"I just came from there. Trust me, Da, e'erything's under control."

When Angus and Andrew went into the house, it was a feery-fary of women cooking and baking. Obviously, Mòrag and Lizzie had already spread the word, and the preparations were well under way for Isobel's wake. Angus sat heavily at the kitchen table, letting out a long sigh. Mòrag and Janet were still hanging on to Andrew for dear life, weeping with relief that he was home safely. It was Maggie who walked over to Angus, and quietly put her arms around his neck to hold him for a minute. He was deeply touched. He patted her shoulder and mumbled his thanks for her thoughtfulness. When she let him go, he caught Lizzie's eyes and just nodded, indicating he was all right.

He walked into the best room, where Isobel was wrapped in a shroud, and laid out on a table surrounded by flowers. His heart stopped, he swore it did. He wasn't prepared for this at all, and was unable to move from the doorway into the room. He just stood there staring at her wrapped form. All the noise from the kitchen had gone silent, he saw nothing around him except Isobel. He never felt the tears stream down his face; he never felt himself crumple to his knees to the floor; he never felt so alone in his life. He hung his head and silently begged her forgiveness.

There's naught to forgive ye for, Angus. This was meant to be. I canna tell ye why just now, but ken that this was for the better.

Angus just nodded, then realized the voice he heard in his head was from Isobel. It startled him for a moment, but the feeling of her was so overwhelming, he couldn't move. "Is it really ye speakin' to me, my love?" he said out loud.

At first there was no answer, but then he heard her again in his head. *Yer daughter will explain it all. And we will see each other again.*

He remembered telling her that when he put his hand on her head in the wagon. She *had* heard him! *Cat would explain it all.* He wondered what that meant. Just then, he heard footsteps coming down the hall, and realized he was on his knees. He wiped away the wetness from his eyes and stood up.

"Shall I leave ye for awhile, *mo charaid?*" Andrew asked softly from behind him.

"No ..." Angus cleared his throat and tried again. "No, come in man. I was just speaking wi' her."

"Wi' who, Angus? There's no one in ..." Andrew stopped mid-sentence, suddenly realizing that Angus meant to Isobel. Andrew was a superstitious man who greatly feared the unknown. Truth be told, he greatly feared Catrìona. He had no understanding of the other side, that the energy of our loved ones walks with us everyday behind an invisible veil that most cannot see through. For those few who are able to see through it, such as Catrìona — and maybe even Angus now — well, he didn't understand how they just didn't go insane. Andrew could actually *feel* Isobel's presence in this room. He wasn't sure if he was imagining it or not, but he couldn't stay! Without a word, Andrew backed out of the best room and quickly walked down the hall into the kitchen, where things were normal, where his wife and daughter were, where life was.

Angus was too preoccupied to notice that Andrew had left. He was in his own world, the one where Isobel still *was.* He stayed there for a long time, just staring at her wrapped body, and letting the spell of the flower-scented room take him. Shortly before sunset, Iain joined him; silent, yet feeling the same presence as his father. Both were content to be where she was until it got too dark to see, then they both lay down on the floor and fell asleep.

❧

Family by family, they started arriving for the *caithris,* and soon *Slios Mìn* was filled to the brim with them. Alexander, with his chieftans and lairds, was in the barn talking politics; each wondering how safe it was for Alexander to be there. The dragoons had been seen lurking around Dùn Alasdair, his second house. The Hermitage at Carie was so run down they probably didn't think anyone would be living there; a good enough place to hide out.

For two days people arrived and camped where they could. Food, ale and whisky were in abundance. They were all gathering outside now, waiting for the sun to set. Isobel's body had been moved back into the wagon to make her final trip to be buried in the ancestral cemetery of the Robertsons; about a mile away under an enormous oak tree. Once there, laments and eulogies would be spoken, tears would be shed, and the Christians among them would say prayers, asking her to stay where she was buried.

As the procession began, Catrìona held onto her father's arm, her brothers walked behind, and Alexander behind them. There were nearly two hundred people there to pay their respects to Angus and his family. About halfway to the cemetery, Angus looked down at Cat and noticed she was smiling. He gave her a little nudge to let her know this was to be a somber time, not one for merriment. Cat looked up at her father and whispered what she had been smiling about.

"Mam just told me that she is verra pleased wi' the turnout."

Angus stared at her, speechless. The look he gave Cat crushed her heart. Cat reached up and put her hand on her father's cheek. Angus gave her a shaky smile, the only reply he could give.

Dusk was upon them as they reached the cemetery. Andrew, Gregor, Donald, and Malcolm lifted Isobel's frail body from the wagon and gently placed her into the ground. Angus and his family moved to surround Isobel's last resting place. Cat had gathered some wildflowers earlier in the day and now sprinkled them over her mother. The vibrant colors were so alive on the linen shroud. Cat was smiling again, but Angus asked her to wait, he wasn't ready for what his wife was saying this time. He told her he wanted to recite a poem first, then cleared his throat and began.

> Isobel's heart is lonely tonight,
> It has been closed to music and merriment.
> The fairy-mound is like an exile
> Without music, a company of singers, or visitors.
> Without a harp made of fragrant wood,
> Without an historian, or baird
> Without laughter or melodious women.
> O, young Isobel, who was taken before her time,
> To speak of you is a weighty matter.
> We will think of you always
> Walking the places you loved.
> Sorrowful is the group that surrounds you.

Cat stared at her father as tears fell from her long lashes. Never before had she heard her father speak so tenderly. She reached her arms around his neck and whispered, "She'll love ye forever, Da."

A few families came over to give their condolences, while most of the others went back to the house. Angus and his family stood in the fading light; silent, although Cat could hear all of the their thoughts as if spoken aloud. *Ye'll need to be strong for our men, Cat,* her mother had said and again she wondered if she herself would be strong enough.

In the darkness, Angus took hold of Cat's arm and quietly asked, "Was she here the whole time?"

Cat couldn't see her father's face, yet somehow knew the anticipation he wore in his eyes.

"Close yer eyes, Da, and call up her face." She gave him a moment. "Do ye see her?"

"Aye," he whispered, unsure if his mind was playing tricks on him or not.

"Now, just listen. Let yer mind remember her voice, then listen to what she wants to tell ye." Cat laid her hand on her father's big chest, she could feel his heart beating fast. She opened her own mind to become a conduit for her parents so they may have one last visit.

Angus, I told ye earlier that my death now was for the better. The reason is simple. The world is changin' fast and I canna bear what will be comin' to ye all. I would only become more of a burden, and ye will hae plenty to take care of soon. I ken that bad things are comin', but dinna ken when they will begin. Catrìona will ken soon enough. I just want one promise from ye, Angus, and that's to no' let our sons fight in any rebellion, it'll only bring heartache to ye.

I canna say more, they are waitin' for me, just ken that I await the time when we can both share our love once again. Until then, live yer life and ken that I'm always in yer heart.

Cat took her hand from her father's chest and put it up to his face. She could feel that he wore a smile. Through her own tears, she smiled as well, knowing she had made the connection for him.

"Thank ye, Cat," he choked, then turned and started walking home.

Catrìona had to stop her brothers from going with him. She told them what their mother said and that he would need some time alone. Cat walked home in silence after her brothers. It wasn't until she was in sight of the house that she heard Seumas speak in an unmistakably bitter tone.

"How can we keep that promise to Mam?" he said to his brothers.

"It would take a verra outnumbered rout against us for me no' to fight," Lachlan said.

"Aye, and an idiot commander wi' no knowledge of war for me to stay out," Iain stated, as if it were inconceivable for that to happen.

"Cat, ye'll let us ken what will happen, aye?" Lachlan asked.

Cat was too preoccupied thinking about how her brothers dismissed their mother's warning so quickly. Lachlan repeated his question to her, and yet she still only heard the last couple of words.

"What?" she asked, realizing Lachlan was speaking to her.

"Ye will tell us what will happen?" he asked for the third time.

"Och, aye. Ye'll be the first to ken, but please think about Mam's warnin'. She wouldna say things from the grave to ye to be let go of so quick."

Iain and Lachlan shuffled their feet in the dirt, glad for the darkness to hide their reddening faces. Had it been light enough, she would have seen Seumas' blatant disdain for her at that moment. None of them thought of it as a dying wish from their mother, and none of them would give thought of it again until events unfolded.

part two

Blair atholl, scotland

hogmanay 1744

PRELUDE TO WAR

Catrìona smiled when she opened her eyes, remembering it was the eve of a new year — her seventeenth year. This morning she decided to treat herself to some leisure time under the covers of the warm bed. She lay in her cocoon thinking of the events the day would bring.

The sun had not quite risen, but the sky was the color of heather blossoms, promising to be overcast for the day, but hopefully no snow. No matter, she would be meeting her father and brothers tonight at the castle for the Hogmanay feast and divination, whatever the weather.

After her third year of living with Anna and learning the ways of Second Sight, she moved back home to *Slios Mìn*. However, one week every month, weather permitting, Cat would make the long trip to Anna's, not only for further learning, but for a woman's company — a mother's company. She was at Anna's now — as usual during all the feasts — to help prepare for the divination. Anna still did all the readings for Alexander; not that he didn't trust Cat's visions, it's just that Anna had always done them, and superstition ruled.

Lying quiet, Cat listened to the comfortable silence of the house, and could tell by the deep, even breathing that Anna was still asleep. At one hundred and three — give or take a year or two — Anna slept more and more. The decline had begun.

They talked about that day once before. Anna told Cat she would choose her own time and place to die when she had completed what she was put on Earth to do. Cat always figured she would see it happen, as with her mother, but still hoped it would not be anytime soon.

During the six years Cat studied with Anna, she learned more than she thought possible; though still not the Tarot. But then, Anna always said she would rather get the answers like Cat did any day, she just did not possess that power. Cat's more direct method resulted in the same answers, with even more clarity and depth. There was no deciphering of who, where, how, or sometimes even when. Cat got specific, accurate answers when asked nearly every time.

As if knowing she was being thought of, Anna woke with a snort, signaling the end of Cat's languishing time. There was plenty to do for the day that wouldn't get done from bed, so Cat slipped out from under the bedclothes and got dressed.

"*Ciamar a tha thu sa mhadainn an-diugh, a Chatrìona?*" Anna asked groggily from the edge of her bed, her hair all a-fluff around her head in a halo.

Cat ignored the greeting, frustrated by her corset strings.

"Why do we put ourselves through this e'ery day, Mistress? For what purpose does it serve us to hae a waist the size o' a wean's? And I canna be the only woman to e'er complain about it. Somethin' must be done to change this ridiculous fashion, I canna even breathe!" she fumed.

Anna got up from bed, grabbed the strings and gave them a good yank, forcing any air left in Cat's lungs to be expelled with a gasp. Anna seemed to find this quite amusing. Cat did not.

"Why do ye bother wi' them, Cat? I ne'er wear one," she said proudly, looking at her reflection in the looking glass.

"Christ O'Jesus, Mistress. I already hae enough trouble keepin' men away wi'out runnin' around loose."

Anna broke into fits of giggles, remembering Cat's run-ins with smitten boys — and now men — vying for her attention.

Cat put her fists on her tiny waist in a vain attempt to stay mad, but always found Anna's laughter too contagious to resist. She joined in with her demented mentor and finished dressing.

٭

It was late afternoon when Alexander's carriage came by to fetch Anna and Cat for the feast and divination. They went directly to Alexander's chambers to do a preliminary assessment of the new year.

Anna worked with her Tarot cards at the table and Cat sat in her favorite chair in the semi-darkness of the other side of the room.

Before Cat could even get herself comfortable, images of huge, frothy waves on the sea — like those she had seen in paintings — were appearing in her mind's eye. Storm-ravaged ships were pummeled by the winds of winter and tossed onto the rocks; men and provisions were swept into the icy waters and lost.

After a few minutes of seeing this same scenario played out three times, Cat attempted to find out where the ships were coming from, and where they were bound. Having never seen the sea, she wondered what any of this had to do with her.

Question after question was presented to no avail; the interrogation needed new input. Anna was about to begin a new spread, so Cat went over and sat across from her.

"A word wi' ye, Mistress?"

"What is it, Cat?" Anna asked, flipping over the first card.

Cat laid her hand over Anna's and gave her the vision. Anna stopped all movement as the scene played out in her mind. When it was over, she sent Cat a tortured look and whispered, "It's begun."

"What's begun?"

"The rebellion."

Cat inhaled sharply, remembering her mother's last words to her father.

"What sort o' madman would attempt to send a fleet o' ships across the sea in the heart o' winter?" Cat asked, getting a pit in her stomach. If King James ordered this, how would this folly possibly win Scotland back?

"Did ye ken why ye saw it play out thrice?" Anna asked.

"Please tell me it wasna because it will happen three times," Cat said shaking her head, unable to comprehend how after seeing the first attempt fail in such disaster, why two more attempts would be made in winter.

"This is indeed a bad omen, Cat. If this is meant to surprise the English, it will only surprise them to ken how foolish 'twould be to take any thought o' a rebellion by the Scots seriously."

"Aye. But at least there wilna be a rebellion. Not wi' all hands lost before they e'er set foot in Scotland. Were they French, Mistress?"

"I dinna ken, but 'twould seem the most likely place to start from. We must give this information to Alexander immediately. I dinna want to wait 'til tonight."

"I'll go fetch him," Cat said, then added, "See if yer wee cards will tell us when this will all occur." Then she bolted from the room.

⁊❧

"And you say it will be tried thrice and each time in winter?" Alexander asked, rubbing his temples. He had started drinking earlier than normal today and the sweetened concoction had gotten to him. Unable to think clear enough because of it, he recited:

"Why have the powerful gods designed

Their likenesses so weak,

That what we drink to ease our mind

Should make our temples ache?"

He paced around the room rubbing his head, severely agitated. "Why have I not heard of this plan? Do they not know that strategies must be readied here? We still do not know who is on whose side, for God's sake!"

Anna and Cat relayed all the information they had attained, even managing to get approximate dates when the ill-fated attempts would be made.

"They'll first set sail in early February, then early March, and the final attempt will be launched at the end o' March. Each endeavor will be thwarted by a gale, and by the last attempt, all backing will be pulled from the cause," Anna relayed.

"I hae one more bit o' information, Alexander," Cat said.

"Well, speak up, lass," he said, downing the last of his whisky in a single gulp.

"It's no' King James leadin' this rebellion — although he's still makin' the plans — 'tis his eldest son, Charles, Prince o' Wales."

At that, Alexander threw his glass into the fireplace and stormed out of the room.

⁊❧

By the end of April, word finally reached Scotland that a rebellion had failed yet again, occurring exactly as Cat and Anna had seen it. To Angus, it was a blessing. Once Seumas, Iain and Lachlan heard what Cat had seen, they were ready to begin the fight, with or without the Prince being in Scotland.

"I canna believe ye still disregard Mam's last words," she scolded the three of them. "And Seumas, ye wi' yer new wife of only two months. What does she think o' ye goin' off to get killed?"

"She has little to say about it, doesna she," he growled, "And since there wilna be a rebellion, what does it matter?"

"Are ye daft, man? Hae ye no' been hearin' my warnings — Mam's warnin'? Christ! What will it take? I swear ye all must be thinkin' wi' yer *prigs* instead o' yer heids!" Her face grew an angry scarlet and her eyes turned deep amethyst.

"Now, now, there's no cause to be usin' profanities on us," Iain said, not sure whether he was hurt or scandalized by his sister's vulgar terminology. Lachlan, on the other hand, tried to hide the smirk on his face by pretending to cough. Cat saw right through him and cuffed him along side his head, just to let him know it was not meant to be humorous.

"Hey, that hurt," he said, rubbing his head.

"I dinna ken how it could hae hurt ye, there's naught inside o' that thick skull — yours or your brothers'. I dinna ken why I even waste my breath on ye." With daggers in her eyes she glared at the three of them, then stormed off.

Later, after she had cooled down, she found Seumas alone in the barn. She really wanted to hear it from his lips. Hear the reason he despised her. Still feeling that old unreasonable blame towards her, she didn't believe that was all there was to it. Coming up behind him, she saw him rubbing his leg, knowing that certain times of the day, it hurt more than others. She walked in front of him and stared at him. He matched her gaze with disdain in his eyes.

"Why do ye do exactly the opposite o' what I tell ye, Seumas? Dinna ye believe me after all that has happened?" Cat asked, getting angry again.

Seumas just looked at her for a moment. Cat could feel his turmoil, his hatred, his indecision whether to speak to her or not. Finally, he gave in and let all the years of pent-up anger spill in an emotional release.

"Ye did this to me!" Angrily pointing to his leg. "Ye made it happen. Ye made Mam die before her time, and just because ye dinna want us to fight, ye made the rebellion fail! If ye hadna said what ye saw, none o' it would hae happened. Ye made it all happen! Ye're naught but a witch, Catrìona Robertson!" He spat furiously on the ground at her feet.

Cat didn't know what to say. Her mouth opened and closed in a kind of shock, incredulous to hear such irrational thought.

"See, ye canna even deny what I hae said can ye?" he shouted, pounding his fist on the railing.

Without dignifying such rubbish with an answer, she whirled around and rushed out of the barn not looking back.

ॐ

After that, Cat refused to pass on another scrap of information to any of them. She couldn't decide whether she was truly angry with them, or just scared, but either way, she skirted them all so much that they barely spoke at all. The silent treatment was inflicted on them throughout the summer, with mealtime being the most awkward. Cat cooked their meals but ate alone in the kitchen. Only when they left the table would she return to clean up. None of them dared enter the kitchen, except Angus.

"How long do ye plan on treatin' them this way?"

"As long as they remain arses. They forget that I can read their minds and naught has changed in them," she said while washing dishes one night. She never told her father what Seumas said to her; how he felt about her.

"I hae tried to reason wi' them, but they're o' the thinkin' that since there wilna be a rebellion now, ye should give them quarter."

Cat turned to face her father, mindless of her hands dripping on the wooden floor, wearing a look that reminded him of Isobel when she was angry, and he smiled, despite the seriousness of the request.

"I'll no' forgive them," she promised, overlooking his smile. "Do they think he'll no' try again? The Prince wants to be King. He canna do that wi'out a kingdom, now can he."

She returned to her dishes, but before her father reached the door, she asked into the warm water, "Do ye really think I look like Mam?"

Angus stopped in mid-stride, and without turning, replied simply, "Aye," then left the room.

ॐ

As the summer melded into fall, the strained silence lessened, but speaking never returned to its former ease. One day, while Cat was milking the cow, Lachlan dared to enter the barn, knowing she was in there. Cat was deep in thought and didn't hear him enter until his footfalls right beside her gave his presence away and startled her back.

"I didna mean to give ye a fright," he said apologetically, taking a step back. "Can I talk to ye, Cat?"

She ignored him, keeping her head against the cow's belly, watching the rich milk squirt into the bucket. After a few moments, she realized he wasn't going to leave until he had his say.

"Aye, what is it?" she asked, in an annoyed tone.

"I miss ye."

Before Cat could say anything, he was gone. She smiled to herself. Ooh, he was good. He knew just what to say without any fluff or mushiness to make it sound false. Maybe nine months was long enough, she decided.

The week before her seventeenth birthday, before she left for Anna's for Samhain divination, Iain and Lachlan presented her with a small, plain wooden box as they sat down to dinner. She was a little skeptical of brothers bearing gifts. After all, she had just started speaking to them again. Seumas was conspicuously missing from the table.

Holding the smooth box in the palm of her hand, she glanced at both of them. They seemed genuinely pleased with themselves, so she dismissed any tomfoolery.

Slowly, she lifted the lid to find a small leather pouch inside. Laying the box on the table, she removed the pouch and loosened the drawstrings to open it. As she gingerly tilted the pouch into her hand, the contents struck her palm with a metallic weight. The silver ring was engraved with a heart-knot interlace pattern and topped with a garnet cabochon.

Her look was just as they hoped it would be; awestruck. Cat stared at them with tears in her eyes and her mouth wide open, unable to find her voice.

Both of them scraped together enough shillings to pay the clan silversmith to create a present which, as they requested, "begged her forgiveness."

"We remembered Mistress Macpherson callin' ye Garnet and hoped this would make ye aware that we love ye dearly, *a ghaoil mo chridhe*," Lachlan said, speaking for both of them.

Cat slid the ring onto her right ring finger and was dazzled.

"If I kent I would get such a rare fine piece o' jewellery for no' speakin' to ye, I'd hae been silent long ago," she whispered.

Angus, unaware of the ring's existence, wore just about the same look his daughter did, but laughed at Cat's comment. He took in his sons' pleased faces, just now realizing how much they missed their sister, and patted Lachlan's shoulder, knowing full well it was he who initiated this gesture. Lachlan smiled, but never took his eyes off Catrìona, as if in looking away, he would miss her approval.

"I dinna ken what to say, but if it's talkin' ye want, it's talkin' ye'll get. 'Tis beautiful. Thank ye," she said, giving them both hugs of appreciation.

☙

The winter passed uneventfully, though a bit harsher than normal. Severe spring storms prevented Cat from travelling to Anna's, though they remained in contact telepathically. It was Beltaine, 1745, before Cat was physically able to return to Anna's.

"I wish ye would stay at the castle during the winter, Mistress," Cat said, unpacking her satchel for the week-long stay.

"Och, ye worry too much for such a young lass," Anna retorted. "I hae ne'er needed anyone but meself. Besides, Gregor checks in wi' me once a week to bring peat and an occasional rabbit. I get along just fine."

"Maybe so, but it would make me feel better to ken ye were watched o'er proper."

"When ye get to be my age and used to just yer own company, ye'll understand, but thank ye. Now, would ye make me some tea? 'Tis nice to be waited on sometimes."

"Hmmmm."

As Cat was making the tea, she started to feel very anxious. By the time she sat at the table with Anna, the feeling became overwhelming. Analyzing what possible disaster could appear so quickly, she glanced at Anna to see if it registered with her as well. Anna was as white as a sheet, alarming Cat even further.

"What's happenin', Mistress?"

Anna didn't answer … or couldn't. She just sat there with such horror on her face, Cat thought it was the end. She reached across the table to touch Anna's hand, hoping to make a connection to see the cause of the anguish. When Cat's fingers touched Anna's, a spark flew across the room, breaking Anna's trance.

"All is lost," she said in a tone so chilling, Cat was sure Anna had seen her own death.

"What is it, Mistress? Are ye all right?" Cat repeated.

Slowly, Anna's eyes met Cat's and held them.

"Did ye no' see it?" she whispered.

"When I sat down to hae my tea, I was near out o' my mind wi' foreboding, but when I saw yer face, my concern was for ye. I thought ye were dyin', Mistress."

"I think it may be a good time to die."

"I dinna understand. Did ye see yer death?" Cat was convinced this was not the case, but was too confused by Anna's state to get to the truth.

Knowing Cat's overwhelming protective nature towards her, Anna gathered in her feelings to allow Cat to see what she saw.

"Try now, Garnet," she said, seemingly back to normal.

Cat released Anna's hand and went to the thinking window. Her hand instinctively reached for a thickness of hair to begin the twirling process. Slowly, she relaxed, letting the feelings diminish to clear her head. What she saw next was more than enough reason for the overpowering feelings she had moments ago.

Tears ran unchecked down her cheeks. She gasped at the brutality of the event, but could not quell the flow of images and feelings flooding into her head and heart. It all happened so fast, as if these men she knew all her life — strong, brave, fearless men — were sheep being led to the slaughter. It couldn't be real. It had to be some kind of mistake. Didn't it?

No matter how hard she tried to get out of the vision, the images drew her in deeper and deeper, until it was more than she could bear. Anna's knobby hand touched her shoulder when she started sobbing.

"Hush, lass, hush. Take some deep breaths and come sit at the table wi' me."

Cat allowed herself to be led back to the table, as if in slow motion, and took her seat. Anna gave her a few minutes to compose herself, waiting for the toot in the handkerchief before pursuing the comparison of visions.

Cat held onto the cooling tea cup with both hands; a grounding force to steady herself with.

"Ye saw the same as I, dinna ye, Mistress?" Cat asked in a mono-tone voice.

"Aye, judgin' from yer reaction, we did. 'Tis no' often that I see ye get that emotional anymore."

"How can it be stopped? It must be stopped. It'll be the end o' the clans if not. Christ, it'll be the end o' Scotland!"

A fire began burning inside of her. Everyone she knew would be affected by this, and no good would come of it. They must all be warned. She had to save her family. They would listen to her. They wouldn't fight after what she told them she saw.

Anna saw that Cat's resolve was even stronger now that she was older. There would be no changing her mind or talking her out of what she was planning. Cat would make it her mission to save her family, whether they could be saved or not.

ॐ

Alexander had indeed heard that the Prince was in no way going to let a rebellion be vanquished by the weather or removal of finan-cial backing. Rumors were spreading through the Highlands that Prince Charles would make another attempt at the Scottish throne, even if he had to come across the English Channel by himself.

"Can ye see when he'll try again to cross?" Alexander asked.

Anna worked her cards, but it was Cat that answered from her place in the darkened corner.

"Early July. And it will no' be an easy voyage."

Anna laid down her cards, letting Catrìona describe her vision in full detail.

"There will be a battle at sea wi' three ships. I see a woman tryin' to save them. How is that possible?"

Anna was tuned into Cat's mind and said "A ship wi' a woman's name."

With that piece of the puzzle solved, and without missing a beat, Cat continued.

"The ship wi' the woman's name holds the men, arms and pro-visions, and it will be badly damaged in the fray. Charles will think that all is lost once again."

"Will the Prince make it to Scotland?" asked Alexander.

"His destination was ne'er to be Scotland, it was Ireland. But I also see that he wilna make it to Ireland."

Cat felt Alexander tense, mistakenly assuming the Prince would be lost at sea.

"The Hebrides," she said, clarifying the location.

☙

Angus was summoned to Alexander's chambers, along with the other lairds and chieftains attending the feast, including the Jacobite Duke of Atholl, Tullibardine, who was at the castle. There they spent the night making strategies to commit the clan to the Prince in the rebellion. During the entire night, Cat gave as much information as she could, but never once spoke to her father. An underlying tension ran through them that only Anna caught. By sunrise, oaths were taken by the chieftans and lairds to commit their men to the Jacobite cause and Prince Charles.

Catrìona left before the oath-taking. She would not sit idly by after telling the roomful of clansmen what she had seen, and go along with their cause. She had to get to her brothers before they heard of this, or she feared they too would get caught up in man's irrational excitement for war.

Anna found Cat in the Great Hall speaking with her friend Janet. Catching Cat's eye, Anna motioned for a meeting.

"What will ye tell yer brothers, Garnet?" she asked.

"I'll tell them if they fight, they'll die on the battlefield. One should only hope that will get their attention," Cat answered, flustered at her inability to locate them in the throng of people.

"What about yer Da?" Anna asked.

"I understand why he feels it's his duty, being a laird and all, but I'm hopin' to convince him no' to take an active role in the battle. The way he rides a horse, maybe he can courier instead o' fight, though I hold out little hope of it," she said, already knowing her pleas will fall on deaf ears.

Cat fondled the ring her brothers gave her, knowing how much it meant to them to remain a family. Maybe as a family, they could convince Angus to stay out of the battle.

"Will ye be comin' back wi' me?" Anna asked.

Cat was too preoccupied to notice the look Anna wore when she asked Cat that question.

"No, no' yet. I must find my brothers and get their solemn oaths that they wilna fight, and I dinna ken how long that will take. Do ye want me to call for the carriage?" Cat asked absently, still trying to locate her brothers.

"No, but dinna be long," Anna said in a strange voice.

Cat glanced over to Anna, but Anna had already turned and was walking away. At that same moment, Cat caught sight of Iain, and Anna was forgotten.

⁊⦿

The spring dawn came early, with no one sleeping during the eventful night. By mid-morning, Cat had promises from Iain and Lachlan that when they got home, they would all talk of what roles they would play in the rebellion, without fighting. Seumas was another matter.

"Are we all ready to go then?" Angus asked his brood.

"I'd like to say good-bye to Anna first," Cat said, wishing she didn't have to cut her stay short. "I'll be back within the hour. Is that all right wi' ye, Da?"

"Aye. It'll take us that long to saddle the horses and say our own good-byes."

With that, Cat was off. When she opened the front door, the air was cool on her face and smelled of fresh earth, grasses and rain. She walked down the carriage trail that led to Anna's cottage noticing that the mountains were shrouded in clouds. She felt better now that most of her family would listen to her about the rebellion, and her steps were light.

About halfway there, Cat was hit with an urgency to get to Anna's. She lifted her skirts and quickened her pace to a jog. Before she got to the crossroads, Cat knew Anna was telling her something was wrong.

"No, no, no!" The words tore from her lips in anguish "Ye canna leave wi'out me!" she shouted, and sprinted the rest of the way.

Cat burst through the door to find Anna lying in bed on her side with the covers up around her neck, unmoving. Kneeling on the floor, Cat gently pushed the bedclothes down and heard Anna moan softly.

With all her willpower, Anna lifted her hand. Cat grabbed it and held it tightly, placing it on her cheek.

"I waited as long as I could for ye, lass," Anna whispered.

"Why didna ye tell me ye were leavin', Mistress?" Cat pleaded. "I would hae seen ye home to be wi' ye."

"Yer place was wi' yer family."

"But, ye are my family."

"Then say good-bye, daughter."

Anna closed her eyes and exhaled a last breath, her hand slackening against Cat's cheek. Tears welled up in Cat's eyes, making her vision blurry as she kissed Anna's hand and placed it gently on the bed.

"'Tis no' good-bye, Mistress, for I ken I'll see ye again."

For a long time, Cat stood at the window where she had learned so much — saw so much. She knew this day would come, it was inevitable, after all. Yet, there is no easy way to leave or be left. Life continues without a pause. What's left is memory. But if you're lucky, conversations can still be carried on for awhile.

Cat wiped her eyes and looked around the small cottage, all clean and cozy. She noticed a rolled parchment on top of a box on the table, and walked over to see what it was. The parchment had Cat's name on it in a fine script. She unrolled it and read Anna's last words.

Dearest Catrìona,

It was time for me to depart from this place. My time, and my reason for being, has been fulfilled. I have ye to thank for that. Ye made my last years a joy to live. I can see the changes that this rising will bring, and I fear none of them are good, so I choose today to die.

Inside the box is a gift to ye. So long ago, I do not recall now, I received this as payment for predicting a profitable outcome for Tullibardine, the Duke of Atholl. I wanted so to give it to ye on yer next birthday, but alas, I cannot wait that long. I ken it will suit ye.

Yer most humble teacher,
Anna

"Mistress, ye had this well planned, didna ye?" she said, the tears starting fresh.

Cat picked up the dark red wooden box, polished to a warm glow. It was heavy and about eighteen inches long, six inches wide and four inches deep. She ran her fingers over the smooth surface, making a circle around the brass inlay engraved with Anna's name.

"The box alone speaks of royalty," she spoke out loud.

Lifting the brass clasp, she opened it. Inside was lined with purple velvet, and resting in the velvet nest lay the most beautiful dirk she had ever seen. This was a ceremonial dirk, encrusted with garnets on the silver pommel and at the ends of the short, curved quillons. It must have been worth a fortune.

She returned the box to the table, and with the care of lifting a newborn, picked the dirk out of its resting place. She held it in her hand, feeling its weight. It was not as long as her own utilitarian dirk, but it weighed about the same. Its balance was mastery.

"'Tis beautiful," she whispered. "Thank ye, Mistress."

At that moment, she felt a warm embrace, and she smiled, knowing it was Anna.

"Mistress, would ye mind terrible if I lived here from now on? Alexander will be needin' a Seer and I would so like to continue yer work."

Cat felt the embrace tighten and knew permission was granted.

"Now I just need to convince Da," she said to herself.

No sooner had she finished that statement, when she heard hoofbeats outside. Lachlan was coming to see what the hold-up was, and she went out to meet him.

Lachlan instantly knew something was wrong when he saw her tear-stained cheeks. He dismounted and walked over to meet her at the door.

"Anna has died," was all she said.

&

Being well-loved by all of the clan, nearly everyone stayed on a couple more days at the castle for Anna's *caithris*. The early May weather was cool and damp, making for a somber affair, but more people arrived daily. These newcomers were the tenants Anna had treated from the far outskirts of clan territory.

Cat helped Mrs. Macgregor with the shroud, and Anna was laid out in the Great Hall for all to pay their respects. Cat remembered many of these people as they filed in to touch or pray over Anna's body. Many came over to Cat afterwards to give her their condolences, and to tell her that they hoped she would continue in Anna's footsteps. She was truly touched by their acceptance. As a rule, Scots are skeptical of everything and don't readily approve of anything new, to say nothing of a seventeen year old Seer.

Anna was buried with all the ceremony of a Chief. Her oak staff was laid on top of her as she had wished, guiding her through to the next world.

After the ceremony, Cat broached the subject to Alexander about taking over Anna's duties and her cottage. She would be eighteen in October — certainly old enough to be on her own, but she wanted his permission first before speaking with her father.

"That would be lovely, cousin," Alexander said. "But there's one thing that must be heeded to before ye may take over Anna's cottage."

"Oh? And what might that be?" Cat asked.

"Since I have no means of protecting ye out there, and certainly could not post a guard, ye must take Argentinus."

"Who is Argentinus?"

"He's Celt's last son. Though less than a year old, he's nearly as big as his sire, and shows great promise. He'll keep guard for ye. Agreed?"

"Och, aye! Is he inside?"

"He should be in the barn. Go get acquainted with him. I have some business to attend to."

He turned to walk away, but remembered to ask, "When will ye be moving in?"

"With Da's permission, next week, if that's all right wi' ye," she said hopefully.

"That'll do."

&

By the middle of May, Catrìona had settled into Anna's cottage permanently. Angus was none too happy about his daughter's decision, but with Alexander backing her, protesting was pointless.

"Da, ye ken that I was born to do this," she tried to reassure her father.

"Aye, I ken it all too well, Cat, and that's what scares me so. Ye ken how the *Sassenachs* hae been harryin' Alexander of late. I just dinna want ye to be alone out there wi' them pokin' around e'erywhere."

"Dinna fash, Da. Alexander gave me Argentinus to protect me. Hae ye seen him? No one would dare try anythin' wi' him around." She hugged her father tight, indicating the subject was closed.

The only thing he could do now was help her move, and help her he did. He tried his best to give Cat nearly every dish, pot, blanket and extra chair in the house.

"Christ O'Jesus, Da, I'm goin' to look like a gypsy!" she said giggling, looking over the wagonload of household utensils he had slated to go. "The cottage isna that big, and in case ye dinna remember, it already has all these things in it from Anna."

"But dinna ye want yer own things wi' ye?" he asked, bewildered.

"Da, they are just things. I dinna hae an attachment to them."

She could tell he was hurt, as if not being constantly reminded of her family would make her forget them.

"Wait Da. Didna Mam hae a lap desk for writin'?"

Angus scratched his head trying to recall what Cat was talking about.

"Remember? It was her Mam's, I think."

His brows flew up in memory. "Oh, I ken what yer talkin' about. Ye want that auld thing?"

"Could I? It would mean a lot," she said, watching her father's expression.

"O' course ye can hae it," he said, delighted he could finally be of service. "I'll go fetch it. Are ye sure there's naught else ye want, though?"

"Da, I dinna ken where I'll be able to find room for all o' this, ne'er mind what else ye hae in mind," she said smiling.

This seemed to appease him and he went upstairs for the lap desk. At that moment, Lachlan walked into the house to see the stacks of items to be put into the wagon.

"Ye canna be serious," he mocked. "Where are ye gonna put all this in that wee cottage?"

"I dinna ken," Cat whispered. "I hae been tryin' to tell him that the house is already full, but he gets upset. What am I goin' to do?"

Lachlan stood in the doorway staring at the stack. An idea was forming.

"Where is he now?" he asked.

"Upstairs fetchin' Mam's auld lap desk I asked for. It's the only thing I really want to take wi' me."

Just then, thumping could be heard above them as items were moved around.

"Quick, while he's up there, let's put as much of this away as we can. He'll no' miss it. He'll just think we loaded it into the wagon already," he said, winking at Cat.

"Ye're a wicked man, Lachlan," she said giggling.

By the time Angus came down with the lap desk, nearly all of what was in the stack to go was returned to its original location.

"Och, a fine job ye did loadin' so much in the wagon, Lachlan," Angus said, none the wiser.

Cat and Lachlan exchanged corrupt looks, but said nothing.

"Are ye ready to go, then?" Angus asked Cat.

"Aye, Da, I'm ready."

"Lachlan, ye hae the list of necessaries to get on the way back?" he asked.

"Aye, Da, I do," Lachlan said, patting his sporran.

"Then off wi' the two o' ye," he said, hugging Cat fiercely and kissing her on the cheek.

Cat headed for the wagon, but Lachlan was held back by Angus for further instructions.

"Stay as long as she needs ye to get settled, aye? And dinna tarry on the way home. I dinna care for the dragoons takin' a fondness for what ye may be carryin'. Hae ye got yer pistols?"

"They're under the seat o' the wagon. Dinna worry, Da, we'll be fine," Lachlan said, doing his best to slip out the door.

After a few more orders were barked from the doorway, Lachlan and Cat set off. It felt a little like when she left for her training nearly six years earlier, only this time she was ready to be on her own.

❧

Lachlan stayed for three days, not because Cat needed him, but because he found great comfort in the small cottage with his sister.

Cat did little to change anything in the cottage. Anna's presence was still there and she didn't want that to go away. The only different thing was the addition of another life force in the house.

Argentinus, a name that hardly rolled off the tongue, got a new, abbreviated name. He was now called Gent, which even he seemed to like better. Gent and Lachlan got along splendidly, and it seemed like severing an appendage when Lachlan left. That, however, didn't last long, for Gent immediately understood what his purpose was with Cat, and he took his task seriously.

Nearly two weeks had passed before Cat was called to duty. Just after dawn, on a rainy June morning, Gent began growling at the door. Cat sensed she would be called upon for a healing today, and was already awake, but still in bed. Hoof beats were not heard yet, so she decided to dress before the rider arrived.

She had just finished with the top button, when she heard foot-falls on the steps. At this, Gent went wild and leaped at the door, throwing his huge body up against it. On the other side, a string of curses were let out by the ignorant visitor. Cat had to stifle her giggles before she could greet the frightened caller. She decided then and there, that Gent would certainly protect her.

the arrival

The first week of July was a stormy one, thunderheads rolled unceasingly through the summer sky. By the beginning of the second week, it finally cleared off and the sun shone warmly into Catrìona's window. Today she planned to spend time in her garden tending to her herbs and vegetables. When she moved in, Alexander had brought over some strange new tubers called potatoes, obtained from one of his contacts in France. Cat planted them immediately and they were blooming now, giving off a sweet fragrance.

After most of the weeds had been pulled, restoring order to her garden, Cat went in for a small lunch, leaving the door open to allow the breeze to remove the peat smoke that perpetually hovered there. Spying Gent on the porch, she caught his ears perking up and heard a low growl emanate from his throat, signaling a visitor. Before she got up to see who it was, Gent's tail started wagging. She resumed eating, knowing it was Alexander.

"Hallò in the house," he said, not waiting for a reply before casually charging in.

"Hallò, cousin. What brings ye out here?" Cat asked, swallowing the last bite of her bannock.

"I was wondering if ye've had any visions of the Prince's journey?" He wasted no time in getting to the point.

Immediately Cat's hackles went up. She hadn't given the Prince and his rebellion a thought since Beltaine.

"No, but I suppose ye want me to find out for ye," she said, a bit more acidly than she meant to. Alexander quirked his eyebrows, clearly meaning, *would you like to rephrase that?* "I'm sorry, Alexander, I had all but forgotten that damned rebellion, and now ye put it right in front o' me again."

He chuckled at her candor, but had no intention of dismissing the question.

"My dear, no one has any word — not even my spies — as to when Prince Charles will make his attempt to the Hebrides. Ye said it would be in the beginning of July, and I should like to know if he has at least left France yet."

"Would ye let me hae a minute?" she asked, already heading to the west window.

"Take whatever time ye need, lass."

Quietly, he took a seat at the kitchen table and watched her. He thought she looked more and more like Isobel all the time, but with more vitality. The sun angling in the window illuminated her, setting her hair on fire against her forest green dress with such intensity he involuntarily sighed at the stunning display. He may not have a fondness for women, per say, but he appreciated beauty when he saw it.

Cat felt Alexander watching her, and turned away from his stare. A lock of hair was pried from beneath her kerch and she began the process of Seeing. At first, she saw two ships, but the Prince was nowhere to be found. Not knowing what he looked like, she employed a different method to locate him. Going beyond the physical, she looked for the metaphysical energy of him, easily locating him disguised as a student. His royal air and confidence, hidden under the drab clothes and humble demeanor, made her smile. She took an instant liking to the way he fit in; never pretentious about his royal status. Sobering a bit, she realized how else could he secretly cross the Channel to start his rebellion.

"How long does it take to cross the Channel?" she asked, her voice muffled by the window she spoke into.

Alexander jumped, startled out of the preoccupation of his own thoughts when he heard Cat speak. "Oh, um, three weeks to a month, depending on weather."

Cat nodded, indicating that she heard him, then a moment later, turned around and joined him at the table.

"The Prince has been at sea for a week. So far it's been smooth sailin' for him, however, my original vision of three ships has no' changed. It just must come later in the voyage. Do ye want me to stop by next week wi' an update?"

"Yes. Yes, next week," he said, still preoccupied with something.

"Ye seem a bit far away, cousin. Is there somethin' I can be helpin' ye wi'?"

"No. I was just wondering which clan he'll be met by when he arrives in the Hebrides. Macdonald's and Cameron's, I suppose."

"Does it matter?" Cat asked.

"I do not know. So many have not made their allegiances as of yet." He got up from the plain wooden chair, and without so much as a "thanks", left the cottage. Cat heard the hoof beats of his horse and knew he was gone.

ॐ

The week advanced at a snail's pace; the Prince and his journey consuming Cat's thoughts — day and night. Dreams haunted her with visions of the sea, battlefields and death. This morning was very different though. This morning, she saw sheep, more sheep than she had ever seen in her life. They covered the countryside from one end of Scotland to the other. Lairds and chiefs were their tenders, driving the clans from their native land to foreign places, making room for the hoards of woolly beasts.

"What in the world was that all about?" she said to no one, tossing away the bedclothes in an attempt to shake off an extremely eerie feeling. Gent eyed her quizzically from the foot of the bed, as if to say, *if* ye *do not know, then I cannot help ye.*

Cat hurriedly dressed, and despite the earliness of the hour, walked to the castle. Following her nose to Mrs. Macgregor's kitchen, she sat at the table, watching bread get kneaded at record speed.

"What's troublin' ye, Catrìona?" she asked, flour dust floating through the shafts of dawn coming in the window.

"Sheep."

"Weel, ye ken what they say about she ..."

"What's this about sheep?" Alexander interrupted, scratching his balding head and yawning widely.

"I had a dream that sheep took over the whole of the country and the lairds and chiefs drove out their own for them."

"Nonsense. Why in the world would I want to run out my own

people to raise sheep? Nonsense. Now, what news have you about our friend?" he asked, vaguely.

"Shall we go to yer chambers?"

Still scratching his head, he turned and walked out towards his chambers, presuming Cat was following close behind. Gent, who appeared from the hallway, followed Cat through the double doors, sitting next to her favorite chair on the dark side of the room.

"How are the two of ye getting along?" Alexander asked of her and Gent, as he poured himself a whisky, minus the honey.

Cat smiled a radiant set of teeth. "Grandly."

"Good. So tell me. What news have ye?" He rolled the whisky glass between his large hands.

"The Prince and his men hae been through a battle. The ship wi' the woman's name saved them, but is no longer escortin' them. It was so badly damaged in the fray, it had to return to France, takin' wi' her the men and arms the Prince hoped to use to begin his rebellion wi'," she said from her shadowed place.

Alexander drained his glass and started pacing in his usual fashion. Gent's eyes followed his every move.

"What of the Prince now?" he asked, rooted beside the fireplace.

"The ship he's on is still seaworthy, and he's sailin' northward as we speak. He should arrive within the week."

"Do you know where he will land — which island?"

Cat had been expecting this question, but having no knowledge of the names of the islands, could not give him an answer.

"Do ye hae a map, cousin?" she asked, rising from her chair to step into the light.

"Hmmm." Behind his desk were rows of parchment. He pulled out a few of the yellowed rolls, laying them onto his desk with a book on each corner to keep them flat. Cat stood over them, seeing her country for the first time.

"Where are we on this map?" she asked, absently tracing her finger around the islands of the Hebrides.

Nearly dead center in the middle of Scotland was Blair Atholl. "Here. And here is *Slios Mìn*," he said, pointing to the northern side of the largest loch west of Blair Atholl. Moving his finger just south of the loch, he pointed out his country estates in Carie. Cat took it all in, memorizing each landmark.

Returning to her initial reason for looking at the map, her attention focused back to the Hebrides. Effortlessly, she placed herself on the ship with the Prince. Closing her eyes, she smelled the fresh sea air and felt the wind in her hair. The sun was warm upon her face, shadowed every so often by a billowing sail, pitted by cannon shot. Looking around the landless expanse of water, it was impossible to get her bearings. On the deck, she listened to the men, hoping their location would be given away, but they remained silent.

Employing a different approach, she walked through the ship, finding it very claustrophobic. Why someone would deliberately embark into this confinement for an entire month was beyond her. Going below decks, she was assailed by rank odors of rotting food, spilled ale, and unclean bodies. She walked through dark, tiny rooms of hammocks not more than two feet apart, where creatures of all sorts scurried in the darkness. Finally finding the captain's quarters, there were maps and ledgers strewn all over his desk. Opening his log book, she read the last few pages, hoping for some information that would tell her their final destination.

Sparingly written with just the facts, the bold script told of the encounter with an English man-of-war named the *Lyon*. It went on to say that the gunship sailing with the Prince — she smiled as she read the name *Elisabeth* — was so badly damaged in the fray, it had to return to Brest, France.

The further she read, the more convinced she was that even the captain wasn't sure where they would land. Searching the map over and over, their destination eluded her. What she needed was a pendulum. Looking around, she found a short length of twine on the captain's locker. Removing her ring, she threaded the twine through it, knotted the end, then instructed the pendulum how to react to the islands she pointed to, while holding the pendulum over the map.

Using her finger as a guide, she pointed to Islay. The pendulum remained stationary. She pointed to Colonsay; it remained still. Isle of Mull, Iona, Tiree, Coll, Rum, Isle of Skie; no movement was detected. She shook her hand to clear it of any interference, then returned it to where she left off. Tracing further north, she pointed to Barra and the pendulum started to move. She was getting close. When she pointed to the tiny island of Erisea, the pendulum made a strong sunwise rotation. Just to be sure, she pointed to South Uist, but the pendulum went quiet again.

Thanking the guides that steered her hand, she re-entered

Alexander's chambers. Cat glanced over at her cousin and noticed the hairs on his arms were all on end.

"I do not want to know where ye were, just tell me ye have the location," he said, rubbing the gooseflesh from his arms.

Cat smiled, patted his shoulder, and pointed to Erisea.

৯

Three days later, a gale blew in from the west carrying with it heavy rains. It was 23 July, 1745.

"Weel, my Prince, ye'll be in for some weather when ye land today," Cat said, tossing a mutton bone outside for Gent, before turning her attention to her own stomach.

Preparing her breakfast, she knew Alexander was on his way over. A few moments later he and Gent walked in, both shaking off the water from their hair.

"What news have ye, lass," he asked, taking a seat at the table. Cat had a cup of tea ready and set it down in front of him.

"I was just about to find out." She walked over to the west window and began her ritual. A few minutes later, she sat beside Alexander at the table with her own cup of tea.

"They'll be landin' tonight and given shelter by a fisherman. The weather, and another English ship, will keep them there for two days. They'll set out at dark on the second day for the mainland … oh, I wish I had a map."

Alexander immediately got up and went outside, calling for the driver to bring in the maps. With the western coast of Scotland on the table, Cat used her pendulum again, tracing her finger along the coast, just east of Erisea.

The Isle of Skie was the first land due east, but the pendulum remained still. Cat continued southwards to Mallaig, then on to Arisaig, where the pendulum started to circle. She went a little further to Moidart, and it continued to circle. As soon as her fingers continued their southward journey, the pendulum stopped.

"Somewhere here," pointing to Loch nan Uamh. "If the English gunship is still after them, this would be a good place to hide, aye?" Their heads were nearly touching as they surveyed the area, trying to put depth to the parchment.

"Aye, and still in Macdonald and Cameron lands," Alexander said, speaking mostly to himself.

"What will ye do now, cousin?"

"We wait for word," he said, tapping the map where the Prince would land. "He'll certainly send riders out to gather supporters for the rebellion. We wait for a rendezvous point."

ॐ

Two weeks after the Prince arrived, word came and the meeting place was set.

"We are to meet at Glenfinnan on the 19th of August," Alexander shouted, dismounting from his horse in the dooryard, startling Cat out of her morning meditation. He walked in as if he owned the place.

"Tell me, cousin," she said, moving from her window to start the tea when he walked in, now that she was thoroughly interrupted. "Did ye make yer entrances this way wi' Anna?"

Alexander took his seat at the table, making himself right at home, undeterred.

"Until you moved into this house, I ne'er stepped foot in it. Truthfully, Anna scared the life out o' me."

"It seems I'll hae to start usin' some o' her tactics, because I canna work wi' ye crashin' in here whene'er ye please," she said, slamming down the pot on the stove to get her point across.

"Point taken, lass," he said, waving his hand in dismissal, but by no means promising never to do it again. "Now, did ye hear what I said about the rendezvous point?"

Cat glared at him for a moment before answering.

"Aye, I did. Glenfinnan. Are ye to bring the men to fight wi' ye, or are ye to go alone?"

"Neither. I'll send word back that Clan Donnachaidh will lend out two hundred men to fight when there is adequate promise from the other clans that it'll not be a folly."

"The future is pushed by the past, aye? Ye're no doubt thinkin' o' the '15."

"That's exactly what I was thinking of," he said, pushing his chair from the table.

When he reached the door to leave, he said in an odd voice, "William, Marquis of Tullibardine is the one who asked for the clan's forces. For him, all the clan will surely fight." He said it as if it were he who had called for the clan to fight, they wouldn't have.

Cat watched him leave with a sinking feeling in the pit of her stomach.

ॽ🐦

A raven cawed nearby before dawn, signaling a message was to be delivered. Cat woke and went to the door in her shift. It was a warm morning for the end of August, but she instantly felt a change in the air, though not from the weather.

The raven sat perched on the lowest branch of the rowan tree near the cottage, waiting patiently for Cat to approach.

"What message hae ye for me wee raven?" She looked into its onyx eyes and prepared herself to receive this rather unusual communication.

Grappling with what the raven observed, her heart sank. Maybe she thought the rebellion would stay away from her home, or maybe she just wished for it so hard, she thought the power of her will could make it so. But now, it was here, as big as life. The entire Stuart army was heading towards Blair Atholl, recruiting men loyal to the Jacobite cause, and King James, from each village and hamlet along the way.

Cat ran back into the cottage and got dressed. From the few times she *met* the Prince, she knew his charisma and energy would lure fighting men in by the hundreds. What she was afraid of was all that enthusiasm seducing her father and brothers into the mob, even though promising not to fight. If she rode hard, she could be back at *Slios Mìn* by nightfall, in an effort to convince her family not to join as soldiers, before the Prince arrived to change their minds.

Recruitment

The sun rose in a troubled sky as Cat saddled her horse. She packed light for the quick trip home, securing her dirk and pistol in her belt. By now, she knew the Hanoverian army would be on the move looking to engage the rebel forces, and did not want be caught out in the open without protection, however confident of her safety.

Knowing Alexander would forbid her to go, traveling past the castle undetected would be the tricky part. To escape unnoticed, she opted to take the trail behind the castle through the mountains. It would be harder travel, but she suspected it would be a less watched route.

Keeping to the trees as much as possible, she traversed the high terrain for about two miles before urging Clot Heid back down to the main trail. Gent, ignoring his natural instincts to chase anything that moved, stayed just ahead of Cat, acting as a scout.

About ten miles into the trip, they stopped for water, remaining in the brush along the river to avoid being seen. When they drank their fill, Cat put her foot in the stirrup, but froze when she saw Gent's hair all standing on end, followed by a deep guttural growl.

"I see them, lad. Stay quiet now, and stay there." He did as he was told.

A small party of dragoons — maybe a half a dozen — dressed in scarlet coats, were on the other side of the river. Scouts, no doubt, searching for the rebel army. As they moved closer to the river, she crossed her fingers, hoping they weren't going to make camp there, or she would be trapped.

Her cinnamon-brown dress hid her well in the scrub brush, and she willed herself to be invisible. Listening for any tell-tale information, she heard them talk about their commander, a General John Cope, and how little faith they had in his abilities to find the rebels; never mind engage them in battle.

Minutes clicked on agonizingly slow, but the men finally filled their water flasks and began to move on. She exhaled the breath she had been holding, Gent even relaxed, until a branch broke behind them. Everything went still. Gent spied intently into the woodland they just passed through, but before Cat could get a fix on what he saw, a band of kilted men screaming like *bean-sidhes* blazed through the brush and splashed across the river, brandishing broadswords, pistols and dirks.

Before they knew what hit them, the Highlanders took the unprepared dragoons captive, quickly disarming them, then marching them across the river towards her. Could she remain invisible or should she make a dash for safer ground? Unfortunately, the only ground ahead of her was open moorland. She would not be invisible there.

With the amount of noise nearly twenty men made crossing the river, she opted for a better hiding place right where she was. Signaling Gent to move into the brush, she dismounted Clot Heid, and as quietly as she could — which in her ears sounded like a small army in itself — coaxed him into the scrub, where they all disappeared.

Within moments, the regiment filed passed noisily, totally unaware of her existence. They moved so close she could smell their odor and hear their labored breathing. Thankfully, they were going in the opposite direction she was.

She waited until they could no longer be heard before venturing out of her hiding place. Gent emerged at the same time, confident they were long gone.

"Well, lads, ye both did verra well, but that was too close for comfort, aye?" she said, scratching Gent's and Clot Heid's ears.

On their way once again, the approaching wide expanse of moorland was actually a welcome sight. She may be more exposed, but then again, so would anyone else. Their steps, a little more hurried, their senses a little more heightened, they crossed the three miles of open boulder-strewn heather, but the rest of the trip was uneventful.

Just after dark, the exhausted, hungry and dusty trio reached *Slios Mìn*. Cat headed straight for the barn, where she met a very startled Iain, who visibly jumped as though he was looking at a ghost.

"What in bloody hell are ye doin' here?" he blasted, bending over to pick up the brush he was using on his horse that flung itself out of his hand at the sight of her.

Cat went over and gave him a kiss on his cheek. "Glad to see ye, too," she said, bringing Clot Heid into a stall and removing his saddle.

Iain went outside to see who came with her, returning even more distressed that she was alone.

"Da's goin' to kill ye, ye ken. What e'er possessed ye to do such a rash thing as travel here by yerself? Dinna ye ken dragoons are all around here? The Prince is in Scotland ye ken. He's mountin' an army ..."

"Iain, if ye just shut up for a minute, I should like to ask ye to feed my horse and come inside when ye're done. I hae some verra important news. Is Da home?"

Iain just nodded, and Cat left him in his bewildered state.

Greeted in the house in nearly the same fashion as in the barn, Cat fixed herself and Gent something to eat under the severe eyes of her father. Sitting at the table to eat the bread and venison Maggie had prepared earlier, she ignored his angry ranting, knowing it was a fear reaction.

As she took the last bite, Iain and Lachlan walked in. Lachlan, sporting a bright smile and always glad to see her, lifted her from her chair, squeezed her tight, and planted kisses in her hair. Cat giggled throughout the process, and Gent furiously wagged his tail, whimpering for the same attention. By the time Gent had been given his due, the household was brought to a more festive atmosphere.

"So, my brave, daft daughter, what was so important that ye risked yer life gettin' here to tell us?" Angus asked, sitting beside her at the table.

She scanned their faces, making sure they would pay attention to the seriousness of her every word, then she began.

"As ye well ken, the Prince is in Scotland. He has wi' him the clans Macdonald and Cameron; men numberin' well into the hundreds. They're on their way to Blair Atholl as we speak, raisin' an army." She searched their eyes for a waver of their promise not to fight. Approving of their resolve, she continued.

"On my way here, by the river in Bohally Wood, I encountered a small scoutin' party o' dragoons." Before she could continue further, she was assaulted with questions and fresh reprimands to her absence of judgement in making the trip alone. She held up her hand, making Angus smile in reminder of himself. "Might I continue or are ye just goin' to keep interruptin'?"

Though just mutters, she was sure they said to go ahead and finish her story.

"As I was sayin'; the dragoons talked of a General John Cope; do ye ken who he is?" she asked her father.

"Weel, o' course. He's the Commander-in-Chief for Scotland; an imbecile, though."

"That's what his own men were sayin' about him, too. Said he would probably no' even *find* the rebels, ne'er mind engage them in battle."

Her father chuckled, "Yep, that would be him." While he was nodding, he began rubbing his chin. Cat could tell he was planning something. "So they sent Cope to squash the rebellion, huh?" he said slyly.

"Da, dinna ye get any ideas in yer heid that ye can make the outcome of this damned war change. I still see the same slaughter as I did at Hogmanay. I still see my brothers — yer sons — dyin' on the battlefield. The only way I ken to change that is to make me a promise once again, no' to fight."

"Now, lass. Ye ken I canna do that, but the lads can — and will," he said to Iain and Lachlan. They in turn shuffled their feet, uncomfortable, leading Cat to believe that having their way would be very different.

"What about Seumas? Can ye make him promise, as well?" she asked, noticing how none of them would meet her eyes.

"Ah, so he's still bent on gettin' himself killed." Making up her mind, she got up from the table and stormed out into the night.

Walking the near mile to get to Seumas' croft, she had lots of time to think about what she would say to him; noting that except for Gent by her side, she was alone in the persuasion.

Reaching the front door, she hollered, "Hallò in the house." A moment later Seumas opened it, carrying a lantern. Caught off guard when he saw who it was, he wasn't sure what emotion to display. He remained blank.

"Come in … are ye alone?" Lifting the lantern higher to see for himself, then opening the door wider for her to enter.

"Gent's wi' me," she said "But, he'll stay outside. Hallò Charlotte."

Charlotte, being as timid as anyone Catrìona had ever known, remained silent in the darkened corner of the one-room croft, holding her round belly. Cat instantly smiled, seeing the small boy growing inside due in two months, but saying nothing else.

"Can I offer ye a *cuppa* tea?" he asked, in an attempt to be polite.

"Och, no. I just finished wi' supper at Da's."

"Why are ye here, Cat?" he asked, bluntly.

"It sounds like ye already ken, dinna ye?"

"Aye, and there's naught a thing ye can say to me to make me change my mind." He turned his back to her, busying himself with the fire in an effort to hide his face.

Oh really, she thought.

"What about yer son, then? Would he be able to change yer mind?" she asked.

He whipped around at the word *son.* "Ye canna ken that for sure," he stated hesitantly, knowing full well her powers.

Cat said nothing; just stared at him with her arms folded under her breasts, playing as dirty as he was. She didn't want to resort to this kind of extortion, but he left her no choice. Cat saw Charlotte rubbing her belly; a slight smile played along her lips indicating she appreciated Cat's means of persuasion, not finding a befitting method of her own.

"Hae ye no' heard who's leadin' the Hanoverian troops, Cat? Cope, for Christ sakes, Cope! He's a fool who couldna lead an army to victory if his life depended upon it. There isna any way we can lose this fight, Cat," he said calmly, defying her to say more.

"I will speak o' it only this one time, *mo bhràthair mòr;* if ye fight, ye will die, and it wilna be under General Cope that the slaughter will come."

He wasn't listening anymore. There was no way to get through if not even his own son could sway him. He was lost to her. She stared at him for a long moment; memorizing his face, his hair, his stance; seeing in her mind's eye hollowness in his future. He was already dead.

Cat turned and, without another word, left the croft; closing the door behind her with a raw finality.

ॐ

A week passed by quietly, with Lachlan being the only bright spot in it, making it his mission to keep her occupied and smiling. The day before she was to return to her own cottage, they went up into the mountains to gather the cattle closer to the house. Her father, at least, believed the Stuart army was heading their way, and did not want to leave his prized herd as food for hundreds of clansmen.

Overlooking the valley, with a clear view of at least twenty miles, Gent started a low growl. Lachlan, closest to him, heard it first, scanning the direction Gent was intent on. Cat sidled up closer to see what had Lachlan's attention. Far in the distance, a long, ragged line of Highlanders moved towards them, following the cattle trails through the mountainous terrain.

"The Prince is frustrated," Cat said.

Lachlan glanced quizzically at his sister and noticed the glazed over look of her amethyst eyes. He wondered what she was seeing, as the hair rose on his neck, but knew not to interrupt while she was in this state.

"He and his men were to engage General Cope at the Pass o' Corrieyairack. An informant told Cope that he was goin' to be ambushed there, so he sought another route, avoidin' the fight. They," she said, pointing to the Highlanders, "are headin' for Blair Atholl, now armed wi' tales of how the English are afraid to fight them."

"Christ, Cat. Wi' the army in such high spirits, men will follow him to the death." His eyes never left the endless string of men heading westward.

"What about ye, Lachlan? Will ye follow him?" Cat whispered, still seeing the outcome, but not the circumstances in between.

"No, Cat, ye ken I wilna … for ye, I wilna fight."

ॐ

The Jacobite Duke of Atholl, William, Tullibardine, and Alexander invited the Prince to stay at Blair Atholl for a week to allow the men to train and officers to make their strategies. The next stop was the ancient capital of Perth.

Catrìona was invited to the castle for a reading of the *clach na brataich*. This was only a formality, since she had already seen the outcome for the clan, and the entire Jacobite Rising.

Alexander pulled Cat aside before going into his chambers with the Prince, the Duke, and the high ranking Chiefs of the Macdonald's and Cameron's.

"Is there any way to tell them of what will happen in Perth, without telling them that they will all have their heads lopped off at the end of this war?" he whispered, threateningly.

"So ye would hae me lie to them?"

Truth be known, she didn't know what she was going to say when she walked into that room, but she wanted Alexander to sweat for this one. He volunteered her for this reading knowing full well the outcome had not changed.

"No, not lie. Just do not tell them anything more than what will happen at Perth. Will ye do that?"

"I'll only tell them what they ask of me, and besides, not *all* will hae their heids lopped off."

Alexander shot her a dirty look, still skeptical about her vagueness, but before he could protest, the Duke opened the chamber doors; further reprimands would have to wait until later. He sent her a last warning look and they proceeded into his chambers.

Cat walked in, and immediately, the Prince, Duke, and the Chiefs rose from their seats. This took her off guard a bit, but she refused to let it show, instead curtsying to them all and taking her seat in the darkened end of the room.

"Will you not come into the light, Catrìona? I would very much like to see to whom I am speaking," said the Prince, in an accent she did not recognize.

Cat felt her face go scarlet. Alexander was warned that she would not do a reading in front of such authoritative men. She gave him a moment to intercede on her behalf, but he remained silent. Fine. The last thing she wanted to do was go against the Prince's wishes, but would if push came to shove …

"Please forgive me, yer Highness, but I canna read the future wi' so many eyes upon me." There, she left no room for debate.

"You may do your reading from the dark, Mistress, but I would like to look at you first," he responded calmly, daring her to argue.

Not willing to push this too far, she acquiesced. Rising from her chair, she crossed the room and stood in front of him.

"That's better. Now, I have heard that you have quite a talent for seeing the future. Is this not true?" He looked her square in the face with a curiosity that made Cat smile. For under his royal character — and purple coat covering a gold-laced shirt — was a man not much older than herself, finding life interesting, and genuinely wanting to learn about what she did.

"Aye, yer Highness, I hae the Sight. What is it ye would like to ken about?" Calmly, she searched his large brown eyes for the question, hoping it wouldn't be the outcome of the Rising.

"I aim to take Perth and then Edinburgh. I would like to know what you see for my plans," he asked, never taking his eyes from hers.

"Since I kent what ye would ask beforehand, yer Highness, I see that both towns will be victorious for ye. In fact, ye'll take them both wi'out a single shot bein' fired or life lost." The royal group clapped their hands together when they saw the Prince smile at the news.

Within a month of the Prince setting foot on Scottish soil, he and his ever-expanding army of Highlanders were an unstoppable force. It seemed the Stuart reign was cinched.

After the private celebration, Cat excused herself, leaving the royal chambers before any more questions could be asked. She wanted to go home, but did not wish to be seen alone. Through the castle walls, the sounds of battle were heard, as the men practiced with their swords. Even Gent may not be enough of a deterrent against men fired up with aggression.

Looking out over the sea of Highlanders, one head stood above most; Seumas'. Softly, she spoke his name from the castle entrance, then waited a minute. He was in the middle of a mock battle, but she could tell he heard her. Making quick work of his opponent due to the distraction, he stepped out of the training for a moment to figure out what just happened. He looked around, almost positive he heard Cat calling his name.

Cat quietly spoke his name again; this time he found her, standing in the last rays of the late summer sun that sparked off her hair. His expression never changed, but she could tell he was not happy to see her. She met him halfway at the gate.

"What are ye doin' here, *piuthar?*" he asked impatiently.

"I just finished a readin' and now I'd like to go home, but I dinna want to walk there alone. Could I trouble ye to take me? 'Tis but a mile from here."

"Alexander couldna spare his carriage for the Seer of the Clan?" he asked bitterly, not feeling particularly chauvinistic.

"I didna ask, besides," she interjected hurriedly, "I would love ye to see my cott."

"Why?" he asked, instantly on guard that she may have had another vision of him.

The hurt in her eyes was evident. He still carried the irrational disdain for her and her gift.

"Ne'er mind, Seumas." Turning in the direction of home before they got into an argument.

"Wait," he said, running his hand through his hair in a turmoil of feeling. "I'd better tell Da where I'll be."

"Da is here? Where?" Stopping to search through the mob, without any luck.

"Last time I saw him, he was in the barn wi' Gregor fashionin' some new kind o' spear. Come on, I'm sure he'd like to see ye." Grabbing her elbow, he guided her over towards the workshop.

Before reaching their destination, her father and Gregor were heard laughing deviously. The first thing she thought of was how men never really grow up. Obviously, creating the most vile weapon of destruction known to man was a fun thing. As they rounded the corner, they almost found out first hand how vile a weapon it was.

Attached to a heavy stick, seven or eight feet long, was a scythe, and they were poking and jabbing it to get the feel of it. As one of these jabs exited the barn, it missed Seumas literally by an inch.

"Jesus!" he swore, jumping back and nearly knocking Cat over in the process. Gent barked furiously, scared by the surge of emotions from everyone.

The stunned looks on the faces of Angus and Gregor indicated the severity of the near miss, but once Seumas saw the simple deadliness in the creation, all rage vanished. This only solidified Cat's previous notion of men never growing up.

"If ye lads are done wi' yer new toy, I'd like to invite ye o'er for supper tonight at my cott. Ye too, Gregor." All eyes fell upon her in disbelief at such an invitation at this inappropriate time. It was as if she had laughed during a hanging.

Reading their thoughts, her only response was, "Hmmm." She started to walk away, remembering at the last minute her mission. "I'll be waitin' for ye in the kitchen for ye to take me home, Seumas." He muttered an acknowledgment under his breath, but was thoroughly preoccupied with the new weapon to really hear her.

"I may as well hae spoken to a stone."

After Cat waited impatiently in the kitchen for almost an hour, Tullibardine walked in to see if he could get Mrs. Macgregor to fix him something warm to eat. His rheumatism was acting up.

"Ye're still here, lass? I thought ye went home hours ago," he said, rubbing his gnarled hands.

"Weel, me laird, 'tis no' for lack o' tryin'. My brother was supposed to walk me home, but has been … well, let's just say he's been detained for the moment. I was about to go see what was holdin' him up."

"Och, nonsense, lass. I'll fetch my driver and he'll take ye home. How far away do ye live?" he asked, curious that she would walk anywhere given the dangerous atmosphere of the area.

"A mile from here, in Anna Macpherson's cottage."

"In Anna's cottage? Well then, how is that brave, dear woman?" he asked, opening the window over the sink to summon his driver.

"Ye did no' hear, me laird? She passed on the first o' June."

The aging Duke stopped waving in mid-stroke, and slowly turned to face Cat. The graveness on his face indicated that he had not heard of her death, making him appear much older than his late sixties. There was something else to the look, yet as quickly as it appeared, it was gone. He turned back to the window and shouted unceremoniously for his driver, who was already on his way inside, but now quickened his pace.

Without as much as a good-bye to Cat, he told his driver to take her home, then strode out of the kitchen, ignoring his quest for sustenance. Cat just stood there for a long moment, open mouthed, totally mystified by what just happened.

The driver cleared his throat, indicating his readiness to leave, which brought Cat back to reality.

"Are ye ready, Miss?" he asked, quietly.

With the bewildered look still on her face, she slowly took notice of the driver. A harder looking man was impossible to imagine. His hewn granite features were shaped by years of servitude and struggle, but when Cat met his malachite eyes, she smiled. They held humor and softness, unexpected compassion.

"Please forgive me, sir," she said, instantly feeling the change in his attitude. "I did no' mean to stare. I ... well ... I was taken in by yer eyes." Cat suddenly felt very self-conscious. For a long moment, they were statues, unable — or unwilling — to move, until Gent walked in, growling deeply at this stranger who seemed to have his partner in an odd emotional predicament. Realizing it was a perfect opportunity to break the paralysis, she said "Aye, I'm ready to go, thank ye."

Cat and Gent settled into the extravagant carriage, with its lush velvet seats and intricately carved woodwork surrounding the windows. Her fingers explored all the textures of this foreign world with child-like wonder. Alexander's carriage was certainly nothing like this.

Feeling the carriage shift as the driver stepped up into his seat, she suddenly remembered she hadn't told him where to take her. He must have realized it too, because his muffled voice came through the ceiling at the same instant.

"Where to, Miss?" he called, his deep voice reminiscent of her father's.

Not wanting to shout at him, she opened the door and peered up at him, again, taken aback by the green of his eyes.

"My name is Catrìona, which I would greatly appreciate bein' called, sir." This time, not only his eyes smiled, but his entire face transformed into more of a rugged oak than solid stone.

"All right ... Catrìona. Where would ye be goin'?" His dark chocolate hair, tied back in a queue, was being ruffled by the stiff breeze, setting free a few thick strands across his forehead. The cleft in his square chin reflected the light like a cliff overlooking the sea.

"Follow the carriage path to the northeast for nearly a mile. I'm in the cott there."

Forgetting his position, he abandoned all social conduct and spoke freely. "Ye're livin' in Anna Macpherson's cott?"

"Aye. Did ye ken who she was?" More than a little curious now to know the relationship between Anna and Tullibardine.

"Och, aye. She and the Duke were verra close," he said, tucking the loose strands of hair behind his ear.

"What's yer name?" Cat blurted out.

Misinterpreting her genuine curiosity for a reprimand, his face returned to stone and he quickly said "Greame Hay ... Miss. We'll be goin' now."

Cat almost made it to her seat when Greame slapped the reins and the carriage lurched forward, throwing her into Gent, who mistook it for play, licking her face severely before she could get off of him.

The mile was not nearly long enough to think of every possible nasty thing to say to him. She fumed, muttering to herself and digging her fingers into the plush seats wishing it was his hair. Gent refused to make eye contact with her, unsure what might have brought on this wrath.

When the carriage finally came to a halt, Cat was out before Greame even tied off the reins. His look of surprise was the exact position she wanted him in.

"What in bloody hell is wrong wi' ye, man? I ask ye yer name and ye treat me like I just asked ye to slit yer own throat! How could askin' yer name be improper? I'm so angry at bein' told I'm improp ..."

Before she could continue any further with the tirade, Greame jumped from the carriage, grabbed her by the shoulders and gave her a teeth-jarring shake.

"There was naught a thing wrong wi' askin' for my name. It was the way ye asked it that I remembered my place. I was bein' too forward wi' ye." He stopped, realizing what he was doing. "Ha, now look at me. I'll be flogged for sure for this."

Releasing her as hard as he grabbed her, she almost fell backwards. In two steps, he was back up on the carriage, grabbing violently for the reins, and slapping them hard enough to rear up the horses.

"Wait!" Cat shouted, but he never looked back. Whether he heard her or not, she didn't know. As quickly as he entered her life, he vanished from it.

For some strange reason, it really bothered her. Hot tears seared her checks, infuriating her even further. "What in hell's name are ye blubberin' about?" she chastised herself, angrily wiping her face with her sleeve.

She went inside with blurred vision. Gent remained out, not wanting to be anywhere near her until she released the anger she was feeling. It made him very uncomfortable.

From the porch, Gent heard things being slammed around inside, and lots of muttering. At one point well into the fury, a shoe flew passed him, landing on the ground just off the porch. Any other time, that would have been a game and he would have fetched it for her. But not today. As a matter of fact, it was getting too dangerous to stay on the porch, and he decided the barn would be a safer place.

By the time dusk enveloped the cottage, Cat had finally cooled down. Gent, returning from his hiding place, quietly stepped up on the porch and listened. All was peaceful. Deciding it was safe, he nosed his way into the house, finding Cat sitting in the rocking chair beside the fireplace. He waited for a response before proceeding further.

"Come on in, lad. I'm sorry for actin' like a spoiled bairn." She got up and lit a few candles. "I dinna think Da will be comin' for supper, so we may as well eat, aye?"

Gent wagged his tail in agreement and order was restored.

❧

Greame Hay was quite caught off guard by her reaction to his physical appearance. Normally, people just meeting him for the first time were afraid of him; they never smiled at him. To say he was intrigued would be an understatement, only now there was a foreign emotion to deal with; self-consciousness.

His looks had always been hard, and he had long ago given up any thoughts of a woman taking notice of him without cringing. No one saw beyond the hardened features to notice that he was a kind, gentle man with a sense of humor. Somehow, she had. In the kitchen they had made a connection he could not fathom, but the rush of emotions they parted with meant he would never see her again.

He pulled the carriage up to the castle gates and stepped down. "Forget her, man. She's already forgotten about ye."

He walked into the castle shaking his head and whispering her name.

in times of war

As Cat predicted, Prince Charles Edward Stuart and his motley looking mob of Highlanders took Perth and Edinburgh by September 17, without resistance. This would be the last time, however.

Lying in bed, fully awake and listening to the rain, Cat's mind was suddenly filled with a scene of a battlefield choked with dragoons. The flat, wide stretch of ground was backed by the sea, and flanked by tall stone walls on the right. There was a large expanse of marsh to the left, seemingly impregnable. It was a trap. With no apparent way in, except through the deadly marsh, the Jacobites would be slaughtered when they got mired in the bog.

Searching further, Cat noticed a pathway. Following it in her vision, it led straight through the marsh onto the higher ground of the field. The Prince and his army had to get this information, but how? She could dispatch a raven, but with no one to decipher the message in its eyes, it might be shot from the sky before reaching its destination. For a moment, she almost wished Lachlan would be there, but quickly cancelled out that thought. Someone else must be able to receive a message from her mind, but at the moment, she did not know who.

Letting the *how* part go for a minute, she continued with the vision. It was nearing dawn now. The stealthy Highlanders entered the marsh on a direct course towards the sleeping dragoons, but before the entire regiment got through, the Hanoverians awoke in total panic. In typical Highlander fashion, they rushed the unprepared confusion of dragoons with bloodcurdling screams and pistols blazing.

What Cat saw after that was a spectacle so repulsive, it was difficult to remain in the vision. With swords, dirks and her father's new weapon — which were nearly all the Highlanders had to fight with — came mutilation beyond any horror she had ever known. The field bled from the severed arms, legs and heads of the Hanoverian army.

When the vision was finally spent, she came to weeping.

"Dear God," she said to herself.

For the rest of the day, she sat huddled near the fireplace, debating whether to tell Alexander, who was still at Blair Castle. It wasn't as if informing him of what she saw changed his mind about fighting. Her breath was wasted on an energy much greater than herself — man's insatiable need to make all others conform to the same belief. Why? Was there something written somewhere that said difference was evil? That hatred and fear had rule upon the land? That man had the right to dominate everything he touched?

She retreated to the place where she lived in her head. It was comforting, nurturing, peaceful and happy there. And there was no war. She returned to the days when she didn't have the Sight; innocent and ignorant of the sinister hearts that lay inside men.

Just before dusk, Cat heard the distinct sounds of Alexander's carriage. The decision was made when he knocked on her door.

"I came by to invite ye to dine with me, Catrìona."

"Well, cousin, I was thinkin' about comin' by the castle to talk wi' ye, anyway. Come in and I'll tell ye of my vision."

"A new one?"

"Aye. A terrible one of a battle to come verra soon. Do ye ken where the Prince is now?" she asked, slumping heavily into her chair at the table, suddenly ravenous at the thought of food.

"The latest news is that he's heading for Dunbar to engage Cope at the earliest convenience. What have ye seen?"

After repeating her vision to him in vivid detail, she added, "And this time, lives will be lost in our ranks as well as theirs."

"Did ye see how many of the Jacobites were killed?" Pacing now, unable to remain seated after hearing about the vision.

"Not near as many as theirs, but more than I care to think about. There is one piece of intrigue, though. How will the Highlanders get through the marsh?"

He sat back down and pondered on that for a moment, watching a mouse dash about near the fireplace, looking for its own route through the maze of items on the floor.

"What about the landowner? He must know of a safe passage through it," he said, thinking like the strategist he was.

"How do we go about gettin' the landowner to get the information to the Prince?"

"Ah, never fear, lass. I'm leaving in the morning with yer father to join up with the Prince. I shall see to it myself."

He got up from his chair and, doing well to remember his invitation for supper, asked, "Well, are ye coming?"

Losing her appetite after learning her father was heading into a battle again, she declined the offer, but Alexander insisted, saying, "It'll do ye good to be with people right now, Catrìona."

Contemplating that for a moment, Cat gathered her shawl and followed Alexander to the waiting carriage.

ð

Life reinvented itself day after day. With or without a war going on, people got sick and needed help. Returning from treating the broken wrist of wee Danny Donachie — joyfully due to playing with his sister and landing the wrong way when he tripped over a rock in pursuit of a frog — Catrìona was summoned by the raven just before dark. She had just unsaddled and fed Clot Heid, and now just wanted to get something to eat for herself and Gent, and go to bed.

"What is it, raven?" she asked, dropping her satchel on the ground beside the apple tree. Gent sat beside her, curiously keen on the raven, as if he too was included in the mindplay.

As the message revealed itself in Catrìona's mind, she saw Alexander in a carriage heading for his country house in Carie. He was returning from the battle of Prestonpans, surrounded by his clansmen. "Wait. What is that?" she said out loud. There was an animal wrapped around him.

Squinting her eyes to get a better view did not help. "Phaa!" she sputtered. Too tired to figure out what that was all about, she continued with the message. Alexander seemed to be all right, but extremely fatigued. As they neared Carie, where the wagon path disappears, the clansmen now carried and pulled the carriage the rest of the way with shear brute strength. Her father was not with them.

"Well, raven, what am I to do wi' this information? Ye're no' tellin' me that he needs my help. What then?" she asked, noticing Gent's questioning look as well.

Since Lachlan was much closer than she was to Carie, she decided to have him check on Alexander to be sure he did not need her assistance. Unwilling to chance a miscommunication, she wrote a short note, tied it to the raven's leg, and sent him on his way, thanking him for his efforts. As a forewarning, she mentally sent a vision to Lachlan that the raven was trying to find him, then went inside.

❧

By the end of September, word spread through the countryside about the invincible Jacobite army annihilating nearly 850 of Cope's men within a quarter hour. Cat noticed the white cockade, symbolizing all that was Stuart, appearing on bonnets everywhere. Some said the women in Edinburgh handed out the white ribbons in the streets.

With no word from her father or Seumas, but sensing they came out of the battle unscathed, she selfishly wished to have the comfort of Iain and Lachlan. Unfortunately, she could not risk the trip home. She also did not want to imperil her brothers by having them cross hostile territory just to keep her company. Besides, with probably all of her father's male tenants fighting, her brothers may well be the only men of the clan around for the protection of those left behind.

She would just have to put them out of her mind and be content to keep herself busy. Most of the garden was now harvested, but there were still herbs to collect and dry. With the weather starting to turn bad, she decided to spend the day in her herb shed sorting and mixing the tonics and ointments needed for the upcoming season.

By mid-afternoon, Gent, who had been keeping himself busy, charged into the herb shed as excited as he could possibly be. With her sleeves rolled up to the elbows, and her hands plunged into a muslin bag of lavender breaking up the dry leaves and blossoms, the most she could do to see what all the fuss was about was turn her head. When she did, she let out a squeal of delight at Lachlan and Iain standing in the doorway with enormous smiles on their faces.

Unmindful of the mess she made ripping her hands out of the

bag of lavender, she ran across the room into the arms of the two most beautiful men she ever laid eyes on.

"What are ye doin' here?" she cried. "Och, ne'er mind, just so long as ye're here!"

After exhausting themselves with hugs and kisses, they explained why they were there.

"The wee raven found me and I did as ye asked," Lachlan said.

"Aye, Alexander's verra tired, but he's unharmed," Iain said. "He's stayin' at the Hermitage for a time. Figures the dragoons wilna find him there, as it looks like a ruin already."

"He did tell us of the battle wi' Cope, though. He told us ye saw the whole thing. From his description, it was a rout, but I would no' hae wanted to see what the bloody end looked like," Lachlan said in all seriousness. It seemed to further solidify his stance on fighting, which made Cat very happy.

"I hae one question about what I saw wi' Alexander," Cat said to the both of them.

"Aye?" they said in unison.

"Why was Alexander wearin' an animal wrapped around him?"

Iain and Lachlan looked at each other and burst out laughing.

"That was no animal. It was General John Cope's fur-lined coat!" Lachlan said, wiping tears from his eyes.

"The spoils o' war," Iain said, chuckling.

"Weel, I dinna think I would hae e'er guessed that one," Cat said, giggling. Wiping her hands on her apron, she put her arms in the crooks of both her brother's elbows and asked, "Are ye hungry?"

Not waiting for a reply, they all walked out of the shed smelling of lavender.

❧

Lachlan and Iain stayed for two days. For Iain, it was the first time he had seen where Cat lived, and now understood why Lachlan was so comfortable there. It had a sort of peace about it, as if the war — or any other malevolent event — could not break through the gentle energy surrounding it.

While they were there, word came that Angus and Seumas came through the battle at Prestonpans unscathed. Though not wanting to hear of the war while in that peaceful place, they rejoiced knowing their family was well.

Battles were being fought all around; each one the Jacobites engaged in, they were surprised at the ease of victory. The Hanoverians were still not taking the rebellion seriously.

Winter began to make its presence be felt in October. It snowed regularly, covering the hills knee-deep, and the fierce winds blew incessantly, making travel by foot a miserable task for both armies.

At the end of November, Angus and Seumas returned to *Slios Mìn* to wait out the worst of the winter. Cat was at the castle when she received a letter from Lachlan.

27 November, 1745
Dearest Catrìona,

Such glorious news I must share with you, that our father and brother have returned from the war to wait out the weather. Seumas told me that the battles were so one-sided as to not be a real war anyway, so why not be warm and dry until the English decide to join in!

It's good to have them home again. Da is worried for you, though, and would so much wish for you to come home until this war is over. He says that he can trust no one, as there is dissension in the higher ranks as to how far the Jacobites are willing to go. He thinks that since the English have little in the way of defense, the Prince will go all the way to London, if left to his own desires, but his Generals and the Chiefs can rarely decide on anything unanimously.

Did you hear what they are saying about the Jacobites? About roasting babes, raping women and killing for the pleasure of it? They do not know us very well.

Do think it over, about coming home, I mean. I do not want to sound like the big brother, but you cannot be safe out there by yourself. The castle has changed hands too many times for my taste. Besides, if the English do decide to make a stand, you could be right in their way. Send the raven if you decide to make the trip and I'll fetch you myself.

Your brother and most humble and obedient servant,
Lachlan

Cat folded the letter and placed it in her lap, thinking hard about what Lachlan said about going home. She was pretty much all alone, and with Alexander in Carrie, no divinations were going on. It was also rare to have someone summon her for a healing in the middle of winter. The more she thought about it, the more her mind was made up.

                                    ❧

On the first of December, in between snow storms, came a brief warm-up. Cat had sent the raven nearly a week earlier with a message that when it was convenient, she would like to have an escort home. Thinking only Lachlan would make the trip, she was quite surprised to see her father and Lachlan trudging through the mud to get her.

"Da!" she squealed, almost tripping over Gent to get out of the house to meet him.

"'Tis good to see ye do hae a good heid on yer shoulders, lass," he said warmly into her hair.

"Aye, well, that and the winter is too long to be alone," she said smiling, crooking her arm through his proffered elbow.

They would leave at first light, but Angus and Lachlan took the rest of the day to warm themselves by the fire, and they all filled their bellies with rabbit stew.

Cat had packed as many herbs, tinctures and ointments as she could carry in her satchel, but wished she could take more. Now that there were two extra horses, she loaded up a couple of blankets with the rest of her precious physics. She had no idea how long she would be away, and did not want to risk having them ruined.

Her father slept in Anna's bed, Cat slept in her own, and Lachlan took the rug in front of the fireplace alongside Gent, who seemed to have a smile on his face when Cat blew out the candles. It was cozy indeed.

By dawn, they were all up having one last breakfast in her cottage. Cat had made some extra bannocks the day before, and there was left-over rabbit so they would all have something to eat for the trip. Dolling out some food to her father and Lachlan, she carefully packed the rest into her saddlebag.

"I'll go saddle the horses, or do ye need more time, Cat?" Lachlan asked.

"No, go ahead, I'm nearly done here," Cat said, cleaning up the kitchen, as Angus smothered the fire. Gent decided he'd rather be with his sleeping partner, so joined Lachlan to the barn.

Within half an hour, Cat was closing the door to her cottage and mounting Clot Heid for what she hoped would not be too long. All of a sudden, she remembered her most prized possession was still under the floor boards inside. She dismounted, fending off good-natured jibes about how a woman's work was never done.

When she emerged with a polished wooden box under her arm, Angus and Lachlan looked at each other curiously, neither recognizing the piece of furniture.

"What hae ye there, lass?" Angus asked, dismounting Uallach to get a better look.

"Hae I ne'er shown this to ye?" she replied, adjusting it in her hands as if to present it to him. He just looked from the box to her, not sure what was expected of him.

"Well, go on, open it, Da. It wilna bite ye," she said, giggling.

Lachlan stood next to Angus wanting to see what his father was so enthralled with. Slowly, Angus lifted the brass clasp and opened the cover, seeming to know exactly what was in it, just not believing it.

"What is it, Da?" Lachlan asked, impatiently.

As the box opened, revealing the garnet-encrusted dirk, Lachlan inhaled at its beauty, much like Cat did when she first saw it.

"Where did ye get this?" Angus asked softly.

"Anna left it to me when she died. She said it was a payment from Tullibardine." Cat had not seen it since that day, and seeing it again was just as awe-inspiring as the first time. "Is there somethin' wrong, Da?"

"I had only heard o' this dirk, but ne'er laid eyes upon it. Most o' the clan think it's no' a real thing, just a myth."

"Where did it come from?" Lachlan asked his father, touching it gently to confirm its reality.

"This belonged to our 4th Chief of the Clan, Grizzled Robert Duncanson. It was his ceremonial dirk, thought lost for ages," Angus said in a quietly reverent voice. "It was given to him by King James II for capturin' Sir Robert Graham, who assassinated his father, King James I, o'er three hundred years ago."

Angus pulled the shimmering blade from its velvet nest and held it in his big hand, feeling its perfect weight and balance. "Well, I dinna ken where Tullibardine got it, but he kent who to entrust it to, didna he," he said gently placing it back in the velvet-lined box and closing the cover.

Cat and Lachlan shared the same expressions at the revelation, but before they could question their father on the dirk's history, he was mounting his horse and telling them to do the same. Cat carefully wrapped the box inside a blanket and tied it to the back of the saddle, while Lachlan quietly waited for her.

"What will ye do wi' the dirk, Cat, now that ye ken what it is?" Lachlan asked.

"I canna think o' why I would do anythin' different than what I was doin' wi' it," she stated in a far off voice.

Lachlan knew she was thinking something other than what she said by her hair twirling rapidly around her fingers. But the subject was closed; for now.

For the next few miles, all three rode silently in single file. Gent took the point position, ever watchful for anything that moved. The weather was almost spring-like and the further they went, the lighter their emotions felt, leaving the questions of the dirk behind.

Just before they reached a clearing, Angus stopped them when Gent's hair rose on his back and he started growling. Angus searched for the intruders with his hand on his pistol, ready for whatever lay ahead. Moments later, over the hill came a band of Highlanders coming from the south. Angus recognized the red, green and brown of the Stewart plaid, and knew they were heading home for the winter like so many others.

"'Tis all right, laddie, they're ours," Angus whispered, preferring not to draw attention to his family; friend or foe.

They waited in the woods until the Stewart men were nearly out of sight before continuing on their way. When they reached Bohally Wood, they stopped to rest. Trudging through six inches of snow was tiring, and in the sunlit warmth, the exerted horses steamed.

"Where are the Jacobites now, Da?" Lachlan asked, fishing for a chew of rabbit meat from his sporran.

"Seumas and I left when we were in Manchester, nearly one hundred miles into England. If I ken George Murray and the Prince, they'll be headin' for London, but I dinna ken exactly where they are right now. Why?"

"Och, no reason. I was just thinkin' o' what it would be like to best the wee German lairdie in his own house."

Angus chuckled at Lachlan's slang terminology for King George. "Aye, weel, if I'm no' present to find out, I'll be a happy man."

"Really, Da?" Cat asked, thinking for the first time that maybe, just maybe, her family will make it through this war safely.

"O' course, lass. I just want to get on wi' the rest o' my life in peace, watchin' my grandchildren grow up."

A look appeared in his eyes for a moment wishing Isobel could be there with him, but he hid it quickly. Cat caught it, but chose to ignore it, and changed the subject. She had forgotten that she was an Auntie now, and asked who the bairn looked like. Lachlan answered proudly, "He looks like a Robertson." Cat giggled and they all mounted their horses to continue their trip.

It was after nightfall when they reached *Slios Mìn*, just in time for the weather to return to winter. A cold rain began as they unsaddled their horses in the barn, and the wind howled through the doors, making an eerie whine.

Loaded with all of Cat's belongings in blankets and satchels, the three were soaked through when they reached the house. Iain opened the door for them, only to be nearly run over by Gent wanting to get out of the icy rain that was beginning to cling to his fur.

They settled in with a hot ale, hot meal and a warm fire, and went to bed happy to be a family again.

≥▲

By the end of December, word came through the Highlands that the Jacobites retreated from Derby, never making a run at London. Cat, who had been in a relative bliss-like state being with her family, was brought back to reality when Alexander sent word he would like her "eyes" on what would happen next to the Prince and his army.

"Damn it to hell!" she swore. "He kens the outcome o' this damned war already. Why does he need me to keep tellin' him?"

Angus waited patiently for her tirade to end before inviting the messenger in, but had to duck when a tea cup flew across the room, smashing on the door.

"Catrìona, are ye quite finished now?" he asked calmly, his hand on the door latch, unsure whether it was safe to open it yet.

With fire in her eyes and a heavy, agitated growl, she nodded and went upstairs to her room to see if there was anything new she could tell Alexander. Willing herself to calm down, she took several deep breaths, but still was not in the proper frame of mind to see. Reaching under her bed, she pulled out the box containing the *clach na brataich*. Holding the crystal, she let its energy remove the anger and wash her in peace.

After a few moments, her calm state returned, and she asked the crystal to give her a vision of the next moves of the war. Slowly, a vision of a long line of Highlanders came into her view. They were heading north, back into Scotland, but not because they were beat. Their rage over retreating before they could engage in battle filled her emotions. Constantly being harried by Hanoverian troops, not only in England, but in Scotland as well, the Jacobite army would not have an easy trip home.

She saw that in January, the Jacobites would take Stirling again, but would also engage in a battle at Falkirk Muir, which would be victorious, yet not seem so at first. Again, the Jacobites would retreat northward towards Inverness, where they would wait out the winter and have no other large military engagements.

Cat got the distinct impression that the Prince was no longer in charge of his army, and he was not pleased with the fact. Would the rebellion just fade away? Going further with the vision, she asked just that. The answer she got was not what she wanted, but it was the answer she knew still existed. The final battle.

silent moor

The remainder of the brutal winter passed with little word of the rebellion. There was little need for Cat's talents during those quiet months and she was glad of it. She felt like a normal person in a normal life, even spending time with Janet Murray, though finding the relationship much changed from when they were younger.

Cat was now very well acquainted with her new nephew, Teàrlach, and was growing very fond of Charlotte. During a family supper in which Seumas and his family were invited, Cat watched as wee Teàrlach fell asleep curled up on the floor with Gent. It was quite probably the most comforting image she had ever witnessed, and it burned itself into her memory, never to be erased. It filled her heart with a maternal longing she knew would never be fulfilled. She had known that all along, and had accepted it, but she was unprepared for the intensity of the feeling that hit her so strong it made her light-headed.

Excusing herself, she went up to her room to lie down, claiming a headache. As she lay there looking up at the beamed ceiling, she thought, not for the first time, about Greame Hay. Was he fighting for the Prince, or for King George? Or was he fighting at all, since he was the Duke's personal servant? It was strange how easily she could recreate his face in her mind. How long had she known the man, ten minutes? And how could that be called "knowing" someone?

"Christ O'Jesus, woman! Snap out o' it," she chastised herself, then got out of bed and went back down stairs.

ಎಲ

When the weather started warming at the end of March, word
came down from Inverness that the Prince was looking for recruits
again. Against all of Cat's pleading, Angus and Seumas headed north
at the end of first week in April to rejoin the Stuart army. Not long
after they left, she started having visions again.

While walking across the yard to the barn the next morning, she
was transported to a different place. She was now on a flat, open
expanse of moorland. It was raining and very raw, sending a shiver
through her. A death-like stillness permeated the air, as if the Earth
herself knew of the impending assault that would take place there.

Looking around, Cat could not understand why this would be
the chosen place to do battle, knowing Highlanders did not fight
well in pitched battles. It was chosen, but not unanimously. In fact,
there seemed to be quite a heated dispute over the site. Again, Cat
had the feeling of the Prince losing control, only now there was a
pettiness about it, as if this moor was chosen in spite of the dispute.

As the vision continued, she saw fires everywhere. They weren't
from the camps, nor were they from the cannons that now cracked
the silence with deafening roars. With mind-shocking clarity, she
realized the fuel for the fires was men. They were in piles, three and
four high, not all dead, but being burned anyway. The apocalypse
was so vivid she saw the faces of the dead. Faces she knew. The acrid
stink of seared flesh burned her nose, and the smoke filled her lungs,
making her cover her mouth and nose with her sleeve. Screams of
the dying pierced her ears, and she fell to the ground in sobbing
blindness.

From the barn, Iain heard her crying and ran out to see what
happened. Rushing to Cat's side, he tried to hold her, but still in the
vision, she struck at him, thinking he was trying to throw her into
the flames with her countrymen. Panicking, Iain ran to the house to
get Lachlan's help, but he was not inside. He raced back out see if
Cat had come out of the vision yet, and found Lachlan cradling her
on the ground where he left her.

"Is she all right?" he asked, breathlessly, still alarmed by the depth
of her state.

Lachlan looked up with fear in his eyes. "This is the worst one I
hae ever seen her go through. She isna comin' out of it."

"What can we do?" Iain asked.

"Help me get her into the house, then we hae to see if we can bring her senses to a different place," Lachlan said, lifting Cat from the cold ground.

Having no previous experience with Cat's visions, Iain was at a loss how to accomplish that, but hooked Cat's arm over his shoulder and helped walk her inside.

They laid her on the settee, and Iain scrambled around for a blanket. Maggie, who had watched them bring Cat in after Iain's frantic burst through the house in search of Lachlan, rushed from the kitchen to take over as nursemaid. She sat next to Cat, brushing the thick locks from her forehead, whispering soothing words in Gaelic.

Lachlan came running down the stairs with an armful of different herbs, and even had the forethought to bring the *clach na brataich*. Setting his armload on the floor, he started opening jars of herbs and running them under Cat's nose. At first he tried the pungent ones, but they only seemed to make her more agitated. Next, he tried some camphor; sharp, to startle her out of her unseen surroundings. While certainly opening her eyes, she was still in the other world.

"Damn it!" he said to the ceiling. "I need some help here!" He closed his eyes to calm down, then took a few deep breaths. When he opened his eyes, he reached for the lavender and the crystal. He placed the crystal on Cat's forehead and instructed Maggie to hold it there. Opening the muslin bag of lavender, he held it under her nose. Slowly, she began to quiet, and all the worried eyes upon her also relaxed.

Slowly, Cat opened her eyes to see her concerned family surrounding her. She smiled shakily, then closed them again. Lachlan knew it was over, and once again looked to the ceiling and said, "Thank ye."

Cat slept for most of the day, her brothers checking in when they could, but Maggie rarely left her side, keeping herself busy with the mending she had been meaning to get to for some time.

When darkness fell and Maggie was in the kitchen preparing supper, Cat got up, still drained from her ordeal, but gaining strength. She walked into the kitchen, ravenous, and startled Maggie, who was just about to bring a bowl of broth to Cat.

"I'll save ye the trip." Retrieving a spoon, she rescued the broth before the contents were upset any further.

"Are ye feelin' better, Catrìona?" Maggie asked, still concerned by her gray pallor.

"Och, aye," Cat said, waving her off as if nothing at all had happened. "This is a fine broth, Maggie."

Moments later, Cat watched Lachlan and Iain walk in for their supper as quietly as they could, in an effort not to wake her. Their eyes opened wide in surprise when they saw her sitting in the kitchen eating.

In amongst their concerns for her state of health, hugs, kisses and nervous looks, came of course, the question. Lachlan was the one who broached it.

"What did ye see, Cat?"

Cat stared at him for a moment, silent. For an instant, she was back in her vision, then shook it off and tried to compose the best way to tell them.

"It doesna matter what I saw, for I care not to return to that horror. But I hae set me mind to one thing, and that is to retrieve Da and Seumas before they die on that battlefield."

She got up from her chair and walked upstairs without any further explanation. Her brothers chased after her with a barrage of questions, coming to a halt in her small bedroom.

Sitting on the edge of her bed preening her fingernails, she refused to answer them in their heated states. Finally, they caught on, and silenced themselves.

"Are ye ready to listen to me, or do ye want to continue on wi' yer chastisin'?" She looked each of them square in the eyes for any leftover debate, but found only a spark.

"Since Da and Seumas left only yesterday morn, we should be able to catch up to them in a couple o' days, right?"

"Aye," they said skeptically.

"Right then. Now, how far is it to Inverness from here?" she asked.

"About 70 miles," Iain answered.

"Good. Not close enough to get caught out on that battlefield if we dinna catch up to them right away."

"What are ye hopin' to say to change their minds about fightin'? Ye remember what Seumas said about the *Sassenachs* no' even wantin' to engage us in battle. Why should this battle be any different than the others?" Lachlan stated, getting agitated again.

"This one's different because it's no' Cope leadin' the Hanoverians, it's the man I told Seumas about a year last. This new commander is no' afraid of the Jacobites, nor will he let his men be afraid o' them, for fear o' his retribution if they fail. He's a hardened soldier who will no' be caught unaware like the others."

"Can ye no' tell us why this is so important now, Cat?" Iain pleaded.

Cat thought about it for a minute, then said "I refuse to hae to look for yer faces in the burnin' stacks o' men when ye are dead."

৯

The three left in a cold rain the next morning, staying to the mountains instead of the new road General Wade built going from Blair Atholl to Inverness. The travel was more difficult, but safer.

By the end of the first day, they had not seen a soul — Jacobite or Hanoverian. Iain figured they covered only about fifteen miles through that high terrain. From their rest stop on the top of a mountain at the northeastern end of Loch Ericht, they could see the road to Inverness. They also saw a village. All of them were frozen to the bone, and did not relish sleeping in the snow-covered heather, but were skeptical about being seen in town. The longer they stayed on their frigid perch, the easier it was to make the decision to find a warm inn in which to spend the night.

The town was called Dalwhinnie, they found out. It consisted of a small inn and a few crofts, but not much more. No matter, they ate a hot meal and shared a room at the top of the stairs, while below, a few hardy Highlanders drank in relative quiet.

By dawn the next morning, the three set out once more, but in more favorable weather. Iain suggested they take the road following the River Truim to make up some time, since no one seemed to be around. Cat and Lachlan agreed, and by mid-day, they had traveled nearly as many miles as they had all the previous day.

Seeing Highlanders only twice in their travels for the day, Cat began to wonder if she had misinterpreted her vision. She had seen that the battle was to be very soon, but a battle with whom? Shouldn't there be Hanoverians everywhere by now?

"Do ye think we missed Da and Seumas? They didna hae as

good travellin' weather as we hae," she thought out loud, getting a little nervous about being so close to mostly Hanoverian Inverness.

Her anxiety seemed to reflect precisely what Lachlan and Iain were thinking, for neither said a word. They travelled on in silence until around dusk, when they reached a small town called Aviemore, near the River Spey. Shelling out money for another night's stay inside seemed to rankle Lachlan, but when it started to sleet, he subscribed to the idea a bit easier.

The Lynwilg Mail was a coaching hotel, though not many coaches were travelling this time of year. Between the snow or the mud, horseback or foot were the only sensible modes of transportation. The three finished their hot ales and warm pasties, but were not quite ready to retire to their room, choosing to sit by the fire to drive the ever-present chill from their bones.

Cat watched the patrons come and go, half expecting to see her father and brother walk through the door. It was not to be. When the clock on the wall struck ten o'clock, Cat relinquished her vigil and allowed herself, and her brothers, to go to bed.

When they got up to their room, Iain announced that Inverness was only a one day ride.

"What will we do when we get there?" he asked Cat.

"If the Prince is truly in Inverness, then his troops will be there as well. We'll just hae to find Da and Seumas there," she stated, confidently.

"But then what?" Lachlan asked.

Cat stood beside the window twirling her hair, the sleet pellets made a scratching noise as they hit the panes.

"I dinna ken."

                                    ❧

Inverness was filled to capacity with Jacobites, having taken over the town and holding it as their own since the end of February. The Jacobite army was now only some forty-five hundred strong. Half of their numbers had returned to their homes to wait out the winter's inactivity and were not reinstated yet. It was April 13.

Just before dusk, the three arrived in the bustling town. Unable to spend the night in an inn since all the rooms in town were taken by the Jacobites, they continued just to the east of town, where they found an old croft in near ruin. It was unoccupied, therefore serving the purpose of getting mostly out of the weather for the night.

Iain gathered some wood for a fire, and Lachlan and Cat built a large lean-to with their blankets. It may not be a bed, but they would be cozy. As the fire started to warm them, Lachlan heard hoof beats heading in their direction. All three of them froze. It was more than likely a Jacobite, but who could be sure?

The hoof beats slowed as they neared the croft, stopping beside it. The unknown rider did not dismount, maybe he was thinking the same as they were. Finally, as the rider's horse started to dance around, a voice called out.

"Hallò in the house," came the muffled request.

Aside from the fact that it was a far cry from a house, Highland manners prevailed.

"Da?" Cat whispered.

The rider dismounted, his footfalls in the crunching grass indicated he was coming in. Iain and Lachlan got up with their hands on their dirks, ready to meet the mysterious man entering their house. Cat sat by the fire with a smile on her face, rubbing her hands together.

As the firelight illuminated the barrel chest, then the face of their father, the previously charged air relaxed considerably. That was until the reality that all of his children were in the danger zone struck him.

"What in bloody hell are ye doin' here?" he boomed.

"Just like home," Cat chuckled.

Angus stood there glaring at her, until she met his eyes. In them, he saw that there was good reason for her being there, and relinquished some of the anger. Taking a seat by the fire, he remained silent for a few minutes, as if composing his request for them to return home immediately. Cat broke the silence and saved him the unnecessary speech.

"I hae seen the final battle, Da. I hae seen what will happen under this new English commander. It will be butchery for the Jacobites, and it will happen verra soon."

"Sooner than ye think, lass. Cumberland is headin' this way wi' an army twice the size of ours. That's what I was on my way to tell the Prince."

"Da, I saw a flat, open moor as the battlefield. Is there such a place near here?"

"Aye, O'Sullivan chose the site today. Culloden. The locals call it Drummossie Muir. Lord George Murray tried to tell the Prince that Highlanders dinna do their best fightin' on that sort o' ground," he said through clenched teeth, tossing another stick into the fire.

"What did the Prince say?" Iain asked, sitting beside his father on a broken stone wall.

"He said his men were invincible, and that his God was on his side."

As he spoke, Cat felt him try to keep his emotions in check. He knew, as she did, that this battle would not be in the Jacobite's favor.

"Is there no way to meet Cumberland somewhere else?" Lachlan asked.

Angus stood up and stretched. "I'm goin' to try to convince the Prince to do just that, lad." He left them, walking through what was left of the doorway into the night. The three watched him disappear, then heard him mount Uallach and trot away.

"Be safe, Da," Cat murmured.

They slept huddled together for warmth in the dilapidated croft, and by dawn, a cold dampness prevailed, echoing their emotions. They didn't bother with a fire, choosing to get to the Jacobite camp as quickly as possible. Cat was hoping that since she had predicted the favorable outcomes for the Prince at Perth and Edinburgh, maybe she could persuade him to change the field of battle to one more suitable for Highlanders. Her brothers thought it was worth a try, and on empty bellies, they rode back to Inverness.

Nearing the Jacobite camps, it looked as though the mob was preparing to leave. The three looked at each other, daring to hope their father got through to the Prince, changing his mind about the location of the battle. It was not hard to tell where the Prince was staying; heavy guards around one of the modest houses gave him away. They headed straight for it, with Cat in the lead.

The guards were not especially concerned with their approach, but would not just let them walk into the house either.

"What business hae ye here, lass?" He was a short, wiry man with flaming red hair and beard.

"I need to speak wi' the Prince."

"That wilna be necessary," came a voice from behind.

All three of them turned around to see their father and Seumas with grins on their faces.

"C'mon, the lot o' ye. Let's get out o' the cold," Angus said, gathering his brood to a nearby inn. "There's only bread to eat, but at least we'll be warm in there."

When they all had taken seats as close to the fire as possible, Iain asked if he had been able to change the Prince's mind. He told them the Prince had wavered a bit, but since being demoted in the field at Falkirk Muir, he was not listening to anyone at this time.

"He wants to see for himself this unfit battlefield, then he'll make his decision," he said. "That's where e'eryone's goin'."

"Are ye no' goin' wi' them, Da?" Cat asked, feeling he had other plans.

Angus moved his head in closer to his children. They all huddled together as he whispered his plan.

"Culloden is about five miles southeast of here. Seumas and I are goin' wi' the rest, then I'm goin' to scout out exactly where Cumberland's army is. Hopefully, I'll return by mid-day."

"What should we do, Da?" Lachlan asked, wishing he could help.

"The three of ye will stay here. This is still the main camp. Wi' any luck, Prince Charles will see the futility of Culloden and move back here to fight Cumberland somewhere better suited to us."

He and Seumas got up to leave, but Cat stopped them with a hand in the air. Seumas nearly knocked over the chair in anger, refusing to hear what she had to say and left, slamming the door behind him. Undaunted, Cat let the vision play out while her father waited.

Cat looked up at her father with deep sorrow in her eyes, ready to tell him what she saw, but before she could say anything, he asked, "How long has that been goin' on?"

"E'er since he got hurt at the Games," Cat stated, waving it off as if it didn't really bother her.

"What? Why?" Angus asked, incredulously, waiting for Seumas to come back inside.

"He thinks I make the things I see happen by tellin' o' them," Cat replied. "He thinks I'm a witch."

"What? This is intolerable. I canna believe this has been goin' on for ... what ... five, six years, now, and I ne'er kent about it. Why hae ye no' come to me about it, Cat? Why do ye think ye hae to carry all the burden?"

"Isna that what Seers do, Da?"

"Oh, Christ, Cat."

Angus looked at Iain and Lachlan and asked them if they knew about Seumas' behavior towards her. Both dropped their heads, indicating they knew all too well.

"He'll be spoken to, as soon as I'm able."

Wanting the subject closed, she got back to recounting her vision. "Da, there's a celebration in the Cumberland camp. Do ye think he thinks he's already won the war?"

"I dinna ken," he sighed deeply, then tried to get back to the business at hand. "Do ye see where he is right now? It would save me a lot of time if I kent exactly where to find him."

Cat closed her eyes in an attempt to get a direction and distance. Her head kept going to the east, but the small lines between her brows indicated she was not really sure about something. When her eyes opened, she said "He's due east o' here, but I dinna ken how far. I only ken it isna too far away. I hope that helps ye, Da."

"Due east, huh. It could be that he's in Nairn, near twelve miles from here," he said, scratching a few days growth of beard on his chin. "Aye, I'll head there first."

Angus left the inn, but Lachlan and Iain were chomping at the bit for something to do to help.

"I just canna sit here all day waitin'," Lachlan said, pacing the floor near the fire. Iain nodded in agreement.

"Ye could go huntin', but ye canna use yer pistols. I dinna ken about ye, but I'm hungry," Cat said, understanding the need to keep busy until word came from their father. Almost before she finished the suggestion, her brothers were out the door. Cat decided to find the innkeeper and see if she could help in the kitchen.

☙

The day turned to night without word from anyone. The town was nearly empty of Jacobites, and it seemed to breathe a sigh of relief. Iain had returned with a grouse and Lachlan with a pair of rabbits. They shared their bounty with the few who remained in the inn.

A rider came into town and burst through the inn's front door with news that the Jacobites were remaining in Culloden to engage Cumberland in the morning.

Cat looked at Iain and Lachlan with a kind of defeat on her face. "Ye canna change fate," she murmured.

"We dinna ken if it's true or no', Cat. Da hasna returned yet and I would rather hear it from him," Iain said.

Noticing the clock on the wall, it read half past eight. She freed a lock of her hair from her kerch and began twisting it. Lachlan started pacing and Iain stared at the fire in the fireplace.

After an excruciating hour, another rider was heard coming near the inn. Cat rushed to the door to greet her father. He walked through the door in a *whoosh* of cold air, sending shivers through her.

He walked over to the corner table and sat down heavily in a chair that did not look like it would hold him, but amazingly did. The three of them followed and took seats of their own.

"We heard the Jacobites are waitin' to fight Cumberland on the moor. Is it true, Da?" Lachlan asked, quietly.

"Aye," he said. "It seems the more the Prince is told what he should do, the more determined he is to do the opposite."

Cat pushed away from the table, but before she left, she asked, "Where did ye find Cumberland?"

"In Nairn. I suggested to the Prince that there was a more suitable battle ground nearby, and that we could catch Cumberland by surprise there. He told me he would sleep on it."

Cat resumed her route to bed in no better spirits than before her father returned.

ૐ

Before dawn, Cat heard a rider leave. Her father. She got up to see if she could help with breakfast, since she was no longer able to sleep. When she got to the kitchen, she was immersed in the smell of onions and bacon, and a woman near her age was kneading bread dough. The woman looked up from her task and smiled.

"Can I be helpin' ye?" Cat asked the dark haired woman with the striking blue eyes behind the butcher's block table.

"Och, aye, I'll no' turn away help," she said in a soft voice. "I'm Sarah Mackintosh."

"I'm Catrìona Robertson. Pleased to meet ye, Sarah." Tying on an apron and putting on her kerch, she was ready to help in any way she could. "What would ye like me to do?"

"Ye can start dressin' those rabbits. I'm near done wi' this bread, then I can finish the stew."

The two worked in amiable silence for a time, stealing glances at each other every so often, taking in each other's appearance and mannerism. When Cat finished preparing the rabbits, she could take it no longer. Obviously, neither could Sarah. At the same time they turned from their tasks and asked, "Do I ken ye from somewhere?" They looked at each other and giggled.

"I dinna think we hae e'er met," Cat said. "I hae ne'er been to Inverness before two days past, but I feel I ken ye."

"'Tis verra strange ye should say that, for I feel I ken ye, as well."

Before Cat could stop it, she found herself saying, "Maybe it was in another life." She was always very careful not to say things like that to people she didn't know. It made some people afraid of her, and that was the last thing she wanted with Sarah. But, to her surprise, Sarah just smiled.

"Aye, maybe it was."

Cat cocked her head and looked inquisitively at Sarah. Sarah had done the same thing as she in the company of "normal" people. She had put herself in a bubble so the uneducated couldn't feel the peculiar energy Seers had.

"When did ye ken that I had the Sight?" Cat asked, very curious about what Sarah knew.

"When I heard ye whisperin' yer thanks to the wee rabbits before dressin' them."

Cat giggled and put the pair of rabbits on the butcher block. Standing next to Sarah, who was a good five or six inches shorter, they shared nearly the same figure. She had never met another Seer even close to her age, and was dying to ask a thousand questions, comparing what they saw and how they saw it. Once again, maybe inadvertently reading each other's minds, they started the question at the same time.

"Weel, I can see we're no' goin' to get much accomplished this way," Sarah laughed.

"I think the secret is to no' think about the question before we ask it, just let it out. Care to try it?" Cat said, pulling a knife from the block to begin butchering the rabbits.

"Aye. Ye first," Sarah said, forming the dough into four round balls and covering them with linens.

"How long hae ye kent ye had the Sight?"

"I had my first vision the day I started my courses. It was so amazin', but it scairt the life out o' me at the same time. How about ye?" Sarah asked, wiping her hands on her apron.

"It was the same thing wi' me. How do ye get yer visions?" Cat asked.

"Ye mean what do I use to get my visions?"

Cat smiled and nodded, remembering that most Seers need tools to see with. "Aye."

"I hae a holy well near my cott. It ne'er freezes so I can use the dark, quiet water to see into. What about ye?"

"I just ask, and I see whate'er it is I ask about. Sometimes, if I canna stay calm, I use a crystal, but no' verra often."

This seemed to scare Sarah a little. Cat felt it and immediately put up her bubble.

"I didna mean to frighten ye, Sarah. I ken that most dinna see as I do. Even my teacher couldna do what I do." She reached over and laid her hand on Sarah's to calm her. It relaxed her a bit, but she remained ill at ease.

"Ye're verra lucky that ye hae no' been found a witch," Sarah whispered.

Cat smiled sadly, realizing that her newfound friend was caught up in the scare tactics of religion. Just then, with his uncanny timing, Lachlan walked into the kitchen in search of food.

"Oh, Lachlan, I'm verra glad ye here. This is Sarah, she can fix ye some breakfast. Where is Iain?" she asked, flustered, flitting uncharacteristically around the kitchen for a moment before excusing herself to fetch Iain.

As soon as she left the warm room, she ran upstairs, trying to get as far away from Sarah Mackintosh as she could. Before making it to her room, Iain stepped into the hallway and they nearly collided.

"Whoa! What's yer rush, Cat? What's wrong?" he asked, grabbing her arm in an effort to stop her.

Cat just looked at him, then saying nothing, wrapped her arms around his neck and cried. A very confused and worried Iain just held her until she was ready to talk. He walked her into his room, closed the door for some privacy, then sat her down on the bed. Within moments, she had calmed down and released herself from his neck.

"Can ye tell me now?" Iain whispered, pulling away the hair that hid her face.

"Och, I was just bein' stupid," she said, angrily wiping the tears from her eyes with her sleeve.

"Well, since I hae no' kent ye to be stupid verra often, can ye tell me what happened, then?" he inquired, offering her a handkerchief from his coat. She waved him off.

"The cook downstairs is a Seer," she said, glancing at Iain to see his reaction. He only quirked his eyebrow. "I was so happy to meet someone near my own age wi' the Sight that I didna take my usual precautions."

"What precautions?" Iain asked.

Knowing Iain was not as keen about her talents as Lachlan was, she explained it as simply as she could. "I told her I didna use any tools to get my visions — somethin' I ne'er do, because nearly all Seers use tools."

"Why should that be a problem to another Seer?" He was perplexed. "Shouldna she want to ken more about it, since it's a better way to do the same task?"

"Some Seers are scairt o' how I work. They think it's witchcraft, like Seumas," she said bitterly. "They go by what the Christians think instead o' rememberin' their pagan past." She got up and angrily paced around the small room. "Doesna she remember that Christians tried to kill all wi' the Sight no' that long ago? They murdered hundreds o' thousands o' innocent people because we scairt them. Does she think that since she uses a *holy well*, she's any different than I am? Does she think they wouldna condemn her for it if they chose to hunt us again?"

"Cat, ye need to calm yerself," he said, watching her go back and forth in front of him. "Ye ken that ye canna change an entire society, ye just need to make it work for ye. Like ye hae been doin'."

"Aye, well, that's all about to change too, isna it. And no' for the better." She sat next to Iain on the bed twirling her hair, but could not remain still. "Och, I need some air."

Iain said nothing to stop her or ask if she wanted company. He knew better. She had to work it out on her own. He decided to go to the kitchen and meet Sarah Mackintosh for himself.

ॐ

Cat was hit in the face with stinging sleet when she walked out to get some air. It was light now, but as dismal as her mood. She wandered aimlessly through streets ensconced in deep silence. Without any concept of time or distance, she looked up to find that she had walked to the shores of the Moray Firth. She stopped and listened to the small waves lap the sand, but the fog was too thick to see very far. In the harbor, ghostly masts lurked in the thickness, creating a surreal dance. Taking a deep breath, she noted the sea-scented air; fresh, akin to that of a passing thunderstorm. Gulls pierced the quiet with their sharp cries, swooping in and out of the grayness.

With each lap of wave ebbing from her feet, she could feel the tension drain from her mind, body and soul. She closed her eyes, finding herself at total peace, the likes of which she had not felt for a very long time. She lifted her arms and raised her smiling face to the sky, mindless of the cold rain, feeling again her connection to the Earth. It had been another lifetime when she felt this close to the natural world. Life kept getting in the way, keeping her from feeling the Mother's warmth and protection.

For a fleeting moment, the fog lifted, the Earth's reward for her appreciation of the place. As far as the eye could see, the land embraced the water on both sides, with a clear view of the slate gray liquid all the way to the horizon. She was awestruck by its beauty. But just as quickly as the shroud lifted, it closed again, protecting the mere mortal from being overwhelmed by its grandeur.

Cat turned with a smile on her face, relieved of her burden, and headed back to town. It was near noon when she returned to the deserted streets. Recognizing Uallach out in front of the inn, she ran the rest of the way, finding her father with a hot ale in his grasp, talking with Iain and Lachlan.

"Oh, good, there ye are," Angus said, wiping the froth from his well-established mustache. "Sit down, we need to talk."

Cat sat next to her father, avoiding both of her brothers' condemning glares. She was quite aware she was gone too long without telling them where she would be, but inwardly smiled at the knowledge that they must have made an excuse for her, since her father wasn't climbing down her throat with questions of her whereabouts for the past four hours.

"I do hope it's good news, Da."

"Well, it just may be. It seems that the celebration ye saw was a birthday party for the Duke o' Cumberland. He's celebratin' as we speak, sippin' brandy in Nairn. The Prince is furious once again."

"Does this mean ye hae convinced the Prince to go to Nairn after all?" Her excitement showed on her face, and her father smiled.

"Lord George has convinced him to meet Cumberland as we did in Prestonpans — unexpectedly. We are to march before nightfall, so I must leave now to rejoin the troops," he said, putting his massive hand over hers. "Is there anythin' I should ken?"

"I'll need a minute," she said, walking over to a quiet corner of the room. After a few minutes, she returned with an expression of concern on her face.

"What is it, Cat?"

"Ye wilna make it to Nairn in surprise, but ye must convince Lord George no' to turn back to Culloden," she stressed. "There's still naught but death there for the Jacobites."

⁊⧫

Iain and Lachlan stayed downstairs after Cat retired for the evening. For a time they were quiet with their thoughts, pushing around items on the table and swirling the dark ale in their mugs. Iain broke the silence.

"I want to help Da convince the Jacobites no' to return to Culloden," he blurted out quickly.

Lachlan's first reaction was of shock, not for the content of the statement, but the for the parallel thoughts he was just having.

"I was thinkin' the verra same thing, but Cat wilna let us go."

"I ken that. It'll hae to done in secret. If we leave now, we can catch up quickly to the army, since most will be on foot. We hae horses and the weather is good." Convincing himself, as much as Lachlan.

"Cat will kill us if we fight," Lachlan said, remembering his promise.

"I ne'er said anythin' about fightin'. But Cat said Culloden is where death is. If we can convince enough men to no' return to that moor, maybe we can save them."

Iain's words were rational, and Lachlan saw the valor in the task. Smiling, Lachlan raised his mug in a toast to the cheating of fate. Iain clinked it together with Lachlan's, swallowing the remaining liquid in a single gulp.

"Let's go, *bràthair beag.*"

Without looking back, they headed into the night in search of the Jacobites. Little did they know that with barely enough food to sustain mice, the Jacobite army was disheartened, to say the least. Many broke ranks to find food, while others curled up in their plaids and slept, hoping provisions would arrive by morning.

The troops that did march to Nairn got a very late start, leaving well after dark. In their cold and hungry state, the trek was punishing. The darkness necessitated a slow pace, and Iain and Lachlan caught up to the mob several hours into the excursion.

Just as they suspected, most of the army was on foot, leaving specter-like Uallach to stand out in the crowd. Iain nudged his horse to catch up to his father; Lachlan following suit. As they got closer, they noticed another rider on a dark horse. It was Seumas. Sidling up to him, Iain saw Seumas' white teeth as he smiled.

"I kent ye would join us, *bràithrean,*" Seumas said softly, patting his brother on the shoulder.

Angus was not as thrilled to see his two sons, demanding they all pull off the road to discuss this fool-hearty plan of theirs.

"Let me guess. Ye didna tell Catrìona ye were single-handedly goin' to save the Jacobite army from destruction, did ye?" Even in the dark, he didn't have to hear them answer. He knew they left her without a word. "Christ! What were ye thinkin'!"

"We didna come to fight, Da, we only came to help ye persuade the army to no' return to Culloden," Lachlan said defensively, thoroughly convinced it was that simple.

"And how do ye propose to stay out o' the fight? Ye hae no idea what it will be like," he growled. "What if we canna keep them from returnin' to Culloden, then what? Do ye think ye can hide from the Hanoverians? Do ye think I can protect ye from bein' hurt?" If there was enough light to see their father's face, they would have seen the tears forming in his eyes. "Yer Mam warned us about this." Shaking his head in hopelessness.

"Da, they'll be fine. I'll keep my eyes on them and keep them out o' danger," Seumas promised.

かん

Angus was just beginning to think Cat may have misinterpreted the journey to Nairn. Only four miles were all that separated the surprise attack on the Hanoverians. On the cusp of dawn, the wind rose in a fury, the scent of rain permeated the air, then came the order that they were turning back. The element of surprise would not be in their favor if they could not reach Cumberland's camp before first light, which was now impossible.

Now began the task of trying to get the Jacobites to stay where they were, hunkering down where they could, and let Cumberland meet them in a much better suited field of battle, the woods. One by one, the Robertson's of Aulich spoke to their clansmen. Some listened, taking off to find food while they could before the fighting broke out, or just finding shelter under the gorse to get some sleep. They were exhausted and bitter, disbelieving that once again, when so close, they were ordered to turn back.

The cold rain started a couple hours after dawn. After catching a little sleep, Angus woke to see that there weren't many Jacobites remaining. Nearly three quarters returned to Culloden, despite his warnings. He tried, but these few tired, cold and hungry men would not be able to hold off Cumberland's army for long. He had to send Iain and Lachlan back to Inverness — out of harms way.

As he started to rouse his sons, a distant thunder rolled, only this was a man-made thunder. He mounted his horse and went to gauge how close Cumberland was to them, but not before instructing Seumas to wake the camp and prepare for anything.

Within a quarter hour, Angus returned with news that some nine thousand Hanoverians were descending upon them, and they must retreat.

"At least we'll be in better shape than those who marched all night wi'out sleep, aye?" he told them, in an effort to boost their spirits.

By the time they broke camp, the sound of the pipes were heard, and the remaining Jacobites from their protected knoll, saw the line of Hanoverians stretching as far as the eye could see. They knew to remain would be futile.

"Iain, Lachlan, ride to Culloden and tell the Jacobite commanders that Cumberland is but a few miles from them. That should give them time to rally."

They mounted their horses, but before they could ride, Angus shouted to them, "The two o' ye listen to me now. Once ye hae alerted the Jacobites, get back to Inverness wi' yer sister. Understand?"

They both agreed, then took off as fast as their steeds could take them.

ॐ

April 16, 1746. Cat woke up crying, though could not remember the dream that upset her so. She got dressed and went to Lachlan's room, only to find it empty. With a sinking feeling, she ran further down the hall to Iain's room. It too was empty. Neither bed had been slept in. With little hope they had too much to drink last night and slept at the table she left them at, she ran downstairs. Finding the innkeeper, she asked if he had seen her brothers.

"Och, no. They left last night," the old man said, brushing crumbs from the tables.

She sat in the nearest chair before her legs gave out from under her. When seeing all the color drain from Cat's face, he quickly brought her a dram and pushed it in front of her. "Drink this, lass."

Cat studied the amber liquid for a moment, then downed it in one gulp. "Did they say where they were goin'?" she asked, hoarse from the burning liquid.

"Left wi'out a word, they did. Dinna fash now, they probably just went to watch the battle."

With that stab of reality, Cat regained herself, the color returning in full bloom to her face. She ran to saddle Clot Heid, all the time wishing for a club to beat her brothers with when she found them. Rage drove her on. Just before she raised her foot for the stirrup, she heard her mother's voice say, "*Ye'll need to be strong for our men, Cat.*"

"I will no' be strong enough to keep them out o' trouble this time, Mam."

Mounting her horse, she headed southeast at breakneck speed, towards Culloden. The rain and wind whipped around her in a wild frenzy, making it difficult to see. Refusing to slow to a safer pace, she pressed on, figuring she would arrive around noon, and hoped it would not be too late.

The road was muddy and slippery, bogging Clot Heid down. Once out of the thick soup, though, he resumed a full gallop, as Cat urged him on. At a sharp bend in the road, not more than two miles from the battlefield, he slipped on a patch of open granite ledge and the two went down hard. Cat was thrown to the side, landing in gorse and granite, knocked unconscious. Clot Heid wasn't as lucky. He had broken his left rear leg, and was thrashing in agony trying to right himself.

In her unconscious state, Cat dreamt of flying. She soared over the open sea — a much better method of travel, she concluded, than a claustrophobic ship. She felt the warm breeze wash over her; shades of blue and green filled her eyes, and she tasted the salt spray as the waves crested with white froth.

For a long time there was only water, but then, off in the distance on the horizon, she began to see the beginnings of a shape. Deep purple at first, but as she flew closer, the mass turned gray, then dark green from the fir trees lining a rock-bound coast. She flew over wide pebble beaches and long, tree-lined coves cut into the coastline. Small villages dotted the shore, but they were not made of stone. The houses were long, made of logs and had rounded tops. This wasn't Scotland. She didn't know where it was, but she knew it wasn't her home country.

A loud noise woke her, interrupting her explorations. She was very cold and wet. Opening her eyes, sparks seemed to fly in front of them, and her head ached terribly. She tried to get up to assess the damage, but excruciating pain seared through her head, making her nauseous. Rolling to her side as carefully as she could, she pulled a few gorse thorns from hand and cheek, then gingerly felt the back of her head. Her fingers came away sticky and red with blood. There was a good size knot there, but she didn't think it was too bad.

She managed to get herself to a sitting position, but kept her head between her legs to retard the waves of nausea. Nearby, she heard labored breathing, intermingled with deep groans. Daring to look up, she found Clot Heid lying on his side, his back leg bleeding from the broken bone piercing through the skin.

"What hae I done?" she whimpered.

Off in the distance, cannon fire tore through the afternoon, affirming Cat's suspicions that she was too late to help her family. All of her pent up frustration was released in heavy sobs, making her head feel like it would explode. She threw up a couple of times, relieving her nausea, but was powerless to help Clot Heid in his agony. She would need all her strength to end his life with just her dirk, and that meant time.

But time she did not have. The gunfire was getting closer. It seemed as though there were thousands and thousands of guns all going off at the same time. How could anyone live through that barrage?

With all her effort, she got to her feet. Deciding that one more shot going off would not be heard through the din, she pulled the pistol from her waist belt and checked the primer. It had managed to stay dry because her cloak covered it when she fell.

Clot Heid was exhausted from his attempts to stand, and remained on the ground. His eyes were wild when he looked at Cat. She bent down and placed her hand on his cheek, rubbing and cooing to calm him.

"It'll be o'er soon, lad," she told him, then cocked the pistol and fired.

{€

The sun had the audacity to show itself periodically on what should have remained a thoroughly bleak day. Concluding it was only early afternoon, Cat had no idea what to do now. The battle must be over, as only sporadic gunfire was still heard. She couldn't chance going to the battlefield in broad daylight, having seen the gruesome butchery of the aftermath of this fight. She would have to wait for dark when she could walk invisible through the carnage.

Starting the walk back to Inverness, she heard women speaking in the distance. Cat waited on the side of the road with her hand on her dirk. Soon, three women came into view, better than averagely dressed. Cat assumed they had not heard of the battle, and stepped into the road for an introduction.

She must have looked a sight; bloody, filthy and not without a bit of a crazed looked in her eyes. Instead of fearing her, they ran to her aid, sending Cat into tears all over again.

"Dear child, what has happened to ye?"

Cat relayed her story to the sympathetic ears, all the while having her head wound cleaned and bandaged.

"I'm Anne Leith. This is my friend, Mrs. Stonor, and her maid, Eppy." The four exchanged pleasantries, then Cat asked where they were heading.

"To tend to the wounded, of which there must be many, if the reports are correct," Anne said.

"But it wilna be safe for ye until dark. They are leavin' no one alive," Cat said weakly, her head hurting fresh from the treatment.

"I must go and help where I can. Will ye be all right on yer own goin' back to Inverness?" Anne said, picking up her basket of bandages and remedies.

Cat thought for a minute. If these women were willing to risk their lives to help, then she would not run away from the danger either. At this point, what did she have to lose?

"No. I'll go wi' ye. I'm a healer and will be able to help." Cat stated, mustering herself up to the task. "What hae ye in yer wee basket besides bandages?"

"Scissors, whisky, Angelica root and Nettle," Eppy declared.

"Good. I hae some Bone Knit in my satchel, but no' much else. Och, I wish I had all my remedies wi' me, but we'll just hae to make do," Cat said, feeling the strength return to her.

"Are ye sure ye are up to it, then?" asked Anne.

"Aye. My Da and three brothers are out there somewhere. I was waitin' 'til dark to look for them, but ye hae given me the spirit I needed to no' be afraid."

The four women headed into a battle of their own. Each knew the risk they took, but nothing prepared them for what they would see.

sending them home

The ground was scorched and bleeding from the wounded and dead Jacobites. Most of the Hanoverians had moved off the battlefield, only to reek havoc in the surrounding countryside. They were killing indiscriminately — men, women and children — in an effort to rid the country of the dirty, shabby, wretched savages.

The few Redcoats who remained ignored Cat and her little group. They were too busy removing the clothes, bonnets and any valuables the Jacobites might have on them, leaving the naked dead on the cold, wet ground. Some had started putting men into piles as Cat had seen in her vision.

Scanning the carnage, she felt herself panic, and grabbed for Anne's hand. Anne didn't seem to notice, she just stood there along with the others, white and staring in disbelief. Cat realized it was her turn to be the strong one. The Hanoverians would not let them tarry for long without turning their attentions to the four women.

"Anne, we must find anyone alive and get them to safety now," Cat whispered.

"Dear God in heaven, Catrìona, where do we begin?" Anne said, wiping the tears from her cheeks.

"I dinna like the soldiers watchin' us. I'm frightened that if we do find one alive, they'll come and kill him in front o' us," Cat said.

Inhaling sharply, Mrs. Stonor said "They wouldna dare ... would they?"

"I care no' to find out," Cat said, moving towards a scrub of gorse.

The three women followed her until they were out of the soldier's view. Mrs. Stonor suggested that they should not call out if they found someone alive. Anne asked if everyone could whistle, and all said they could. They worked out a call signal, and feeling a bit safer, they split up to search the woods.

Right off, Eppy whistled from a thicket nearby. All the women gathered in to see if the wounded man could be mended. He was lucky, having only received a bullet in his shoulder. He would live — if they could get him out without being seen. For now, he was treated and left in his hideout.

Spreading out once again, Cat was the one who whistled this time. This man's arm was hacked off, and he was bleeding badly. He was given some whisky and bandaged, but Cat was not confident about his prognosis. Eppy opted to stay with him, reasoning that she hoped to have the same consideration in her final hours.

This same scene played out over and over. After dark, lanterns were seen coming from all directions like fireflies. It was the Jacobite women, risking rape, beatings, even death, to look for their men.

The more time that passed, Cat dared to hope that the vision of her family dying was wrong. Maybe they managed to get out, as they were nowhere to be found. There certainly weren't enough men on this moor to account for all of the Jacobite army. Many must have escaped. That idea led to other horrors that Cat was not ready to think about just yet.

As the cold dawn came, Cat and her entourage had treated dozens of wounded men and seen nearly that many die. Scanning the battlefield for Hanoverians, the four women, aided by several Jacobite women, helped get the wounded off the moor. The Jacobite women came equipped with two wagons to bring home their dead. Cat, Anne and the others hid the wounded men in among the dead, and hoped the Hanoverians would not stop them on their journey home.

During the night, the pyres of the dead burned as in Cat's vision. She tried her best to stay up wind of the stench, but even this morning, it burned her nasal passages indelibly. She had to find out if any of her family were among those who were in those ashes. Finding a sheltered scrub of gorse, she crawled into it, out of sight, so she could do what she had hoped she would never have to.

Where were they? She was sure they would have stood together in the fight. With blinding intensity, the scene manifested itself.

Cannon fire, grape shot and musket balls whizzed at her from all sides, making her duck.

She watched as chaos reigned in the Jacobite ranks. Exhausted, cold and hungry from the night's march on empty stomachs, the Jacobites somehow mustered their energy for the suicide mission. Men ran towards the enemy with little or no chance of making it through the barrage alive. Those in the front of the line were cut down immediately, blocking the way for their countrymen to engage in battle before they too were slashed by the deadly bombardment of iron.

From out of the smoke, Cat saw four men running shoulder to shoulder straight into the fray of musket fire; swords brandished in one hand and dirks gleaming in the other, screaming, *"Garg'n uair dhuisgear!"*

First to be hit was Seumas. Grapeshot took him in the chest leaving nothing but a gaping bloody hole where his ribs used to be. Angus, Iain and Lachlan were still on a dead run, blinded by their mission. In the next instant, Iain and Lachlan were taken down by musket fire. Lachlan died instantly, a perfectly round hole pierced his forehead, but Iain was only wounded in the leg. He crawled over and held Lachlan to his chest, until two bullets hit him in the back, crumpling him on top of Lachlan in protective cover, even after death. Her brothers died not twenty-five feet apart. But where was her father?

Searching the field, she found him near the enemy line. He somehow made it through the musket balls and grapeshot unscathed, and was now entertaining two Redcoats with his sword. Cat could see his face, his features so contorted by rage that she barely recognized him. Although giving the seasoned soldiers a run, he tired quickly and was bayoneted in the back by a third Redcoat, and went down hard. Seeming to have spurred the Hanoverians on, they gave him a few more jabs with their swords for good measure.

Cat could take no more. She felt the weight of the world on her shoulders, not just for being unable to change the fate of her family, but oddly, she felt as though she let her mother down by not protecting them. She sat in her hideout and cried for hours, never hearing Anne calling for her. There was still work to do.

Crawling from the gorse and making sure she was alone on the silent moor, Catrìona stood and called for her family. It didn't matter anymore that their physical bodies could not be found. Their true selves — their life energy — was no longer in their bodies, it was waiting to cross over. Closing her eyes, she let the tears run unabated down her cheeks.

Soon, in her mind's eye, she saw her brothers appear in front of her, still looking alive and well. They knew why she was there. She was sending them home. The three knelt at her feet, bowing their heads as if taking an oath. She rested her hands on Seumas' and Iain's heads and said "Go ye now to the next place, the place where ye are but light, the place where there is no pain or sufferin', the place o' yer new life." She repeated the same with Lachlan, then they were gone.

She waited there for her father, but he did not appear. With a spark of hope, Cat wondered if he managed to live. If he did, how, and where was he now? Was he taken prisoner? She soon realized that a vision to get those answers was impossible, for there was a line of dead in front of her, all wanting to be sent home, to be released from this world.

℥

When darkness started to creep onto the lonely moor, Cat, hungry, cold and exhausted, started back for Inverness. It did not take too long to realize that it was not a wise idea. Along the way, she saw the aftermath of the Hanoverian fury on the Highlanders. She found many dead along the side of the road. Not just men, but women, children, the old, no one was spared, slaughtered and left naked where they fell, incomprehension still registering on their faces.

Keeping off the road, she noticed the crops had been trampled, the land razed and crofts burned. They left nothing for the Highlanders to live on or in, just as in her visions, only now it was real, and even more devastating.

In the distance, she heard sporadic gunfire. No, Inverness would be too dangerous tonight. She needed a safe place to sleep and clear her head to find her father, if he truly was alive. She also desperately needed something to eat, but would have to forgo her stomach until morning.

Ahead, she saw what appeared to be a cave, but couldn't be sure in the fading light. Walking up the hill for a closer inspection, a cave may have been stretching it, for it was more of an outcropping not much bigger than herself, but at least it was dry. She gathered some grass that managed to escape the fires, and spread it out to lie on. Wrapping herself tightly in her cloak, she settled in for the night.

Scanning her surroundings, she noticed fires dotting the hillsides. More than likely, they were Hanoverian camps, which sent a shiver down her spine. She felt numb. Even though she had seen the entire event unfold well in advance, seen the gruesome slaughter and aftermath, she felt as though it were still just a bad dream. Hoping to wake and find it was all a big mistake, she fell asleep.

In her dream, her father was indeed alive, but he was aboard one of those horrible ships. He was hurt badly and not being cared for properly. She felt his anguish, felt his will to live fading. After seeing his sons killed and not knowing the condition of his daughter, he was giving up.

Cat searched for him in Inverness, but the ship must have already sailed, but bound for where? No one would tell her, they just said they were glad to be rid of the Rebels, and where they went was of no consequence to them. Raging, Cat demanded to see the ships' manifests for his name. They laughed at her, saying most wouldn't survive the trip to London, never mind where they were headed.

Waking with a start just before the sun rose, still feeling the anger of her dream, she needed a plan. Sitting up with her arms folded around her knees, she watched the sun get swallowed by the vermilion and charcoal-colored clouds.

"Where are ye, Da?"

The first thing she decided to do was get back home. Alexander would know what to do. She also knew she should not travel alone, not that she would be safe with anyone at this point. The thought of traveling at night didn't thrill her either, and in her state of mind, wasn't sure making herself invisible was possible. There was too much uncertainty in her ideas, fueling the anger she already felt.

"Well, lass, ye better buck up and be strong, 'cause this wilna be an easy task," she admonished herself.

This called for all of her internal resources. Clearing her mind, she meditated on her safe return to *Slios Mìn*. Staying to the mountains, there was cover and a good vantage point to see trouble coming. Without a horse, the trip would take nearer to four days, and that's if the weather cooperated. She was sure she could find roots and tubers to eat, which reminded her stomach that it had not eaten in two days, and began to make itself be heard. She patted it, and went on with her plan.

With the Hanoverian army on the move, she had to make it home quickly. She hoped Alexander would be able to get some news on where the government would take the prisoners, then she would go there. Cat knew it wouldn't be nearly as simple as the way she planned it, but she would make adjustments along the way. Now, it was time to move.

⃦❤

For the next three and a half days, Cat managed to stay out of sight of everyone. She kept to the trees as much as possible, was able to find edible plants and roots, and the weather, while stormy, aided her by keeping visibility down to a minimum.

On the southern tip of Loch Ericht, on the last few miles of her journey, she was hit with a vision. She sat next to a clump of Alders and proceeded to see the same rocky coast covered with fir trees and strange long, rounded roofed houses made of logs.

This time she saw the inhabitants of those houses. They were dark skinned, with straight black hair and black eyes. They wore animal skins, not tartan cloth, and lived amongst each other as a large family.

"C'mon. Who are ye? Where are ye?" she asked out loud.

The vision continued with a ship; a ship she was on to get to this new place. She looked around for her father, but he was not on it. She was alone, but felt as though where she was going was where her father was. Then the vision ended.

"So, now we are goin' for a sail. Great," she said, not enthused by the prospect of traveling in a dank, dark, claustrophobic tub.

Getting up, she resumed her trek towards home. When she got there, the strange silence of emptiness was deeply felt. At least she beat the government troops, but would have to hurry to collect the few things she knew she had to take with her.

Running upstairs, she went straight to her bedroom. Pushing the bed as close to the wall as she could, she lifted the floorboard, pulling out the box that held the garnet dirk, and set it down on the floor. Reaching back into the small space, she snatched the *clach na brataich* and wrapped them both in a linen before placing them in her satchel.

Walking down the hall with her precious cargo, she passed

Seumas' room, and caught a movement out of the corner of her eye. She stopped in her tracks and backed up, looking inside his room to see what had captured her attention. Sitting on the edge of his bed was her brother. His head was hung low in sadness.

"Seumas?"

Slowly he looked up, his eyes full of remorse. Cat froze, just stood in the doorway, as if to move would make him disappear. Without moving his lips, she heard him softly say, "I'm sorry, Cat."

"Sorry? Sorry for what, Seumas?" she whispered.

Again, the voice from him came without movement of his lips. "For my pettiness, for my mistrust o' ye, for judgin' ye … for blamin' ye for e'erything that happened to me."

Cat stared at him for a long moment, trying to put into words how she felt.

"I hold no ill feelin's towards ye, Seumas. I kent that ye didna understand the Sight — didna understand me. There's naught to forgive. I can see now that from the other side ye hae been set free o' the prejudice ye carried. Take that freedom and move on wi' the knowledge that I will always hae ye in my heart."

Slowly, as if melting away, he vanished, but as he was leaving, Cat felt his warm embrace, acknowledging the love that she would indeed hold within her.

Hoof beats outside startled her back to reality, breaking the connection to the dead. She went to the window to see who it was, careful not to move the curtains to give away her presence.

It was Gregor. Had he not fought at Culloden? She ran downstairs and whipped open the front door, startling him as he was just about to step down from his horse.

"Jesus Christ in heaven, woman!" he blasted.

"I'm verra sorry, Gregor, but I was so happy it was ye, and no' some Redcoat."

"Hae ye seen any around, lass?" he asked, scanning the area with a keen eye.

"No' here. I left them all in Inverness, but no' for long I fear."

"Where's yer Da?"

Cat immediately broke down, unable to tell him what happened. He walked her into the house, sitting her down at the kitchen table until she had spent all her tears. He was patient, sitting next to her, rubbing her back.

After a few minutes, releasing all the tension she held in from the past week, she relived the horror one more time. Gregor's face visibly hardened, but he listened without interruption. When Cat finished telling the story, he got up to leave.

"Wait. What did ye come here for?" Cat asked.

"I hae been comin' here e'eryday, hopin' to find yer Da safe. Now I ken I dinna need to do that anymore," he said, his voice cracking as he turned away from her.

"Gregor?"

After a moment, he answered her.

"Did ye no' fight?"

He turned and faced her now, with the proud face of a Highlander. "I am the guard of our thirteenth Chief. He's no' well. I fought in Prestonpans wi' him, then carried him home to Carie, where he is right now. I'll no' leave his side."

Cat stood in the doorway with tears starting afresh. Wiping them away, she asked, "Do ye hae a horse ye can spare? I'll be needin' one to find my Da."

He held out his hand, she took it and folded herself into his arms, both getting comforted. He knew she would go after him. He knew he would help her in any way he could, but first they had to tell Alexander.

"Get what ye need to take wi' ye. I'll be waitin' here."

ॐ

Alexander had moved from his run-down estate in Carie to his Dùn Alasdair estate a few miles away to recuperate. Cat had not been there in a very long time, and smiled at the verse carved over the gate.

> *In this small Spot whole Paradise you'll see,*
> *With all its Plants but the forbidden Tree;*
> *Here every Sort of Animal you'll find*
> *Subdu'd, but woman who betrayed mankind;*
> *All Kinds of Insects too their shelter take*
> *Within these happy Groves, except the snake;*
> *In fine, there's nothing pois'nous here inclos'd*
> *But all is pure as heav'n at first dispos'd;*
> *Woods, Hills, and Dales, with Milk and Corns abound.*
> *Traveller, pull off thy Shoes. 'Tis holy Ground.*

"He must hae been in love once to hae been hurt so badly as to compose those biting remarks," Cat said, chuckling into Gregor's back.

He stopped the horse in front of the house and Cat slid off the rear. Taking a look at the place she only remembered from her childhood, she noticed Gent on the front stoop, looking as if he had been expecting her for days, but didn't move. She lifted her satchel from the front of the saddle, and stood for a minute attempting to look remorseful.

"I'm verra sorry for leavin' ye for so long, lad."

With her apology out of the way, he bounded over to greet her with an excited look on his face. She set her satchel down, gave him a hug and a duly deserved rub-down. All was right again until she looked up to find a much older-looking Alexander.

"Thank God ye're all right, lass. I've been worried sick o'er yer fate." He looked around puzzled, expecting to see the rest of her family.

"Let's go inside and I'll tell ye all that has happened," Cat said, hoping this would be the last time she would have to relay the story to anyone.

After several mugs of ale, angry pounding on the table, pacing the floor, and questions not easily answered, Alexander asked Gregor to search for Angus with her.

"And ye say ye saw him on a ship?" Alexander asked.

"Aye. It must hae left from Inverness, but I dinna ken where it was bound," Cat said.

"Do ye ken for sure it did leave?" Gregor asked.

Cat stared at him for a moment. Why had she not thought of that? He could be in Inverness right now, dying of his wounds, and she was seventy miles away.

"Damn it!" she shouted, throwing her mug across the room. It made a loud crash as it hit the archway to the hall.

Alexander and Gregor looked at each other with startled expressions, never seeing this side of her before. Gent whimpered; he'd seen it before.

Gregor smiled and nodded. "We'll leave in the mornin'."

⁊

Cat thought all night long about the trip back to Inverness. She thought about her invaluable burden — the garnet dirk and the ensign stone. She couldn't risk taking them with her, but she knew leaving them with Alexander was not a good idea either. She needed to hide them so well that only she would know where they were. But where?

By morning, she had the perfect spot chosen. Gregor would not like going that far out of the way, but her mind was made up.

The sun chose to return to a cloud-free sky for the first time in over a week. Cat took it as a good omen, and even Gregor seemed amiable about the extended trip. He understood that the priceless items entrusted to Catrìona were the clan's property, and she was protecting them from falling into enemy hands.

Leaving with Alexander's blessings and a small leather pouch of coins, the two rode off towards Blair Atholl. Gent stayed on as Alexander's protector now that Gregor was leaving. Alexander said it was a fair trade, though Gregor wasn't sure if being replaced by a dog said anything for him or not. Cat just giggled, unwilling to open Pandora's box.

They rode on in silence for a time, comfortable in each other's company. After a few hours, Gregor asked what he had been pondering since they left.

"What does the dirk look like, Catrìona?"

"Let's rest for a while and I'll show ye."

Dismounting by the river, they watered their horses and Cat pulled the box from her satchel. Holding it like she was presenting it to him for the full effect, Gregor looked from her to the box, just like her father had. It made her smile when she had to give him permission to open it.

Slowly, he lifted the cover to reveal the glowing garnet-encrusted silver. He didn't say a word, but his unveiled look of awe betrayed his thoughts. He went to touch it, then stopped and looked at Cat for permission.

"Ye may take it from its nest, Gregor."

Like a child in wonder, he slowly lifted it from the velvet and held it in his hands, feeling its weight and balance, just as everyone who has ever touched it had.

"'Tis a magnificent thing. And it truly belonged to King James II?" he asked, turning it so the garnets refracted the sunlight in a deep red light show.

"That's what Da said."

Shaking his head, he carefully placed the dirk back into its noble keep and closed the cover.

"I dinna think I hae e'er seen such a thing o' beauty. Ye're a wise woman, Catrìona."

"Wise? Why am I wise?" she asked, perplexed by his chosen word, returning the box to the satchel.

"Wise, because for one so young, ye ken the value of somethin' like that to the clan enough to protect it," he said, mounting his horse.

Cat didn't know how to respond to that. What else would she have done with it?

⁊

A few miles before reaching Blair Atholl, they headed up into the mountains. First, the Hanoverians had siezed the castle, then the Jacobites, and at the moment, Gregor didn't know who had possession of it, and didn't want to risk being seen by anyone.

"Where are we goin' anyway?" he asked.

"To the Faerie Dùn. Do ye remember the Pictish dwellin' Lachlan and I found up there?"

"Aye," he said, thinking about how much had happened since then. "Ye're goin' to hide it there?"

"Aye. There are only four people in the world who ken about the place; me, ye, Alexander and Da. 'Tis perfect," she stated, hoping there were still four.

They came around to the waterfall entrance, Cat once again amazed at the perfect secrecy of the place. Dismounting, she led her horse through the guarding oaks and behind the gorse. Glancing behind for Gregor, she found he wasn't there. She tied her horse to the scrub, and walked out to see what was keeping him. He was still mounted, but when he saw her return, his face lit up with a smile she never knew existed in that magnitude.

"Are ye comin?" Cat asked, unable to keep the smile from her own face.

"Do ye ken how many times I hae ridden by this place?" he asked, astonished how something could hide in plain sight.

Cat laughed and replied, "That's exactly what Alexander said."

Gregor dismounted and followed her to the waterfall. Cat looked back a couple times, smiling at his expression of delight.

Once inside, Cat lit the lantern that was left when she visited the last time. They crouched down the narrow hall to the stairs, then up into the room with the wooden floor, where they could stand up straight.

Catching Gregor's expression once again, Cat laughed and said "Didna ye e'er hae this much fun when ye were a bairn?"

"No," he said candidly. "Ne'er."

Cat laughed some more, then they went on to more serious things. Where to hide the dirk and the crystal. Since there was no sign of anyone being there since she and Lachlan had found it over six years ago, she didn't think she had to put much thought in finding a hidden spot. She opted to place it on the wooden table, next to the wooden bowls.

"That's where ye are goin' to *hide* yer treasures?" Gregor asked.

"No one kens o' this place, and besides, where else am I to *hide* it? Do ye see anyplace in this room where somethin' could be hidden?"

Gregor walked around the room, holding the lantern high. He ran his big hand over the stones on the wall in sort of awe of the place. Cat watched him curiously. She would have never guessed he would be amazed by anything, but this place seemed to speak to him. And he was listening.

Cat closed her eyes, letting the ancient place draw her in. Once again, she saw the families who lived here; the men with blue faces. This time, including Gregor in her mind, she heard him inhale sharply as he saw what she projected.

She opened her eyes to make sure he was not panicking — he wasn't. He stood there, unmoving, in the middle of these ancient warriors that stood only as high as his chest. They carried on with their life, oblivious of his presence. He glanced at Cat, looking for an explanation. Stopping the vision, she told him about the people who lived here so long ago in as much detail as she knew. Gregor was fascinated, but a bit spooked. Cat decided it was time to go.

Leaving the same way they entered, Gregor looked back, shook his head and said "I would ne'er hae believed it if I hadna seen it wi' my own eyes."

Cat agreed with him and they began their trek to Inverness.

❧

There was a definite path of destruction left by the government troops. Cat and Gregor stayed to the mountains, out of sight, but wondered how the people of the Highlands would survive. All their crops were decimated, the land burned, even crofts burned. Several times, Cat and Gregor came across women and small children huddled next to their ruined crofts; out in the open, nowhere to go, nothing to eat, withering.

It was a quiet trip, each keeping their comments to themselves, as if to voice them, the same fate would befall them. They had a mission; find Angus and get him to safety. After that was incomprehensible.

By the third day of travel, they remained in the hills overlooking Inverness to devise a plan. Since Inverness was held by government troops, Gregor, looking too much like a Highlander, was probably not safe going into town. No changing that for the moment.

Cat transformed herself into a lady; a quick wash, her best dress, and put her hair up the way ladies did. She was fully intent on going into town alone to meet Anne Leith and her friends. Being allies, she hoped they could tell her where the prisoners were being held.

Gregor didn't like it, but could not see a better way in broad daylight. They worked out a signal and a place to meet after dark, hopefully relaying news to each other on her father's whereabouts.

"Wish me luck," Cat said in her bravest voice.

Gregor said "Och, lass, ye'll be fine. Ye dinna look like a Rebel, so they shouldna bother ye."

"Remember, nine o'clock," she said, after squeezing his hand. Wrapping her cloak around her for strength, she started down the hill into town.

She remembered where Anne said she was staying, and found her way there. Gregor was right, because no one gave her a second glance.

Just as Cat was going to knock on the door, it opened, startling her and Eppy. Before Cat could apologize, Eppy hauled her inside.

"Dear me, lass. What are ye doin' here?" she whispered.

"I came to see Anne and ask her for help to find my Da. He was taken prisoner," Cat said, unaware she was whispering.

"Who are ye talkin' to, Eppy?" Anne quietly asked from another room, but instead of waiting for an answer, she came to find out for herself, followed by Mrs. Stonor.

When Anne saw Cat standing in her suite, she put her hand to her chest and smiled the sweetest smile Cat had ever seen.

"I hae prayed ye were no' dead," she said quietly, then hugged Cat ferociously.

Cat giggled and hugged her back. "No, I'm no' dead."

Sobering a bit, Cat released Anne and asked if this was a good time to talk. Anne recognized the cryptic tone in her voice and whispered, "No' here."

Anne grabbed her cloak, asked Eppy to watch her son, then shuffled Cat out the door with her finger to her lips for silence.

Once out on the street, Anne took Cat to a busy tea house. Cat wasn't sure she could talk loud enough for Anne to hear her over the gossiping of the women in the warm room. They took off their cloaks and found a table near the window.

"I'm sorry we couldna talk in the privacy of my room, but the walls are too thin, and ye ne'er ken who's listenin'."

"Is it that bad here?" Cat asked, as quietly as she could.

"Well, it is for us Jacobites. What are ye doin' here?"

Cat recounted her plight to a very sympathetic Anne.

"Well, Catrìona, they dinna call me the Grand Rebel for naught."

Cat grinned widely, "Really?"

"Aye, and I'm rather proud o' it," she said smiling. "But on to yer quest. The prisoners' are no' on ships yet. Since the gaols are all full, they are bein' held in cellars, churches; anywhere they'll fit. There are o'er three thousand and no' a one bein' treated for their wounds. They are bein' denied food, clothin', and blankets. Many wilna live to see the gallows," she said through gritted teeth.

Cat went white at the barbarity of it. Anne patted her hand which seemed to shake Cat out of it, bringing high color to her cheeks.

"That's all I need to see," Anne said, a determined grin on her face.

"What's all ye need to see?" Cat asked.

"Yer will to follow through wi' findin' yer Da."

"Och, dinna worry for me, Anne," Cat said defiantly. "Ye canna keep me from findin' him — wi' or wi'out ye."

Anne rose and Cat followed suit, wrapping themselves in their cloaks, they left the tea room and walked passed the gaol.

"I'll need some time to find out if he's in there, or bein' held elsewhere," Anne said.

"I dinna ken why I canna *see* him," Cat said out loud, looking up at the formidable stone fortress.

Anne took her statement the wrong way, and said "They're no' lettin' anyone see the prisoners."

Cat let it go, not willing to divulge her abilities for some reason. Either way, if her father was in that gaol, there was no way she and Gregor were getting him out. She needed a new plan.

After getting a generalization of what the townspeople looked like, she was sure she could alter Gregor's appearance to fit in. Asking for Anne's help with a few supplies, and giving her Gregor's description, she began planning his transformation.

She found lodgings in a hotel near Anne's on Church Street, and told the clerk on duty her father would be joining her tonight. She went up to her room with a smile on her face. She could hardly wait to see Gregor's face when she told him.

At nine o'clock, she waited in front of Balnain House for Gregor. He lurked in the shadows, making sure no one was in sight before giving the signal, then Cat joined him with her satchel containing his new image.

With a few curses and mutterings at having his hair put into a proper queue, Gregor emerged from the shadows sporting a pair of breeks, clean linen shirt and jacket.

When he stepped into the light where Cat could see her handiwork, she was astonished. He was actually a very handsome man. The strong bone structure of his face was evident when his thick hair was pulled away from it, rather than obscuring it.

"Wait," she commanded.

"What now?" he barked, thoroughly displeased by his apparel.

"Ye'll need this ribbon for yer queue," turning him around to get to his hair.

"Christ, woman, must ye?" he said, visibly shaking, he was so mad.

She didn't say anything, just tied his hair with the dark blue ribbon, crooked her arm through his, and guided him towards her hotel. Glancing at him when they went near a lantern, she thought he cut a fine figure, but telling him so didn't quell his mood.

Walking into the hotel, the clerk looked up, remembering Cat said her father was joining her tonight, and greeted the two of them with a nod, then went back to his books.

When they entered Cat's room, Gregor caught his image in the mirror over the dresser, stopping him cold. He looked at himself critically from all angles, adjusting his jabot. Cat watched as his expression softened to the point of almost smiling.

"Do ye like what ye see?" Cat asked coyly.

He glared at her for a second, before returning his gaze back to the mirror. "Actually, ye did fine, lass."

ॐ

Nearly a month after Anne Leith said it would take some time to ascertain the whereabouts of Angus Robertson, she knocked on Catrìona's door with news of his confinement. Anne may have had many enemies among the Loyalists, but she also had some very influential relatives with sympathies for the cruel treatment of the Jacobite prisoners.

Anne went to the prisons every day with bread and blankets. This morning, she wanted Cat to go with her. Gregor did not like the idea, because up until now, Cat was not known in town as a Jacobite supporter, she was just a Scotswoman enjoying Inverness with her father.

"I'll no' find him if I dinna look for him, Gregor," Cat said, filling her satchel with the bread Anne brought over.

"How will ye explain yerself to the guards?" he asked.

"Och, I'll do that," Anne said. "They all ken me there, and I'll just tell them that Catrìona is just helpin' me distribute bread because there's so much to pass out. She'll no' be in any harm, I promise."

"How did ye get in to see them?" Gregor asked, still skeptical of Cat's role in this.

"I hae written many curt letters to my relatives in the Hanoverian aristocracy demandin' better treatment of the prisoners, and hae told them I would continue my efforts until they receive it. The guards are forewarned to let me in and give the prisoners what little I can."

"I still dinna like it."

Cat hoisted her satchel over her shoulder, and patted Gregor's arm, "I'll see ye in a few hours. Go out and get some fresh air." She left him standing in the doorway.

ॐ

Cat stood in front of the church, wondering how many times she had walked passed it during her stay. It was May fifteenth, four weeks after the battle. Her father has been in that cold, damp, dark basement with forty three other prisoners since then.

"Come on, then. Or do ye just want to stare at the place?" Anne chided.

Once through the main doors, the stench of human filth was so overpowering, it almost made Cat vomit. Anne handed her a scented handkerchief and told her to breath through it. Cat did as she was told, but it seemed the odor was indelibly burned into her nasal passages.

Without saying a word, Anne followed a guard down the stairs, through a long hallway, then down another set of stairs that led to the prisoners. Cat wanted to cry, as the sounds of the wounded, sick and starving men wafted to her.

Reaching the hastily barred rooms where no lights were used, Anne lit a lantern left from her previous excursions there, then proceeded to pass out the bread. Not long after she began her task, the guard left, going back up the stairs, unwilling to subject himself to the stench for long. Anne had obviously become a staple there, so he figured she would be all right to leave alone.

When the door closed at the top of the stairs, Anne grabbed Cat's hand and guided her over to the corner of the cell.

"Is this yer Da?" she asked, quietly.

Cat grabbed the lantern, thrusting it into the face of a man she did not recognize. He had long dark hair and a full beard, but was so thin and filthy, she didn't think it possible to be her father.

"Da? Da, it that ye?" she whispered to the barely conscious man.

The man cracked open one eye to see who the angel was who was speaking to him. His eye was blue, but there was little life left in it. With all the energy he had, he lifted himself up onto his elbow, then Cat saw he only had one arm. Holding the lantern closer so he could see her, both his eyes flew open in recognition.

"*Catrìona, mo nighean,*" he whispered, in the same voice she remembered, husky and deep. Tears ran down his cheeks, and his strength to remain in an upright position failed, dropping him onto the leg of another man.

Despite his filth, Cat hugged him tightly to her breast and they cried together for a moment. She wanted to check his wounds, so asked the man he fell on to roll him over onto his side so she could see his back. Without a word, he obliged. The light from the lantern splashed onto ugly red gashes, somehow healing despite this totally inhumane treatment. She laid her hands over them, willing them to heal.

"We've got to be leaving soon, Catrìona," Anne whispered, both satchels empty of their burden.

Cat turned to the young man next to her father, who seemed to be very coherent, and asked his name. He told her he was Donald Haldane of Lanrick.

"Well, Donald Haldane, I'll be askin' for yer help verra soon." She didn't elaborate any further, because the door at the top of the stairs opened and the footfalls of the guard descended to remove her and Anne from their task. Donald nodded and whispered in Gaelic, "I'll take care of him."

&c.

The next day, Cat once again helped Anne with the prisoners, only this time, she managed to smuggle in an herbal poultice for her father's wounds, and a bit of beef the Loyalists were saying was poisoned by the Jacobites. Cat herself had eaten some the night before and lived to tell about it.

She made sure Donald Haldane got some too. It would keep him interested enough in keeping her father alive until they could devise a plan to help him escape.

Gregor raged when Cat told him the conditions her father was forced to endure. He walked her and Anne to the church daily, noting guard changes and scouting out possible escape routes. He was pretty sure he had a plan, but had to get Angus stronger to make the trip.

"How long do ye think before yer Da is able to walk on his own?" Gregor asked after two weeks of Cat secretly feeding her father.

"He was able to stand on his own yesterday, but he's still verra weak. I hope by the end o' this week, he'll be fit for travel."

"Good. We'll set his escape for the second week in June."

&c.

Three days later, Cat and Anne began their rounds, and to their horror, the prisoners at the church were gone.

"What do ye mean they hae been taken away!" Anne shouted at the guard. "Taken where?"

He pointed to the quay. There were seven ships anchored in the harbor waiting to transport the prisoners to London for trial.

Cat fainted.

ॐ

How she got back to her hotel room, Cat didn't know, but Gregor was hovering over her like a hen. She tried to sit up, but was still a bit fuzzy, and slid back down into a reclining position.

"What's happenin'?" she asked, as Gregor laid a fresh, cool linen on her forehead.

"Ye fainted."

"I did? Why?"

"I dinna want to tell ye for fear ye may do it again," Gregor said, concern edging in his eyes.

"Christ, man," she said, making another attempt to sit up, this time making it. "Tell me. I promise I'll no' do it again."

He looked at her with a critical eye; her color was back — so was her temper. In his determination, she should be fit enough to hear the news.

"They took yer Da and the other prisoners to the ships where they will be sent to London for trial."

She went white again, but stayed upright. He waited for the ranting about a rescue attempt, but she remained quiet.

"Are ye all right, lass?" he asked.

Cat looked at him with immeasurable sadness. He saw hope flee from her. After all this time it took to find him, losing her father again was more than she could bear. She sat there in a kind of daze, seeming to age in front of him. He didn't have a clue how to bring her around, so he sat with her, holding her hand, hoping he would have an answer if she asked what they should do. No such question was asked.

Gregor didn't realize that Cat was somewhere else. She had been unable to have a vision of her father, until now. She saw the orders that came in from the Hanoverian government.

Give them no special attention, and if they die, they are to be sent overboard, with no further thought. The less that come to trial, the less of a nuisance it will be. Feed them only the barest amounts of oatmeal, bread, cheese and water.

Cat returned in a rage, startling Gregor, who had never seen Cat have a vision.

"I wilna let this happen," she ranted, pacing the floor, twirling her hair in a frenzy of emotion.

All Gregor could do was sit there until she vented whatever it was she was furious about. He didn't dare interrupt. He just watched her go back and forth, sometimes sitting, all the time thinking, planning, fuming. If he wasn't so involved, he would have thought it rather amusing, but he had seen a glimpse of her temper, and did not want to invite that wrath upon himself. So he waited, unmoving, blending into the settee until she was finished.

Finally, she sat next to him in resolution, put her hand on his, looked him square in the eye and said, "We'll be needin' a boat."

Booking passage

Having spent no time around the sea, Gregor didn't know where to begin. Who could be trusted? Once again, Anne Leith was called upon for advice. Her brothers were fishermen and had connections in matters such as this.

"They're called Privateers," Anne said to Cat and Gregor. "Ye pay them to take ye where ye want to go, and if stirrin' up a bit o' trouble is involved, all the better, especially with the English."

"How much do they need to get us to London?" Gregor asked.

"I hae a meetin' set up wi' my brother, Abraham, tomorrow at dusk on the quay where he keeps his boat. We'll find out then."

Cat shot a glance at Gregor implying they may need more money. Reading her mind, he just shrugged, indicating he didn't know where they would get it. They had used up nearly all Alexander had given them. They would just have to wait for the meeting tomorrow to find out just what they needed before getting worried about it. It would be a long day.

ॐ

When dusk rolled in with the fog, Anne, Cat and Gregor were already on the dock waiting for Abraham and his crew. Through the thickness, a longboat rowed in with three men aboard. Anne waved and the fair-haired man in the front waved back.

They tied up on the far end, and quietly hopped up on the wooden decking. Introductions went around, then business began quickly. By the end of the hushed conversation, a price had been set and a date had been arranged. They would leave in a week, and the fee was a fair day's work from Gregor aboard ship. Cat volunteered to help with the cooking and tend to the sick or wounded. It was a fair bargain.

"It's rather excitin', is it no', Gregor?" Cat asked, as they walked back to their hotel.

"Och, aye. Real excitin'." His voice dripped with sarcasm.

Cat giggled. It was an unfamiliar sound lately, and Gregor smiled inwardly for its return.

When they returned to their room, Cat decided to write to Alexander and let him know what had happened during the past two months. She also wrote of their plan to go to London, positive she would be well on her way before he could do anything about it.

§

The third week of June started off warm and pleasant — perfect sailing weather for the pair of landlubbers. The seven government ships remained in the harbor for only two days. Permission to get bread to the prisoners while they were aboard ship was denied, and Cat hoped her father would not slip back into his malnourished state on the journey.

Abraham assured Cat that they would arrive in London well in advance of those tubs, which would give them time to formulate a plan to get her father out of wherever they would remand him to while awaiting his trial.

Setting the sails, Cat stood at the bow of the ship, getting the full feel of the wind in her face. It was a freeing experience. If she closed her eyes, she could almost imagine herself flying. She took deep breaths of the sea-scented air, determining right then and there, that the sea was where she would spend the rest of her days. Not aboard a ship, though, for the thought of having to go below still made her feel anxious and closed in, but she would live near the sea.

She thought again of the vision she had of the strange land and people. Savages, they were called by the English. *Phaa!* They called everyone savages, even Highlanders. A determination would be made on her own of what they were when she got to wherever it was.

The first night on board was a strange experience. Gregor seemed to take yanking on ropes all day in stride, but was asleep as soon as he got into his hammock. It took Cat quite a while to get used to all the creaks and groans of the wooden hull before she finally dozed off.

By the first light of day, thuds from above her head woke her. At first, she didn't know where she was. Opening her eyes, she let them adjust to the dimness, then the odors of rum, tar, men and rotten wood assailed her senses. Pinching her nose, she wondered how she slept at all in that pungent concoction.

The ship was coming alive again. Men were scrambling to their posts, so Cat swung out of her hammock and went to see if she could be of help in the galley.

❧

Jack, the cook, was a short, stocky fellow, with arms too long for his body. He had a long white queue, and the top of his head was covered by a tight fitting red scarf, the tails hanging down either side of his plait. He turned when he heard her enter his world. His black eyes held a mischievous twinkle, and Cat instantly liked him.

He stopped stirring the porridge for an instant, absorbing Cat's entire appearance in that short span of time. His clean-shaven face belied his white hair, for he looked no older than her father. He smiled, showing many gaps in his grin, but it was friendly smile, inviting her into his station.

"What'll be yer name, lass?" he asked. His voice was raspy and light.

"Catrìona."

"Won't do."

Cat cocked her head, lifted her brows in question and waited for what would do.

"Ye look like a jewel," he said. "A simple name like Catrìona is no' doin' ye justice." He rubbed his chin with the end of the wooden spoon he was stirring the porridge with.

Cat smiled, giving him the name Anna had given to her so long ago.

"Ah, Garnet. Aye, that suits ye fine, lass, just fine."

He returned his attention to the pot, and the rest of the breakfast was cooked in silence, save for barking orders at her.

The twelve men aboard ship were called to breakfast at the long table in the mess room. There was no talking, no ceremony, no wasting of time dawdling over the food. They ate and returned immediately to their stations. When the helmsman was relieved, he came down to take his food, and ate as the others had, returning as soon as he was finished.

"That didna take long," Cat mused, bringing the dirty dishes into the galley to be washed.

"Ye should see 'em in a storm," he chuckled, sounding like a rusty hinge.

ॐ

For the next week, the routine was the same, always keeping to an orderly schedule for everything. Gregor came up from below decks, washed and cleanly shaven, to stand next to Cat on the quarter deck as they entered the Thames River to the English port of London. He had donned his breeks and jacket, and held out a comb and the ribbon for his queue. Cat smiled, took the proffered comb, and instructed him to sit on one of the barrels to complete her task.

"When do ye think the transport ships will get here?" Cat asked, trying to tame Gregor's thick locks.

"Abraham said it could take another two weeks, he wasn't sure. Do ye ken which ship he was on?"

"The *Margaret and Mary.*"

"Then, when we get to London, I'll get a job on the quays and learn of when it arrives." It sounded like he had a plan.

"We'll need to ken where they'll take the prisoners. They must hae a place already chosen for the task. That'll be my job," Cat announced.

"Ye must promise me to be careful. London's a big place. I dinna want to lose ye there."

Cat tied the ribbon in his hair, and placed a kiss on his cheek. He didn't say anything, but she saw his neck turn scarlet. He stood quickly, without looking at her, and went aft. Cat giggled and shouted, "Thank ye for carin' about me, Gregor." He waved and picked up his pace, making Cat laugh.

ॐ

Sailing through the ever narrowing river, Cat got a strange feeling as they passed through the marshy estuary just beyond Canvey Island. The river made a sharp left turn, then a sharp right turn, narrowing further still. Coming up on the north side of the Thames, a fortification began to appear. Quickly finding Abraham, she asked him what that place was.

"Tilbury Fort. They store gunpowder and arms there. Why?"

"This is where my Da will be brought."

He looked at her, but remained silent for a minute, trying to figure out if she was for real. He decided to ask.

"Do ye *see* him there?

Cat knew exactly what he was asking. She looked him square in his light blue eyes, and said "Aye. I *see* him there."

Abraham continued analyzing her, then nodded, determining she was for real. "If that's true, then there isna any need o' goin' into London town, is there?"

"No' if there's a place to stay around here to wait for the ships to come in," she said, not looking at him.

Gregor joined the two at the rail and was briefed on the change of plans.

"Och, and I was so lookin' forward to workin' the docks," his sarcasm revealing itself again.

Abraham put his hand on Gregor's shoulder in a show of condolence. Cat smiled and went below. After she was out of earshot, Abraham asked Gregor about his companion. Gregor gave him only as much information as he needed to know, assuring him that if she says she sees or knows something, it should be taken very seriously.

They moored just outside the fort, and Abraham took a few of his crew members ashore to secure lodgings for Cat and Gregor. As captain, he would remain aboard his ship for the duration of their stay.

&

Cat was going crazy waiting for the prison ships. It had been three weeks since she and Gregor arrived in Tilbury. It wasn't as if the ships could have snuck in without someone seeing them, the channel was too narrow.

While in town, Cat had gotten to know most of the townspeople by sight, if not by name. Gregor spent most of his time around the docks and in the public house. It was the best way to get information, but Cat thought he may be a bit overzealous about his job. She remained quiet about it. After all, Gregor did not have to help her.

Mid-afternoon at the beginning of the fourth week, Gregor came bounding up the stairs of the hotel and burst through Cat's door with news.

"Ships hae just been sighted!"

Without any further explanation, Cat followed Gregor down

the stairs to the quay. Abraham was just rowing in, hopefully with more definitive news. Gregor lent him a hand up and the three walked to a private spot near the shore.

"Seven ships are comin' in. The lead ship is the *Margaret and Mary*. Isna that the ship yer Da is on?"

Cat, too preoccupied to answer, was trying to get a sense of her father and the other prisoners. Inside the ships hold, they laid in their own filth, there were several dead, or near death. Her father wasn't one of them. He seemed to have recovered from his wounds, but was still not well.

"He's alive," she said to Gregor and Abraham. They looked at each other, but said nothing.

Nearly two hours later, the *Margaret and Mary* sailed in and moored not far from Abraham's ship. The other six ships also moored near the fort, but further up stream. Abraham shook his head in amazement, and said to his first mate, "'Tis just like she said."

⁊⁊

"His majesty directs that 300 of the rebel prisoners should be taken to Tilbury Fort to be kept there until his majesty's further pleasure. It is signed by the Secretary at War." Gregor read the banner that he "acquired" from one of the guards. Cat didn't ask, nor did she care how he got it.

"Why are they no' takin' them off the ships? It has been two weeks since they hae arrived."

"I dinna ken, but surgeons are bein' allowed to board all the ships to tend to the sick."

"Really?" Cat asked, hopeful for the first time that the prisoners may finally receive proper treatment.

"Aye. When the guards complained about the prisoner's hardship and treatment, the doctors made an adamant plea to tend to them."

"Has Abraham seen any o' the prisoners from his ship when they're let out o' the hold?"

"Aye, and he's seen several one-armed men, but is no' sure if one is Angus."

That was all Cat had to hear. In the morning when they let the men out of the hold, she would be on Abraham's ship to see her father.

૨૧

"I canna see him anywhere," Cat complained. "Are ye sure ye counted all o' them?"

"Wait! There he is," Gregor whispered, passing the scope to Cat. She fiddled with the focus, then found her mark and smiled.

"It's him," she said. "He's so thin, though, I nearly didna recognize him."

She watched him for a long time from her hiding spot up in the sails, invisible from the guards. He slowly walked the deck, taking deep breaths of fresh air, although Cat could smell the reek even from where she was and couldn't imagine what it was like below decks. "I hae got to get him off that ship."

૨૧

Another week passed before four of the ships were relieved of their cargo. The *Margaret and Mary* was not one of them. The fort was filled, and the rest of the prisoners would remain aboard their ships awaiting trial. Lots were now being drawn for every twentieth man to be tried, though word coming from the trials was that none of the prisoners would be spared unless they joined the English army. So far, there were no takers.

As if on display, a ferry from Westminster was now taking sightseers to visit the prison ships. The onlookers were handed scented handkerchiefs, and each day they would come to heckle men barely able to stand. Cat and the others aboard Abraham's ship were appalled.

It was now the end of September, and some of the hangings had begun. The public was taking great joy in the festivities; the drawing and quartering being a favorite. Four of the Jacobite Clan Chiefs were beheaded in London, their heads put on display for all to see.

Ship by ship, the guards went through and pulled off the unlucky souls who had managed to survive up until now, and brought them before the court to have their sentence proclaimed. Most were being put back onto their ships, though, not taken to the gallows.

Cat had a sinking feeling as she watched the proceedings day by day, week by week. She couldn't fathom what they would do with the prisoners who were not to be hung. Her father was not one who was sent to trial, probably figuring he was already just half a man due to his lack of appendage.

Abraham had returned to his ship with news from the court on sentencing of the prisoners. He took Cat and Gregor aside and said "They're takin' the prisoners who hae returned to their ships to the colonies."

Cat went white, and Gregor didn't look much better. They knew what that meant. Slavery for the rest of their lives. Servants for masters not much better than those who were tending them now.

"No' all will hae a life sentence," Abraham said, sensing their thoughts. "Many are bein' given just seven years of servitude, then they will be free men."

"When will they be transported?" Cat asked, regaining some of her color.

"Two days. They canna chance the weather to hold for much longer, " Abraham said, then walked away.

Gregor had no words. Sworn to protect Alexander, leaving Scotland was not an option, but how could he let her go there by herself? He was torn between duty and doing the right thing.

Cat laid a hand on his cheek, feeling his anguish. "Ye hae gone as far as ye're to go, *mo charaid*. I'll be fine, Gregor, ye ken I will be, but I must go where Da is goin'." She hugged him then, a sort of desperation hug, trying to keep him with her just a little longer. Releasing her hold and stepping back, she looked long at him, memorizing yet another face, another moment. No arguments were uttered from him. He had given in.

"The clan's history is in yer hands now. Tell Alexander where the sacred objects are hidden. I dinna think I will e'er see them again." She rushed away before the tears started flowing.

❧

Walking towards the crowded docks, her thoughts now turned to the voyage. A voyage she did not want to embark upon, but one she had to take. She looked in her purse to see how much money she had on her; a shilling and three pence. Hardly enough to book passage to America. How else would she get there? Her thumb rubbed the ring — the garnet glowed deep red in the carved sterling. It was the only thing she had left from her family. She raised her eyes to the sky as if asking permission from her brothers to sell it so she may retrieve their father. In her mind she saw the three of them — their faces appearing from the shadows of the other side. They smiled at her, but it was Lachlan's voice she heard.

Remember why we gave the ring to ye, Cat. It was so ye would forgive us for bein' — as ye so delicately put it — pricks. Da is more important than that reminder, aye?

Cat choked out a laugh as the tears streamed down her cheeks. "Thank ye, Lachlan."

It took a few minutes to regain her composure, then she went to the booking agent to see when the next ship to America was to sail. Informed that the last ship to the colonies for the year was sailing on tomorrow's tide, she asked if her ring would be payment enough for passage.

"Let me see it," the round-faced man with very little hair asked her.

Cat removed the precious treasure from her finger and handed it to him. He looked at it with an appraising eye, noting the expert craftsmanship and the quality stone.

"A garnet, yes?"

"Aye," she answered. "In sterling."

He nodded, turning it in his stubby fingers, his face remaining blank as to its value. He looked up at her then, still contemplating. Cat knew right away it would not be enough for the full fare. She pulled out her purse and handed over the shilling and three pence, hoping that would make it adequate.

"'Tis all I hae, sir. Will it be enough?" she said, quietly.

"What will you do for your food, Miss?" he asked, wondering why he was making an exception for her. It wasn't nearly enough, but for some reason, he wanted to help her.

"What do ye mean?"

"What will you use to buy your food with for the voyage?"

Cat looked at him dumbfoundedly. "I hae to bring my own food?"

The man nodded, still fingering the ring. "Don't you know that most will not survive this trip? Bad food, bad water, disease, vermin, not to say anything of the weather this time of year. The ones that live stay in good health by bringing as much of their own food as they can."

"How long does it take to get to America?" Cat asked, trying to stave off a sinking feeling.

"Nearly two months."

Cat thought for a moment and nodded. She could gather enough food from somewhere between now and tomorrow morning. He just needed to let her passage be paid in full.

"I'll get enough to last me, sir, if ye just get me passage."

He was still deciding.

"'Tis no' like I want to go, I *must* go, sir … please."

He pulled out a ticket and stamped it Paid In Full, then handed it to her. Cat looked at it through misty eyes and slowly took it between both hands, letting her fingers touch his, then turned to see if Abraham was still at the docks.

ॐ

The morning dawned fair and cool. Cat stood at the rail of the *Jonathan A. Winthrop* with her satchel filled with as much hard tack, dried fish, bannocks and cheese as she could carry. Abraham had been able to supply her for the two month voyage from the galley of his own ship. They had grown quite close in the months together. "Besides," he said, passing her another round of cheese, "Anne would hae me heid if I didna help ye as much as I could."

As the anchor was weighed and the sails were hoisted, Cat felt the ship start to drift from the quay. A flurry of activity bustled around her. She was on the stern deck, tucked in between the cargo out of the way of the crew as they busily heaved on ropes, climbed up the rigging, and did every other imaginable thing to keep this tub afloat. The fresh air, she knew, was going to be a rarity once she went below decks, so she wanted to remain in it for as long as possible.

With a sudden lurch as the wind caught the sails in the harbor, they were off. Cat looked back towards the shores of the only place she'd ever known. But it wasn't home anymore. Within minutes, the distance made the buildings meld into each other; the skyline became more like a distorted mountain range. The color of the land turned from gray-green to blue-gray; the color of the past. Her focus returned to her father. She turned from her homeland to face the bow of the ship, to the future, to the new land she would call home. America.

Gàidhlig Glossary

A Ghaoil = a ghooil = my love

A Ghaoil mo Chridhe = a ghooil mo cre-ee = love of my heart

An dà Shealladh = an daah shay-lagh = the two sights (literally) or Second Sight

Arisaid = arisaitch = long tartan covering that women wore over their dress that folded up over their heads like a shawl

Abaisd = ah-pasht = brat

Bean-sidhes = ban-shees = banshee

Beurnag = bee-yur-nak = wild, mean woman

Bodhran = bo-rahn = drum

Bràithrean = bray-hren = brothers

Brighid = bree-geet = Bridget the saint

Bràthair Beag = bray-hair beck = little brother

Caithris = kay-reesh = wake

Catrìona = katreena = Catherine

Ceilidh = kay-lee = party or visit

Ciamar a tha thu? = kimmar ah ha oo = how are you? (familiar)

Ciamar a tha shibh? = kimmar ah ha shiv = how are you? (proper)

Ciamar a tha thu sa mhadain an-diugh? = kimmar ah ha oo sa'vah-teen an-joo = how are you this morning?

Clach na Brataich = clack na bra-teck = ensign stone

Clan Donnachaidh = clan don-a-key = children of Duncan

Cuppa = coopa = cup

Garg 'n Uair Dhuisgear = garg-en oor ghooskar = fierce when roused

Glè Mhath = glay vah = very good

Iain = ee-ine = John

Lachlan = lahk-lan

Madainn mhath mo nighean mhaiseach = mah-deen vah mo nee-an vash-eck = good morning my beautiful girls

Mo Bhalach = mo vah-lack = my son

Mo Bhràthair Mòr = mo vraa-hair more = my big brother

Mo Charaid = mo kar-eetch = my friend

Mo Ghille = mo ghilly = my boy

Mo Shionnach = mo shon-nack = my fox

Piuthar = pee-oor = sister

Sassenach = sah-sen-ach = English

Seumas = shay-mus = James

Sgian Dhu = skee-an doo = black knife

Shaeumais = hay-mish = James

Sìdhichean = shee-ican = faeries

Sionnach = shon-nack = fox

Slìo Mìn aig Aulich = slees meen ek aw-lick = smooth slope at Aulich

Tapadh Leibh = tah-pah leeve = thank you (proper)

Here are a few words in broad Scots:

Kine = cows

Ken = know

Kent = knew

Dinna = don't